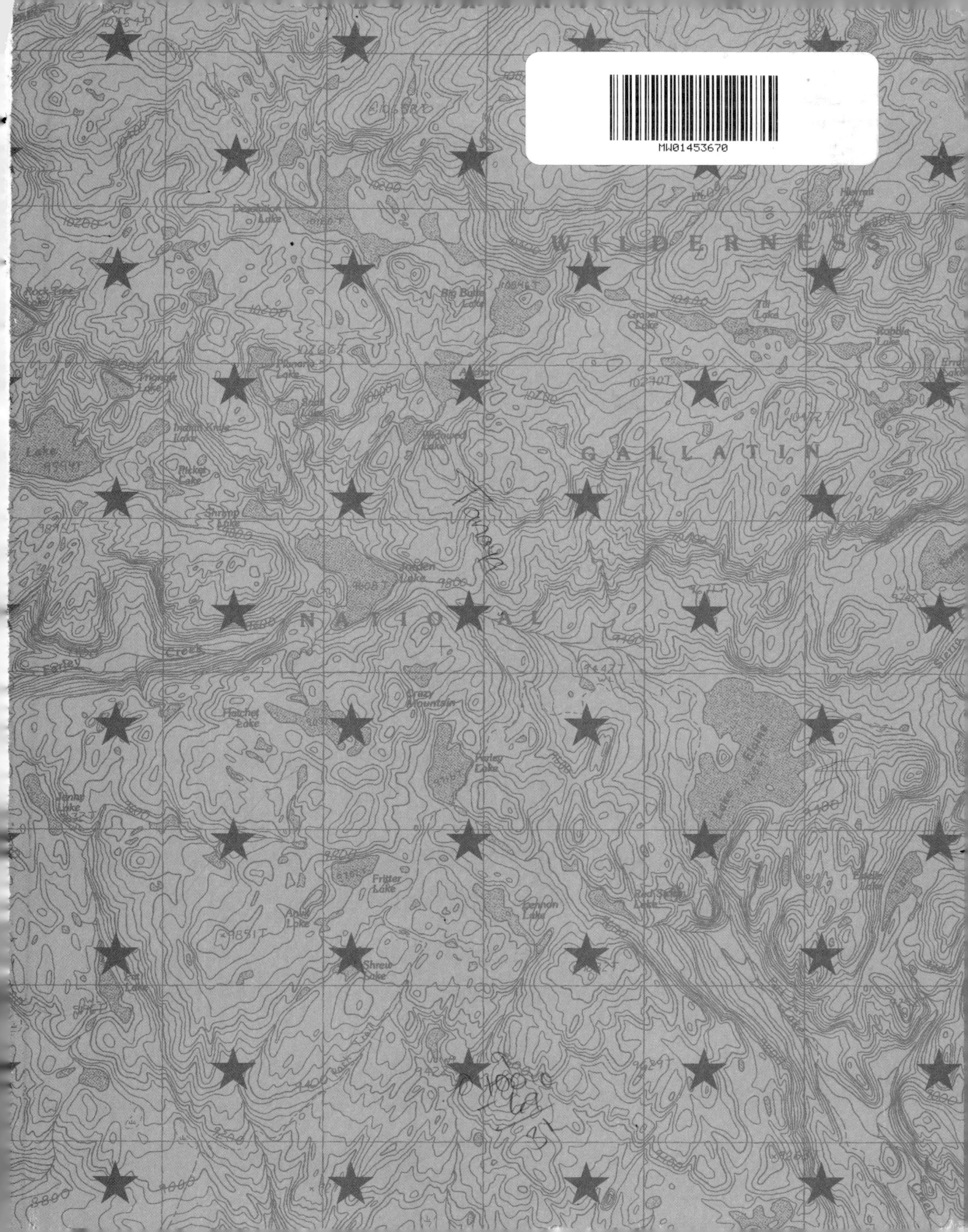

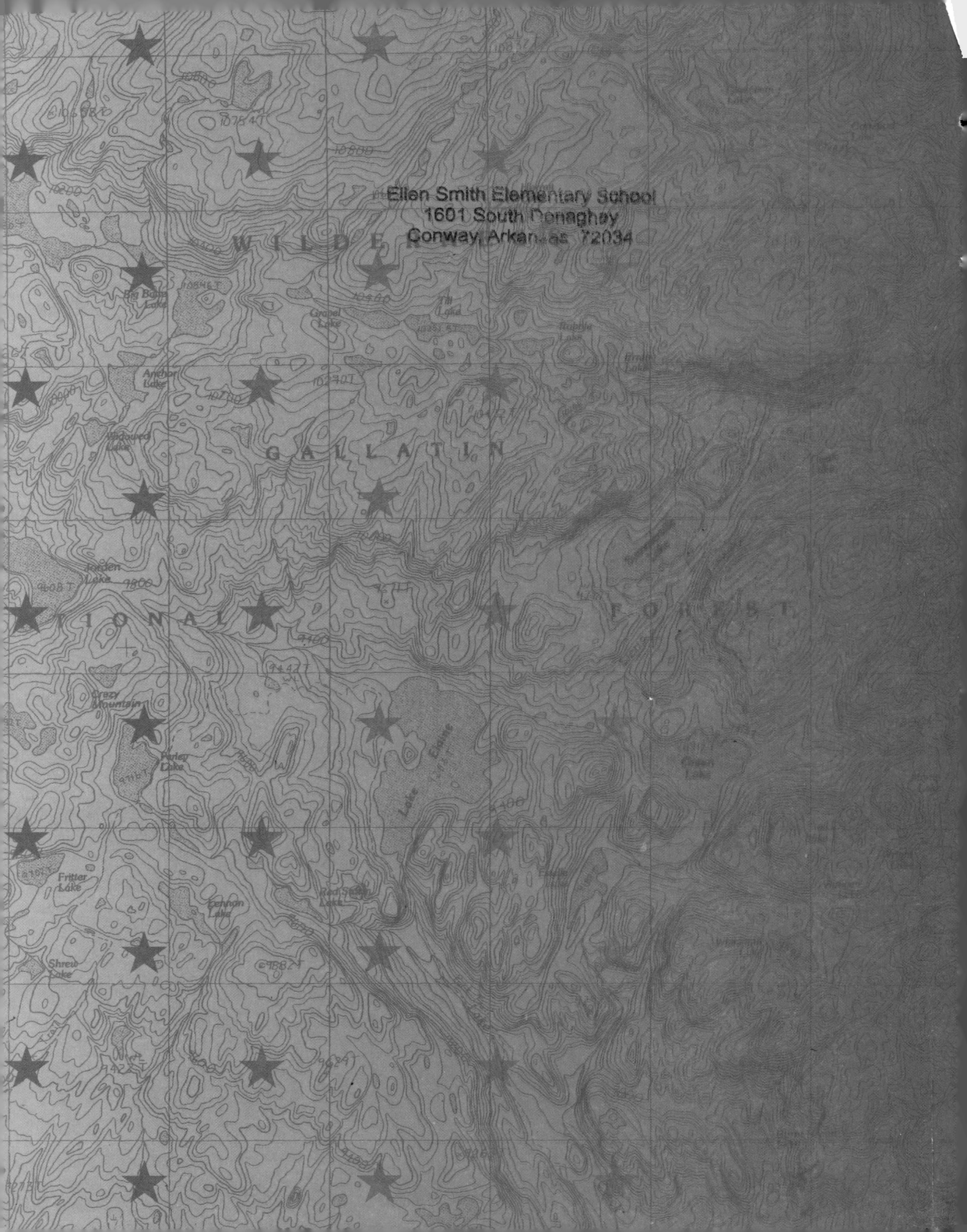

Ellen Smith Elementary School
1601 South Donaghey
Conway, Arkansas 72034

HOUGHTON MIFFLIN

SOCIAL STUDIES

LIBERTY EDITION

★ Arkansas Studies ★

Visit **Education Place®**
www.eduplace.com/kids

HOUGHTON MIFFLIN   BOSTON

★ ★ ★ ARKANSAS ★ ★ ★

★ AUTHORS ★

Senior Author
Dr. Herman J. Viola
Curator Emeritus
Smithsonian Institution

Dr. Cheryl Jennings
Project Director
Florida Institute of
Education
University of North Florida

Dr. Sarah Witham Bednarz
Associate Professor,
Geography
Texas A&M University

Dr. Mark C. Schug
Professor and Director
Center for Economic
Education
University of Wisconsin,
Milwaukee

Dr. Carlos E. Cortés
Professor Emeritus, History
University of California,
Riverside

Dr. Charles S. White
Associate Professor,
School of Education
Boston University

Consulting Authors

Dr. Dolores Beltran
Assistant Professor
Curriculum Instruction
California State University, Los Angeles
(Support for English Language Learners)

Dr. MaryEllen Vogt
Co-Director
California State University Center for
the Advancement of Reading
(Reading in the Content Area)

HOUGHTON MIFFLIN
SOCIAL STUDIES

LIBERTY EDITION

★ ARKANSAS STUDIES ★

HOUGHTON MIFFLIN — BOSTON

ARKANSAS

Consultants

Philip J. Deloria
Associate Professor
Department of History
  and Program in
  American Studies
University of Michigan

Lucien Ellington
UC Professor of Education
  and Asia Program
  Co-Director
University of Tennessee,
  Chattanooga

Thelma Wills Foote
Associate Professor
University of California,
  Irvine

Stephen J. Fugita
Distinguished Professor
Psychology and Ethnic
  Studies
Santa Clara University

Charles C. Haynes
Senior Scholar
First Amendment Center

Ted Hemmingway
Professor of History
The Florida Agricultural &
  Mechanical University

Douglas Monroy
Professor of History
The Colorado College

Lynette K. Oshima
Assistant Professor
Department of Language,
  Literacy and Sociocultural
  Studies and Social Studies
  Program Coordinator
University of New Mexico

Jeffrey Strickland
Assistant Professor, History
University of Texas Pan
  American

Clifford E. Trafzer
Professor of History and
  American Indian Studies
University of California,
  Riverside

Teacher Reviewers

Charlene Holman
Elmdale Elementary
Springdale, AR

Tracey J. Nelson
Oaklawn Magnet School
Hot Springs, AR

© 2008 Houghton Mifflin Company. All rights reserved.

No part of this work may be reproduced or transmitted in any form or by any means, electronic or mechanical, including photocopying and recording, or by any information storage or retrieval system, without the prior written permission of Houghton Mifflin unless such copying is expressly permitted by federal copyright law. Address requests for permission to reproduce Houghton Mifflin material to School Permissions, Houghton Mifflin Company, 222 Berkeley St., Boston, MA 02116.

Printed in the U.S.A.

ISBN-13: 978-0-618-90628-4   ISBN-10: 0-618-90628-2

2 3 4 5 6 7 8 9 DW-13 12 11 10 09 08

Social Studies Curriculum Framework

GEOGRAPHY

1. Physical and Spatial

Students shall develop an understanding of the physical and spatial characteristics and applications of geography.

G.1.4.1 Discuss the difference between *relative* and *absolute location*

G.1.4.2 Locate and describe physical characteristics of the six natural *regions* of Arkansas:
- Arkansas River Valley
- Crowley's Ridge
- Mississippi Alluvial Plain
- Ozark Mountains (plateau)
- West Gulf Coastal Plain
- Ouachita Mountains

G.1.4.3 Locate each of the five *regions* of the United States and describe each *region's* major physical features:
- Northeast
- Southeast
- Midwest
- Southwest
- West

G.1.4.4 Determine *absolute locations* (*latitude* and *longitude*) of places studied using a grid map

G.1.4.5 Locate several countries in each of the four *hemispheres*

G.1.4.6 Explain the difference between a continent and a country

G.1.4.7 Locate major mountain ranges in the United States:
- Appalachian
- Rocky

G.1.4.8 Locate major mountain ranges in the world:
- Andes
- Alps
- Himalayas
- Rocky

G.1.4.9 Locate major rivers in the United States:
- Mississippi
- Ohio
- Arkansas
- Hudson
- Missouri
- Colorado

G.1.4.10 Locate major rivers in the world:
- Nile
- Amazon
- Mississippi
- Yangtze
- Ganges
- Volga
- Rhine

G.1.4.11 Explore weather changes in various *regions*

G.1.4.12 Explain the purpose of *historical* and *political maps*

G.1.4.13 Utilize the map *key/legend* to interpret *historical* and *political maps*

G.1.4.14 Interpret a map using *cardinal* and *intermediate directions, map scales, legends,* and titles to locate places on contemporary maps

G.1.4.15 Identify and label *political map* features:
- boundaries
- capitals
- cities

G.1.4.16 Create a *political map* that includes the following:
- title
- *compass rose*
- *legend/key*

Social Studies Curriculum Framework

GEOGRAPHY (continued)

2. Culture and Diversity

Students shall develop an understanding of how cultures around the world develop and change.

G.2.4.1 Research elements of *culture* in a community, state, or nation (e.g., food, clothing, housing, language, sports/recreation, customs, traditions, art, music, religion)

G.2.4.2 Describe the *cultural* characteristics of diverse populations in the United States

G.2.4.3 Discuss the advantages and disadvantages of life in a *suburban* area

G.2.4.4 Compare and contrast the human characteristics of early settlements and contemporary communities in the five regions of the United States

3. Interaction of People and the Environment

Students shall develop an understanding of the interactions between people and their environment.

G.3.4.1 Examine different types of transportation and communication links between communities in Arkansas

G.3.4.2 Discuss the reasons for human settlement patterns (e.g., jobs, *climate,* family)

G.3.4.3 Explain how communities share ideas and information with each other

G.3.4.4 Explain how people are influenced by, adapt to, and alter the environment (e.g., agriculture, housing, occupation, industry, transportation, communication, acid rain, global warming, ozone depletion)

G.3.4.5 Describe the social impact of extreme natural events on human and physical environments (e.g., fires, volcanoes, earthquakes, floods, hurricanes, tornados, tsunamis)

G.3.4.6 Research ways in which the school and community can improve the physical environment by practicing conservation

CIVICS

4. Government

Students shall develop an understanding of the forms and roles of government.

C.4.4.1 Compare and contrast the purpose and function of government at the local, state, and federal levels

C.4.4.2 Compare responsibilities of local, state, and federal government officials

C.4.4.3 Identify the three branches of government:
- executive
- legislative
- judicial

C.4.4.4 Describe how United States citizens apply fundamental principles of *democracy* (e.g., people rule themselves, power of government limited by law, people exercise their authority directly through voting and indirectly through elected officials)

C.4.4.5 Recognize that there are different forms of government throughout the world

5. Citizenship

Students shall develop an understanding of how to participate, develop, and use the skills necessary for effective citizenship.

C.5.4.1 Identify and explain the role of the Founding Fathers in writing the founding documents:
- Benjamin Franklin
- John Hancock
- Thomas Jefferson
- James Madison
- George Washington

C.5.4.2 Identify and explain the purpose of the founding documents:
- Declaration of Independence
- Articles of Confederation
- United States Constitution

C.5.4.3 Examine the meaning of the Pledge of Allegiance

C.5.4.4 Examine characteristics needed for active citizenship

C.5.4.5 Analyze components of the election process:
- candidacy
- primary
- general

C.5.4.6 Demonstrate the proper flag etiquette for the American flag

HISTORY

6. History

Students shall analyze significant ideas, events, and people in world, national, state, and local history and how they affect change over time.

H.6.4.1 Discuss the meaning of the state motto of Arkansas

H.6.4.2 Examine the history of the State Seal of Arkansas and its components

H.6.4.3 Examine historical settlements in Arkansas:
- Arkansas Post
- Old Washington
- Fort Smith

H.6.4.4 Name the major causes of the American Revolutionary War:
- taxation
- distance
- lack of communication

H.6.4.5 Identify George Washington as the lead general in the Revolutionary War

H.6.4.6 Identify events that led to Arkansas' involvement in the Civil War:
- excise taxes
- state's rights
- slavery

H.6.4.7 Identify major historical events that occurred during the 20th century (e.g., World War I, Great Depression, World War II, Space Exploration, Civil Rights)

H.6.4.8 Discuss how differences between people lead to conflict (e.g., social, political, economic)

H.6.4.9 Evaluate data presented on a *timeline* of Arkansas history

H.6.4.10 Examine *artifacts* relating to events in Arkansas history

H.6.4.11 Discuss advances in technology (e.g., communications, space travel, medical)

H.6.4.12 Analyze changes in Arkansas from past to present

H.6.4.13 Understand the transition of the thirteen colonies into thirteen separate states

H.6.4.14 Identify and describe the Arkansas Indian Tribes:
- Osage
- Quapaw
- Caddo

H.6.4.15 Identify the reasons for the decline of the native populations of Arkansas (e.g., influenza, small pox, competition for land)

H.6.4.16 Describe how new forms of transportation and communication impacted the Westward Expansion of the United States (e.g., pony express, railroads, telegraphs)

H.6.4.17 Identify areas in Arkansas that were explored by the following:
- Hernando Desoto
- La Salle/De Tonti
- Marquette
- Joliet

H.6.4.18 Identify European nations that claimed authority over territorial Arkansas:
- France
- Spain

H.6.4.19 Discuss the causes and effects of Westward Expansion (e.g., economic opportunity, resources, forced removal, unclaimed lands, religion)

H.6.4.20 Compare the area of the United States before and after the Louisiana Purchase

H.6.4.21 Identify the following individuals and their roles in the Louisiana Purchase:
- Thomas Jefferson
- Napoleon
- Lewis and Clark
- Sacagawea

H.6.4.22 Discuss similarities and differences among the American Indians and Pilgrims:
- housing
- clothing
- foods
- traditions
- tools

Social Studies Curriculum Framework

ECONOMICS

7. Choices
Students shall analyze the costs and benefits of making economic choices.

E.7.4.1 Evaluate the priority of economic wants and consequences of the *opportunity cost*

E.7.4.2 Analyze how *scarcity* caused early exploration (e.g., gold, spices, silk)

E.7.4.3 Recognize and use the *decision making model* to make an economic decision:
- state the problem
- list the alternatives
- state the criteria
- evaluate the criteria
- make a decision

8. Resources
Students shall evaluate the use and allocation of human, natural, and capital resources.

E.8.4.1 Discuss *productivity*

E.8.4.2 Compare the increase in *productivity* when improved *human capital* is available

E.8.4.3 Examine the impact of *scarcity* of *natural resources* on production decisions

E.8.4.4 Analyze how *capital resources* are used to produce *goods* and *services*

E.8.4.5 Identify Arkansas *entrepreneurs*

E.8.4.6 Describe how profit is an *incentive* for *entrepreneurship*

9. Markets
Students shall analyze the exchange of goods and services and the roles of governments, businesses, and individuals in the market place.

E.9.4.1 Discuss the characteristics of money:
- *portability*
- *divisibility*
- *durability*
- *uniformity*

E.9.4.2 Describe the reasons for saving money in a financial institution:
- interest
- safety

E.9.4.3 Research the *productive resources* that go into the production of a product

E.9.4.4 Research public *goods and services* that are provided by taxes

E.9.4.5 Explain why countries trade

E.9.4.6 Explain the benefits of *specialization* and *interdependence*

E.9.4.7 Discuss the effect of *supply* and *demand* in a community

E.9.4.8 Define *inflation*

E.9.4.9 Identify imported and exported goods

E.9.4.10 List exported goods associated with Arkansas (e.g., rice, chicken, auto parts)

E.9.4.11 Explain how foreign trade affects daily life

Arkansas Databank

The Bald Eagle is the national bird and is also known as the American Eagle.

The banner reads, "Regnat Populus," which means, "The people rule." This is Arkansas's state motto.

The steamboat represents Arkansas's industries.

The beehive, plow, and wheat show the importance of Arkansas's agriculture.

Arkansas Facts

Population, 2005 (Rank)	2,779,154 (32nd)
Total Land Area (Rank)	52,075 square miles; 134,874 square kilometers (27th)
Capital	Little Rock
Postal Abbreviation	AR
Economy	**Agriculture:** Rice, soybeans, cotton, corn, wheat, poultry and eggs, hogs, cattle, dairy products **Industry:** Food processing, electric equipment, metal products, machinery, paper products, chemical products
Motto	"The people rule."
Nickname	"The Natural State"
Songs	"Arkansas (You Run Deep in Me)" by Wayland Holyfield, "Oh, Arkansas" by Terry Rose and Gary Klaff

Arkansas Symbols

State Flower
Apple Blossom

State Animal
White-Tailed Deer

State Insect
Honeybee

State Gem
Diamond

State Bird
Mockingbird

State Tree
Loblolly Pine

Contents

Contents .... xii–xxi

▶ **Constitution Day** .... xxii–xxiii

Bringing the world to your classroom!

UNIT 1 Arkansas's Land and First People

CHAPTER 1   Geography of Arkansas 2

Vocabulary Preview   **Reading Strategy:** Predict and Infer 2

Lesson 1 | Core   Five Themes of Geography 4

      Map and Globe Skills   Review Map Skills 10

Lesson 2 | Core   Regions of Arkansas 12
         | Extend   **Geography:** The Mighty Mississippi 16

Lesson 3 | Core   People and Land 18

Chapter 1 Review and Test Prep 22

CHAPTER 2 Arkansas's Early People — 24

Vocabulary Preview **Reading Strategy:** Monitor and Clarify 24

Lesson 1 | Core — The First Arkansans 26
         | Extend — **Primary Sources:** Digging Up the Past 30

Study Skills Write a Report 32

Lesson 2 | Core — Arkansas Indians in the 1600s 34

Graph and Chart Skills Make and Interpret a Line Graph 38

Chapter 2 Review and Test Prep 40

Unit 1 Review WR **Current Events Project** 42

xiii

UNIT 2   Arkansas History   44

CHAPTER 3   Arkansas: Exploration and Settlement   46

Vocabulary Preview   **Reading Strategy:** Summarize 46

Lesson 1 | Core   European Explorers 48
         Extend   **Economics:** The Columbian Exchange 52

Lesson 2 | Core   Arkansas Post 54

Graph and Chart Skills Make a Timeline 58

Chapter 3 Review and Test Prep 60

CHAPTER 4   A Nation and a State   62

Vocabulary Preview   **Reading Strategy:** Question 62

Lesson 1 | Core   A New Nation 64
         Extend   **History:** Saying "No" to Britain 70

Lesson 2 | Core   The Louisiana Purchase 72

Reading and Thinking Skills Identify Cause and Effect 76

Lesson 3 | Core   Arkansas Becomes a State 78

Chapter 4 Review and Test Prep 84

xiv

CHAPTER 5   Arkansas in War and Peace   86

Vocabulary Preview   Reading Strategy: Monitor and Clarify 86

Lesson 1 | Core | The Civil War 88
         | Extend | **Economics:** North and South 94

Lesson 2 | Core | Reconstruction 96

Citizenship Skills Understand Point of View 100

Lesson 3 | Core | A Changing State 102

Chapter 5 Review and Test Prep 108

Unit 2 Review   **WR**   **Current Events Project** 110

UNIT 3 Arkansas Today 112

CHAPTER 6 People and Culture 114

Vocabulary Preview **Reading Strategy:** Question 114

Lesson 1 | Core Progress in Arkansas 116

Citizenship Skills Resolve Conflict 122

Lesson 2 | Core Arkansas Culture 124
Extend **Biographies:** The Pride of Arkansas 128

Chapter 6 Review and Test Prep 130

CHAPTER 7 Government in Arkansas 132

Vocabulary Preview **Reading Strategy:** Summarize 132

Lesson 1 | Core United States Government 134

Study Skills Identify Primary and Secondary Sources 138

Lesson 2 | Core State and Local Government 140
Extend **Citizenship:** Symbols of Arkansas
and the Nation 146

Lesson 3 | Core Good Citizenship 150
Extend **Citizenship:** Forms of Government 154

Chapter 7 Review and Test Prep 156

xvi

CHAPTER 8   Understanding Economics   158

Vocabulary Preview   **Reading Strategy:** Question 158

Lesson 1 | Core   Arkansas's Economy 160
         | Extend   **Readers' Theater:** Money and Banks 164

Lesson 2 | Core   Arkansans at Work 168
         | Extend   **Economics:** Making Choices 172

Citizenship Skills   Make a Decision 174

Chapter 8 Review and Test Prep 176

Unit 3 Review   **Current Events Project** 178

UNIT 4 The Land of the United States 180

CHAPTER 9 An Overview of the United States 182

Vocabulary Preview **Reading Strategy:** Predict and Infer 182

Lesson 1 | Core Earth's Land 184

Map and Globe Skills Use Latitude and Longitude 190

Lesson 2 | Core Many Regions, One Nation 192
 | Extend **Geography:** Borders and Boundaries 196

Chapter 9 Review and Test Prep 198

CHAPTER 10 The Southeast and Southwest 200

Vocabulary Preview **Reading Strategy:** Monitor and Clarify 200

Lesson 1 | Core People of the Southeast 202
 | Extend **Geography:** Gulf Coast Hurricanes 208

Reading and Thinking Skills Distinguish Fact from Opinion 210

Lesson 2 | Core People of the Southwest 212

Chapter 10 Review and Test Prep 218

CHAPTER 11 The Northeast, Midwest, and West 220

Vocabulary Preview **Reading Strategy:** Summarize 220

Lesson 1 | Core People of the Northeast 222

Lesson 2 | Core People of the Midwest 228

Map and Globe Skills Use a Special Purpose Map 234

Lesson 3 | Core People of the West 236
 | Extend **History:** Lewis and Clark 242

Chapter 11 Review and Test Prep 244

Unit 4 Review **WR** **Current Events Project** 246

xviii

References

Citizenship Handbook

Pledge of Allegiance R2

Character Traits R4

Arkansas Governors R6

Arkansas Counties R9

Biographical Dictionary R13

Resources

Geographic Terms R16

Atlas R18

Glossary R32

Index R36

Acknowledgments R45

Extend Lessons

Connect the core lessons to an important concept and dig into it. Extend your social studies knowledge!

Geography
The Mighty Mississippi	16
Borders and Boundaries	196
Gulf Coast Hurricanes	208

Primary Sources
Digging Up the Past	30

Economics
The Columbian Exchange	52
North and South	94
Making Choices	172

History
Saying "No" to Britain	70
Lewis and Clark	242

Biography
The Pride of Arkansas	128

Citizenship
Symbols of Arkansas and the Nation	146
Forms of Government	154

Readers' Theater
Money and Banks	164

Skill Lessons

Take a step-by-step approach to learning and practicing key social studies skills.

Map and Globe Skills
Review Map Skills	10
Use Latitude and Longitude	190
Use a Special Purpose Map	234

Skill Practice: Reading Maps
13, 19, 35, 50, 65, 74, 91, 103, 185, 186, 214, 230

Study Skills
Write a Report	32
Identify Primary and Secondary Sources	138
Apply Critical Thinking	

Skill Practice: Examining Artifacts
28, 55, 80

Skill Practice: Reading Visuals
27

Graph and Chart Skills
Make and Interpret a Line Graph	38
Apply Critical Thinking	
Make a Timeline	58

Skill Practice: Reading Graphs
204

Skill Practice: Reading Charts
97, 136, 141, 232

Reading and Thinking Skills
Identify Cause and Effect	76
Apply Critical Thinking	
Distinguish Fact from Opinion	210
Apply Critical Thinking	

Citizenship Skills
Understand Point of View	100
Apply Critical Thinking	
Resolve Conflict	122
Apply Critical Thinking	
Make a Decision	174
Apply Critical Thinking	

Reading Skills/Graphic Organizer

Compare and Contrast
4, 34, 78, 96, 140

Cause and Effect
12, 64, 184, 222

Main Idea and Details
18, 54, 102, 160, 212

Sequence
26, 48, 88, 202, 228, 236

Draw Conclusions
72, 192

Problem and Solution
116, 134

Categorize
124, 150, 168

Visual Learning

Become skilled at reading visuals. Graphs, maps, timelines, infographs and fine art help you put all of the information together.

Maps

Latitude and Longitude	6
State of Arkansas	10
Arkansas Regions	13
Arkansas Resources	19
Arkansas Map and Globe Skill	23
American Indian Nations in Arkansas	35
Exploration Routes	50
The British Colonies, 1763	65
Proclamation Line of 1763	71
The Louisiana Purchase	74
Confederate and Union States	91
The Great Migration	103
The Continents	185
U.S. Geographic Regions	186
Lines of Latitude	190
Lines of Longitude	190
New Orleans (Latitude and Longitude)	190
United States (Latitude and Longitude)	191
United States Interstate Highways	193
Missouri Latitude and Longitude	199
Spanish Territory	214
American Indian Nations, 1600	223
The Thirteen Colonies	224
Northwest and Louisiana Territories	230
Mineral Resources of the Midwest	234
The Oregon Trail	238
Lewis and Clark	242
Crystal Lake Beach Special Purpose Map	245
Great Lakes Industries	246

Charts and Graphs

Arkansas State Parks	21
U.S. American Indian and Alaska Native Population, 1900–2000	39
Population of American Indians and Alaska Natives in Arkansas, 1960–2000	39
Population in Arkansas Cities	42
Arkansan's Population	83
Railroad Equipment Made in the U.S., 1861	94
Cloth Made in the U.S., 1861	94
Amendments	97
Three Branches of Government	136
Arkansans' Basic Rights and Freedoms	141
Arkansas's Governor Election Results, 2002	153
Unlimited and Limited Government	154
Cotton-related Jobs in the Southeast	204
Manufacturing Workers	232

Diagrams and Infographics

The Mighty Mississippi	16
Digging Up the Past	30
The Columbian Exchange	52
Arkansas Post Trade	55
Points of View about Statehood	82
Sharecropping	98
Writing the Constitution	135
World Trade	162
Supply and Demand at the Movies	169
Borders and Boundaries	196
Pueblo Village	213
Haudenosaunee Longhouse	222
Water-powered Mill	225
Resources in the Valley	237

Timelines

Chapter Opener Timelines
46, 62, 86

Lesson Opener Timelines
48, 54, 64, 72, 78, 88, 96, 102, 202, 212, 222, 228, 236

Lesson Review Timelines
51, 57, 69, 75, 83, 93, 99, 107, 207, 217, 227, 233, 241

Chapter Review Timelines
61, 85, 108

xxi

SPECIAL HOLIDAY

Constitution Day

★ ★ ★ ★ ★ ★ ★ ★ ★ ★ ★ ★ ★ ★ ★ ★ ★ ★ ★ ★

What are all the things a government should do? That's a big question. More than 200 years ago, leaders of our new nation had to decide the answer. Their goal was to write a plan for the United States government. They wanted a government that would protect the common good and serve the people. The plan that they created was called the Constitution of the United States. They signed it on September 17, 1787. A special part of the Constitution, called the Bill of Rights, listed rights that the Constitution would protect.

Today, the Constitution still guides our government and protects our rights. We celebrate Constitution Day and Citizenship Day during the week of September 17.

Visitors can view the original Constitution at the National Archives Building in Washington, D.C.

The Constitution begins with the words "We the People," which shows that it was written by and for the people of the United States.

Today, the Constitution has 4,440 words. It is the oldest and shortest written constitution in the world.

Two of the people who worked on the Constitution, George Washington and James Madison, later became Presidents of the new country.

Activity

WHAT ARE YOUR RIGHTS? The Bill of Rights protects many important rights, including freedom of religion, freedom of speech, and freedom of the press. Choose one of these rights and make a display. Use images and captions to show the ways in which people enjoy this freedom.

UNIT 1

Arkansas's Land and First People

The Big Idea

How did early people use Arkansas's land and water?

"The Arkansas or Quapaw Indians . . . built large, multifamily dwellings covered with bark. . . ."

—S. Charles Bolton, writer

Unit 1

1

Chapter 1: Geography of Arkansas

Technology

e • word games
www.eduplace.com/kids/hmss/

Vocabulary Preview

geography
Geography is the study of our world and our place in it. It describes the land, water, and living things that surround us.
page 4

plain
Much of eastern Arkansas is a large **plain.** This flat land runs along the Mississippi River.
page 14

Reading Strategy

Predict and Infer Use this strategy as you read the lessons in this chapter.

Quick Tip Look at the pictures in a lesson to predict what it will be about. What will you read about?

natural resources

Natural resources provide people with food, fuel, shelter, and clothing. Examples include water, soil, and crops.
page 19

conservation

When people collect and reuse things that are thrown away, they are working for **conservation.** This helps protect the environment.
page 21

Core Lesson 1

The Themes of Geography

VOCABULARY

geography
environment
region
relative location
absolute location

Vocabulary Strategy

<u>geo</u>graphy

Geo- is from a word that means "earth." The study of the earth is **geography**.

READING SKILL
Compare and Contrast Chart how relative location and absolute location are alike and different.

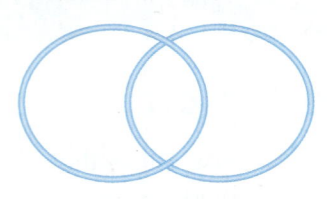

Build on What You Know How would you describe the place where you live? You could talk about where it is, what it is like there, or what you do there.

Welcome to Geography

Main Idea Geographers use different themes to understand and describe places and people.

What is geography? **Geography** is the study of the people and places on Earth. It explains the forces that shape the land. It explores how living things are connected to the places where they live.

Geography helps us understand our environment. An **environment** includes all the surroundings and conditions that affect living things. Water, land, plants, animals, and weather are all part of the environment.

Geographers study geography. They use five themes, or big ideas, to think about Earth. Using these themes can help us understand the world in which we live.

Globe These students are using a globe to learn about geography.

4 • Chapter 1

Place

One theme of geography is place. Every place on Earth has its own special features. Understanding a place means knowing what the things and people there are like.

Geographers talk about physical features, or characteristics. Physical characteristics include landforms, such as mountains and valleys. They also include bodies of water, such as lakes and rivers. Other physical characteristics are animals and plants.

Geographers also talk about human characteristics. These features include the kinds of communities people build, the languages people speak, the beliefs they hold, and the religions they practice. Both human and physical characteristics can change over time.

Region

Regions are another theme of geography. A **region** is an area that shares one or more features. These shared features make one region different from another. For example, a farming region is different from a region with big cities.

A region may be defined by both physical and human characteristics. A physical region could include places that have the same kind of landforms, such as a mountain region. A human region might be one where people speak a certain language.

You can learn more about regions by comparing and contrasting them. Knowing about one region can help you understand others.

REVIEW What are two ways that a region can be defined?

China The way people in a region do something is a human characteristic of the region. In China, many people ride bicycles to work.

Latitude and Longitude

Lines of latitude are called parallels.

Lines of longitude are called meridians.

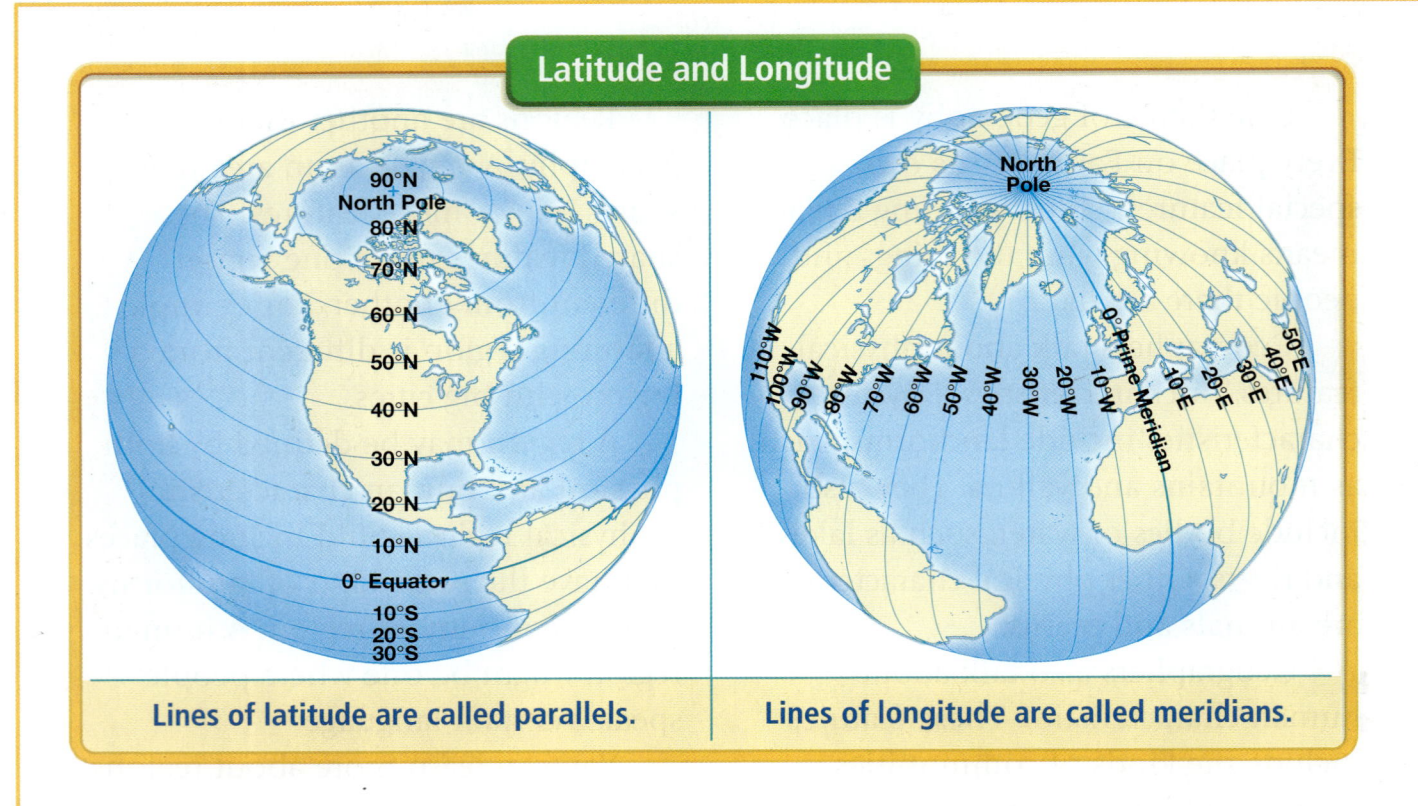

Location and Movement

Main Idea Location and movement are two important themes geographers use.

A place's location refers to where that place is. When you describe what your home is near, you are giving its relative location. **Relative location** is the location of one place in relation to other places. "Next to the school" or "north of Louisiana" are examples.

To tell the exact spot in your town where your home is, you would give your street address. Geographers use absolute location to name the "address" of every place on Earth. **Absolute location** is the exact spot on Earth where a place can be found. To name an absolute location, geographers use two sets of imaginary lines on maps and globes.

Lines of latitude circle the globe from east to west. Lines of longitude run between the North and South Poles. Each line has a number. These numbers are called degrees. The equator is 0 degrees latitude. Other latitude lines are measured in degrees north or south of the equator. The line at 0 degrees longitude is called the prime meridian. Other longitude lines are measured in degrees east or west of the prime meridian.

To give the absolute location of a place, find the lines of latitude and longitude that cross there. For example, the city of Little Rock, Arkansas, is located at about 34 degrees north, 92 degrees west. This absolute location can be written 34°N, 92°W.

6 • Chapter 1

Highways Cars and trucks carry people and products from one place to another along Interstate 30 and other highways in Arkansas.

Movement

People, products, and ideas move from one place to another. So do animals and plants. Physical features on Earth move too, although much more slowly. Movement is the fourth theme of geography.

Sometimes people move within a country. For example, in the 1800s, large numbers of people moved from the states of Kentucky and Tennessee to the new state of Arkansas. In recent years, many people in the United States have moved from northern and eastern states to states in the South or the West.

People also move from one country to another. Throughout the history of the United States, people from other countries have moved to the United States to build new lives. When people move into an area, they bring their ideas and customs with them.

Understanding movement means finding out why people move. Sometimes problems such as war, unfair leaders, or lack of jobs push people out of one place. Peace, freedom, job opportunities, or the chance to buy land can attract people to another place.

The physical environment affects the movement of people and goods. Natural barriers such as mountain ranges, canyons, or raging rivers can make moving from place to place difficult. Oceans, lakes, flat land, and easily traveled rivers can make movement easier. Cars, airplanes, and trains have made it easier for people to move between countries.

REVIEW What are some reasons why people might move to a new place?

Relationships Within Places

Main Idea People change places and places affect people.

The fifth theme of geography is the relationship between people and the environment. Geographers study the ways people change places. They also study the way the environment affects people.

For example, humans have built dams across rivers in Arkansas to make floods less likely. The dams have also supplied water to towns and cities and have provided electricity.

Not every change is helpful. A dam can change the flow of a river. This can affect fish, plants, and animals living in or near the river.

The environment affects people, too. People build communities near things they need, such as water or farmland. Early settlers built homes near rivers in parts of Arkansas that were good for farming. Farmers used rivers to ship their crops to places where they could be sold.

Today, people often move to places where they can find jobs. Cities and towns located on rivers in Arkansas have many different kinds of jobs.

Dam Water flowing through the Bull Shoals Dam in Arkansas makes electricity to power homes and businesses.

Adapting to the Environment

People also adapt to their environment. To adapt means to change in order to fit in. In the past, people who lived near oceans learned to fish. People built homes using materials they found around them. Some people were able to eat food that grew nearby, while other people had to move from place to place to find food.

Today, technology allows people to change the environment in new ways. Technology is the use of scientific knowledge. Air conditioning lets people live comfortably in hot climates. Jets and fast ships carry fresh fruits and vegetables from one place to another. Geographers study the changing relationships between people and places.

REVIEW What is one example of how people are affected by the environment?

Lesson Summary

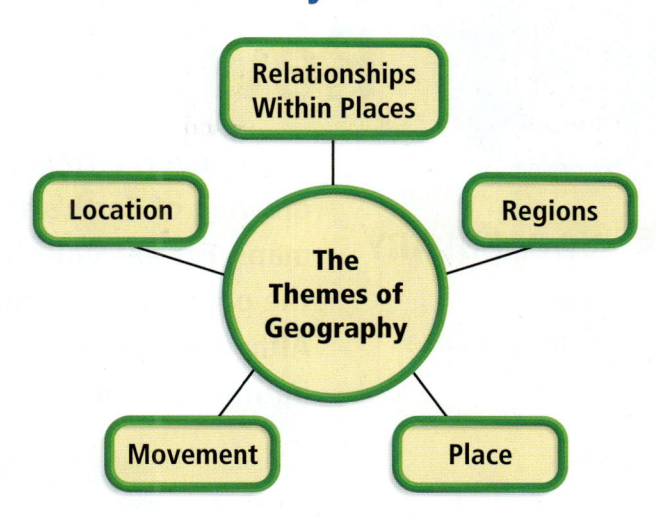

- Relationships Within Places
- Location
- Regions
- The Themes of Geography
- Movement
- Place

Why It Matters...

The five themes of geography help people understand and describe people, places, and environments in the past and present.

Lesson Review

1. **VOCABULARY** Use **region** in a sentence about where you live.

2. **READING SKILL** Give the relative location of Arkansas in relation to the state of Louisiana.

3. **MAIN IDEA: Geography** What is one way the physical environment can affect movement of people?

4. **MAIN IDEA: Geography** In what ways can people alter the environment?

5. **CRITICAL THINKING: Analyze** Identify two regions in your town or city. Explain the features that make each one a region.

WRITING ACTIVITY Describe the place where your school is. Think about landforms, buildings, streets, and bodies of water.

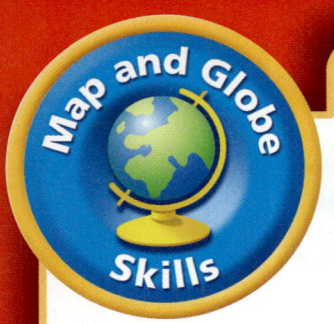

Skillbuilder
Review Map Skills

Map and Globe Skills

A globe is a round model of our planet, Earth. A map is a flat drawing of Earth's surface. There are many different types of maps. For example, historical maps show places or events from the past. Political maps show cities, states, and countries. Although different types of maps show different types of information, most maps share certain elements.

▶ **VOCABULARY**
legend
compass rose
scale

State of Arkansas

MISSOURI
Beaver Lake
• Fayetteville
• Fort Smith
Greers Ferry Lake
ARKANSAS
★ Little Rock
Hot Springs •
Lake Ouachita
• Pine Bluff
Arkansas River
Ouachita River
Red River
Mississippi River
• Jonesboro
OKLAHOMA
TEXAS
LOUISIANA
TENNESSEE
MISSISSIPPI

Compass rose: N, NE, E, SE, S, SW, W, NW

km 0 30 60
mi 0 30 60

LEGEND
★ State capital
• Major city

10 • Chapter 1

Learn the Skill

Step 1: Read the main title to find out what the map shows.

Step 2: Look at the legend. A <mark>legend,</mark> or map key, tells you what symbols on the map mean.

LEGEND
★ State capital
• Major city

Step 3: Use the <mark>compass rose</mark> to find cardinal directions such as north, east, south, and west. Intermediate directions are located between cardinal directions.

Step 4: Use the map <mark>scale</mark> to find the distance between locations.

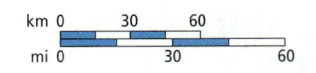

Practice the Skill

Use the political map on page 10 to answer the questions.

1. What is the purpose of this map?
2. What symbol is used to show a city?
3. What state is north of Arkansas?

Apply the Skill

Use the map on page 13 to answer the following questions.

1. What is the title of the map?
2. Using the scale of the map, what distance is represented by three-fourths of an inch on this map?

11

Core Lesson 2

Regions of Arkansas

VOCABULARY

plateau
erosion
plain

Vocabulary Strategy

plateau

Look for the word **plate** in **plateau**. A plate is nearly flat. A plateau is an area of high land that is mostly flat on top.

READING SKILL

Cause and Effect As you read, chart the effects of rivers on Arkansas's land.

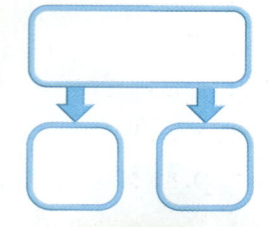

Build on What You Know Have you ever visited another part of Arkansas? What did you see? Was it flat or hilly? Forest or farmland?

Arkansas's Regions

Main Idea The state of Arkansas can be divided into six regions.

Geographers divide Arkansas into six regions. These are the Ozark Mountains, the Arkansas River Valley, the Ouachita Mountains, the Mississippi Alluvial Plain, Crowley's Ridge, and the West Gulf Coastal Plain.

Each region has certain physical features such as landforms and bodies of water. The three regions that contain mountains and valleys are known as the highlands. The three regions that contain hills and lower, flat land are known as the lowlands.

Highland Many oak and hickory forests are found in the Ozark Montains region.

12 • Chapter 1

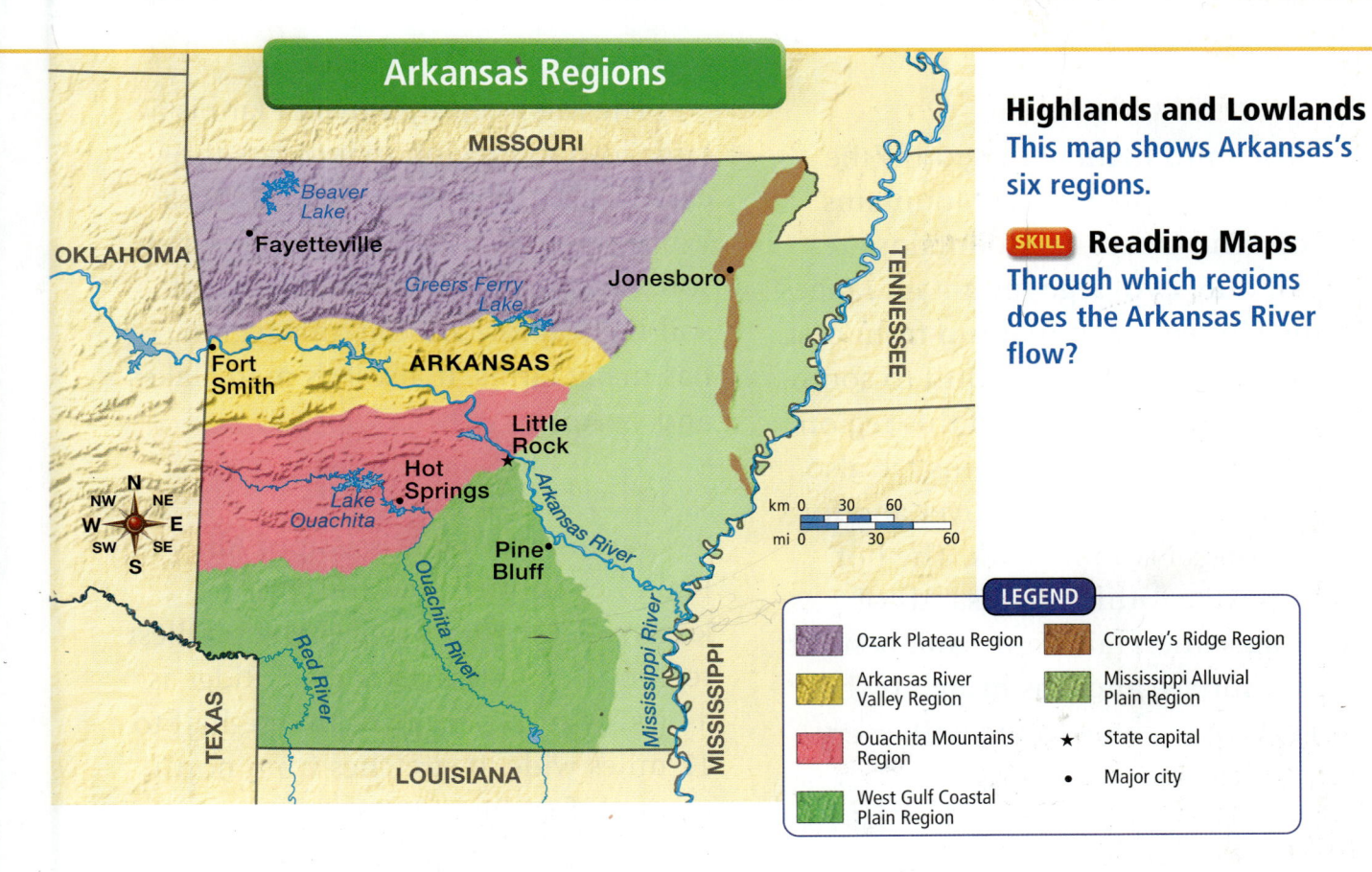

Arkansas Regions

Highlands and Lowlands This map shows Arkansas's six regions.

SKILL Reading Maps Through which regions does the Arkansas River flow?

LEGEND
- Ozark Plateau Region
- Arkansas River Valley Region
- Ouachita Mountains Region
- West Gulf Coastal Plain Region
- Crowley's Ridge Region
- Mississippi Alluvial Plain Region
- ★ State capital
- • Major city

The Ozark Mountains

The Ozark Mountains region is Arkansas's largest highland region. Most of the land here is a plateau. A **plateau** is a high, mostly flat area of land. Over millions of years, erosion carved deep valleys into the region's flat and forested land. **Erosion** is the process of wearing away rock and soil. The region's many rivers, such as the Buffalo, caused some of this erosion.

The Ozark Mountains include the rugged Boston Mountains and Mammoth Springs—one of the largest springs in the world. A spring is a source of underground water. The Ozark Mountains also have many caves. Every year, people tour the region's Blanchard Springs Caverns. Like the valleys in the Ozark Mountains, these caves were formed largely by erosion.

The Arkansas River Valley

The Arkansas River Valley is another highland region. Although rolling hills cover most of this valley, the region does contain some mountains, including Magazine Mountain. This mountain's peak is the highest point in the state. The valley also has forests and prairie areas. A prairie is a dry, mostly flat grassland with few trees.

Much of this region has been shaped by the state's largest river, the Arkansas. The Arkansas River runs through this region on its way to meet the Mississippi River to the east.

REVIEW Describe the Arkansas River Valley region.

The Ouachita Mountains

The third highland region is the Ouachita (WASH ih tah) Mountains region. The Ouachita Mountains are one of only two large mountain ranges in the United States that run from east to west instead of from north to south. Pine forests cover much of this region.

The Ouachita Mountains are also known for the Ouachita River and for Hot Springs National Park. The hot springs were formed thousands of years ago when rainwater sank beneath Earth's surface and was heated by hot rocks. People come to the park every year to bathe in the springs.

The Mississippi Alluvial Plain

Arkansas's largest region is the Mississippi Alluvial Plain. A **plain** is a large area of flat land. Alluvial describes the rich soil left behind by rivers.

The Mississippi Alluvial Plain is a large lowland region that covers the eastern part of the state. The Arkansas, White, and Mississippi rivers carry rich soil into the region. Because alluvial soil is good for farming, this region has many farms. It also has many lakes and swamps.

Crowley's Ridge

Within the flat Mississippi Alluvial Plain lies another lowland region known as Crowley's Ridge. The smallest region in Arkansas, Crowley's Ridge is a narrow strip of hills from one-half to 12 miles wide. It stretches from north to south for about 200 miles.

Crowley's Ridge was formed when windblown dust and soil known as loess (LUSS) covered ridges of alluvial soil. Over time, water erosion has carved the land around Crowley's Ridge so that the region now rises about 200 feet above the surrounding plain.

Lowland The Mississippi Alluvial Plain lies along the Mississippi River.

4 • Chapter 1

Crater of Diamonds On average, two diamonds are found at this state park each day.

West Gulf Coastal Plain

Arkansas's third lowland region is the West Gulf Coastal Plain. This region covers the southern part of the state and continues into Oklahoma, Texas, and Louisiana. The land here is slightly higher than that of the Mississippi Alluvial Plain. Hills, pine forests, and farmland cover much of the plain.

Diamonds are found in this region at the Crater of Diamonds State Park. People can come to the park to find their own diamonds.

REVIEW In what way are the Mississippi Alluvial Plain and the West Gulf Coastal Plain similar?

Lesson Summary
- Geographers divide Arkansas into six regions.
- The Ozark Mountains, the Arkansas River Valley, and the Ouachita Mountains are highland regions.
- The Mississippi Alluvial Plain, Crowley's Ridge, and the West Gulf Coastal Plain are lowland regions.

Why It Matters...

The physical features of a region affect the ways that people work and live in the region.

Lesson Review

1. **VOCABULARY** Describe the difference between a **plateau** and a **plain.**

2. **READING SKILL** What **effect** did rivers have on the land in the Ozark Mountains region?

3. **MAIN IDEA: Geography** Which regions in Arkansas make up the highlands? Which make up the lowlands?

4. **MAIN IDEA: Geography** Which two regions in Arkansas have pine forests?

5. **FACTS TO KNOW** What is the highest point in Arkansas?

6. **CRITICAL THINKING: Compare and Contrast** In what ways is Crowley's Ridge different from the Mississippi Alluvial Plain?

ART ACTIVITY Make a map of Arkansas that shows the state's six regions. Label the Arkansas and Mississippi rivers.

Extend Lesson 2
Geography

The Mighty Mississippi

The Mississippi River flows through ten of the fifty states. It starts in Minnesota and ends in Louisiana at the Gulf of Mexico. People use the river for many purposes. Its water is used for drinking, for making electricity, and for transporting people and goods. Barges on the Mississippi carry grain, coal, gravel, petroleum products, chemicals, paper, wood, coffee, iron, and steel. This powerful river provides many benefits, but people can never completely tame it.

Water
The Mississippi is a source of fresh water for millions of people who live in nearby towns and cities.

Agriculture
Farmers use water from the Mississippi to grow cotton, corn, soybeans, and rice. Others use the water to raise catfish.

Transportation
For hundreds of years, the river has been like a highway. Today, there is more traffic than ever. Each year, people ship about 500 million tons of cargo on the river.

Recreation
Every year people visit the Mississippi to boat, fish, and enjoy the scenery. These visitors create jobs for people who live near the river.

Floods and Levees
The U.S. government has built levees along the river. A levee is a high river bank that stops a river from flooding. However, levees prevent natural wetlands from soaking up extra water. This may make flooding worse downstream.

Towns
Many towns are along the river. When people built levees, they thought it was safe to build near the river's edge. However, flooding still takes place sometimes. Some people think that homes should be built on higher ground.

Activities

1. **DRAW YOUR OWN** Draw a picture of life on the Mississippi. Show people using the river in at least three ways.

2. **RESEARCH IT** Find out about dams and locks. How do they work? Why are they used? How many are there on the Mississippi? Write about your findings.

Core Lesson 3

People and Land

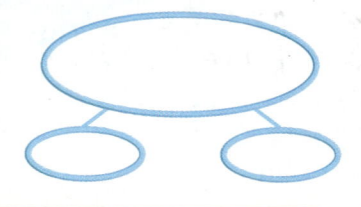

Build on What You Know Have you ever dug a hole or dammed a stream of water? People change the environment every day.

VOCABULARY

climate
natural resources
population
pollution
conservation

Vocabulary Strategy

natural resources

Natural means relating to nature. A **resource** is something that people can use. **Natural resources** are things found in nature that are useful to people.

READING SKILL
Main Idea and Details Record details about the ways in which people alter the environment.

People Adapt

Main Idea People have learned ways to adapt to Arkansas's environment.

What is it like outside today? What will it be like six months from now? As the weather changes, people adapt. For example, people wear warmer clothing when the weather grows colder. They use fans and air conditioning when the weather is hot.

People have found many ways to adapt to Arkansas's mild climate. **Climate** means the usual weather conditions in an area over a long period of time. This means that the state has warm summers and cool winters. Arkansas also receives plenty of rain.

Winter Weather People in Fayetteville have to wear warmer clothing during the winter months.

18 • Chapter 1

Natural Resources

People depend upon natural resources. **Natural resources** are things from the natural environment that people use. Arkansas is rich in natural resources. Arkansans use them to adapt to their environment.

One of Arkansas's most important natural resources is its fertile soil. Fertile means good for growing plants. Farmers in Arkansas use fertile soil to grow crops such as rice and soybeans.

Crops are renewable resources. Renewable resources can be replaced. Nonrenewable resources cannot be replaced. Earth has only a limited supply of such resources.

Coal, oil, and natural gas are nonrenewable resources found in Arkansas. All three are used as fuels to provide energy that heats homes and businesses and powers cars, buses, and other vehicles.

REVIEW What are some of Arkansas's nonrenewable resources?

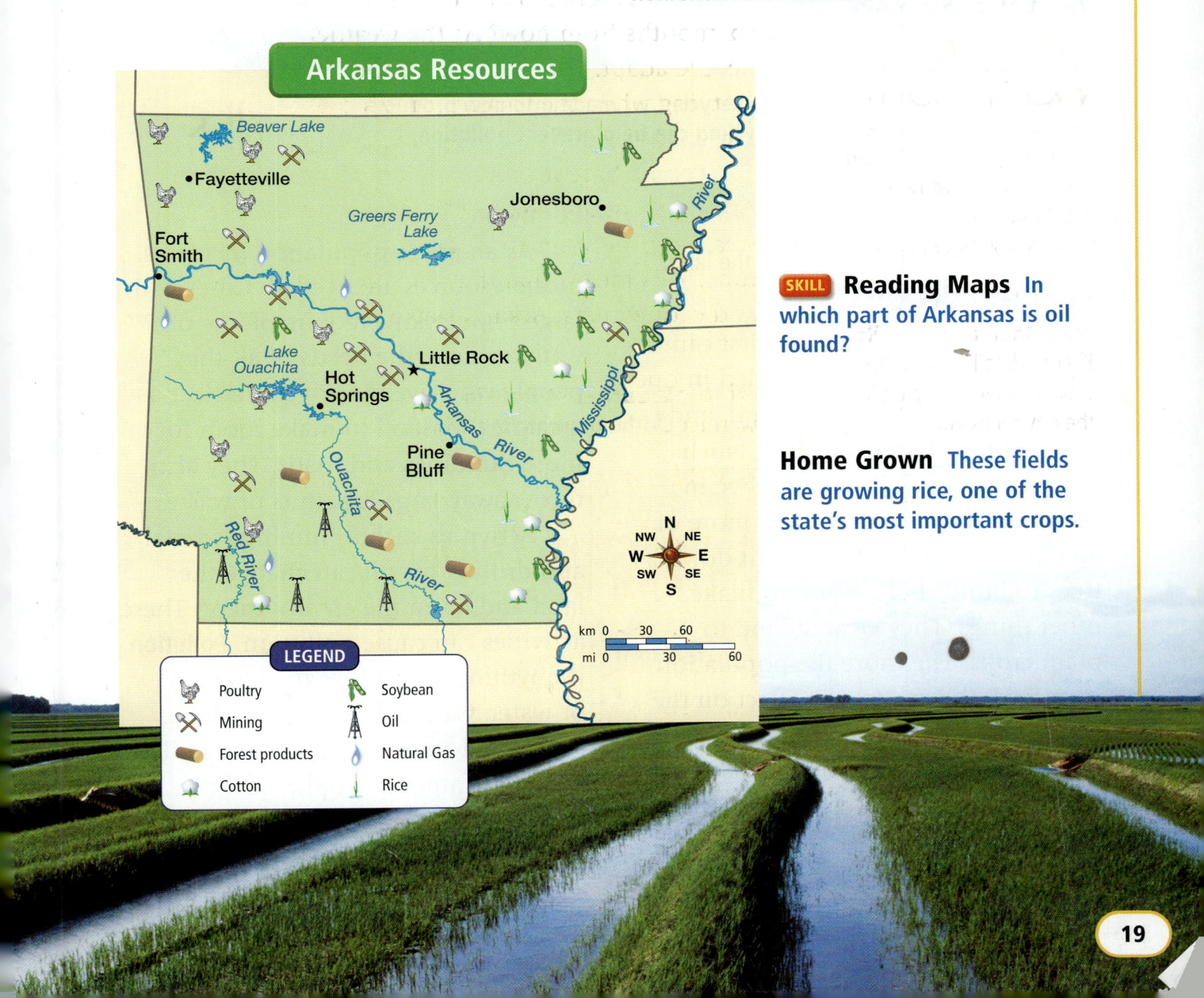

Arkansas Resources

LEGEND
- Poultry
- Mining
- Forest products
- Cotton
- Soybean
- Oil
- Natural Gas
- Rice

SKILL Reading Maps In which part of Arkansas is oil found?

Home Grown These fields are growing rice, one of the state's most important crops.

19

Recycling Many products can be recycled, or made into new products, after people have used them. Recycling can help prevent pollution.

Effects on the Land

Main Idea When people change the land, they can harm the environment.

Long ago, when people first came to Arkansas, they seldom settled in one place. They moved to find food, and they did not change the land much.

As more people came to live in Arkansas, they began to have more of an effect on the land. They cut down trees to build shelters and to make other things. They cleared land to plant crops. The more the population increased, the greater the effect on the environment. **Population** is the number of people who live in an area. Not all of the changes that people make are harmful, but many are.

Pollution

As an area's population increases, more resources are needed. Cities with large populations require plenty of water to meet the needs of all the people who live there. People clear a great deal of land to make room for more buildings and roads. They also throw away large amounts of waste.

Activities such as mining for coal and drilling for oil can change the land and harm the environment. These activities can cause pollution. **Pollution** is anything that dirties the land, air, or water. Cars and machines release fumes and smoke that can also pollute the environment. People must use resources wisely to protect against pollution.

Protecting the Land

At one time, people thought that natural resources would last forever. Today, people know that resources can be used up and polluted. Many Arkansans practice conservation to prevent using up or destroying natural resources. **Conservation** is the careful use and protection of natural resources. Practicing conservation means using only as much of a resource as is needed.

Arkansas is also taking steps to protect the environment. The state has passed laws requiring businesses to produce less waste and pollution. Wilderness areas as well as numerous state parks and six national parks have been created to protect the land, water, and wildlife in the state.

REVIEW How do cars and machines affect the environment?

Arkansas State Parks

Park and Region	Highlights
Devil's Den, Ozark Plateau	hiking, biking, boating
Crater of Diamonds, West Gulf Coastal Plain	digging for diamonds and other minerals
Village Creek, Crowley's Ridge	horseback riding, hiking, fishing

Lesson Summary

People adapt to the environment to survive. Human activities change the land and can hurt the environment. Many Arkansans work to protect the environment.

Why It Matters...

When you understand how human activity affects the environment, you can make wise choices about how to protect Arkansas for the future.

Lesson Review

1. **VOCABULARY** Use the terms **pollution** and **population** in a sentence.

2. **READING SKILL** Use **details** from your chart to describe ways that people have changed Arkansas's environment.

3. **MAIN IDEA: Geography** How do people in Arkansas adapt to their physical environment at different times of the year?

4. **MAIN IDEA: Government** What does the state do to help protect the environment?

5. **CRITICAL THINKING: Synthesize** In what ways does Arkansas's environment influence the crops raised by farmers?

HANDS ON RESEARCH ACTIVITY Use the library or Internet resources to research ways in which your school and community can improve the environment by practicing conservation.

Chapter 1 Review and Test Prep

Visual Summary

1. – 3. ✏️ Write a description of each item named below.

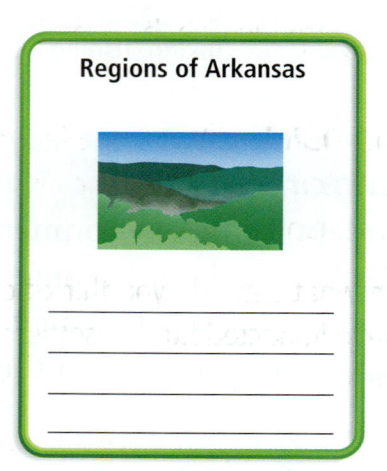

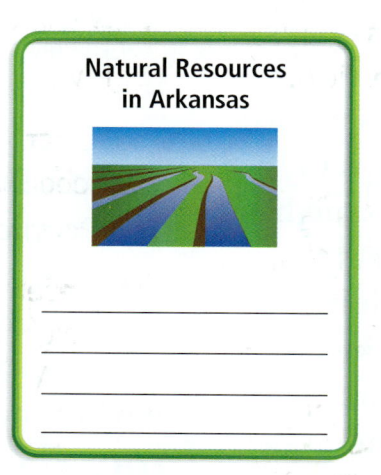

Regions of Arkansas

Natural Resources in Arkansas

People and the Environment

Facts and Main Ideas

✓ **TEST PREP** Answer each question with information from the chapter.

4. **Geography** Explain your town's location relative to two other cities or towns in Arkansas.

5. **History** Why did early settlers in Arkansas build their homes near rivers?

6. **Geography** What makes Crowley's Ridge different from other lowland regions?

7. **Economics** Name three of Arkansas's most important natural resources.

Vocabulary

✓ **TEST PREP** Choose the correct word from the list below to complete each sentence.

region, p. 5
plateau, p. 13
climate, p. 18

8. A _____ is the usual weather conditions that a place experiences over a long period of time.

9. A _____ is an area that is defined by certain physical features.

10. A _____ is a high, mostly flat area of land.

Apply Skills

✅ **TEST PREP** **Map and Globe Skill** Study the map below. Then use your map skills to answer each question.

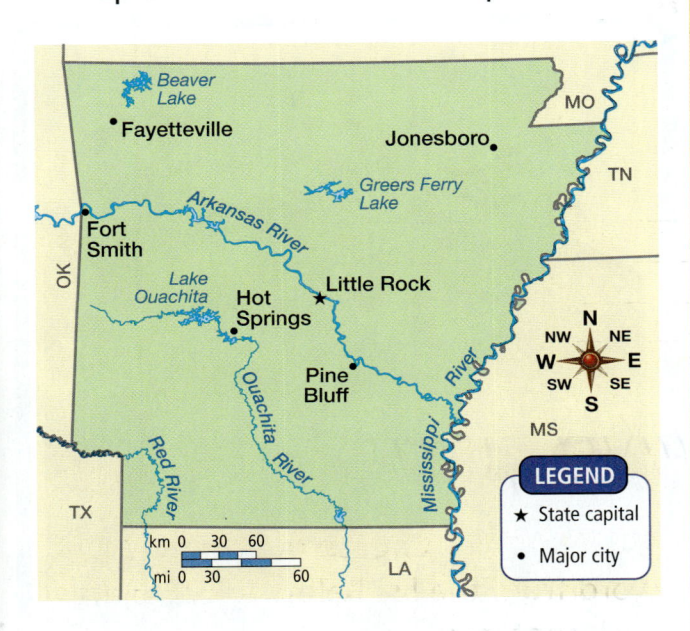

11. ✅ Look at the map legend, then at the map. What is the capital of Arkansas?

    A. Pine Bluff
    B. Jonesboro
    C. Hot Springs
    D. Little Rock

12. In which direction should a person travel to go from Fort Smith to Hot Springs?

    A. northeast
    B. east
    C. southeast
    D. south

Critical Thinking

✅ **TEST PREP** Write a short paragraph to answer each question below.

13. **Fact and Opinion** Write one fact about a region in Arkansas. Then write an opinion about that fact.

14. **Infer** In what ways do you think floods might have impacted human settlement in Arkansas?

Activities

HANDS ON **Map Activity** Create a political map of Arkansas. Include a title, compass rose, and legend. Then label the state's boundaries, capital, and major cities.

Writing Activity Write a magazine article describing Arkansas's six regions.

Technology Writing Process Tips Get help with your writing at: www.eduplace.com/kids/hmss/

23

Chapter 2
Arkansas's Early People

Vocabulary Preview

Technology
e • word games
www.eduplace.com/kids/hmss/

artifact
Studying an **artifact** helps scientists learn how people lived in the past. People long ago made tools such as the adze, or ax. They used this tool to chop and carve wood. **page 27**

mound
Woodland Indians built some **mounds** to mark important places or for burials. Mississippian Indians built bigger mounds with large buildings on top. **page 28**

Reading Strategy

Monitor and Clarify Use this strategy to check your understanding.

Quick Tip: As you read, pause to ask yourself if you understand what you have read. If not, read the passage again.

culture

To understand the **culture** of Arkansas Indians long ago, look at their houses, clothing, tools, and art work. The Quapaw made many kinds of pottery, including teapots such as this one. **page 34**

transportation

Arkansas Indians used canoes for **transportation.** They traveled on rivers and streams to hunt, fish, and trade.
page 37

25

Core Lesson 1

First Arkansans

Build on What You Know Where do people in your community get food? The first Arkansans did not have stores or farms. How do you think they got their food?

The Ice Age

Main Idea Early people in Arkansas moved from place to place to find food and adapted to their environment.

Many scientists think that people first came to North America during the Ice Age. That was a time long ago when ice covered much of Earth. So much water was frozen that the seas were lower than they are today. Low water levels opened a land bridge between Asia and North America. Some scientists believe that people came to North America by walking across this land bridge. Others think that people sailed by boat along the coasts. Slowly, people spread across the land. Most scientists agree that the first people reached Arkansas about 13,000 years ago.

Ice Age Animals Early people hunted large animals, such as the woolly mammoth.

VOCABULARY

artifact
trade
agriculture
mound

Vocabulary Strategy

agriculture

The word part **agri** means "field." You can think of **agriculture** as using fields to raise crops or animals.

READING SKILL

Sequence List the early peoples who lived in Arkansas in order, starting with the most ancient.

26 • Chapter 2

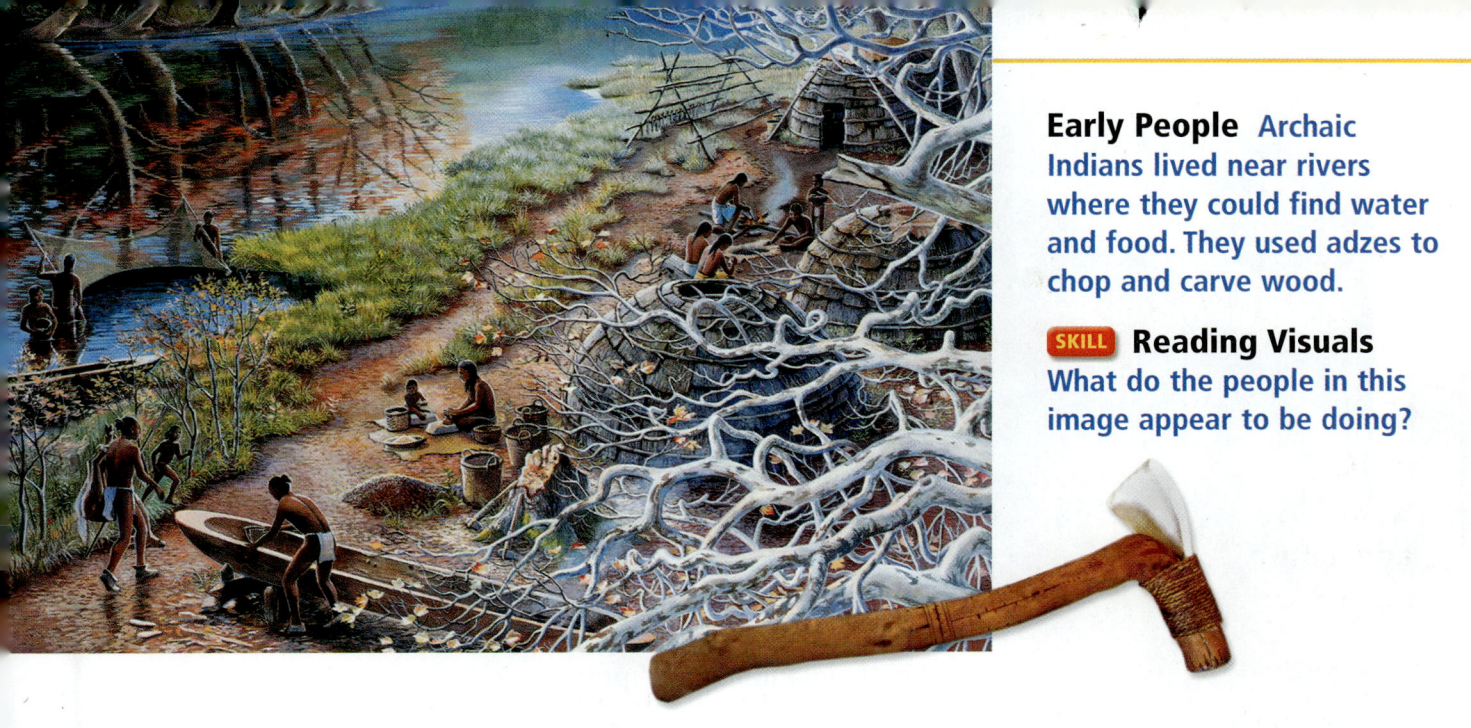

Early People Archaic Indians lived near rivers where they could find water and food. They used adzes to chop and carve wood.

SKILL Reading Visuals What do the people in this image appear to be doing?

Paleoindians

The earliest people to live in Arkansas are known as Paleoindians. These early people did not write down their history. To learn about them, scientists called archaeologists study artifacts. An **artifact** is an object made by people long ago. Artifacts such as spear points provide clues about how Paleoindians lived.

Paleoindians were hunter-gatherers. A hunter-gatherer hunts wild animals and gathers wild nuts, plants, and seeds for food. Paleoindians were nomads. This means that they lived in small groups that moved from place to place to find food. They often camped near streams and lakes. There, they found fresh water and fish.

The Paleoindians lived at the end of the Ice Age. During that time, the climate began to warm. Plants and animals that Paleoindians used for food died out. To survive, Paleoindians had to adapt to the new environment.

Archaic Indians

The people who adapted and lived in Arkansas about 11,000 years ago are known as Archaic Indians. Archaic peoples were also hunter-gatherers. Since more plants and animals lived in the warmer climate, Archaic Indians did not have to travel as far as Paleoindians.

Like Paleoindians, Archaic Indians made tools from stone, bone, shell, and wood. They also began using an ax-like tool called an adze to chop and carve wood. From soft stone and gourds, they made containers. A gourd is a kind of plant, such as a squash.

Many archaeologists believe that Archaic Indians began to trade with one another. To **trade** means to exchange things. Archaic Indians carved canoes from large tree trunks for travel on waterways. About 2,000 to 4,000 years ago, Archaic Indians began collecting seeds to grow plants.

REVIEW What kinds of food did Paleoindians and Archaic Indians eat?

27

Toltec Mound Woodland Indians built this mound near Little Rock about 1,000 years ago. This turtle bowl shows the Woodland Indians' pottery skills.

SKILL Examining Artifacts From what material does this bowl appear to be made?

Mound Builders

Main Idea Woodland and Mississippian Indians built towns and farmed.

Woodland Indians

About 2,500 years ago, people known as Woodland Indians stopped moving around as often. They began changing from hunter-gatherers to settled farmers. Woodland Indians hunted, fished, and gathered nuts and seeds. Agriculture became an important source of food. **Agriculture** means farming. To farm, Woodland Indians had to stay in one place longer.

Woodland Indians grew squash, barley, ragweed, and other plants. As they grew more food, they could feed more people. Their population increased. Many families began living together in large towns.

Woodland peoples also made clay jars, bowls, and pots called pottery. They used pottery to store and prepare food. They made new tools, such as the hoe for farming and the bow and arrow for hunting.

Late Archaic people had begun building mounds to mark important places. A **mound** is a pile of soil, stones, and other material. Woodland Indians continued to build mounds. Some mounds served as burial sites. Others were used as platforms for special events.

Woodland Indians traded with other early peoples. They exchanged things that they made for shell beads from the Gulf Coast and copper from the region near the Great Lakes. Like Archaic peoples, Woodland Indians traveled by canoe along rivers and other waterways.

28 • Chapter 2

Mississippian Indians

As the mound builders' population increased, their towns grew. This growth led to more changes. By 1,000 years ago, the people known as Mississippian Indians lived in Arkansas. Mississippians built large towns and cities. Huge mounds held buildings where leaders lived or worked.

Mississippians raised crops on large farms near their cities. Corn was the main food crop. They also traveled by canoe and traded with distant peoples. Their pottery and crafts became more detailed over time. They often decorated them with figures of animals and people.

REVIEW In what ways did Woodland communities change over time?

Early Art Mississippians carved this spider disc out of shell about 1,000 years ago.

Lesson Summary

- Paleoindians and Archaic Indians were hunter-gatherers who moved around in search of food.
- Woodland and Mississippian Indians farmed and built towns.

Why It Matters...

Learning about the first Arkansans helps us understand how communities grow and change over time.

Lesson Review

1. **VOCABULARY** Use **artifact** and **agriculture** in a sentence about Woodland Indians.

2. **READING SKILL** Use your **sequence** chart to identify who lived in Arkansas first: Mississippian or Woodland Indians?

3. **MAIN IDEA: Geography** Why did Paleoindians move from place to place in small groups?

4. **MAIN IDEA: Culture** Why did the population of the Woodland Indians increase?

5. **FACTS TO KNOW** When do scientists think that the first people reached Arkansas?

6. **CRITICAL THINKING: Compare and Contrast** Compare and contrast the ways in which Archaic Indians and Mississippian Indians adapted to their environment.

RESEARCH ACTIVITY Learn more about one of the large animals that lived in Arkansas during the Ice Age. Write a paragraph summarizing what you find out. Find a picture of the animal to share with the class.

Extend Lesson 1

Primary Sources

Digging into the Past

Everywhere you look, there are clues to the past. Archaeologists study artifacts and other remains to learn about people long ago. They search land and water for bits of bone, stone, clay, metal, and other materials. They keep everything they find—anything might be a clue.

A Mississippian Indian town once stood along the St. Francis River in northeastern Arkansas. Today, the place is known as Parkin Archaeological State Park. Archaeologists explore, dig, and study at the 17-acre site. Mounds, wooden structures, and pottery provide clues about the people who once farmed, traded, and raised families here. This illustration shows one artist's view of what the town may have looked like.

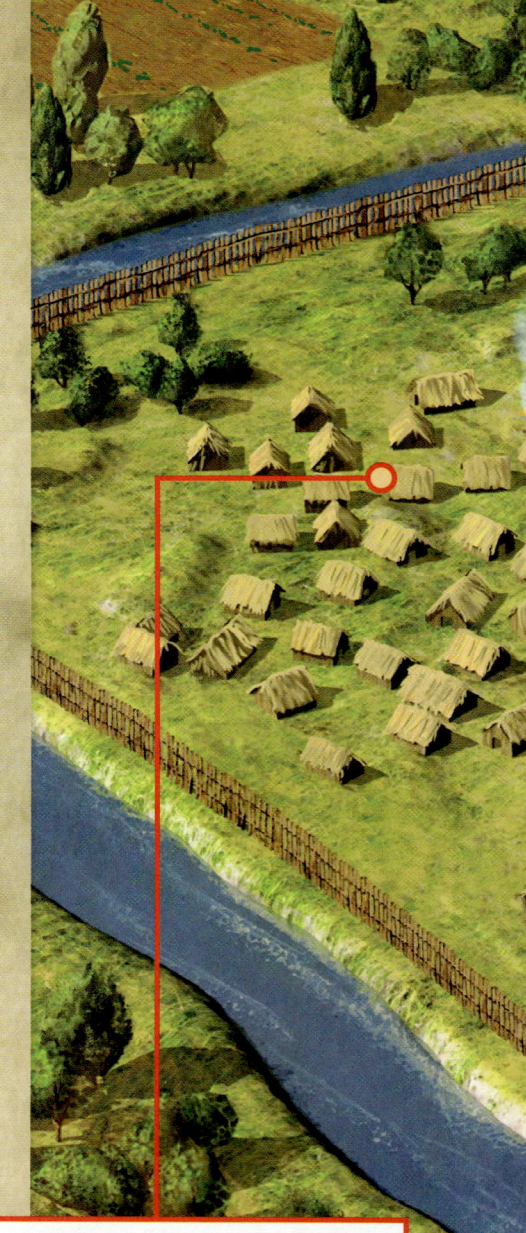

Discovery Archaeologists record every detail about digs. They dig in small spaces. They use string to mark sites so they can map the locations of artifacts. This helps them identify each item's age and purpose.

Pottery The Mississippians were skilled craftspeople. They made bowls in animal and human shapes. Often, archaeologists find head pots such as these in burial sites.

Important buildings once topped this large flat mound. These buildings overlooked a large central plaza. Smaller houses surrounded the plaza. The town's leader may have lived on the mound.

Mississippian Indians competed for land and resources. They built walls and dug moats for protection. Archaeologists found the remains of a wooden wall around this town. They also found a moat around three sides of the town. The St. Francis River protected the fourth side.

PRIMARY SOURCES

Activities

1. **TALK ABOUT IT** What details do you see in the head pots shown? Why do you think Mississippians made pottery shaped like humans and animals?

2. **WRITE ABOUT IT** Choose three "artifacts" that belong to you. Write an essay describing what information archaeologists in the future might learn about you from these items.

Skillbuilder
Write a Report

VOCABULARY
report

You have heard about the importance of Mississippian Indians, but you want to learn more. What did these people do? What kinds of crafts did they make? What makes them special? You can answer these questions by writing a report. A **report** presents information that you have researched. Writing a report is a way to share what you have learned with others.

Learn the Skill

Step 1: Choose a topic. Then brainstorm key words and ideas about your topic.

Step 2: Use your key words and ideas to find information in reference materials.

Step 3: Take notes. Be sure to write down the name of the source. Then organize your notes according to main ideas and details. The details in these notes support the main idea that Mississippians made many unique crafts.

> Source: Encyclopedia Britannica
> What art and craft items did Mississippian Indians make?
> —used copper, shell, stone, wood, clay
> —made headdresses, pipes, pottery, masks, sculptures called effigies
> —added designs, such as serpents, spiders, patterns, human faces

Step 4: Write your report. Start with an opening paragraph that introduces your topic and main ideas. Then, write a separate paragraph for each main idea. Support the main ideas with details. Finally, write a closing paragraph that summarizes what you have written.

> Mississippian Indians made many unique crafts. They used copper, shell, stone, wood, and clay. Artisans made headdresses and masks to wear. They made pottery and small sculptures. They decorated many of their items with patterns and animal designs.

32 • Chapter 2

Mississippian Pottery

Practice the Skill

Use these notes to write a sample paragraph of a report on Mississippian Indians.

Source: Encyclopedia Britannica
What makes Mississippian Indians special?
— They lived in many states throughout the eastern United States.
— They built large towns and cities.
— Their culture lasted about 700 years.

Apply the Skill

Use what you have learned to find information about Toltec Mounds Archaeological State Park in Arkansas. Write a report about the topic.

Core Lesson 2

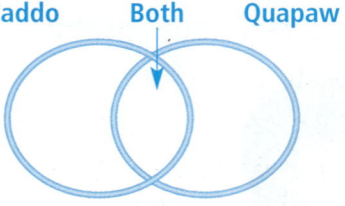

Arkansas Indians in the 1600s

VOCABULARY

culture
harvest
goods
transportation

Vocabulary Strategy

trans**porta**tion

Find **trans** and **porta** in **transportation**. These word parts mean "across" and "to carry." Transportation carries people across land or water.

READING SKILL
Compare and Contrast Use the Venn diagram to record similarities and differences among American Indians in Arkansas.

Caddo Both Quapaw

Build on What You Know Do you know anyone who can hunt, fish, farm, or make pottery or baskets? Can you? Arkansas Indians learned these skills and taught them to their families.

Sharing the Land

Main Idea During the 1600s, four American Indian nations lived in present-day Arkansas and adapted to the environment.

Over time, other American Indians replaced the Mississippians. By the late 1600s, four main nations, or peoples, lived in Arkansas. These were the Caddo (KAY doh), the Quapaw (KWAW paw), the Osage (oh SAYJ), and the Tunica (too NEE kuh). Each of these nations lived by farming, hunting, and fishing. However, each developed its own unique culture. **Culture** means the way of life of a particular group of people. A group's culture includes its language, beliefs, tools, and crafts. People pass along their culture by teaching one another their skills, beliefs, and traditions.

Caddo Community The Caddo made houses from natural resources such as wood and grass.

34 • Chapter 2

American Indian Nations in Arkansas

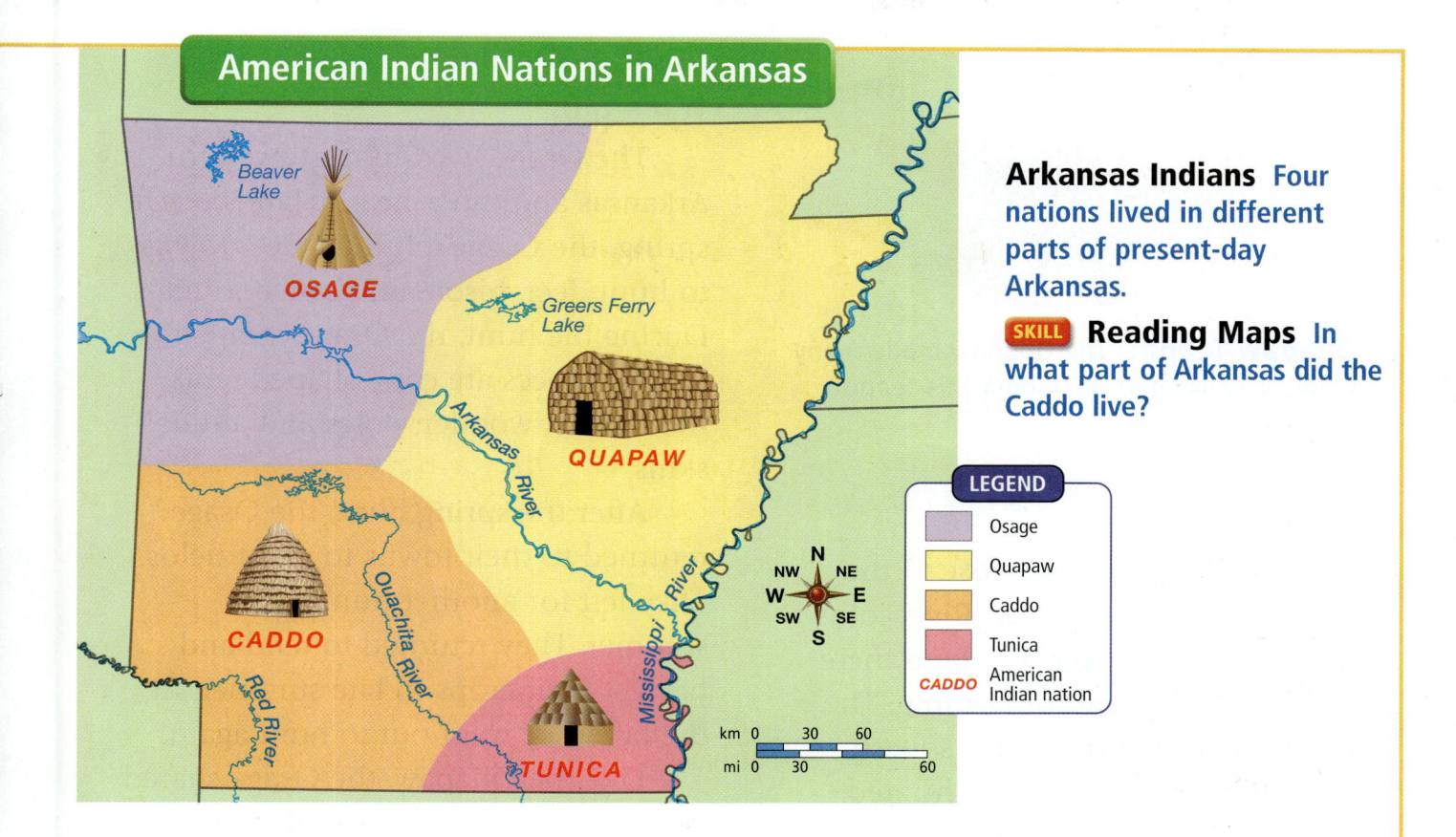

Arkansas Indians Four nations lived in different parts of present-day Arkansas.

SKILL Reading Maps In what part of Arkansas did the Caddo live?

The Caddo

The Caddo first lived in Arkansas about 1,000 years ago. Their culture developed at about the same time as that of Mississippian Indians. The Caddo changed slowly from hunting and gathering to farming. They settled in small communities rather than in large towns.

The Caddo learned to make salt. Ancient oceans had left large amounts of salt underground in the Ouachita River valley. The salt sometimes came to the surface in water. The Caddo learned to boil this salty water, called brine. As the water boiled away, it left the salt behind. The Caddo used salt on food and in trade with other American Indians.

By the late 1600s, thousands of Caddo lived in Arkansas. They had small farming communities along rivers and streams. Caddo families shared large circular houses with cone-shaped roofs. Each household kept its own fields for farming and its own woodlots. A woodlot is a section of forest from which people get wood.

The Caddo planted fields in the spring. They harvested crops in late summer and fall. To **harvest** means to gather crops that are ripe or ready to eat. They stored food such as corn in pits and sheds to eat during winter. Throughout the year, they hunted and fished. The Caddo traveled by canoe. They built small mounds for burials and special buildings.

REVIEW What special skill did the Caddo learn?

35

Quapaw Teapot The Quapaw made many kinds of containers, including this teapot shaped like a deer.

The Quapaw

The Quapaw lived close to the place where the Arkansas River joins the Mississippi River. The land there provided good soil for farming. The Quapaw grew corn, beans, squash, and other crops. They also hunted, fished, and gathered nuts and fruits throughout the year.

The Quapaw built towns around central plazas. Plazas are open areas. Each town contained rectangular longhouses. Several families lived in a single longhouse. The Quapaw made longhouses from wooden poles. They covered them in bark. They held special events in large community buildings. Walls surrounded their towns for protection.

The Quapaw traded animal furs and other goods. **Goods** are items that people exchange in trade or buy and sell for money. They decorated much of their pottery in red and white designs. Like the Caddo, they traveled by canoe.

The Osage

The Osage lived in northwestern Arkansas and other nearby lands. Each spring, the Osage left their river towns to hunt deer, bison, and other animals. During the hunt, the Osage camped in tepees. Tepees are cone-shaped tents made from wooden poles and animal skins.

After the spring hunt, the Osage returned to their towns to plant fields. They left for another hunt in the summer. They returned to tend and harvest their crops in late summer. In the fall, they went out to hunt again.

Like the Quapaw, the Osage shared longhouses in their towns. They traded animal hides, meat, and oil to other American Indians. The Osage made beaded earrings, armbands, and other items to wear.

Osage Hunting Party This painting shows an Osage hunt. The Osage went out several times during the year to hunt bison and other animals.

The Tunica

The Tunica lived in southeastern Arkansas. They farmed, hunted, fished, and gathered wild plants. Corn and squash were their main crops. The Tunica lived in towns. They built round houses from wood, clay, and grass. The Tunica held special events such as feasts and dances in central plazas.

Like the Caddo, the Tunica made salt. They traded items such as salt and animal furs with other American Indians. They used canoes for transportation. **Transportation** is the act of moving people and goods from place to place.

REVIEW What means of transportation did all four American Indian nations use?

Lesson Summary

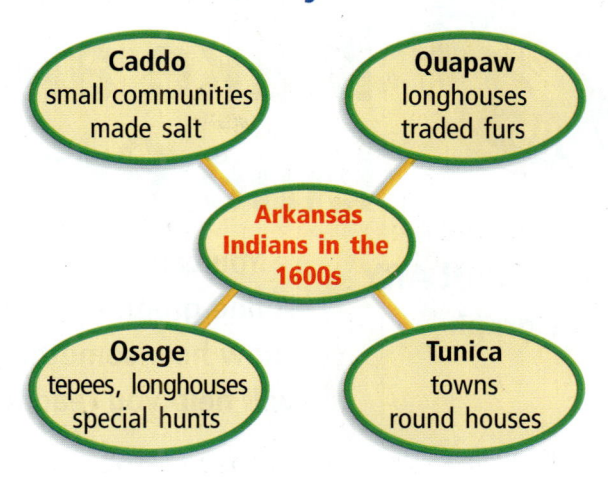

- **Caddo** small communities made salt
- **Quapaw** longhouses traded furs
- **Arkansas Indians in the 1600s**
- **Osage** tepees, longhouses special hunts
- **Tunica** towns round houses

Why It Matters...

Arkansas Indians helped shape the culture of Arkansas and the nation.

Dugout Canoe The Tunica carved canoes like this one from large tree trunks.

Lesson Review

1. **VOCABULARY** Use culture in a sentence about the Quapaw.

2. **READING SKILL Compare and Contrast** Use your chart to list one similarity and one difference between the Caddo and the Quapaw peoples.

3. **MAIN IDEA: History** What four American Indian nations lived in Arkansas in the 1600s?

4. **MAIN IDEA: Geography** In what ways did American Indians in Arkansas adapt to their environment?

5. **CRITICAL THINKING: Generalize** Describe the communities in which American Indians in Arkansas lived. How are these communities different from your community today?

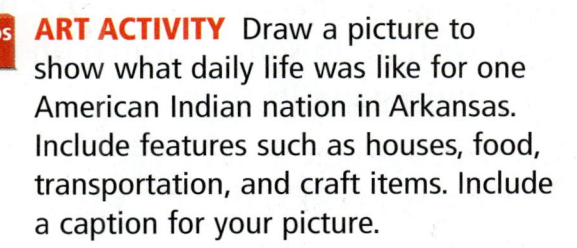

ART ACTIVITY Draw a picture to show what daily life was like for one American Indian nation in Arkansas. Include features such as houses, food, transportation, and craft items. Include a caption for your picture.

Skillbuilder

Make and Interpret a Line Graph

> **VOCABULARY**
> line graph

You can learn about change by studying a <mark>line graph.</mark> A line graph is a kind of graph that uses lines and dots to show how something changes over time. The steps below will help you read a line graph.

Learn the Skill

Step 1: Read the title of the line graph. The title tells what kind of information is on the graph.

Step 2: Read the words and numbers along the side and bottom of the graph. The numbers along the side tell you the amount of what is measured. The numbers along the bottom show the time period.

Step 3: Look at where the dots fall on the graph. The dots show an amount at a specific point in time.

Step 4: Trace the line with your finger. The line shows the change in amount from one time to another.

Step 5: Think about the shape of the line. Does it make sense? You may wish to do some research on the Internet or at the library to help you understand its shape.

Apply Critical Thinking

Practice the Skill

Use the line graph to answer these questions.

1 What time period does the line graph cover?

2 What does the line show about the American Indian and Alaska Native population in the United States?

3 About how many American Indians and Alaska Natives lived in the United States in 1900? in 2000?

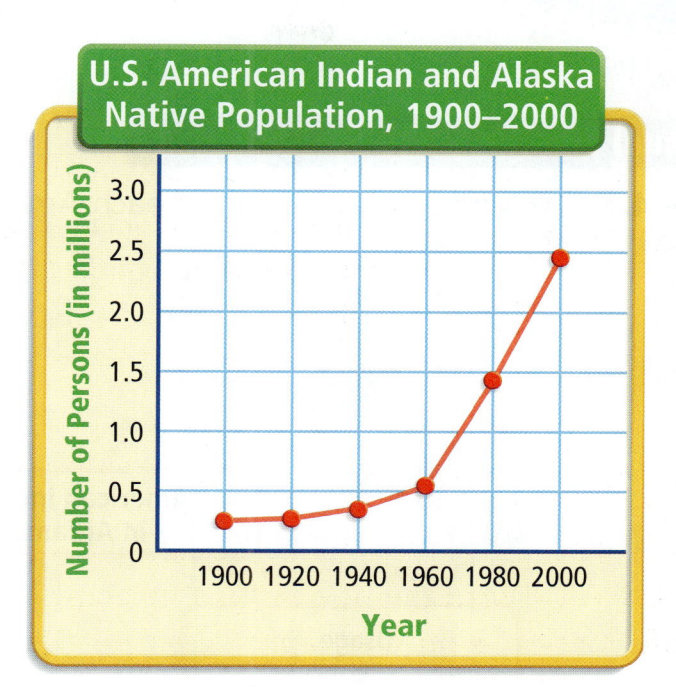

U.S. American Indian and Alaska Native Population, 1900–2000

Apply the Skill

Look at the table describing the number of American Indians and Alaska Natives in Arkansas from 1960 to 2000. Make a line graph using this information. What does the graph show you about the number of American Indians and Alaska Natives living in Arkansas from 1960 to 2000?

Population of American Indians and Alaska Natives in Arkansas, 1960–2000

Year	Number of Persons
1960	580
1970	2,014
1980	9,428
1990	12,530
2000	17,808

39

Chapter 2 Review and Test Prep

Visual Summary

1. – 4. Write a description of each American Indian nation.

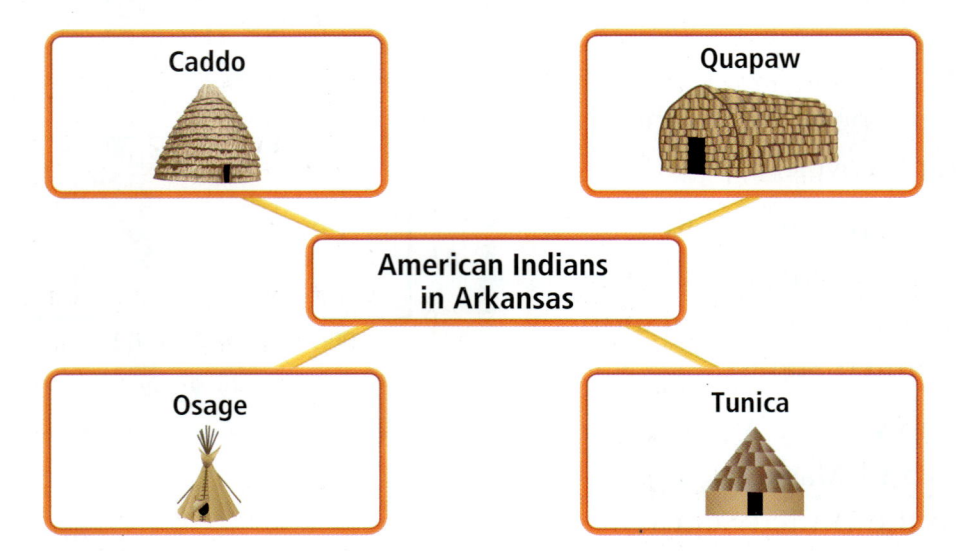

- Caddo
- Quapaw
- Osage
- Tunica

→ American Indians in Arkansas

Facts and Main Ideas

✓ **TEST PREP** Answer each question below.

5. **Geography** How did early people first come to North America and Arkansas?

6. **Culture** Why do archaeologists study artifacts?

7. **Technology** What kinds of tools did Paleoindians and Archaic Indians use?

8. **Economics** What kinds of items did American Indians in Arkansas trade?

Vocabulary

✓ **TEST PREP** Choose the correct word from the list below to complete each sentence.

trade, p. 27
agriculture, p. 28
transportation, p. 37

9. Canoes provided _____ for American Indians in Arkansas.

10. The Quapaw used animal furs for _____.

11. Early Arkansans shifted from a life based on hunting and gathering to one based on _____.

40 • Chapter 2

Apply Skills

✓ **TEST PREP** **Write a Report** Use what you have learned about writing a report to answer each question.

> What was family life like among American Indians in Arkansas?

12. What is the main purpose of writing a report?

    A. to persuade
    B. to share information
    C. to tell a story
    D. to solve a problem

13. Review the topic question on the note card above. Which set of key words should you use to research this question?

    A. resources, trade, transportation
    B. family, household, children
    C. beliefs, stories, traditions
    D. houses, mounds, towns

Critical Thinking

✓ **TEST PREP** Write a short paragraph to answer each question below.

14. **Summarize** Describe how early people in Arkansas changed from the Paleoindians to the Mississippians.

15. **Synthesize** In what ways did the Caddo, Quapaw, Osage, and Tunica use natural resources?

Activities

Research Activity Learn more about American Indians who lived in other parts of the United States during the 1600s. Prepare a visual display to share what you learn about one nation outside Arkansas.

Writing Activity Write a short story in which an Arkansas Indian goes on a hunt, helps build a town, or conducts trade. Use details from the chapter to make your story interesting.

Technology
Writing Process Tips
Get help with your writing at:
www.eduplace.com/kids/hmss/

UNIT 1 Review and Test Prep

Vocabulary and Main Ideas

✓ **TEST PREP** Write a sentence to answer each question.

1. What is the difference between **relative location** and **absolute location?**
2. In what ways do **environment** and **climate** affect where people live and what activities they do?
3. What effect can **population** growth have on **pollution?**
4. Which two early peoples in Arkansas relied heavily on **agriculture?**
5. What type of **transportation** did American Indians in Arkansas use?
6. In what way did the **culture** of the Caddo differ from that of the Quapaw?

Critical Thinking

✓ **TEST PREP** Write a short paragraph to answer each question.

7. **Predict** How do you think conservation efforts in Arkansas will affect the environment? What efforts can members of your school and community take to improve the environment in your area?
8. **Compare and Contrast** Identify similarities and differences between the cultures of the Caddo and Osage.

Apply Skills

✓ **TEST PREP** Study the line graph below. Then use your graph skills to answer the questions that follow.

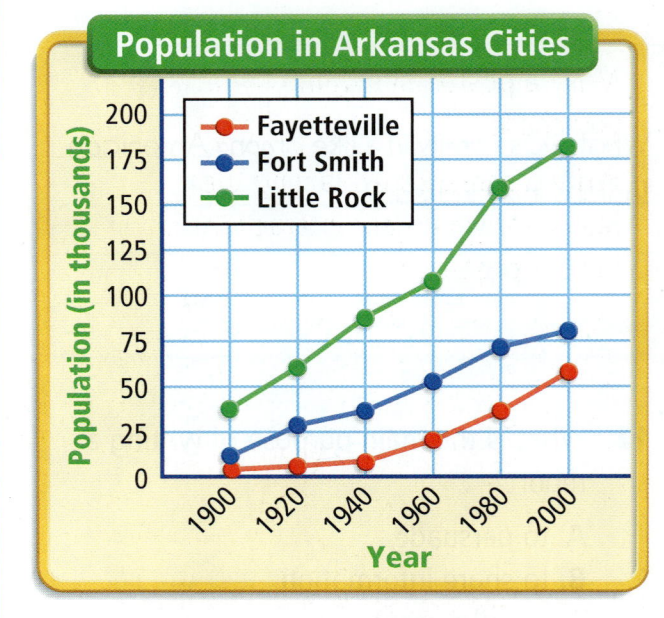

Population in Arkansas Cities

9. What was the population of Fort Smith in 2000?

    A. about 75
    B. about 750
    C. about 7,500
    D. about 75,000

10. Which city's population grew the most between 1900 and 2000?

    A. Fayetteville
    B. Fort Smith
    C. Little Rock
    D. They all grew by about the same amount.

Unit Activity

Make an "Early Arkansans and Their Environment" Poster

- List the ways in which early people in Arkansas used land and water.
- Choose one activity from your list.
- Make a poster illustrating the activity you chose.
- Write a sentence explaining the human-environment interaction shown in your poster.

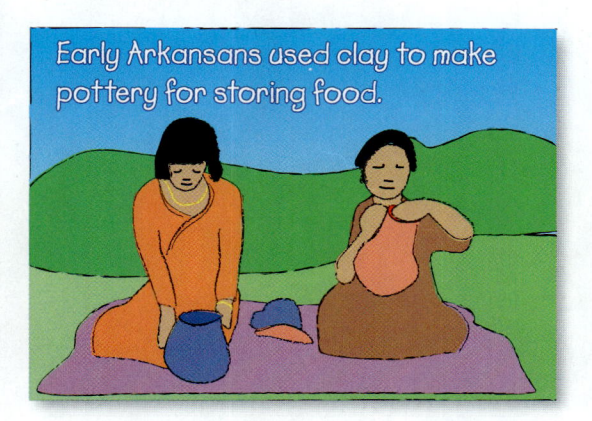

Early Arkansans used clay to make pottery for storing food.

At the Library

Look for this book at your school or public library.

Nations of the Southeast by Molly Aloian and Bobbie Kalman

Discover fun facts about the lifestyles of American Indian nations that lived in Arkansas and other states in the southeastern United States.

CURRENT EVENTS WEEKLY WR READER

Current Events Project

Design a brochure that shows the ways in which people interact with the environment in Arkansas.

- Look for images in newspapers, magazines, and brochures that show the ways in which Arkansans interact with their environment today.
- Select four to six images to include in your brochure.
- Write a description for each image. Explain what is happening and how the image shows human-environment interaction.
- Use your images and descriptions to put together a four- to six-page brochure.
- Think of a fun title for your brochure.

Technology
Weekly Reader online offers social studies articles. Go to: www.eduplace.com/kids/hmss/

UNIT 2

Arkansas History

The Big Idea

Why do people move to new places?

"*Their country is very beautiful, having abundance of peach, plum and apple trees ....*"

—Sieur de La Salle, French explorer, in 1682

Christopher Columbus
1451–1506

Columbus and his crew landed on an island in a place that Europeans did not know—North America.
page 48

History Makers

John Pope
1770–1845

As governor of the Arkansas Territory, Pope worked hard to bring more people there. That way, Arkansas could become a state. **page 82**

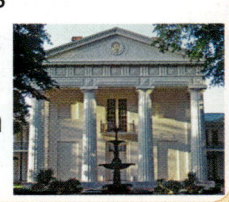

Florence Lee Brown Cotnam
1865–1932

Women couldn't vote? That didn't seem fair, so Cotnam traveled the nation, calling for women's right to vote. **page 103**

Chapter 3: Exploration and Settlement

Technology
e • word games
www.eduplace.com/kids/hmss/

Vocabulary Preview

expedition
Marquette and Jolliet led an **expedition** down the Mississippi River. They hoped that the river would lead to the Pacific Ocean.
page 49

colony
De Tonti started the first European **colony** in present-day Arkansas. He named the settlement Arkansas Post.
page 51

Chapter Timeline

- 1492 Columbus lands in the Americas
- 1541 De Soto enters present-day Arkansas

1400 — 1450 — 1500 — 1550 — 1600

Reading Strategy

Summarize As you read, use this strategy to focus on important ideas.

Quick Tip Take notes as you read. Then highlight the most important information.

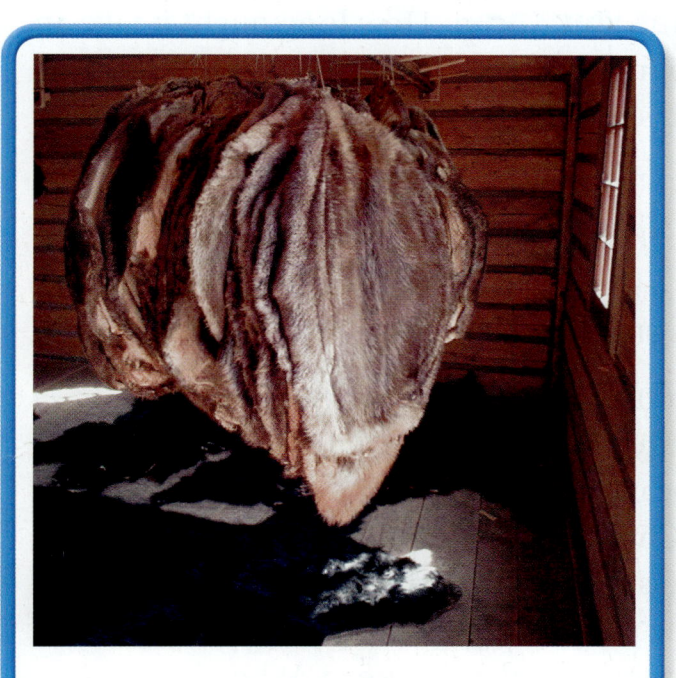

trading post
The French and the Quapaw exchanged items such as metal tools and animal furs at a **trading post** along the Arkansas River.
page 54

ally
During the French and Indian War, the Quapaw nation fought on the side of the French as an **ally.** Other American Indians fought as allies of the British.
page 56

1686
De Tonti starts Arkansas Post

1763
Spain takes control of Arkansas Post

1650 — 1700 — 1750 — 1800

47

Core Lesson 1

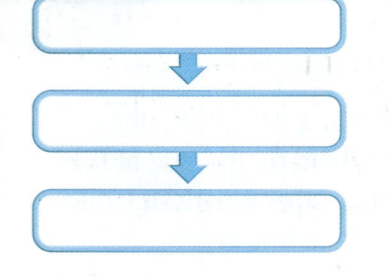

European Explorers

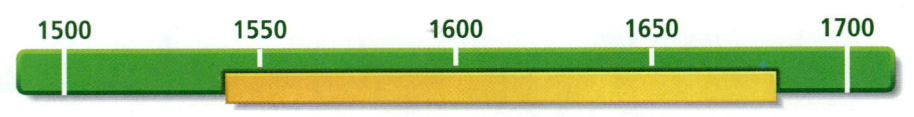

VOCABULARY

scarcity
route
explorer
expedition
colony

Vocabulary Strategy

route

A **route** can be a path, a road, or a trail. Explorers found new routes to reach Arkansas.

READING SKILL

Sequence List events from the lesson in the proper sequence.

1500   1550   1600   1650   1700

1541–1682

Build on What You Know How long might it take an airplane to fly from Europe to Arkansas? In the 1500s, it took Europeans months to reach present-day Arkansas.

The Spanish

Main Idea Spanish explorers traveled to the Americas in search of spices and gold.

In the 1400s, there was a scarcity of spices in Europe. **Scarcity** means a lack of supplies. To get spices, Europeans traded with Asia.

In 1492, **Christopher Columbus** and his crew set out to find a fast water route to Asia. A **route** is a way to go from one place to another. Columbus sailed west from Spain across the Atlantic Ocean. When his ships reached land, he thought he was in Asia. He had actually landed in the Americas.

Columbus's Voyage It took more than two months for the ships to reach land in the Americas.

48 • Chapter 3

De Soto's Expedition De Soto reached the Mississippi River on May 8, 1541. He came looking for gold, which Spain's rulers used to make coins like the one shown here.

Hernando de Soto

In the 1500s, European rulers needed gold and silver to buy goods, such as spices and silk, from Asia. European explorers discovered that the Americas had valuable resources, including large amounts of gold and silver. An **explorer** is a person who travels to an unknown place to discover new things. Spain sent many expeditions to the Americas to find these riches. An **expedition** is a journey for a specific reason.

Hernando de Soto [deh SOH toh] was a Spanish explorer who came to the Americas. De Soto landed in present-day Florida in 1539. He spent four years looking for gold in what became the southeastern United States.

As they traveled, de Soto and his men fought with and captured many American Indians. The Spanish forced them to serve as guides and to provide them with food.

In 1541, de Soto and his men crossed the Mississippi River. They entered present-day Arkansas. The Spanish found many American Indian villages, but not the treasure they wanted.

In 1542, de Soto became sick and died in present-day Louisiana. His group continued down the Mississippi River to the Gulf of Mexico. Although the Spanish claimed the lands that they saw, they did not stay in Arkansas. To claim land means to declare that certain land belongs to you or another country.

REVIEW What lands did de Soto explore?

The French

Main Idea French explorers came to the Mississippi River valley to increase trade.

More than 100 years passed before Europeans returned to Arkansas. This time, the explorers came from France. Like the Spanish, the French had come to North America looking for wealth. They did not find gold, but they did find animal furs. A scarcity of furs in Europe led French explorers to trade with American Indians. French traders claimed lands in present-day Canada. From there, they traveled south along the Mississippi River.

Marquette and Jolliet

In 1673, France sent **Louis Jolliet** [loo EE JOH lee eh], a trader, to explore the Mississippi River. The French hoped that the Mississippi would lead to the Pacific Ocean. They wanted to expand the fur trade.

Jolliet took with him **Father Jacques Marquette** [jahk mahr KEHT]. Marquette was a missionary. A missionary is a person who travels to teach religion. French missionaries wanted to teach American Indians about Christianity.

Marquette and Jolliet set off from the Great Lakes region with five men in two canoes. Jolliet mapped the river and surrounding land along the way. The French explorers met the Quapaw in present-day Arkansas. The Quapaw told them that the river emptied into the Gulf of Mexico, not the Pacific Ocean. Marquette and Jolliet turned back.

Exploration Routes

LEGEND
- Land claimed by France, 1700
- De Soto, 1539–1543
- Marquette and Jolliet, 1673
- La Salle, 1682

SKILL Reading Maps
Along what river did all three European expeditions travel?

Sieur de La Salle

In 1682, **René-Robert Cavelier, Sieur de La Salle** [ruh NAY roh BAIR kah vuh lee AY SIHR duh luh SAL], led another group down the Mississippi River. La Salle reached the mouth of the Mississippi. The mouth of a river is the place where it opens into another body of water. La Salle claimed the entire river valley, including present-day Arkansas, for France. He called the land "Louisiana."

La Salle tried but failed to set up a colony at the mouth of the Mississippi. A **colony** is a land or settlement ruled by another country. One of La Salle's partners would start the first colony in present-day Arkansas several years later.

REVIEW What area did Jolliet map?

Lesson Summary

Explorer	Nation	Purpose
Columbus	Spain	water route to Asia
de Soto	Spain	gold
Jolliet and Marquette	France	fur trade, religion
La Salle	France	mouth of the Mississippi, claiming land

Why It Matters...

The arrival of Europeans changed the way of life for Arkansas's native peoples. It opened the way for further settlement.

Lesson Review

1492 — Columbus in the Americas
1541 — De Soto in Arkansas
1682 — La Salle in Arkansas

1450 — 1500 — 1550 — 1600 — 1650 — 1700

❶ **VOCABULARY** Choose the correct words to complete the sentence.

expedition   route   colony

Marquette and Jolliet hoped to find a(n) _____ to the Pacific Ocean on their _____ down the Mississippi River.

❷ **READING SKILL** Use your **sequence** chart to list the expeditions from the lesson in order of occurrence.

❸ **MAIN IDEA: Economics** Why did de Soto come to the Americas to find gold?

❹ **MAIN IDEA: History** Why did French explorers come to the Americas?

❺ **TIMELINE SKILL** Which explorer reached Arkansas first?

❻ **PEOPLE TO KNOW** What explorer landed in the Americas while sailing west to find a new way to Asia?

❼ **CRITICAL THINKING: Infer** Why did the French hope that the Mississippi River connected to the Pacific Ocean?

WRITING ACTIVITY Record details from the lesson explaining why Europeans came to the Americas. Use your notes to write a paragraph summarizing the roles of scarcity and trade in European exploration.

Extend Lesson 1

Economics

The Columbian Exchange

From Americas to Europe

- Turkeys
- Beans
- Llamas
- Peanuts
- Corn
- Tomatoes

Potatoes Potatoes made it possible to feed the growing population of many European countries.

Imagine a place without corn, potatoes, or turkeys. Before Columbus sailed to North America, Europeans had never eaten these foods. American Indians introduced them to European explorers. The explorers, in turn, brought plants and animals from Europe that were new to American Indians.

We call this trade the Columbian Exchange because it began with Christopher Columbus's voyages. It changed the lives of people in both places. For example, European farmers began growing South American potatoes. Potatoes could feed more people than grain. American Indians learned to ride horses. They found hunting on horseback much easier than hunting on foot.

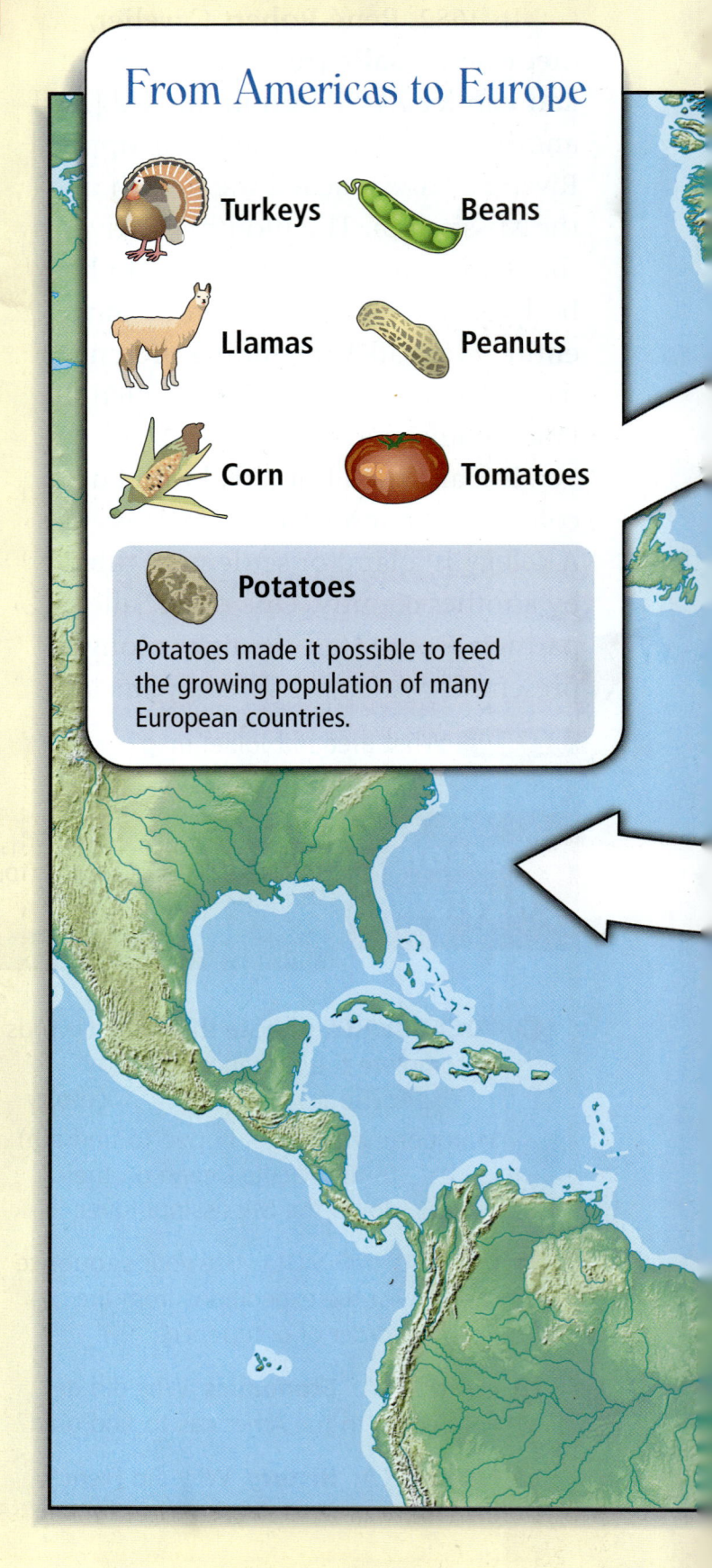

52 • Chapter 3

From Europe to Americas

- Cattle
- Chickens
- Sheep
- Wheat
- Pigs
- Oranges

Horses
Over time, American Indians began keeping large herds of horses.

Atlantic Ocean

ECONOMICS

Activities

1. **DRAW IT** Draw a picture of people using two of the plants or animals from the Columbian Exchange.

2. **WRITE ABOUT IT** Choose one of the foods that came from North America. Describe what it would be like to eat it for the first time.

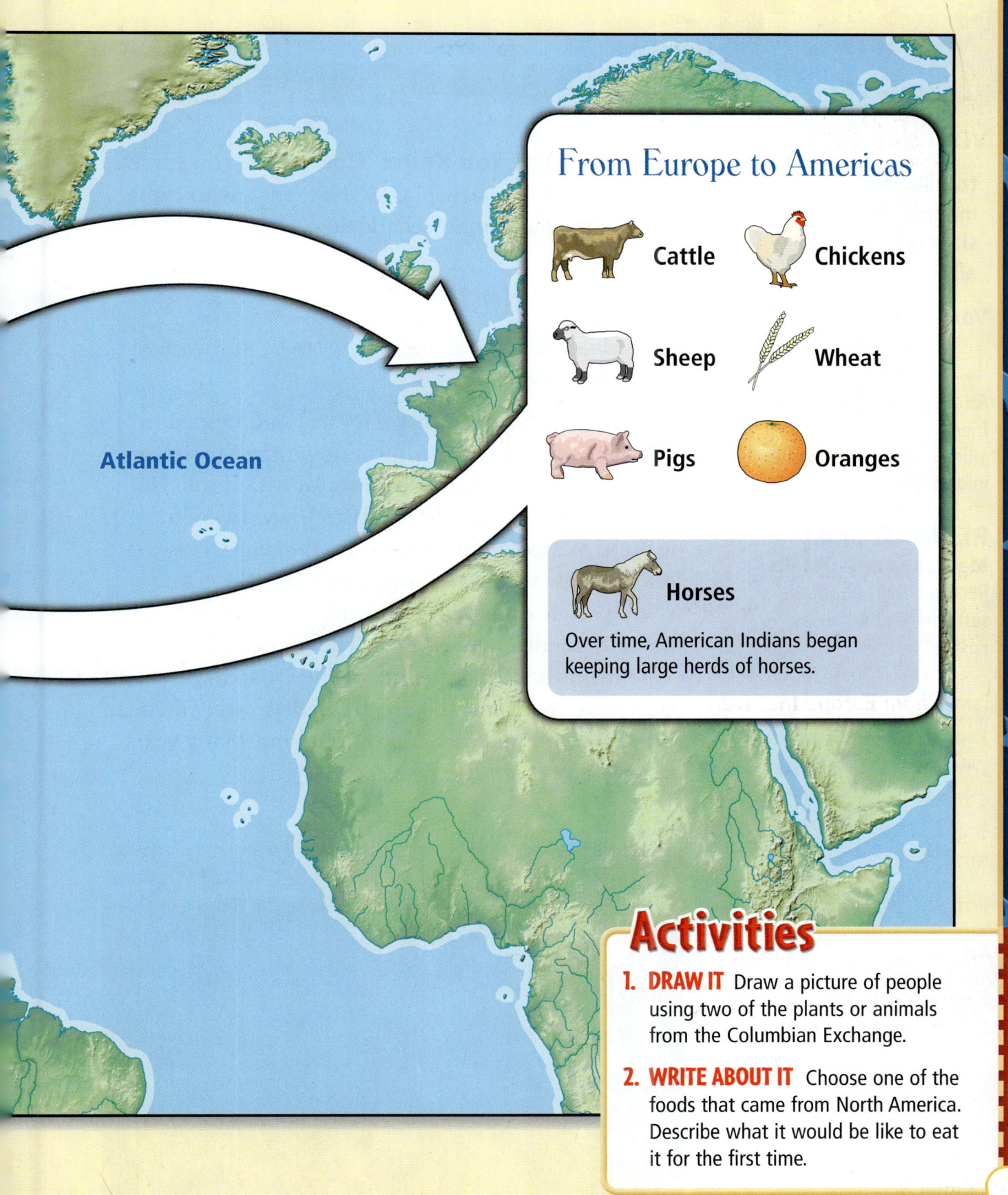

53

Core Lesson 2

Arkansas Post

1600　1650　1700　1750　1800

1686–1783

VOCABULARY

trading post
indentured servant
slavery
ally

Vocabulary Strategy

ally

An **ally** is a partner or a friend. People who are allies support one another in disputes.

READING SKILL
Main Idea and Details Record details about the settlement at Arkansas Post.

Arkansas Post

Build on What You Know How would you survive if you moved to a new place? The French who came to Arkansas faced many challenges.

European Settlement

Main Idea Arkansas Post became a place for the French and the American Indians to trade.

　　Henri de Tonti [duh TAHN tee] had helped La Salle oversee the expedition down the Mississippi River. La Salle rewarded de Tonti for his efforts. He gave him land along the Arkansas River. In 1686, de Tonti started a trading post on this land, close to a Quapaw village. A **trading post** is a place where people exchange goods. De Tonti named this settlement Arkansas Post. The name *Arkansas* came from the French name for the Quapaw. It meant "downriver people." The French traded with American Indians for animal furs and other items. Many years passed before more settlers came.

Arkansas Post The post had one small wooden house run by six traders.

54 • Chapter 3

Arkansas Post Trade

What American Indians Traded	What the French Traded
furs	pots and pans
porcupine quills	beads
salt	iron axe hatchet

SKILL **Reading Visuals** What do these artifacts show about the wants of American Indians and the French?

The Company of the West

In 1717, French rulers put one man, **John Law,** in charge of trade in French Louisiana. Law's Company of the West built a town called New Orleans at the mouth of the Mississippi River. This town quickly became a center of trade. New Orleans grew so quickly that the company decided to start other settlements in the Mississippi River valley.

In 1721, Law decided to turn Arkansas Post into a farming center. He sent 100 indentured servants and enslaved Africans there. An **indentured servant** was a person who agreed to work for a number of years in exchange for a trip to the Americas.

Unlike indentured servants, enslaved persons had no control over where they went. At the time, slavery was practiced in the Americas and many other parts of the world. **Slavery** is a cruel system in which people are bought and sold and forced to work without pay. Many Europeans forced enslaved Africans to work for them in the Americas.

Law's plan to turn Arkansas Post into a farming center failed. His company did not run its business well. Most of the people who had come to Arkansas Post for the company left. They moved closer to New Orleans.

REVIEW Why did John Law's plan to create a farming center at Arkansas Post fail?

55

Growth and Change

Main Idea Arkansas Post continued to grow in the 1700s.

Some indentured servants who had been freed stayed in the area. They hunted bears, farmed, and continued to trade with American Indians. Over time, more people came to the post.

The French brought many changes to the Mississippi River Valley. French traders and other Europeans carried diseases, such as influenza and small pox, which were new to American Indians. Many American Indians died from these diseases.

The American Indian population fell, but the European population grew. In 1731, French colonial leaders sent a group of soldiers to strengthen Arkansas Post. They built buildings called barracks to house the soldiers.

In 1749, the Chickasaw (CHIHK uh saw) attacked Arkansas Post. The Chickasaw were allies of the British. An **ally** is a person or group that joins with another to work for the same goal. In response to this attack, French leaders moved the post farther up the Arkansas River to the cliffs at Écores Rouges (AY cohr roohz). This location was closer to the Quapaw, France's allies, and harder to attack.

France and Britain both had colonies in North America. In 1756, the two nations went to war because they both wanted to control the land and trade. During the French and Indian War, American Indians fought on both sides. Because of the war, the French moved Arkansas Post back down the Arkansas River. They wanted to be closer to the Mississippi River so they could watch for attacks.

France and Britain at War The British sent troops to fight for control of lands near the Mississippi River valley. British settlers along the Atlantic Coast wanted to move farther west.

Spanish Rule

After seven years of fighting, France lost the French and Indian War. The French gave control of French Louisiana to Spain, which had other colonies to the south and west. Many French traders and settlers chose to stay at Arkansas Post. In 1768, 114 men, women, and children lived at the post. They swore loyalty to Spain.

In 1779, flooding of the Arkansas River caused the Spanish to move Arkansas Post back to Écores Rouges. That same year, the Spanish king decided to join a war that had started between Britain and its colonies. The Spanish king hoped to weaken British power by supporting the colonists.

REVIEW What effect did European diseases have on American Indians in Arkansas?

Lesson Summary

- Henri de Tonti established Arkansas Post to trade with American Indians.
- More French traders came to the Arkansas area in the 1700s.
- Arkansas Post was moved several times to avoid flooding and to defend against attack.
- Arkansas Post changed to Spanish rule in 1763.

Why It Matters...

French and Spanish settlers helped shape Arkansas's culture. They started settlements that would grow into Arkansas's towns and cities.

Lesson Review

1686 De Tonti establishes Arkansas Post
1763 Spain takes control of French Louisiana

1600 — 1650 — 1700 — 1750 — 1800

1. **VOCABULARY** Use **trading post** in a sentence about Arkansas Post.

2. **READING SKILL** Write three **details** about the settlement at Arkansas Post.

3. **MAIN IDEA: History** Why did de Tonti establish Arkansas Post?

4. **MAIN IDEA: History** Why did the French and Spanish move Arkansas Post?

5. **TIMELINE SKILL** For how many years did France control Arkansas Post?

6. **CRITICAL THINKING: Infer** Why do you think that the French and the Quapaw became allies?

RESEARCH ACTIVITY Research two of the following: the food, clothing, building styles, or types of transportation used by American Indians and settlers in Arkansas. Identify and describe two similarities and two differences.

Graph and Chart Skills

Skillbuilder
Make a Timeline

People often look at a timeline to find out when important events took place. A timeline shows events in the order in which they happened. Timelines are usually divided by years, decades, or centuries. A **decade** is a period of 10 years. A **century** is a period of 100 years. You can use a timeline to find out the amount of time between events.

▶ **VOCABULARY**
decade
century

Learn the Skill

Step 1: Some timelines have titles. If there is a title, read it to learn the subject of the timeline.

Step 2: Look at the beginning date and the ending date to find out how much time the timeline covers.

Step 3: Look at the events described in the timeline. Read the dates on the timeline to find out when the events happened. Figure out the ways in which the events relate to one another.

Events at Arkansas Post

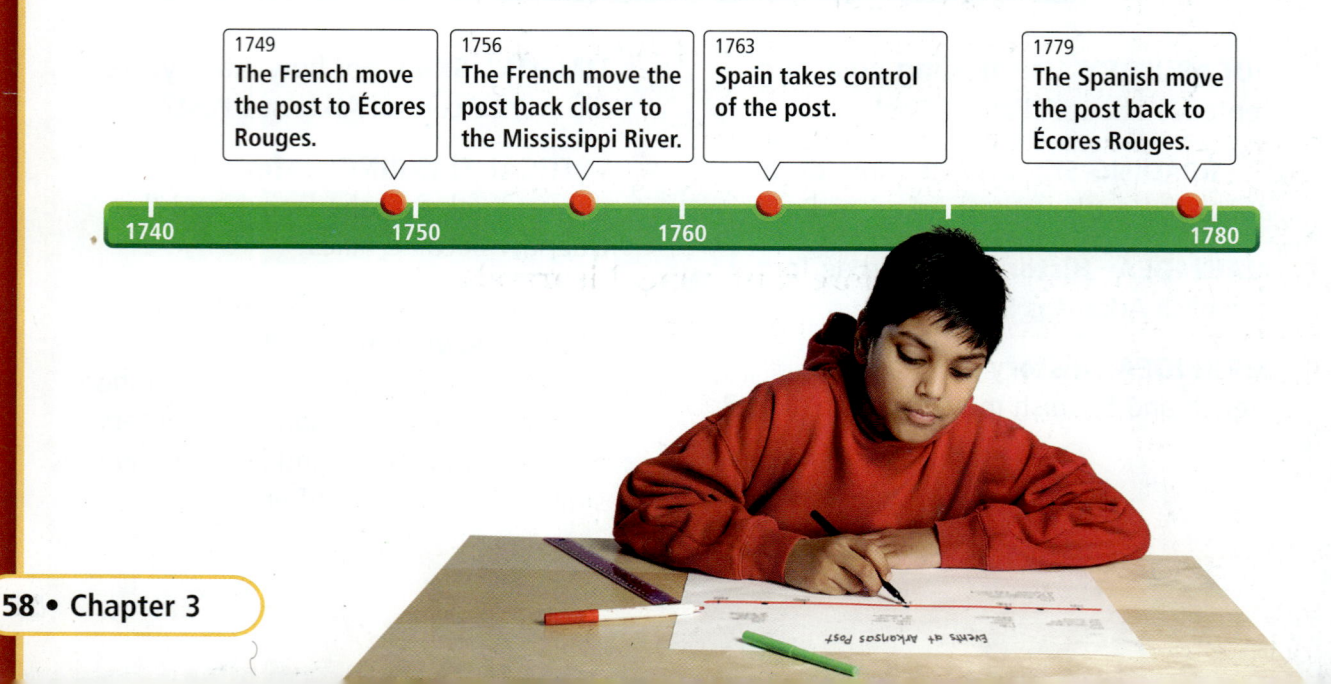

- **1749** The French move the post to Écores Rouges.
- **1756** The French move the post back closer to the Mississippi River.
- **1763** Spain takes control of the post.
- **1779** The Spanish move the post back to Écores Rouges.

1740 — 1750 — 1760 — 1780

58 • Chapter 3

Practice the Skill

Use the timeline on page 58 to answer the questions.

1. What does the title tell you about the events in the timeline?
2. How many years does the timeline cover?
3. When did Arkansas Post first move?
4. How many times did Arkansas Post move?
5. How many years passed before the French moved the post from Écores Rouges back closer to the river?

Apply the Skill

Read the paragraph below. List the events and their dates in the order in which they happened. Trace the timeline below on a separate sheet of paper. Then use your list to complete the timeline.

> Henri de Tonti, known as the "father of Arkansas," was born in Italy around 1649. Soon after his birth, his family moved to France. In 1668, de Tonti joined the French Army. Ten years later, de Tonti came with Sieur de La Salle to North America. In 1682, de Tonti helped La Salle explore the Mississippi River valley. When La Salle returned to France, de Tonti stayed in present-day Illinois. In 1686, he decided to journey back down the Mississippi and establish a trading post. He stayed at Arkansas Post only a year before continuing his travels. He made many other expeditions before settling in French Louisiana in 1700.

| 1640 | 1650 | 1660 | 1670 | 1680 | 1690 | 1700 |

Chapter 3 Review and Test Prep

Visual Summary

1. – 4. Complete the chart with descriptions of each explorer's goals and achievements.

Explorer	Goals	Achievements
De Soto		
La Salle		

Facts and Main Ideas

TEST PREP Answer each question below.

5. **Economics** Scarcity of what items led European explorers to search for better routes to Asia?

6. **History** What caused the deaths of many American Indians in the Mississippi River valley?

7. **Geography** Why do you think de Tonti chose to found Arkansas Post where he did?

8. **History** For what reasons did the British and French go to war in 1756?

9. **History** In the past, what two European nations claimed present-day Arkansas?

Vocabulary

TEST PREP Choose the correct word from the list below to complete each sentence.

explorer, p. 49
colony, p. 51
slavery, p. 55

10. _____ was a cruel system of forced labor practiced in the Americas and much of the world.

11. Hernando de Soto, a Spanish _____, came to the Americas to find gold.

12. La Salle claimed the Mississippi River valley for France but did not start a _____.

60 • Chapter 3

CHAPTER SUMMARY TIMELINE

1492	1539	1686	1763
Columbus reaches the Americas	De Soto lands in Florida	De Tonti starts Arkansas Post	Spain takes control of Arkansas Post

1450 — 1500 — 1550 — 1600 — 1650 — 1700 — 1750 — 1800

Apply Skills

✓ **TEST PREP** **Graph and Chart Skill**
Read the paragraph below. Then use what you have learned about making a timeline to answer each question.

> In 1541, de Soto became the first European to cross the Mississippi River into Arkansas. Marquette and Jolliet reached the mouth of the Arkansas River in 1673, and La Salle sailed down the entire length of the Mississippi in 1682. La Salle's partner, de Tonti, founded the first European settlement in Arkansas in 1686.

13. How many years would a timeline need to span in order to show all the dates mentioned?

   A. 100
   B. 200
   C. 300
   D. 400

14. What title would be best for a timeline showing this information?

   A. American Indians in Arkansas
   B. Journeys on the Mississippi River
   C. The French Founding of Arkansas Post
   D. European Exploration in Arkansas

Critical Thinking

✓ **TEST PREP** Write a short paragraph to answer each question below.

15. Synthesize In what ways did scarcity lead to European exploration in the Americas and Arkansas?

16. Summarize What changes took place at Arkansas Post over time?

Timeline

Use the Chapter Summary Timeline above to answer the question.

17. How many years after de Soto's exploration did Arkansas come under Spanish rule?

Activities

Technology Activity Prepare a poster comparing one type of transportation used in the 1600s with a modern type of transportation. Explore the speed, building materials, and power source of each type.

Writing Activity Write a journal entry in which an explorer from this chapter describes his experiences. Think about the people and landscape that the explorer encountered.

Technology
Writing Process Tips
Get help with your writing at:
www.eduplace.com/kids/hmss/

61

Chapter 4
A Nation and a State

Vocabulary Preview

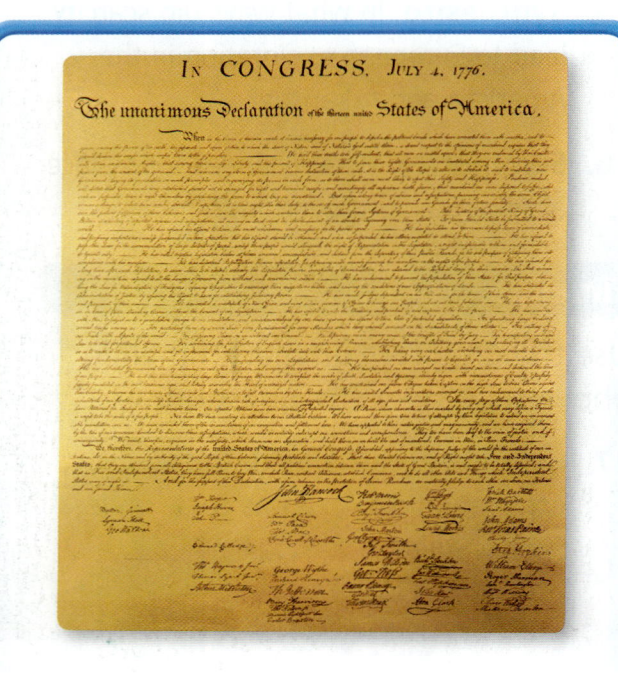

Technology
e • word games
www.eduplace.com/kids/hmss/

declaration
In 1776, Thomas Jefferson wrote the **Declaration** of Independence. This document stated that the American colonies were free from British rule.
page 66

port
To keep the **port** of New Orleans open to American ships, the United States bought the Louisiana Territory from France in 1803. The port is on the Mississippi River.
page 72

Chapter Timeline

- 1776 Declaration of Independence
- 1783 Treaty of Paris
- 1803 Louisiana Purchase

1750 — 1770 — 1790

62 • Unit 2

Reading Strategy

Question Use this strategy as you read the lessons in this chapter.

Quick Tip List any questions that you have. When you have finished reading, go back and find the answers.

capital

Little Rock became Arkansas's **capital** in 1821. State leaders still meet and work together in Little Rock today.
page 78

governor

William Fulton was Arkansas Territory's fifth and last territorial **governor.** His term ended in 1836, when Arkansas became a state.
page 78

1819 Arkansas Territory established

1836 Arkansas becomes a state

1810 — 1830 — 1850

63

Core Lesson 1

A New Nation

1750　1760　1770　1780　1790　1800

1754–1791

Build on What You Know Why do people in the United States celebrate July Fourth? Do you know what important decision the nation's founders made on July 4, 1776?

The Thirteen Colonies

Main Idea The British established thirteen colonies and fought the French on land in North America.

While the French settled in the Mississippi River valley, the English started colonies along the Atlantic Coast of North America. Like the Spanish and French, many English settlers hoped to make money in the Americas. Others, such as the Pilgrims, came to the colonies to practice their religion freely.

The thirteen British colonies had local governments. (In the 1770s, England became better known as Britain.) A government is a system for ruling. Although the colonies belonged to Britain, they mostly governed themselves.

VOCABULARY

tax
revolution
declaration
independence
election

Vocabulary Strategy

declaration

Find the root word **declare** in **declaration**. It means "to announce something." A declaration announces an idea.

READING SKILL

Cause and Effect As you read, note the cause that leads to the American Revolution.

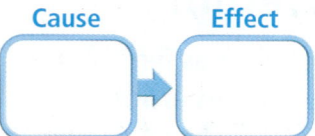

Cause → Effect

Jamestown The first successful English settlement in North America was in present-day Virginia.

64 • Chapter 4

The British Colonies, 1763

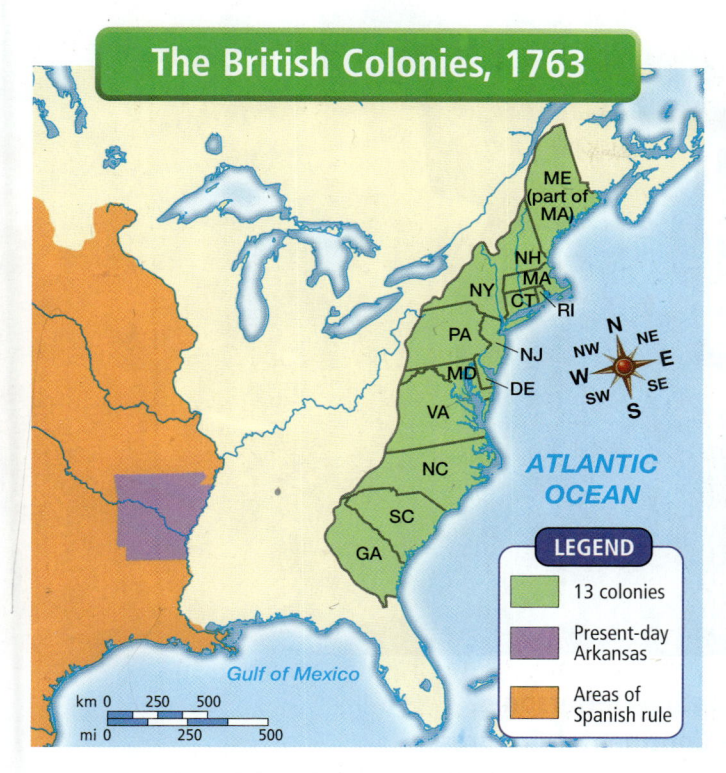

The Thirteen Colonies Britain established thirteen colonies along the Atlantic Coast of North America. **SKILL** Reading Maps Look at the legend. What is the purpose of this historical map?

Protest in the Colonies

The British victory in the French and Indian War had cost the British a great deal of money. The British government decided that the American colonies should help pay for the war. They passed laws to create new taxes. A **tax** is money that people or businesses pay to support the government. The new laws taxed sugar, paper, tea, and other goods.

The colonists believed that the new taxes were unfair. Colonists did not have a representative in the British government. A representative is someone chosen to speak and act for others. Without a representative, the colonists had no say in tax laws. Many colonists believed that the colonial government, not the British government, should decide on taxes for the colonies.

American colonists strongly resisted the new British taxes. They argued that they should be canceled. Colonists refused to buy certain goods such as sugar to avoid paying taxes on them. To protest the British tax on tea, colonists dumped tea into the harbor in Boston, Massachusetts. This event is known as the Boston Tea Party.

The physical distance between Britain and the colonies also created problems. Communication between the British and the American colonists was poor. Over time, some colonists started to lose feelings of loyalty towards Britain.

REVIEW Why did Britain tax the American colonies?

The Boston Tea Party In 1773, colonists dumped 342 chests of tea into Boston Harbor.

The Declaration of Independence In this painting, Jefferson presents the Declaration of Independence to the Continental Congress.

War and Independence

Main Idea The American colonies declared themselves free from Britain in 1776.

In 1774, delegates from 12 colonies met. A delegate is a representative. They discussed whether the colonies could remain loyal to the British government. The delegates at this meeting, known as the First Continental Congress, included **George Washington.**

Tensions grew at this time between colonists who opposed British rule and colonists who wanted to stay loyal to Britain. In April 1775, British soldiers fought colonists at Lexington and at Concord in Massachusetts. These battles were the beginning of the American Revolution, or Revolutionary War. A **revolution** is a fight to remove a government from power.

In 1776, the Continental Congress met again. It chose Virginia delegate **Thomas Jefferson** to write the Declaration of Independence. A **declaration** is a written or spoken statement. **Independence** is freedom from rule by someone else. The purpose of the Declaration of Independence was to state that the American colonies were free from British rule. It also stated that all people are created equal and have the right to "life, liberty, and the pursuit of happiness."

On July 4, 1776, delegates to the Second Continental Congress voted to accept the Declaration and signed their names to the document. Among these delegates was **John Hancock,** the president of the Continental Congress.

Surrender at Yorktown This painting shows British general Charles Cornwallis surrendering to the Continental Army, which was commanded by General George Washington (right).

The American Revolution

The war between Britain and the colonies lasted almost nine years. General George Washington led the colonial soldiers. They were known as the Continental Army.

In 1781, the Continental Army defeated the British at the Battle of Yorktown in Virginia. This was the last great battle of the American Revolution.

Most of the fighting during the American Revolution took place in the thirteen colonies. Yet in 1783, the British and their Chickasaw allies attacked Arkansas Post. This was because Spain, which owned Arkansas Post, supported the colonists. The attack was the westernmost battle of the American Revolution.

In September 1783, Britain and the United States signed the Treaty of Paris. A treaty is an agreement between nations. The treaty ended the American Revolution. It stated that the United States was an independent nation. The treaty also gave the United States more land. The new nation now reached north to British Canada, south to Spanish Florida, and west to the Mississippi River.

In 1789, the United States chose a President for the first time. People voted for George Washington in an election. An **election** is a process by which voters choose government leaders.

REVIEW What was the purpose of the Declaration of Independence?

67

Delegates to the Constitutional Convention Benjamin Franklin of Pennsylvania (left) and James Madison of Virginia (right) helped write a new plan for a stronger national government.

Building a United Country

Main Idea The Constitution was a written plan for the government of the new nation.

After the American Revolution, the thirteen English colonies became independent states. Congress wrote a document called the Articles of Confederation that gave most of the power to the states. For example, the U.S. Congress was not allowed to tax the people. Because of this, the United States had trouble paying for the American Revolution.

The states realized that they needed to change the Articles of Confederation. In 1787, delegates met in Philadelphia, Pennsylvania, to discuss these changes. This meeting later became known as the Constitutional Convention.

The delegates included George Washington, who was elected president of the convention. Other delegates included **Benjamin Franklin** and **James Madison.** Both Washington and Madison wanted to do more than change the Articles. They wanted a new plan that would give the United States a stronger national government. After months of work, the delegates completed the Constitution.

The Constitution is the plan for government in the United States. It sets up a system in which the national government shares power with the states. The Constitution explains the laws and decisions that the national government can make. It also explains the matters that states can decide for themselves.

The Bill of Rights

Many people in the United States wanted to make sure that the government would protect the rights of citizens. Several states refused to approve the new Constitution until the delegates promised to add protections for citizens' rights.

In 1791, ten amendments, or changes to the Constitution, were ratified. To ratify means to accept. These ten amendments are known as the Bill of Rights. The Bill of Rights protects important rights. These rights include the freedom of speech and the freedom of the press, which allow people to share information and opinions.

REVIEW Who were three delegates that helped write the Constitution?

Lesson Summary

- American colonists felt that the British government taxed them unfairly.
- The American colonies declared their independence from Britain in 1776.
- The United States won the American Revolution and gained independence.
- In 1787, delegates met in Philadelphia and wrote the Constitution.

Why It Matters...

Colonists fought for the rights that citizens in the United States enjoy today.

Lesson Review

1775 — American Revolution begins
1783 — Treaty of Paris

1770 — 1780 — 1790

① VOCABULARY Write a sentence about Thomas Jefferson and the **Declaration of Independence.**

② READING SKILL What **caused** problems between the British and the American colonists?

③ MAIN IDEA: History Why did colonists believe that the new British taxes were unfair?

④ MAIN IDEA: Government What were the Articles of Confederation?

⑤ PEOPLE TO KNOW Who was John Hancock?

⑥ TIMELINE SKILL How long did the American Revolution last?

⑦ CRITICAL THINKING: Summarize Why are the Constitution and Bill of Rights still important today?

RESEARCH ACTIVITY Use library and Internet resources to learn more about distance and lack of communication between England and her thirteen colonies as causes of the American Revolution. Write a short report about what you learn.

69

Extend Lesson 1
History

Saying "No" to Britain

Obey the Proclamation of 1763? Many American colonists did not want to! The British government wrote this proclamation to keep settlers from moving west of the Appalachian Mountains. The decision to reserve land for American Indians upset many people who lived east of the Appalachians. They thought this was unfair because they had fought the French in order to open western lands to settlement. They believed that they should be allowed to settle the land.

People from the East without land wanted to take land and start farms beyond the Appalachian Mountains. Wealthy people also wanted to buy western lands. They wanted to divide large areas of land into smaller sections to sell to settlers. The proclamation led many colonists to start opposing the decisions of the British government.

Daniel Boone Many people ignored the Proclamation of 1763. In the early 1770s, Daniel Boone led a group of settlers from North Carolina across the Appalachian Mountains. This group built a road called Boone's Trace along an American Indian trail from present-day Virginia to present-day Kentucky. The road was also known as the Wilderness Road.

70 • Chapter 4

George Washington

As a young man, George Washington mapped and measured land in the Ohio Valley so people could start farms and towns. He also bought land there. The Proclamation of 1763 was one reason that Washington became unhappy with the British government.

Activities

1. **THINK ABOUT IT** Why did people think that they should be allowed to settle western lands?

2. **RESEARCH IT** What effect did more settlers have on Arkansas's environment?

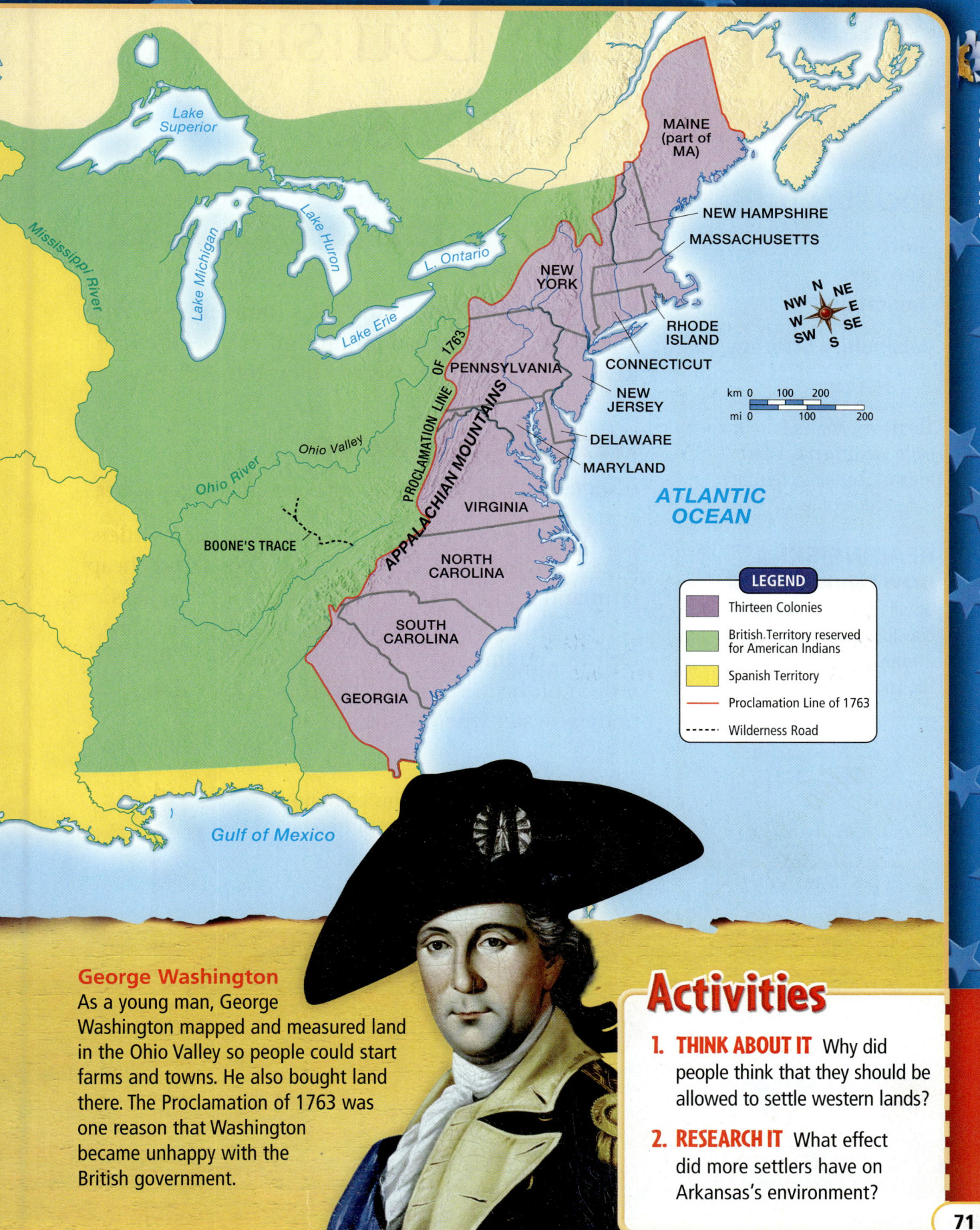

Core Lesson 2

The Louisiana Purchase

VOCABULARY

port
territory
migration

Vocabulary Strategy

terr*itory*

Territory comes from the Latin word **terra,** which means "earth." A territory is a section of land.

READING SKILL

Draw Conclusions List details that help you draw conclusions about why President Jefferson bought the Louisiana Purchase.

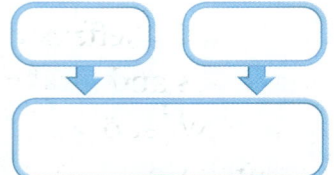

1800 1810 1820 1830 1840 1850 1860
1803–1819

Build on What You Know Has someone new ever joined your class or community? After the American Revolution, many new people moved to Arkansas.

Westward Expansion

Main Idea In the early 1800s, the United States grew larger.

After the American Revolution, American settlers began moving west. They looked for good and cheap farmland in the Ohio and Mississippi River valleys.

One place in which Americans settled was New Orleans, an important port city located near the mouth of the Mississippi. A **port** is a place along a body of water where ships can dock.

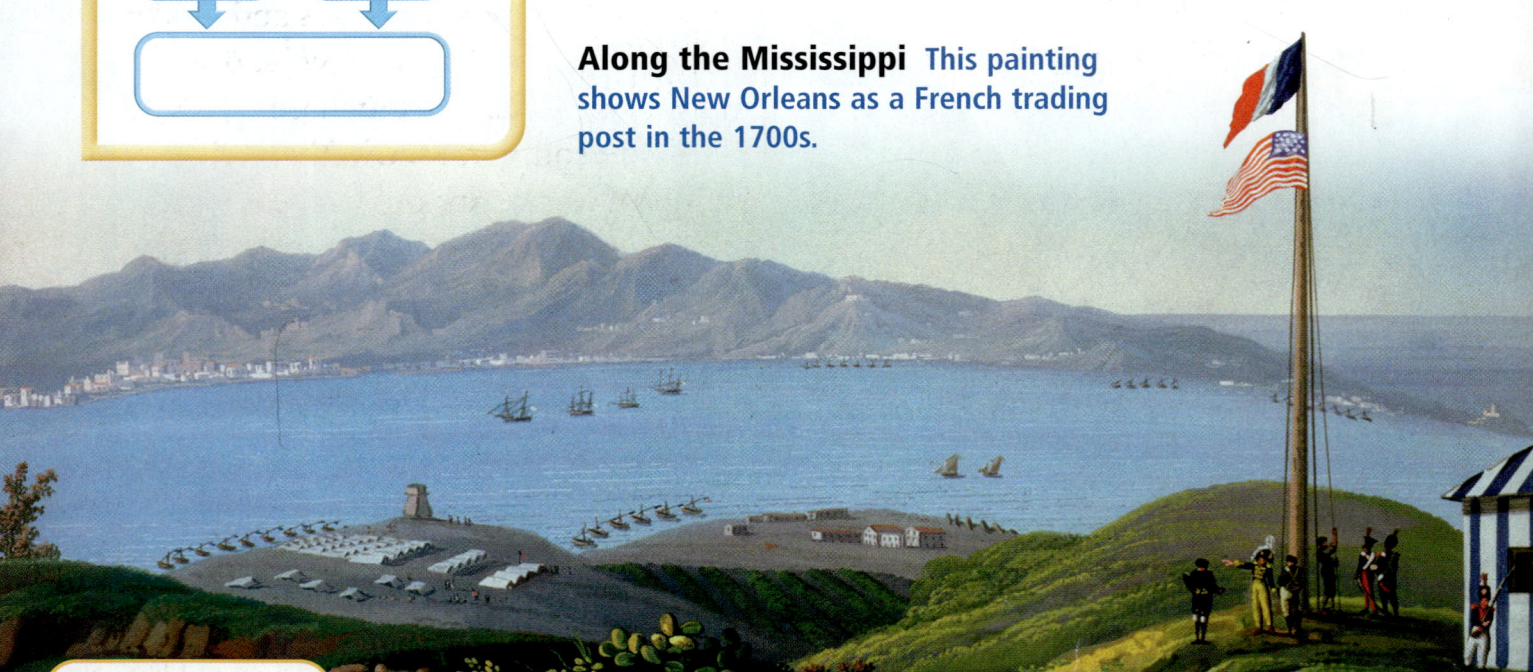

Along the Mississippi This painting shows New Orleans as a French trading post in the 1700s.

Exploring the Louisiana Purchase The Lewis and Clark expedition set out from St. Louis in 1804. It traveled across land to the Pacific coast.

France Sells Louisiana

When the American Revolution ended, Spain controlled most of the land west of the Mississippi River. This included New Orleans. Spain kept the port open to the United States. However, in 1800 Spain returned control of New Orleans—and the rest of Louisiana—to France.

People in the United States depended on the Mississippi River for trade and travel. President Jefferson was concerned that the French would close the port of New Orleans to them. Because of this, Jefferson sent representatives to France to try to purchase New Orleans in 1803.

This led to **Napoleon Bonaparte,** the ruler of France, offering the United States all of its land in North America, not just New Orleans! In 1803, Jefferson bought present-day Arkansas and much more land as well. The new land was called the Louisiana Purchase.

Jefferson sent **Meriwether Lewis** and **William Clark** on an expedition to explore this land. Lewis and Clark were helped on their expedition by a Shoshone Indian woman named **Sacagawea** (sak uh guh WEE uh). Sacagawea knew several American Indian languages and translated for the expedition.

REVIEW Why did many settlers move west in the early 1800s?

73

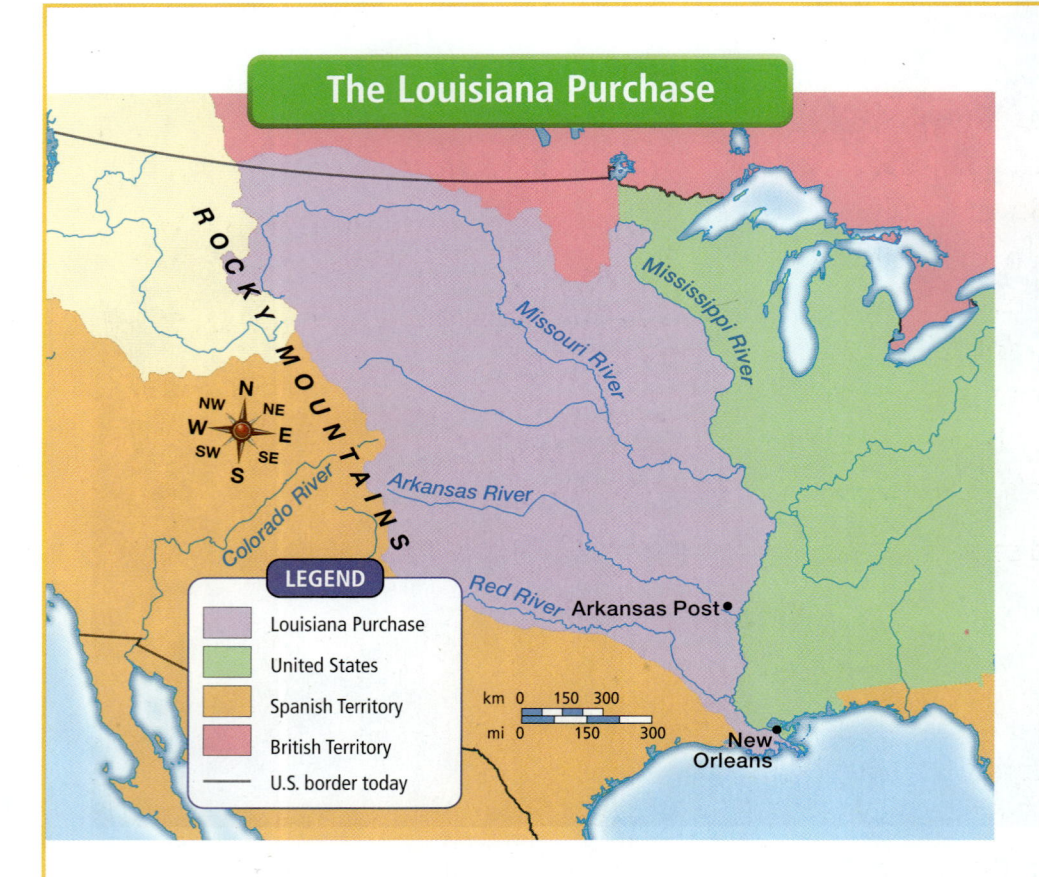

The Louisiana Purchase

LEGEND
- Louisiana Purchase
- United States
- Spanish Territory
- British Territory
- U.S. border today

SKILL Reading Maps
Look at the legend. What mountains helped form a border to the west of the Louisiana Purchase?

The Louisiana Territory

Main Idea Arkansas's population changed in the early 1800s.

The Louisiana Purchase stretched for hundreds of miles west of the Mississippi River. To govern this large area, the United States divided it into the Territory of Orleans and the Louisiana Territory. A **territory** is a part of the United States that is not a state. Arkansas was part of the Louisiana Territory.

Arkansas's population changed during this time. A new group of American Indians, the Western Cherokee, began a migration to Arkansas. A **migration** is a movement from one place to another.

The Western Cherokee came from the East and began settling land between the Arkansas and White rivers. Many settlers also migrated to Arkansas during this time. They cleared large areas of forest to create farmland. As a result, they changed the land in Arkansas.

In 1812, part of the Louisiana Territory became the new state of Louisiana. The land that was left became known as the Missouri Territory to avoid confusion with the new state. In 1819, part of the Missouri Territory applied for statehood. It became the new state of Missouri. At that time, the part of the Missouri Territory that is present-day Arkansas became the Arkansas Territory.

74 • Chapter 4

Life in the Arkansas Territory

Life was not easy for settlers in Arkansas. The New Madrid Earthquakes hit northeast Arkansas in 1811 and 1812. A fault, or break, in Earth's crust caused the ground to move suddenly. Farms and forests sank, and lakes and swamps formed. Yet more settlers came to the Arkansas Territory because they wanted to farm the area's rich soil.

REVIEW In what way did settlers change the land in Arkansas?

Lesson Summary

- The United States purchased Louisiana from France in 1803.
- Many American settlers moved to the new Louisiana Territory.
- Arkansas became a separate territory in 1819.

Why It Matters...

The Louisiana Purchase doubled the size of the United States.

New Madrid Earthquake
This picture shows a boat trying to travel along a river after the 1812 earthquake.

Lesson Review

1803 Louisiana Purchase
1819 Arkansas Territory established

1800 — 1810 — 1820

1. **VOCABULARY** Use **migration** in a sentence about settlers who came to Arkansas during the early 1800s.

2. **READING SKILL** What **conclusions** can you **draw** about why Jefferson bought the Louisiana Purchase?

3. **MAIN IDEA: History** Who did Jefferson send to explore the Louisiana Purchase?

4. **MAIN IDEA: Geography** In what ways did the New Madrid Earthquakes impact the environment in Arkansas?

5. **PEOPLE TO KNOW** Who was Sacagawea?

6. **TIMELINE SKILL** How many years passed between the Louisiana Purchase and the formation of Arkansas Territory?

7. **CRITICAL THINKING: Draw Conclusions** Why do you think Napoleon Bonaparte agreed to sell French land in North America to the United States?

MAP ACTIVITY Make a map showing the United States in 1803 and the Louisiana Purchase. Compare the area of the United States before and after the Louisiana Purchase.

Skillbuilder

Identify Cause and Effect

VOCABULARY
cause
effect

Historians often want to know why events happened. They look for causes and effects of events. A **cause** is an event that makes another event happen. An **effect** is what happens as a result of a cause. Sometimes a cause can have more than one effect. Sometimes an effect can have more than one cause. Sometimes an effect of one event can become a cause for another.

Cause
The British government passed laws to create new taxes in the colonies.

→

Effect
As a result of the taxes, the colonists refused to buy certain goods.

Learn the Skill

Step 1: Look for clue words that tell whether an event is a cause or an effect.

Clue Words

Causes
because
led to

Effects
so
as a result

Step 2: Identify the cause of an event. Check to see if there is more than one cause.

Step 3: Identify the effect. Check to see if there is more than one effect.

76 • Chapter 4

Apply Critical Thinking

Practice the Skill

Reread page 73 of Lesson 2 about the Louisiana Purchase. Then answer the following questions and fill in the rest of the diagram below.

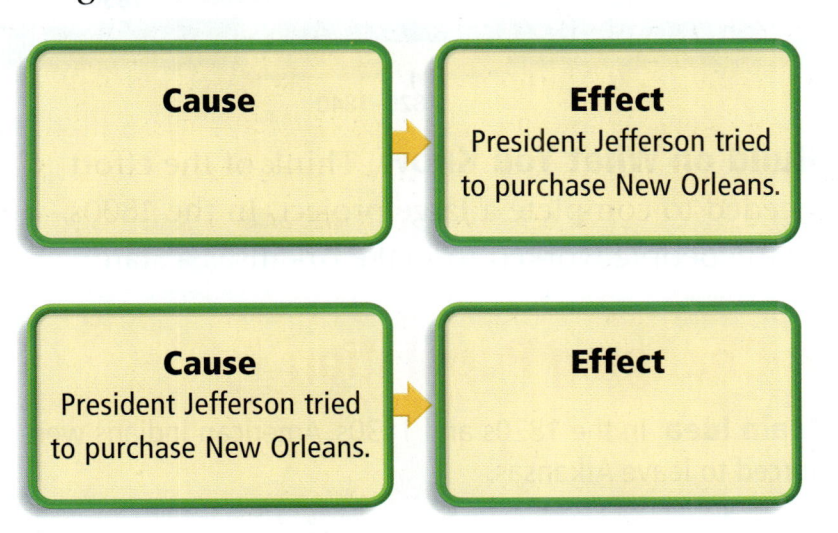

Cause

→ **Effect** President Jefferson tried to purchase New Orleans.

Cause President Jefferson tried to purchase New Orleans.

→ **Effect**

1. What caused President Jefferson to try to purchase New Orleans?
2. What was the effect of Jefferson's offer to Napoleon Bonaparte?
3. What helped you to figure out what the causes and effects were?

Apply the Skill

After the United States bought the Louisiana Purchase, more people began to settle in Arkansas. Reread pages 74 and 75. Then make a chart that shows causes and effects. Name some of the clue words that helped you figure out the causes and effects.

Core Lesson 3

Arkansas Becomes a State

VOCABULARY

capital
governor
squatter

Vocabulary Strategy

squatter

One meaning of **squat** is to settle on land without permission. A squatter is a person who settles on land without permission.

READING SKILL

Compare and Contrast Note similarities and differences between the growth of Fort Smith and Washington.

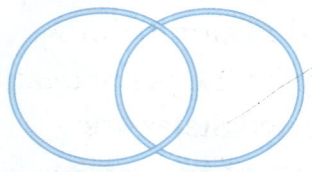

Fort Smith   Washington

1800 1810 1820 1830 1840 1850 1860

1820–1840

Build on What You Know Think of the effort needed to complete a large project. In the 1800s, many people worked to make Arkansas a state.

A Changing Population

Main Idea In the 1820s and 1830s, American Indians were forced to leave Arkansas.

When Arkansas became a territory, Arkansas Post became its capital. A **capital** is a place where the government meets. **James Miller** became the first governor of the Arkansas Territory. A **governor** is the leader of a state or territory.

Arkansas's territorial government passed laws for the people in the region. It also helped Arkansas Territory prepare to become a state. The Arkansas Territory continued to grow, and Arkansas Post became a busy town. By 1820, more than 14,000 people lived in the Arkansas Territory.

Settlers In the 1800s, people came to Arkansas overland and by river. Some traveled on flatboats such as the one shown here.

78 • Chapter 4

Fort Smith Steamboats carried people to and from the settlement along the Arkansas River.

Fort Smith

As more Western Cherokee settled in Arkansas, conflicts arose. They fought with the Osage over land and hunting rights. To stop the fighting between the two groups, the United States army built Fort Smith. It was in western Arkansas, where the Arkansas and Poteau rivers meet. Soldiers from Fort Smith also guarded Arkansas's border with present-day Oklahoma.

The United States government called this area Indian Territory. Settlers came to live near Fort Smith. A town grew up. Businesses in the town helped meet the needs of both the soldiers in the fort and the American Indians in the area.

Most settlers came by wagon, but some arrived by steamboat. In 1822, the *Robert Thompson* became the first steamboat to reach Fort Smith. That same year, members of the Western Cherokee and Osage groups met at the fort. They agreed to stop fighting. Governor Miller signed the peace treaty.

In 1824, the United States army left the fort. The town of Fort Smith continued to grow and attract settlers. Today, Fort Smith is one of Arkansas's largest cities. People visiting the city can see the remains of the original fort at the Fort Smith National Historic Site.

REVIEW Describe how the town of Fort Smith was settled.

The Town of Washington

Many of the earliest American settlers came to Arkansas Territory from Missouri. They traveled by wagon along the Southwest Trail. This route stretched northeast from St. Louis, Missouri, all the way down to the Red River in southwest Arkansas. The Southwest Trail was also called the Arkansas Road, the National Road, and the Red River Road. The main towns along the Southwest Trail in Arkansas Territory were Little Rock, Jackson, and Washington.

Settlers founded the town of Washington in 1824—on February 22, the birthday of George Washington. The town became an important center for agriculture in southwest Arkansas. Farmers in the area raised farm animals and grew crops such as corn and cotton.

Most settlers in the Arkansas Territory bought land from the United States government or private sellers. Other settlers were squatters on unclaimed land. A **squatter** is a person who settles on land without permission.

Old Washington Historic State Park People can learn more about life in early Washington at this state park. Visitors can see furniture and ceramic dishes used by settlers in the 1800s.

SKILL **Examining Artifacts** What does the man on the saucer on the right appear to be doing?

80 • Chapter 4

Trail of Tears This painting shows American Indians being forced to move to Indian Territory. Indian Territory was located in present-day Oklahoma.

American Indians

Over time, conflicts over land in Arkansas Territory grew between American settlers and American Indians. For example, many settlers wanted to grow cotton on land owned by the Quapaw. In 1825, the United States government took the side of the settlers and made the Quapaw sign a treaty. This treaty required that the Quapaw give up all their land in Arkansas Territory. The Quapaw moved south to Louisiana.

Other American Indians were also forced out of Arkansas Territory. In 1828, the territorial government of Arkansas forced the Western Cherokee to sign a treaty that gave up their lands in Arkansas. The Western Cherokee moved west to Indian Territory.

In 1830, **Andrew Jackson,** the United States president, signed the Indian Removal Act. This law forced all American Indians east of the Mississippi River to move west to Indian Territory. American settlers took their land. During that forced migration, many American Indians traveled through Arkansas Territory. Some of them passed through Fort Smith and Washington. Today we call their difficult journey the Trail of Tears.

REVIEW Why did American Indians leave Arkansas in the 1820s?

Points of View about Statehood

William Fulton

Fulton opposed statehood for Arkansas. He did not think that Arkansas had the people or the resources to become a state.

Ambrose Sevier

Sevier initially opposed statehood for Arkansas. He changed his mind when Michigan applied to join the nation. At the time, states had to join in pairs. Sevier worried that too many years would pass before another territory was ready.

Statehood

Main Idea Arkansas became the twenty-fifth state in 1836.

By 1835, more than 50,000 people lived in Arkansas Territory. Many people wanted Arkansas to prepare for statehood. New states were admitted to the Union when they had 60,000 people. The Union is another name for the United States.

John Pope, the third territorial governor, supported statehood and helped the territory grow. He made sure that people in territorial government positions were elected instead of chosen. This attracted more people to move to the area.

Ambrose Sevier, Arkansas's territorial representative to the U.S. Congress, also supported statehood.

Some people, such as **William Fulton**, the fourth territorial governor, opposed statehood. They did not believe that Arkansas's government was ready to take over many of the services provided by the United States government. These included building roads and keeping people safe. People opposed to Arkansas statehood declared that taxes would increase if Arkansas had to take over these responsibilities.

Despite Fulton's opposition, many Arkansans pushed for statehood. Because of flooding at Arkansas Post, Arkansas's capital had been moved to Little Rock in 1821. By 1836, Arkansas Territory had the 60,000 people it needed to apply for statehood. Lawmakers met in Little Rock to write the state's constitution. On June 15, 1836, Arkansas became the 25th state.

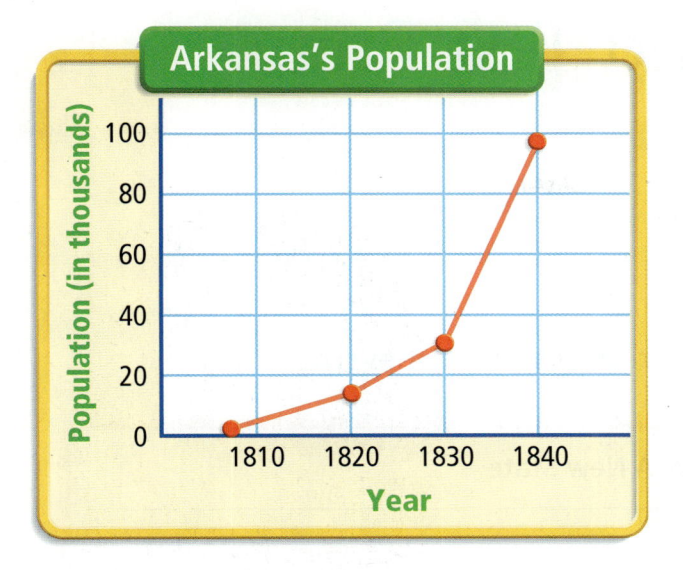

Arkansas's Population

(graph showing population in thousands vs. year from 1810 to 1840)

Lesson Summary
- In the early 1800s, growing numbers of settlers moved to Arkansas Territory.
- Conflicts over land led the territorial government to force American Indians out of Arkansas.
- In 1830, the national government required all American Indians east of the Mississippi River to move west to Indian Territory.
- Arkansas wrote a state constitution and became a state in 1836.

Arkansas's First Constitution

Arkansas's first constitution was based upon the nation's Constitution. It explained the plan for state government. Lawmakers would be elected by Arkansas citizens. Only adult white men could vote. It also made slavery legal.

REVIEW What did John Pope do to help Arkansas become a state?

Why It Matters...

Becoming part of the United States helped Arkansas continue to grow. As a state, Arkansas has shared the history of the nation.

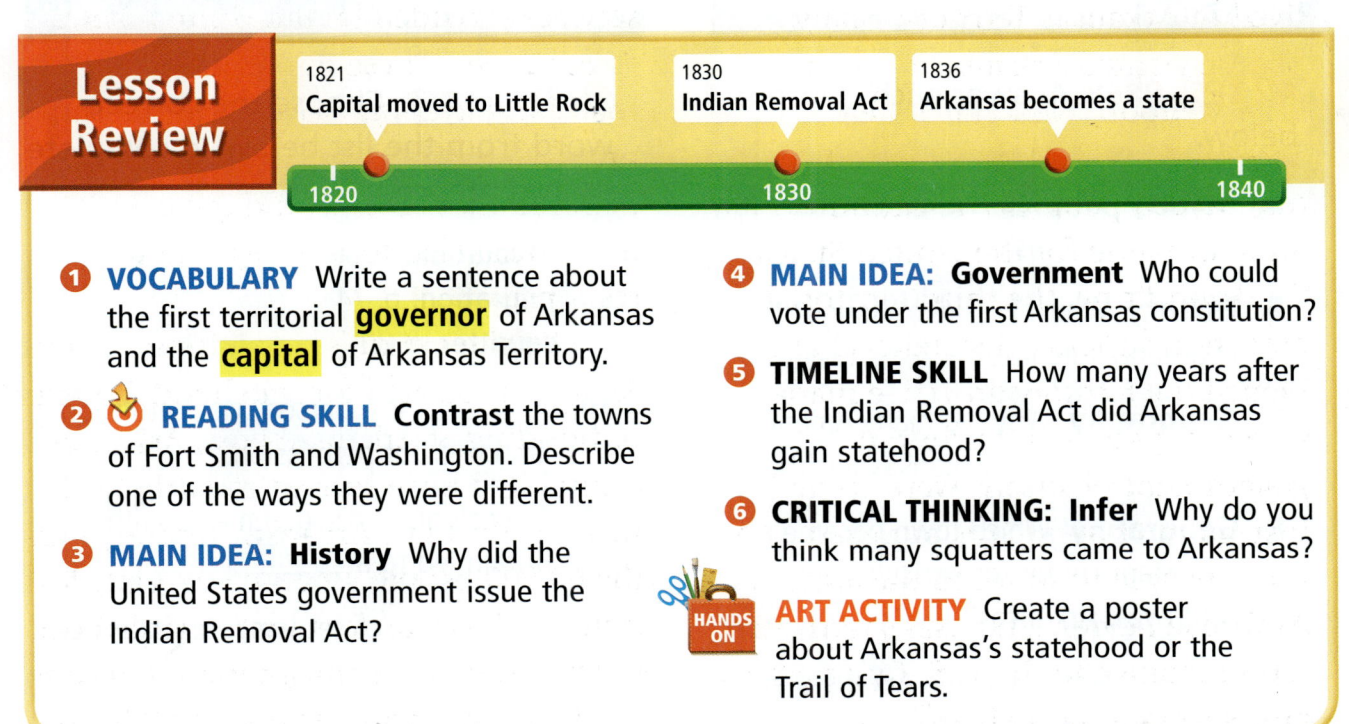

Lesson Review

Timeline:
- 1821 Capital moved to Little Rock
- 1830 Indian Removal Act
- 1836 Arkansas becomes a state

1 VOCABULARY Write a sentence about the first territorial **governor** of Arkansas and the **capital** of Arkansas Territory.

2 READING SKILL Contrast the towns of Fort Smith and Washington. Describe one of the ways they were different.

3 MAIN IDEA: History Why did the United States government issue the Indian Removal Act?

4 MAIN IDEA: Government Who could vote under the first Arkansas constitution?

5 TIMELINE SKILL How many years after the Indian Removal Act did Arkansas gain statehood?

6 CRITICAL THINKING: Infer Why do you think many squatters came to Arkansas?

ART ACTIVITY Create a poster about Arkansas's statehood or the Trail of Tears.

Chapter 4 Review and Test Prep

Visual Summary

1.–4. Complete the chart with descriptions of each event.

A New Nation, A New State	
American Revolution	
Louisiana Purchase	
Arkansas Territory	
Arkansas Statehood	

Facts and Main Ideas

TEST PREP Answer each question below.

5. **History** Who led the Continental Army against the British?

6. **History** Which President bought the Louisiana Purchase?

7. **Geography** Why did many American settlers migrate to Arkansas Territory?

8. **Geography** Which town became an important center for agriculture in southwest Arkansas?

9. **Government** Why did Arkansas enter the Union as a slave state?

Vocabulary

TEST PREP Choose the correct word from the list below to complete each sentence.

revolution, p. 66
migration, p. 74
squatter, p. 80

10. A _____ is a person who settles on land without permission.

11. The colonists' disagreements with Britain led to a _____ .

12. The _____ of settlers into Arkansas increased the territory's population.

CHAPTER SUMMARY TIMELINE

1776 Declaration of Independence
1803 Louisiana Purchase
1819 Arkansas Territory formed

1775 — 1800 — 1825

Apply Skills

TEST PREP **Cause and Effect** Read the passage below. Then use what you have learned about cause and effect to answer each question.

> As settlers moved west, they sometimes fought with American Indians. This led to Congress passing The Indian Removal Act in 1830. This law allowed settlers to force some American Indian groups off their land. As a result, they had to move west of the Mississippi River. Many became sick and died as they traveled. American settlers moved onto their land.

13. Which of the following caused Congress to pass the Indian Removal Act?
    A. the forcing of some American Indian groups off their land
    B. the traveling of American Indians west of the Mississippi River
    C. fights between settlers and American Indians over land
    D. sickness among the American Indians

14. Which word or phrase provides a clue about the effects found in the passage?
    A. allowed
    B. as a result
    C. this led
    D. to force

Critical Thinking

TEST PREP Write a short paragraph to answer each question below.

15. **Compare and Contrast** In what ways were the Articles of Confederation and the Constitution different?

16. **Cause and Effect** What effect did the increase in American settlers have on Arkansas?

Timeline

Use the Chapter Summary Timeline above to answer the question.

17. In what year did the land that is now Arkansas become part of the United States?

Activities

Drama Activity Prepare a scene of a debate between settlers who want Arkansas to become a state and those who do not.

Writing Activity Write a summary explaining the transition of the thirteen colonies into thirteen separate states as a result of the American Revolution.

Technology
Writing Process Tips
Get help with your writing at:
www.eduplace.com/kids/hmss/

85

Chapter 5 Arkansas in War and Peace

Technology
e • word games
www.eduplace.com/kids/hmss/

Vocabulary Preview

abolitionist
Frederick Douglass escaped from slavery and became an **abolitionist.** He spent many years working to end slavery.
page 90

citizen
After the Civil War, African Americans gained their rights as **citizens** of the United States. For the first time, African American men were able to vote and run for office. **page 97**

Chapter Timeline

1861 Civil War begins

1877 Union troops leave the South

1850 — 1875 — 1900

Reading Strategy

Monitor and Clarify Use this strategy to check your understanding of events.

Quick Tip: After you read a passage, pause to ask yourself if you understand what you have read. If you are confused, reread or read aloud.

immigrant

During the early 1900s, an **immigrant** might find work in a factory, on a railroad, or by starting a business. Many newcomers from Europe came to Arkansas to make better lives for themselves. **page 102**

depression

The Great **Depression** was a time of economic hardship. Many businesses failed, and people could not find work. **page 104**

1929 Great Depression begins

1941 United States joins World War II

1925 — 1950

Core Lesson 1

The Civil War

1800 | 1820 | 1840 | 1860 | 1880 | 1900
1840–1865

Build on What You Know You know that people sometimes disagree about issues. In 1861, disagreements between people in northern and southern states led to war.

The Rise of Cotton

Main Idea In the mid-1800s, Arkansas's most important crop was cotton grown by enslaved Africans.

In the early and mid-1800s, most people in the South worked in agriculture. Small farms in northeastern Arkansas grew crops such as corn. Farmers in southern and eastern Arkansas grew cotton in the rich soil along the Mississippi and other rivers. Cotton planters could sell large amounts of cotton to factories throughout the United States and Europe. These factories used cotton to make yarn, cloth, and other items. By the mid-1800s, cotton growing had become the South's most important industry. An **industry** is a group of businesses that provide one kind of product or service.

VOCABULARY

industry
abolitionist
tariff
secede
inflation

Vocabulary Strategy

abolitionist

The word **abolish** means "to end." An **abolitionist** is a person who wants to end slavery.

READING SKILL

Sequence List in order events that led to and took place during the Civil War.

1	
2	
3	
4	

Steamboat Arkansas farmers shipped cotton and other crops to distant cities.

88 • Chapter 5

Lakeport Plantation By 1860, 155 enslaved Africans lived here. Despite cruel conditions, enslaved Africans tried to keep their culture alive, playing musical instruments such as this banjo.

Life on the Plantation

Cotton made some people in Arkansas very wealthy. However, enslaved Africans did most of the work on cotton plantations. A plantation is a large farm. Southern planters were able to grow large amounts of cotton in part because they used enslaved workers. Enslaved Africans were forced to work without pay.

Plantation life was hard. Planters forced enslaved people to clear land, plant and pick cotton, and weed fields. Adults and children worked all day, often in hot weather. When not working in the fields, enslaved workers tended farm animals and did many other tasks.

Enslaved Africans had few comforts. They shared small, crowded cabins with dirt floors and little furniture. They had few things of their own and were forced to depend on planters for clothing and food.

Resisting Slavery

Many enslaved Africans fought against the cruelties of slavery. They often ran away from plantations. Some enslaved people carried out work slowdowns. This means that people broke equipment or did other things to slow the pace of work.

Plantation owners could sell enslaved Africans at any time. Many parents were separated from their children. Despite these cruel conditions, enslaved people worked to pass on their history and culture. They told stories, played music, and kept up other traditions. By 1860, more than 100,000 enslaved people lived in Arkansas.

REVIEW What was plantation life like for enslaved people?

89

Working for Freedom The efforts of abolitionists such as (left to right) Harriet Tubman, Harriet Beecher Stowe, and Frederick Douglass helped make slavery a national issue.

A Nation Divides

Main Idea People in the North and South had different beliefs about slavery.

By the mid 1800s, people in southern and northern states lived and worked in different ways. More than four million people were enslaved in the South. Most northern states had outlawed slavery by 1804.

The South was an agricultural society. It had many farms and plantations. The North had farms, too. However, many people worked in factories that were built as society industrialized. Northern factories made clothing, iron goods, and other items.

As people moved west, the United States gained more land. Abolitionists tried to stop new states that joined the Union from allowing slavery. An **abolitionist** is a person who works to end slavery.

One abolitionist, **Frederick Douglass**, had escaped from slavery. He spent years writing and speaking against it. **Harriet Tubman** also escaped from slavery. She returned to the South to guide other people to freedom on the Underground Railroad. The Underground Railroad was a system of escape routes and hiding places that enslaved Africans used to travel to free states. In 1852, abolitionist **Harriet Beecher Stowe** published a novel that became a best-seller. *Uncle Tom's Cabin* described the cruelty of slavery.

By the mid-1800s, many Northerners believed that the federal government should make slavery illegal in all new states. Most Southern leaders argued for states' rights. They believed that each state should decide for itself about slavery and other important issues. The two sides could not agree.

Arkansas Leaves the Union

In 1860, **Abraham Lincoln** was elected President. Lincoln wanted to stop the growth of slavery. Southern leaders believed that Lincoln would end slavery. Lincoln also supported tariffs. A **tariff** is a tax on trade goods. Tariffs would make European goods that southerners wanted too expensive to buy. Tariffs would also increase the cost of southern cotton.

After Lincoln's election, seven southern states seceded from the Union. To **secede** means to separate from a country and form a new nation. These states formed the Confederate States of America, also known as the Confederacy.

Many Arkansans supported states' rights and wanted to keep slavery legal. Others did not want to divide the Union. Arkansas leaders decided to secede only if Lincoln's government tried to force Confederate states to rejoin the Union.

On April 12, 1861, Confederate troops attacked Union soldiers at Fort Sumter in South Carolina. The Civil War had begun. President Lincoln called for troops from Union states to stop the uprising. Arkansans felt that this was an act of force. On May 6, Arkansas voted to join the Confederacy. By May 20, eleven states belonged to the Confederacy.

REVIEW Why did Arkansas join the Confederacy?

Secession Arkansas joined 10 other states in seceding from the Union.

SKILL Reading Maps Which state was the last to join the Confederacy?

Confederate and Union States

LEGEND
- Union state
- Confederate state / Date of secession
- Territory

Secession dates:
- VA: April 17, 1861
- NC: May 20, 1861
- TN: May 7, 1861
- SC: Dec. 20, 1860
- AR: May 6, 1861
- GA: Jan. 19, 1861
- MS: Jan. 9, 1861
- AL: Jan. 12, 1861
- TX: Feb. 1, 1861
- LA: Jan. 26, 1861
- FL: Jan. 9, 1861

Arkansans at War On January 11, 1863, Union troops captured Fort Hindman at Arkansas Post. During the war, Confederate states began printing their own paper money, such as this Arkansas dollar note from 1862.

The War in Arkansas

Main Idea Arkansans fought for the Union and the Confederacy during the Civil War.

The Civil War lasted from 1861 to 1865. Both the Union and the Confederacy valued Arkansas because of its location along the Mississippi River. It also bordered Union-controlled Missouri. Important battles, such as those at Pea Ridge and Prairie Grove in 1862, took place in Arkansas.

About 58,000 Arkansans fought for the Confederacy. However, many Arkansans remained loyal to the Union. More than 12,000 Arkansas soldiers joined the Union army. Six thousand African Americans from Arkansas also joined the Union army. About 2,000 women served as nurses for both sides during the war.

During the war, Arkansans often ran short of food and other goods. Confederate states began printing their own money. This led to inflation. **Inflation** means that a nation has more money than it has goods to buy. This causes high prices. During the war, inflation made many goods too expensive to buy.

On January 1, 1863, President Lincoln issued the Emancipation Proclamation. Emancipation means the freeing of enslaved people. The proclamation, or statement, declared that all enslaved people in states fighting the Union were free. From that point on, slavery was the central issue of the war. The proclamation helped stop Britain and France from giving aid to the Confederacy.

The War Ends

Also in 1863, Confederate troops lost Arkansas Post, Fort Smith, and Little Rock. These losses ended Confederate control of much of Arkansas. Confederate Governor **Harris Flanagin** moved the state's capital to Washington, Arkansas.

Meanwhile, voters elected **Isaac Murphy** as governor of Union-controlled areas. Murphy formed a state government loyal to the Union. For the rest of the war, two governments controlled different parts of the state.

In April 1865, the Confederate States of America surrendered. The Union won in part because it had more troops, more resources, and stronger industries than the Confederacy.

However, the war resulted in great losses for both sides. About 350,000 Union soldiers and 250,000 Confederate soldiers died. Many more were wounded.

REVIEW What effect did inflation have on the Confederacy?

Lesson Summary

- Arkansas seceded from the Union and joined the Confederacy.
- Not all Arkansans supported secession. Some remained loyal to the Union.
- The Civil War caused great loss of life.

Why It Matters...

The Civil War helped to end slavery and led to many changes in Arkansas and the nation.

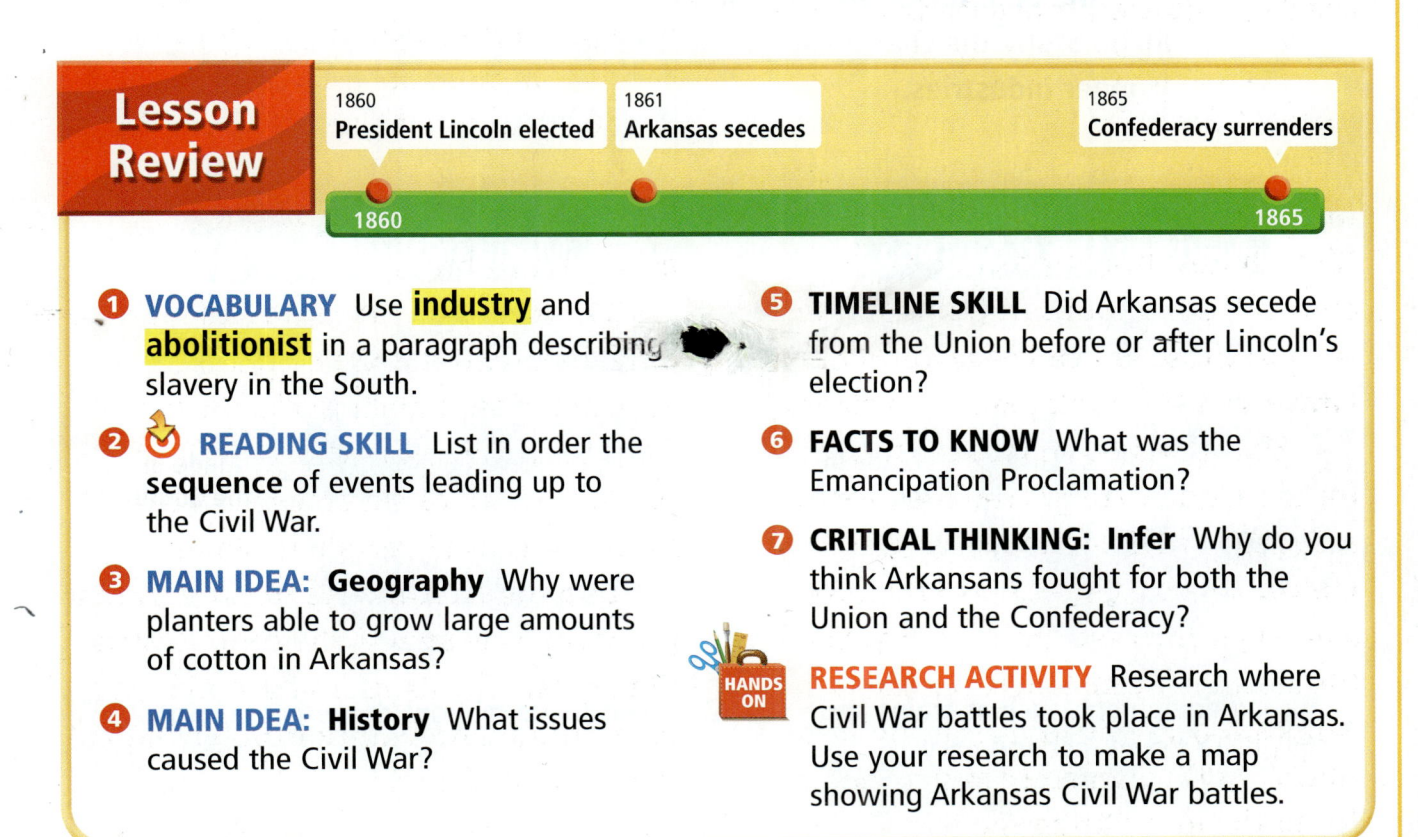

Lesson Review

1860 President Lincoln elected
1861 Arkansas secedes
1865 Confederacy surrenders

1. **VOCABULARY** Use **industry** and **abolitionist** in a paragraph describing slavery in the South.

2. **READING SKILL** List in order the **sequence** of events leading up to the Civil War.

3. **MAIN IDEA: Geography** Why were planters able to grow large amounts of cotton in Arkansas?

4. **MAIN IDEA: History** What issues caused the Civil War?

5. **TIMELINE SKILL** Did Arkansas secede from the Union before or after Lincoln's election?

6. **FACTS TO KNOW** What was the Emancipation Proclamation?

7. **CRITICAL THINKING: Infer** Why do you think Arkansans fought for both the Union and the Confederacy?

RESEARCH ACTIVITY Research where Civil War battles took place in Arkansas. Use your research to make a map showing Arkansas Civil War battles.

Extend Lesson 1
Economics

North and South

Why did the South think it could win the Civil War?
There were 22 Union states and only 11 Confederate states. At the beginning of the war, the Confederates won many battles. The Confederate army seemed powerful and had skilled generals and soldiers.

Over time, it became harder for the South to keep fighting, however. They did not have enough factories to make weapons and cloth. The North had more people and more factories.

In the end, the South surrendered to the more powerful North. Study the charts and pictures to see why the North had stronger industries.

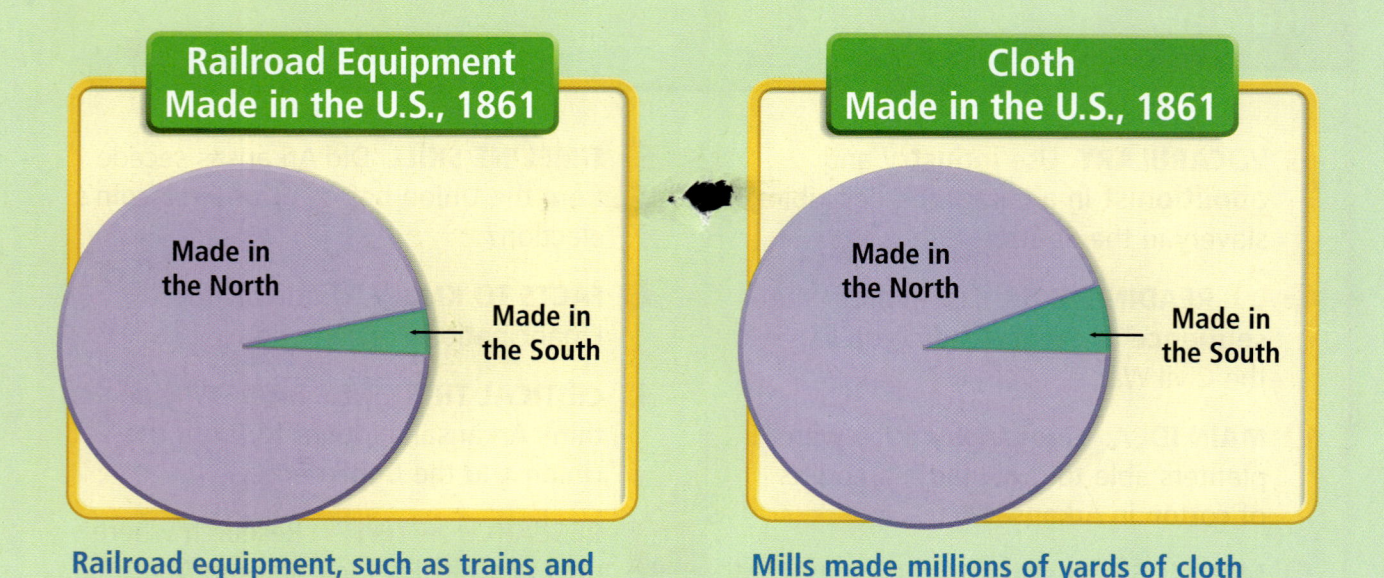

Railroad Equipment Made in the U.S., 1861

Made in the North — Made in the South

Railroad equipment, such as trains and rails, made travel fast and easy.

Cloth Made in the U.S., 1861

Made in the North — Made in the South

Mills made millions of yards of cloth each year.

The North

Rivers provided water power for large factories in the North. Railroads delivered supplies quickly from the factories to the Union army.

The South

The South had many large cotton plantations and few industries.

ECONOMICS

Activities

1. **THINK ABOUT IT** Think about why it would be important to be able to make large amounts of cloth during a war.

2. **CHART IT** Find out more about the differences between the industries and agriculture of the North and the South. Make a chart showing these differences.

Core Lesson 2

Reconstruction

1800 1820 1840 1860 1880 1900

1865–1877

Build on What You Know Think of a time when you had to clean up a big mess. After the Civil War, people in Arkansas worked hard to clean up and fix many homes, farms, and businesses in the state.

After the War

Main Idea To rejoin the United States, Arkansas wrote a new constitution that recognized the rights of African Americans.

After the Civil War, the United States needed to rebuild. The country began a time of Reconstruction. **Reconstruction** refers to the period following the Civil War when Confederate states rejoined the Union.

President Lincoln planned to bring the South back into the Union without punishing it. Yet on April 14, 1865, just after the end of the war, the President was shot. He died the next day. The new President, **Andrew Johnson**, wanted to use Lincoln's ideas. Many lawmakers in the U.S. Congress, however, believed that Lincoln's plan should be tougher. They wanted to protect African Americans' rights and punish Confederate states for the war.

VOCABULARY

Reconstruction
citizen
sharecropping
economy
manufacturing

Vocabulary Strategy

re**construct**ion

The prefix **re** means "back" or "again." **Construct** means "to build." Reconstruction was a time of building the South again.

READING SKILL

Compare and Contrast
Contrast the lives of African Americans before and after the Civil War.

Before Civil War	After Civil War

Abraham Lincoln

Andrew Johnson

96 • Chapter 5

Amendments

Thirteenth Amendment, 1865	Outlawed slavery
Fourteenth Amendment, 1868	Made it illegal to deny any citizen his or her rights
Fifteenth Amendment, 1870	Made it illegal to deny voting rights to citizens because of race or color

Important Changes Congress passed three important amendments for African Americans. **SKILL Reading Charts** Which amendment protected voting rights?

Arkansas Changes

During Reconstruction, Congress divided the South into five areas. The Union army controlled each area. Arkansas and Mississippi were grouped together. Confederate leaders were not allowed to take part in government.

Isaac Murphy was governor of Arkansas during this time. Murphy worked with Union military leaders to keep order. He wanted the state to rejoin the Union quickly. However, to do so, Arkansas had to protect the rights of African Americans.

Before the end of the Civil War, Congress had passed the Thirteenth Amendment to the Constitution. This amendment made slavery illegal. It freed all enslaved people. However, for African Americans, the end of slavery was only the first step toward full freedom. Many people did not want to grant African Americans equal rights. This made progress for African Americans slow and difficult.

In 1868, Congress passed the Fourteenth Amendment. This amendment recognized African Americans as citizens. A **citizen** is a person who is born in or swears loyalty to the nation. In order to rejoin the Union, Congress required former Confederate states to approve the amendment.

After several months of debate, Arkansas lawmakers passed a new state constitution. The 1868 constitution gave African American men the right to vote. It also approved the Fourteenth Amendment. Arkansas citizens voted for the new constitution. On June 22, 1868, Arkansas rejoined the United States.

REVIEW Why was it hard for Arkansas to rejoin the Union?

Citizenship During Reconstruction, African American men gained the right to vote.

Rebuilding Arkansas

Main Idea Arkansas and the South had to rebuild their economies.

The Civil War destroyed homes, farms, factories, roads, and ports in the South. All had to be rebuilt.

To help some poor farmers, the government gave them land. However, many African Americans began sharecropping. **Sharecropping** is a system in which a landowner provides land, tools, and seed for a share of a farmer's crops. Often, landowners treated the sharecroppers unfairly.

Arkansas's economy changed in other ways. An **economy** is the way that people use an area's resources. During Reconstruction, Arkansans started new businesses and went to work in new industries.

Charlotte Andrews Stephens Stephens taught in Little Rock for 70 years.

The state provided money to build railroads. More people went to work in the lumber and mining industries. Manufacturing also increased. **Manufacturing** means making goods such as cloth and canned foods.

Some southerners supported the Union government in Washington during Reconstruction. They were called scalawags. Many northerners traveled south during Reconstruction. Some wanted to help rebuild the South. Others just wanted to make money. They were known as carpetbaggers. Most southerners disliked both scalawags and carpetbaggers.

In 1868, the first free public schools in the state opened. During this time, African Americans attended separate schools from whites. **Charlotte Andrews Stephens** became the first free African American teacher in Little Rock.

Sharecropping

Landowner provides farmer with…
- Seed
- Tools
- Land
- Animals

Farmer gives landowner…
- Bales of cotton

98 • Chapter 5

Reconstruction Ends

During Reconstruction, African Americans began serving in Arkansas's government. In the 1870s, however, lawmakers who were against Reconstruction regained power in southern states. These officials passed unfair laws that limited African Americans' rights. Some people also used violence to stop African Americans from voting, doing business, or living in certain places.

When U.S. troops left the South in 1877, African Americans lost most of the freedoms that they had gained. After little more than ten years, Reconstruction had ended.

REVIEW What was sharecropping?

Lesson Summary

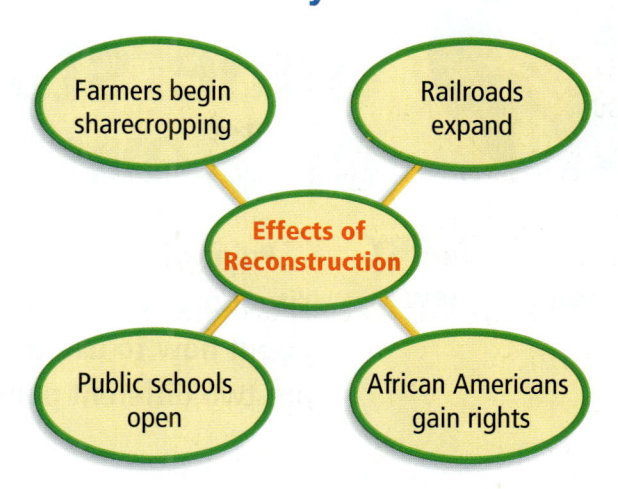

- Farmers begin sharecropping
- Railroads expand
- Public schools open
- African Americans gain rights

Effects of Reconstruction

Why It Matters...

Many years passed before African Americans gained the full rights promised them during Reconstruction.

Lesson Review

Timeline:
- 1865 Civil War ends
- 1868 Arkansas rejoins the Union
- 1877 Union troops leave the South

(1865 – 1870 – 1875 – 1880)

❶ **VOCABULARY** Write a sentence about Arkansas after the Civil War using **Reconstruction**.

❷ **READING SKILL** Use your chart to **contrast** the ways in which African Americans worked on farms before and after the Civil War.

❸ **MAIN IDEA: History** What did Arkansas have to do to rejoin the Union?

❹ **MAIN IDEA: Economics** In what ways did Arkansas's agriculture and industry change during Reconstruction?

❺ **TIMELINE SKILL** For how many years did Union troops stay in the South after the Civil War ended?

❻ **FACTS TO KNOW** Which constitutional amendment abolished slavery?

❼ **CRITICAL THINKING: Analyze** How did the end of Reconstruction make life harder for African Americans in Arkansas?

HANDS ON

SPEAKING ACTIVITY Prepare a speech that Governor Murphy might have given to persuade Arkansans to support Reconstruction. Provide reasons why Arkansas should rejoin the Union and all citizens should have the same rights.

Skillbuilder

Understand Point of View

VOCABULARY
point of view

Point of view is the way that someone looks at a topic or situation. For example, people often have different points of view about how to use the land in their region. The statements below are two different points of view about a place called Riverside Park.

Andrea's Point of View

"Our community is growing fast. We need more homes, schools, stores, and roads for all the people who want to move here. I think the best solution is to build at Riverside Park. It's a big area, so there's plenty of room. Plants, birds, and other animals could still live in areas where there are no buildings. The new homes and stores will help the economy of our community."

Carlos's Point of View

"Many people want to move to our beautiful region. Riverside Park is one thing that makes it special. Building on this land would be a huge mistake. The area provides a home for many plants and animals. Covering the land with roads and buildings will harm our environment. Worse, our grandchildren will not be able to enjoy the natural beauty of the park."

Apply Critical Thinking

Learn the Skill

Step 1: Read the statements carefully. Figure out the subject of the statements.

Step 2: Look for phrases like "I think," "in my opinion," or "I believe." These phrases signal the author's opinion. Also look for positive or negative words that give you more clues about the author's feelings.

Step 3: Describe the author's opinion about the subject.

Step 4: Look for facts that support the author's point of view.

Practice the Skill

Use the statements on page 100 to answer the questions.

1. What is the subject of both passages?
2. Describe each person's point of view on the subject.
3. What facts do Andrea and Carlos present? Do those facts support their points of view?

Apply the Skill

What is your point of view about building and land use in your community? Write a paragraph that states your point of view. Be sure to provide good reasons for your opinion.

Core Lesson 3

A Changing State

1800 1825 1850 1875 1900 1925 1950 1975 2000 2025

1875–Today

VOCABULARY

immigrant
discrimination
depression
suburb

Vocabulary Strategy

depress**ion**

Depress means "to decrease" or "to lessen." In an economic **depression,** prices decrease, businesses fail, and workers lose their jobs.

READING SKILL

Main Idea and Details List details to support the idea that Arkansas went through many changes in the 1900s.

Changes in Arkansas in the 1900s

Build on What You Know Think about people you know who have just moved to your community. The population of Arkansas has changed as people from around the nation and the world have come to the state.

Arkansas in a New Century

Main Idea Arkansas grew and changed during the early 1900s.

Building railroads helped Arkansas's economy and population to grow. More people and goods traveled to and from Arkansas in less time. However, railroad companies and other industries needed workers. They wanted immigrants to come to Arkansas. An **immigrant** is a person who leaves one country to live in another country. During the late 1800s, many people moved to Arkansas from European nations such as Russia, Germany, and Poland. Some immigrants also came from China.

Immigrant Workers This man came to Eureka Springs and earned money by selling eggs.

102 • Chapter 5

The Great Migration

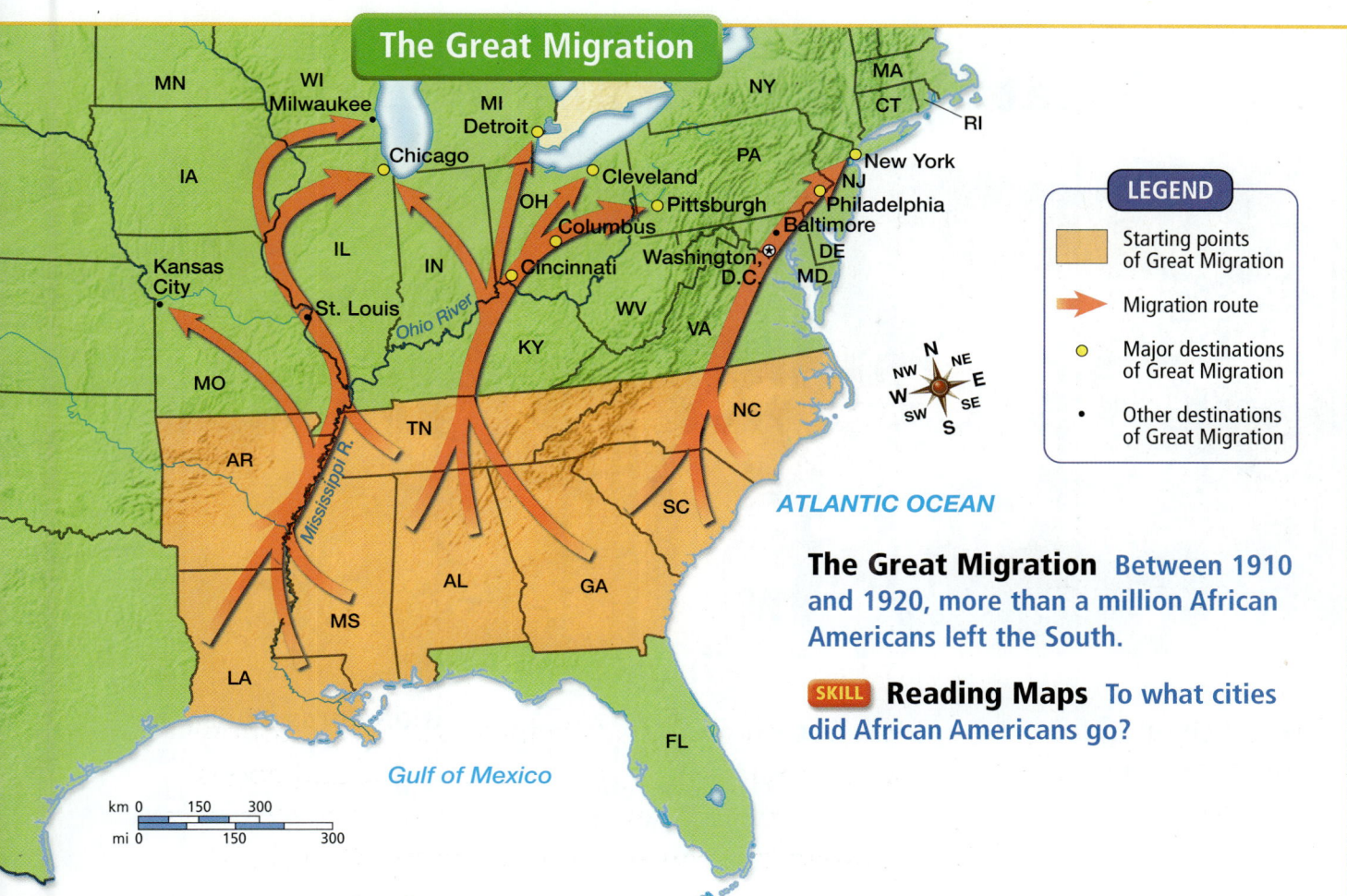

The Great Migration Between 1910 and 1920, more than a million African Americans left the South.

SKILL Reading Maps To what cities did African Americans go?

World War I and Arkansas

In 1914, World War I began in Europe. Three years later, the United States entered the war. More than 70,000 soldiers from Arkansas went to war. Other Arkansans worked as nurses, made supplies, and grew food for the troops.

During the war, so many working men became soldiers that American factories needed more workers. Many women filled empty jobs in factories. African Americans also filled jobs in northern cities. Since the early 1900s, African Americans had been leaving the South and moving to northern cities. This migration increased during the war. It became known as the Great Migration.

Many African Americans who moved north hoped to avoid discrimination and find better jobs. **Discrimination** is the unfair treatment of a group of people. Southern states unfairly limited African Americans' rights.

Women in the United States also faced discrimination. However, in 1917, Arkansas granted women the right to vote. **Florence Lee Brown Cotnam** of Little Rock worked to win the right to vote for all American women. In 1919, Congress passed the Nineteenth Amendment. The law gave women voting rights in all elections. It went into effect in 1920.

REVIEW Why did African Americans leave the South during the Great Migration?

The Great Depression and World War II

Bread Lines In 1931, the American Red Cross provided food for 180,000 families in Arkansas.

Civilian Conservation Corps During the Great Depression, the government put many people to work building state parks, roads, and other public projects.

Hard Times

Main Idea Arkansans struggled through hardship during depression and war.

The years after World War I were difficult for Arkansas. In 1927, the Mississippi River flooded. Water covered two million acres of land in Arkansas. A severe drought followed. A drought is a long dry period without rain.

Flooding and drought left farmers without enough crops to eat or sell. These conditions hurt farmers. Factories that made goods from crops also suffered. Many city workers lost their jobs or earned less money. Then in 1929, the Great Depression began.

A **depression** is a period of time when businesses fail, prices drop, and many people lose jobs. The Great Depression lasted for many years and made conditions in Arkansas worse. More workers lost jobs. Farmers lost land. Many people needed help.

Organizations such as the American Red Cross provided food, clothing, and shelter for many people. Under President **Franklin Delano Roosevelt**, the government started programs such as the Civilian Conservation Corps and the Works Progress Administration. These programs put people back to work. Still, most people struggled to support themselves and their families.

104 • Chapter 5

Victory Gardens During World War II, posters such as this one encouraged Americans to help the war effort by growing their own food.

Women in the Factory Many Arkansas women went to work making machines.

World War II

In 1939, World War II began in Europe. The war soon spread to parts of Africa and Asia. In 1941, Japan bombed Pearl Harbor, a United States military base in Hawaii. In response to this attack, the United States went to war.

More than 195,000 men and women from Arkansas served in the military during the war. Women worked as mechanics, radio operators, clerks, and nurses. African American men and women also served, but they were separated from whites and given less important jobs. The unfair treatment of African Americans in military service caused more people to demand their full rights as citizens.

During the war, Arkansas's economy began to improve. Farms produced crops to feed soldiers. Factories made tools, clothes, and other supplies. Arkansas mines produced coal for fuel as well as large amounts of bauxite. Bauxite is a mineral that can be turned into aluminum. Factories used aluminum to build military airplanes.

Thousands of women filled jobs left by men who had gone to fight. They built ships, airplanes, and other machinery. When the war ended in 1945, many women did not want to give up their jobs to returning soldiers.

REVIEW What jobs did women who served in the military during World War II do?

The Space Race The United States and the Soviet Union competed to launch the first satellite in space (right) and send the first person to the moon.

Post-War Arkansas

Main Idea The mid- and late 1900s brought many advances to Arkansas and the nation.

After World War II, soldiers returned home from the war. In 1944, Congress passed a law called the G.I. Bill. It provided money for military men and women to go to college, start businesses, and buy homes. Families started looking for homes to buy, but cities had a scarcity of housing.

Builders responded by building suburbs. A **suburb** is a community that develops near a city. In 1946, Bralei Homes built 84 new houses in three months in Park Hill, a suburb of Little Rock. These homes sold for less than $6,000. Other suburbs grew quickly, too.

A system of highways helped suburbs grow. Highways made it possible for people to live in suburbs and drive into cities to work. Many businesses, such as grocery stores and gas stations, opened to serve people who lived in suburbs.

After World War II, the United States and the Soviet Union competed for power around the world. This led to the "space race." During the space race, both nations sent satellites and astronauts into space. A satellite is a spacecraft that orbits, or circles, Earth. The Soviet Union launched the first satellite, *Sputnik I*, in 1957. Just over ten years later, an American named **Neil Armstrong** became the first person to walk on the moon.

Looking Ahead

Arkansas and the United States continued to change in the late 1900s. The use of personal computers grew rapidly in the 1980s. In the 1990s, the Internet connected computers around the world. The Internet lets people get information from all over the globe and send electronic mail, or e-mail, to one another.

In the 1990s, many immigrants came to Arkansas from Mexico and countries in Central America. They helped to increase the diversity in Arkansas. Diversity means variety. In 2006, almost three million people lived in Arkansas.

REVIEW What was the space race?

Lesson Summary

World War I and the Great Migration

The Great Depression

World War II and economic growth

Suburbs, the space race, and new technologies

Why It Matters...

The events of the 1900s helped shape the government, industries, and population of modern Arkansas. Today, national and world events continue to affect the people of Arkansas.

Lesson Review

1917 United States enters World War I
1929 Great Depression begins
1941 United States enters World War II

1910 — 1930 — 1945

1 VOCABULARY Write two sentences to describe Arkansas's economy in the 1900s, one using **depression** and the other **suburb**.

2 READING SKILL Identify two **details** that support the **main idea** that national and world events caused changes in Arkansas's economy.

3 MAIN IDEA: Technology What was the effect of railroads on Arkansas in the early 1900s?

4 MAIN IDEA: Technology What advances did Arkansas and the nation experience in the late 1900s?

5 TIMELINE SKILL How many years after the United States entered World War I did the Great Depression start?

6 CRITICAL THINKING: Infer How do you think the growth of suburbs might have affected cities?

RESEARCH ACTIVITY Learn more about the culture of one group of immigrants that came to Arkansas in the 1900s. Research the customs, language, food, music, dance, art, and religious beliefs of that group. Share what you learn in a class discussion.

107

Chapter 5 Review and Test Prep

Visual Summary

1. – 3. Write a description of each item named below.

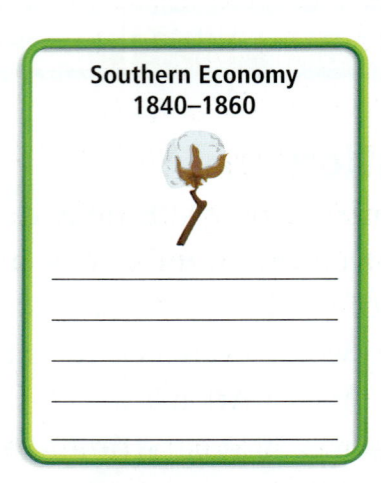

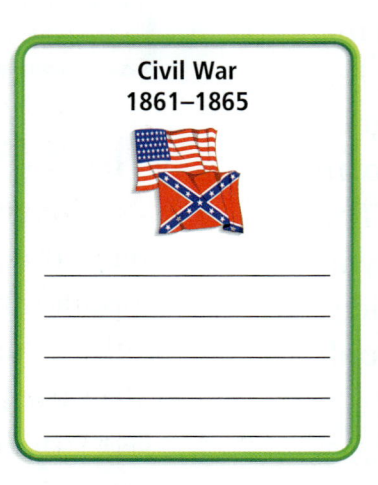

Southern Economy 1840–1860

Civil War 1861–1865

Reconstruction 1865–1877

Facts and Main Ideas

TEST PREP Answer each question below.

4. **History** Why were farmers in southeastern Arkansas able to grow large amounts of cotton?

5. **Economics** Why were many people in the South against tariffs?

6. **History** How did the failure of Reconstruction delay African Americans from gaining their full rights as citizens?

7. **History** Why did suburbs in Arkansas grow quickly after World War II?

Vocabulary

TEST PREP Choose the correct word from the list below to complete each sentence.

inflation, p. 92
sharecropping, p. 98
manufacturing, p. 98
immigrants, p. 102

8. During the Civil War, high rates of _____ made many goods too expensive to buy.

9. Farmers who began _____ had to give some of their crops to the landowner.

10. In the early 1900s, _____ from countries in Europe came to Arkansas.

11. During World War II, _____ industries made supplies for the military.

108 • Chapter 5

CHAPTER SUMMARY TIMELINE

- **1861** Arkansas secedes from the Union
- **1868** Arkansas rejoins the Union
- **1917** Women in Arkansas win the right to vote

1840 — 1860 — 1880 — 1900 — 1920

Apply Skills

✓ **TEST PREP Understand Point of View** Read the letter below. Then use what you have learned about understanding point of view to answer the questions that follow.

> Dear Mother,
> I just signed on with the Civilian Conservation Corps. I'll be working on the state park at Petit Jean. Soon, I'll be able to send money home! And the Corps provides food and housing. In my opinion, we'll all get out of this Depression yet. We just have to hold on a bit longer!
>
> Your son,
> Jakob

12. Which statement best summarizes Jakob's point of view?
- **A.** There is no hope.
- **B.** President Roosevelt does not know what to do.
- **C.** Jobs will help people recover.
- **D.** People are working too much.

13. What words provide a clue that Jakob is giving his point of view?
- **A.** I just signed
- **B.** I'll be working
- **C.** I'll be able
- **D.** In my opinion

Critical Thinking

✓ **TEST PREP** Write a short paragraph to answer each question below.

14. Synthesize In what ways did Reconstruction change life in Arkansas?

15. Summarize Describe the challenges that Arkansans faced in the early and mid-1900s.

Timeline

Use the Chapter Summary Timeline above to answer the question.

16. How long was Arkansas not part of the United States?

Activities

Citizenship Activity Find out the steps that people must take before they can vote. Make a poster showing what you learn. Explain why you think people worked to win voting rights for themselves and others.

Writing Activity Choose one invention from the 1900s, such as the airplane or the Internet. Write an essay explaining the ways in which this technology benefits people.

Technology
Writing Process Tips
Get help with your writing at:
www.eduplace.com/kids/hmss/

UNIT 2 Review and Test Prep

Vocabulary and Main Ideas

✓ **TEST PREP** Write a sentence to answer each question.

1. What role did **scarcity** play in the **expedition** of Columbus?

2. Why did the French and the Quapaw become **allies?**

3. For what purpose did the Founders write the **Declaration** of **Independence?**

4. Why did the United States order the forced **migration** of American Indians under the Indian Removal Act?

5. Why did southern farmers begin **sharecropping** during **Reconstruction?**

6. What impact did the Great **Depression** have on Arkansas's **economy?**

Critical Thinking

✓ **TEST PREP** Write a short paragraph to answer each question.

7. **Analyze** Why did people settle in Arkansas in the early 1800s?

8. **Summarize** What issues and events led Arkansas into the Civil War?

Apply Skills

✓ **TEST PREP** Read the paragraph below. Then use what you have learned about making timelines to answer the questions that follow.

In 1860, voters elected Abraham Lincoln to be President. Eleven southern states decided to secede. They formed the Confederate States of America in 1861. The Civil War between Confederate and Union states lasted four years. After the war, Arkansas's leaders wrote a new constitution. The state rejoined the Union in 1868. Still, Union troops remained in the South until 1877 when Reconstruction ended.

9. How many years would a timeline need to cover to include all the dates?

    A. 10
    B. 20
    C. 30
    D. 40

10. Which event would be second?

    A. Reconstruction ends.
    B. Abraham Lincoln is elected.
    C. Confederate States of America is formed.
    D. Arkansas rejoins the Union.

Unit Activity

Make a "Why I Came to Arkansas" Postcard

- Choose an explorer, a settler, or an immigrant who came to Arkansas.
- Find out why that person came and what he or she did.
- Make a postcard showing one or more sights that the person would have seen.
- Write a short message from the person. Explain why he or she came to Arkansas and what he or she did.

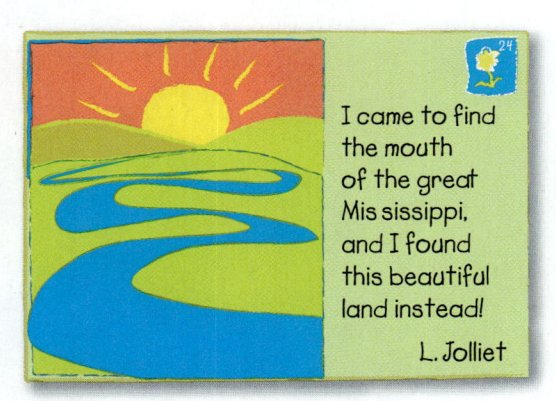

At the Library

Look for these books at your school or public library.

In Defense of Liberty: The Story of America's Bill of Rights by Russell Freedman
Learn the history of the Bill of Rights.

Divided in Two: The Road to Civil War, 1861 by James R. Arnold and Roberta Wiener
Explore the issues that led to war.

CURRENT EVENTS — WEEKLY WR READER

Connect to Today

Celebrate Arkansas's cultural diversity.

- Find pictures of events, such as sporting activities, celebrations, and folk festivals, that reflect the cultures of different groups of people who live in Arkansas today.
- Select two pictures to share with the class.
- Write a brief description of each image. Make sure to check the accuracy of your information.
- Post your selections and your descriptions on a class bulletin board to help celebrate Arkansas's cultural diversity.

Technology

Weekly Reader online offers social studies articles. Go to: www.eduplace.com/kids/hmss/

UNIT 3

Arkansas Today

The Big Idea

What part will you play in Arkansas's future?

"*Our destiny is bound up with the destiny of every other American.*"

—President Bill Clinton, 1991

John H. Johnson
1918–2005

Johnson was the first African American to start a successful publishing company. In 1996, he received the Presidential Medal of Freedom. **page 120**

History Makers

Mike Huckabee
Arkansas Governor Mike Huckabee worked to improve the lives of all Arkansans. In 2004 he started the "Healthy Arkansas" program. **page 145**

Steven M. Anthony
This businessman runs a large company in Arkansas that produces lumber. He took over from his father, who started the company in 1973. **page 170**

Chapter 6: People and Culture

Technology
e • word games
www.eduplace.com/kids/hmss/

Vocabulary Preview

segregation
In 1957, nine African American students began attending Little Rock's all-white Central High School. They helped to end **segregation** in Arkansas.
page 116

politician
Politician David Pryor worked for the good of Arkansas for over thirty years. He served as both a member of Congress and as state governor.
page 118

114 • Unit 3

Reading Strategy

Question Use this strategy as you read the lessons in this chapter.

Quick Tip Ask yourself what you want to know more about. Write your question, and go back to it when you have finished reading.

entrepreneur

Maura Lozano-Yancy is an **entrepreneur.** In 2000, she started Arkansas's first statewide Spanish-English newspaper.
page 120

heritage

Art is a part of Arkansas's **heritage.** Artist Carroll Cloar's paintings help Arkansans remember what rural life in the state was like in the past.
page 124

Core Lesson 1

Progress in Arkansas

VOCABULARY

segregation
civil rights
politician
entrepreneur

Vocabulary Strategy

civil rights

The word **civil** has the same root as "citizen." **Civil rights** are rights belonging to citizens.

READING SKILL
Problem and Solution List problems that African Americans faced during the 1950s and 1960s and the solutions that they found.

Problem	Solution

The Little Rock Nine
Elizabeth Eckford was one of nine African American students who helped end school segregation in Arkansas.

Build on What You Know Have your ever wanted to change a rule that you thought was unfair? Many Arkansans worked to change laws that they thought were unfair to African Americans.

The Struggle for Civil Rights

Main Idea Many Arkansans have worked hard to gain equal rights for all citizens.

After World War II, segregation was legal in many places in the United States. **Segregation** is the separation of people based on race. For example, in some places, African Americans could not use the same restaurants and schools as whites.

In the early 1950s, African Americans and others joined together in a struggle for their civil rights. **Civil rights** are the freedoms that belong to all citizens of a nation.

116 • Chapter 6

Working for Change Daisy Bates (left) and Dr. Martin Luther King, Jr. worked to end segregation.

Civil Rights Leaders

In 1954, the U.S. Supreme Court decided that the segregation of schools was illegal. White schools in Little Rock, however, did not open to all. In 1957, nine African American students and their families tried to change things. The students chose to go to Central High School. They became known as the Little Rock Nine.

Protesters tried to keep the Little Rock Nine out of the school. **Daisy** and **Lucious Bates** helped protect them. Daisy was a writer and civil rights leader. Lucious published a newspaper. President **Dwight Eisenhower** also helped. He sent soldiers to guard the Little Rock Nine on their way to school. One of the students, **Ernest Green**, made Arkansas history by becoming the first African American student to graduate from Central High School.

Dr. Martin Luther King, Jr. believed that peaceful protests could win people the rights that the Constitution said that they should have. In 1963, King organized a protest march in Washington, D.C. More than 200,000 people took part.

In 1964, Congress passed the Civil Rights Act. This law made segregation in schools, workplaces, restaurants, and other public places illegal.

Women, American Indians, and people with disabilities have also fought for civil rights. **Kerry George**, an Arkansas teacher, works locally and nationally to ensure that disabled children receive equal treatment and education. The struggle for civil rights continues even today.

REVIEW What groups of people have fought for civil rights?

Political Leaders

Main Idea Politicians have worked to make life better in Arkansas.

Many politicians in Arkansas have worked to make life better for all Arkansans. A **politician** is a person who takes part in government or has an elected position.

Some of Arkansas's important politicians have been judges. A judge hears and decides cases in court. Judges also decide punishment when laws are broken. In 1873, **Mifflin Wistar Gibbs** became the first African American city judge elected in the United States. Gibbs later worked as a diplomat for the United States. A diplomat is a politician who represents his or her country while in another country.

Other important Arkansas politicians have represented the state in Congress. In 1932, **Hattie Wyatt Caraway** became the first woman elected to the Senate. As a senator, Caraway helped the state's economy by making sure that air bases and factories were built in Arkansas during World War II.

After the war, Arkansas senator **William Fulbright** started the Fulbright Exchange Program. This program gives teachers and students in the United States a chance to study in other countries. The program also gives students from other countries a chance to study in the United States. Today, more than 270,000 people have been able to participate in the Fulbright Exchange Program.

NOTABLE ARKANSAS POLITICIANS

Mifflin Wistar Gibbs

Hattie Wyatt Caraway

John McClellan

Senator **John McClellan** represented Arkansas in Congress from 1942 to 1977. This was longer than anyone else in the state's history. McClellan helped create a system of dams on the Arkansas River. The dams made shipping on the river easier and better.

Governors have also worked to improve life in Arkansas. **Winthrop Rockefeller** served as governor from 1967 to 1971. During this time, he fought for equality in Arkansas schools and government offices. Rockefeller also helped increase the amount of money that workers in Arkansas earned.

Like Rockefeller, Governor **David Pryor** struggled for equal rights. In the 1970s, Governor Pryor chose many African Americans and women for government positions.

Bill and Hillary Clinton

One of Arkansas's most famous governors was **Bill Clinton.** During the 1980s and early 1990s, he worked to improve education and to create more jobs in the state. In 1993, Clinton became the first President of the United States from Arkansas. During his two terms as President, he helped the United States have the longest period of economic growth in its history.

As Bill Clinton's wife, **Hillary Clinton** was the First Lady of Arkansas and the First Lady of the United States. In 2001 she became a senator for the state of New York. She was the first First Lady of the United States elected to the Senate.

REVIEW In what way did Bill Clinton help Arkansas's economy?

Bill and Hillary Clinton

Winthrop Rockefeller

Maura Lozano-Yancy She started ¡Hola! Arkansas, the first statewide Spanish-English newspaper in Arkansas.

Other entrepreneurs have started magazine and newspaper businesses. In 1945, **John H. Johnson** started *Ebony*, a successful magazine for African Americans. He later built one of the nation's largest African American-owned businesses.

Entrepreneurs have also opened stores. In 1962, **Sam Walton** opened his first Wal-Mart store in Rogers, Arkansas. Because of the success of Wal-Mart stores, Walton became the richest person in the United States.

Not all entrepreneurs start a business for profit. In 2000, **Maura Lozano-Yancy** started a newspaper called *¡Hola! Arkansas*. Lozano-Yancy started *¡Hola! Arkansas* to help Spanish-speaking and English-speaking people in the state understand each other.

Entrepreneurs

Main Idea Arkansas has been home to many business leaders.

Many entrepreneurs have improved life in Arkansas by creating jobs. An **entrepreneur** is a person who takes a risk to start a business. Most entrepreneurs start a business to earn a profit. A profit is the money left over after a business pays its expenses.

Some entrepreneurs in Arkansas have worked in agriculture. In the 1930s, **John Tyson** started a business raising chickens. His company helped make poultry one of the state's most important industries.

Sam Walton The first Wal-Mart store opened in Arkansas in 1962.

Educators and Doctors

Arkansas has also been home to many important educators and doctors. In the 1950s, Arkansan **Samuel Lee Kountz** became one of the first African Americans to attend the University of Arkansas medical school. Kountz went on to develop a way to improve kidney transplants.

In 1966, **Samuel Massie** became the first African American professor at the United States Naval Academy. A professor is a college teacher. In 1993, **Nannerl Keohane** became the first woman president of Duke University.

REVIEW Name four entrepreneurs from Arkansas.

Samuel Massie He taught chemistry at the United States Naval Academy.

Lesson Summary
- Arkansans have worked for equality and civil rights.
- Politicians and entrepreneurs in Arkansas have helped improve life in the state.
- Many important educators and doctors have come from Arkansas.

Why It Matters...
Arkansans have made important contributions in civil rights, politics, business, education, and medicine.

Lesson Review

1. **VOCABULARY** Write a sentence about the 1950s and 1960s, using the term **civil rights**.

2. **READING SKILL** Name one way that people tried to **solve the problem** of segregation.

3. **MAIN IDEA: Citizenship** What did Daisy and Lucious Bates do to fight for civil rights?

4. **MAIN IDEA: Economics** Why do most entrepreneurs start a business?

5. **PEOPLE TO KNOW** Who is Samuel Massie?

6. **CRITICAL THINKING: Analyze** In what way did differences between people lead to conflict at Little Rock's Central High School?

ART ACTIVITY Make a drawing or another piece of artwork showing something that politicians from Arkansas have done to improve life in the state.

121

Skillbuilder

Resolve Conflicts

Sometimes, differences in opinions and beliefs can lead to a conflict. A **conflict** is a disagreement between groups of people or individuals. By working together, both sides in a conflict can overcome their disagreements and find a solution.

▶ **VOCABULARY**
conflict
compromise

Learn the Skill

Step 1: Identify the conflict.

Conflict: The softball team and the school band want to use the auditorium after school on Tuesdays.

Step 2: Understand the reasons for the conflict. Have the people involved in the conflict state their goals.

Goal: The softball team wants to hold meetings on Tuesdays.

Goal: The school band wants to rehearse on Tuesdays.

Step 3: Think of all the possible ways to solve the conflict.

Possible Solution: The softball team offers to hold meetings every other Tuesday.

Possible Solution: The school band offers to practice at a later time.

Step 4: Choose the plan or compromise that is most acceptable to everyone involved. Each side may need to **compromise** on its goals. To compromise means to give up something that you want in order to move closer to an agreement.

Solution: The softball team will hold meetings every other Tuesday. The band will practice in the evening on the days that the softball team has meetings.

122 • Chapter 6

Apply Critical Thinking

Rain forests help keep the air clean, and they help support many plant and animal species. Rain forests also hold many valuable resources. Some people want to cut down rain forests to build houses, create farmland, and sell timber. Others think that this will harm the environment. They want to keep people from disturbing the rain forest.

Practice the Skill

Read the paragraph above. Then answer the questions.

1. Identify the conflict. What differences in opinion do people have about rain forests?
2. What are the goals of the people involved in the conflict?
3. Brainstorm ways that both groups can work together to resolve this conflict.

Apply the Skill

Find out about a conflict that exists in your community. Learn about ways that people have tried to compromise in order to find a solution.

Core Lesson 2

Arkansas Culture

Build on What You Know You have probably heard country and blues music. Both are part of Arkansas's culture.

Arkansas and the Arts

Main Idea Writers and painters contribute to the culture of Arkansas.

People in the United States share a common heritage. **Heritage** means the traditions that people have passed down to each other for many years. The arts, such as writing, painting, and music, are part of this heritage.

People in Arkansas come from different backgrounds and cultures. They all add to the shared heritage of Arkansas and the United States. They also help make Arkansas a multicultural state. **Multicultural** means having many cultures.

VOCABULARY

heritage
multicultural

Vocabulary Strategy

multicultural

The prefix **multi-** means "many." **Multicultural** means "of many cultures," or ways of life.

READING SKILL

Categorize As you read, categorize the achievements of Arkansans.

Type of Achievement	Examples

Maya Angelou This famous poet and writer grew up in Arkansas.

124 • Chapter 6

Painting Arkansas Carroll Cloar's paintings are based on memories of his childhood in Earle, Arkansas.

Writers and Painters

Arkansans **Maya Angelou** and **John Grisham** are well-known writers. Growing up in Arkansas and the South influenced them both.

Maya Angelou was born in St. Louis, Missouri, in 1928. As a child, she moved to Stamps, Arkansas. There she saw African Americans living under segregation. Angelou later wrote about equality and civil rights in her poetry, stories, books, and plays. In 1993, she read these words at President Bill Clinton's inauguration:

> Lift up your hearts
> Each new hour holds new chances
> For new beginnings.

John Grisham was born in Jonesboro in 1955. His parents had been cotton farmers. After going to law school, Grisham became a lawyer and a politician. Today, he is known for his popular fiction works about the legal system.

Important painters have also come from Arkansas. **Carroll Cloar** was born near Earle in 1913. Many of his paintings are based on photographs of people and buildings in Earle. In 1993, a painting by Cloar was chosen to honor the inauguration of President Bill Clinton.

REVIEW Who are two writers from Arkansas?

125

Entertainers and Athletes

Main Idea Musicians, actors, and athletes are part of Arkansas's multicultural heritage.

Arkansans have entertained people across the United States and the world. Musician **"Sonny Boy" Williamson** first rose to fame in the 1940s while performing on the *King Biscuit Time* radio show. This show was broadcast from Helena. Williamson played the blues, a type of music developed by African Americans in the South.

Johnny Cash was born in Kingsland in 1932. Cash played country music. Country music grew out of the folk music brought by Scottish and Irish settlers. Cash had many hit songs in the 1950s and 1960s, including "Ring of Fire." In the 1980s he was elected to both the Country Music Hall of Fame and the Songwriters Hall of Fame.

Mary Steenburgen

Some Arkansas entertainers have been actors and actresses. One example is **Mary Steenburgen,** from Newport. Steenburgen won an Academy Award in 1981 for her role in the movie *Melvin and Howard*. Steenburgen also helped make *End of the Line,* a movie filmed in Arkansas.

Talented Arkansans "Sonny Boy" Williamson (below, center) and Johnny Cash (right) entertained people with their music. Mary Steenburgen (above, right) works in film.

Arkansas Athletes

Basketball player **Hazel Walker** rose to fame as part of a women's basketball team called the All-American Red Heads. **Scottie Pippen** played basketball at the University of Central Arkansas. Later, he won six NBA championships with the Chicago Bulls. **Jerry Jones** played football at the University of Arkansas before becoming the owner of the Dallas Cowboys. Walker, Pippen, and Jones have all been elected to the Arkansas Sports Hall of Fame.

REVIEW Who are two musicians from Arkansas?

Lesson Summary

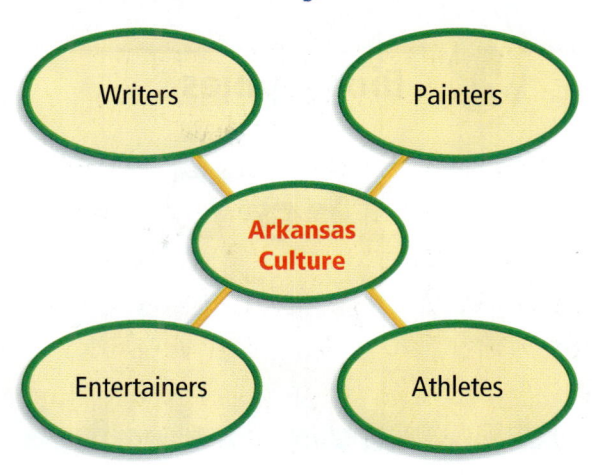

- Writers
- Painters
- Arkansas Culture
- Entertainers
- Athletes

Why It Matters...

Learning about Arkansas's heritage helps people to understand and respect one another. Arkansas writers, painters, musicians, actors, athletes, and other artists and entertainers have helped shape the culture of the state and nation.

Basketball Star Scottie Pippen of Hamburg was named one of the "50 Greatest Players in NBA History."

Lesson Review

1. **VOCABULARY** Write a sentence about Arkansas, using the words **heritage** and **multicultural**.

2. **READING SKILL** For what **category** of achievement did Mary Steenburgen become famous?

3. **MAIN IDEA: Culture** What does Maya Angelou write about in her poetry, stories, books, and plays?

4. **MAIN IDEA: Culture** What heritage did the music of "Sonny Boy" Williamson reflect?

5. **PEOPLE TO KNOW** Who is Hazel Walker?

6. **CRITICAL THINKING: Draw Conclusions** In what ways did African Americans and Scottish and Irish settlers add to Arkansas's musical heritage?

RESEARCH ACTIVITY Use the library or Internet resources to learn more about art and music in your community, state, and nation. Write a report about what you learn.

Extend Lesson 2
Biographies

The Pride of ARKANSAS

To be a great state, Arkansas must have great people—and it does! People from Arkansas have made their mark helping others, starting businesses, taking part in government, making music, writing, and painting, and in many other ways. Great Arkansans, including the three on these pages, are the pride of Arkansas.

Al Green (1946–)

The son of a sharecropper, Al Green was born in Forrest City in 1946. Today, he is considered one of Arkansas's finest singers. Over his long career he has sung rhythm and blues, pop, and gospel music. Green has won eight Grammy awards for his music. A Grammy Award is a special honor given to people who work in the music industry. He was elected to the Rock and Roll Hall of Fame in 1995 and to the Gospel Hall of Fame in 2004.

Natalie Smith Henry (1907–1992)

Malvern native Natalie Smith Henry became famous during the Great Depression for her paintings and murals. A mural is a large painting that covers a wall or several walls. In 1939, the U.S. Treasury Department's Section of Fine Arts asked Henry to paint a mural called "Local Industries" for the Springdale post office. Today, Arkansans can see Henry's paintings in Springdale at the Shiloh Museum of Ozark History.

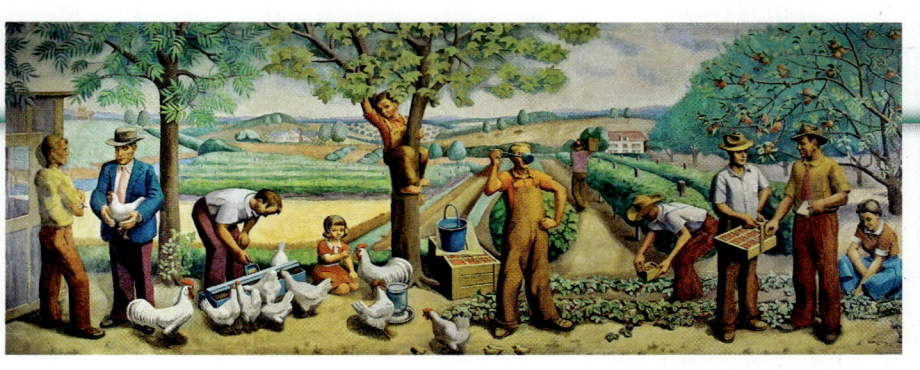

"Local Industries" Henry completed this painting in 1940.

Harry Scott Ashmore (1916–1998)

Harry Scott Ashmore first joined the *Arkansas Gazette* in 1947 as a reporter. He soon became the paper's lead editor. During the 1950s, Ashmore wrote front-page articles in the *Gazette*, urging people to end discrimination and allow African Americans to attend all-white schools in Arkansas and across the United States. For his efforts, Ashmore was awarded a Pulitzer Prize. Columbia University in New York awards the Pulitzer Prize to people in journalism, literature, and music. Until his death in 1998, Ashmore continued to speak and write in favor of civil rights.

Activities

1. **TALK ABOUT IT** Why do you think these three people are considered the pride of Arkansas?
2. **WRITE A LETTER** Write a letter to one of these people. Tell the person what you think about his or her achievements.

BIOGRAPHIES

Chapter 6 Review and Test Prep

Visual Summary

1. – 3. Write a description of each item named below.

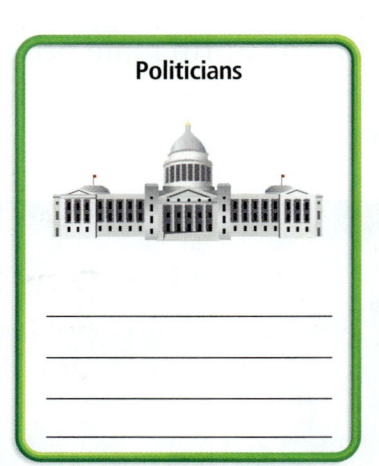

Civil Rights Leaders

Politicians

Entertainers

Facts and Main Ideas

TEST PREP Answer each question below.

4. **Citizenship** Who was Dr. Martin Luther King, Jr.?

5. **Government** What did Bill Clinton do as governor of Arkansas?

6. **Economics** What magazine did entrepreneur John H. Johnson start?

7. **Culture** Who spoke at President Bill Clinton's inauguration in 1993?

8. **Culture** What sport did Hazel Walker play?

Vocabulary

TEST PREP Choose the correct word from the list below to complete each sentence.

politician, p. 118
entrepreneur, p. 120
heritage, p. 124
multicultural, p. 124

9. Music and painting are part of Arkansas's _____.

10. Sam Walton is a(n) _____ from Arkansas.

11. A governor is a type of _____.

12. Different cultures help make Arkansas a(n) _____ state.

130 • Chapter 6

Apply Skills

✓ **TEST PREP** **Resolve Conflicts**
Use what you have learned about resolving conflicts to answer each question.

> Four friends are deciding what to do on Saturday. One wants to go to a movie. One wants to go to a cultural festival. Two want to go to a music concert.

13. Which statement describes the conflict?

  A. Friends want to see different movies.
  B. Friends want to go to different music concerts.
  C. Friends have no idea what to do.
  D. Friends have different ideas about what to do.

14. Which circumstance would help the friends reach a compromise?

  A. The friends discuss the choices and find an activity most of them can agree on.
  B. Each friend makes a choice without discussion.
  C. One friend makes a choice for everyone.
  D. All friends avoid talking about the conflict.

Critical Thinking

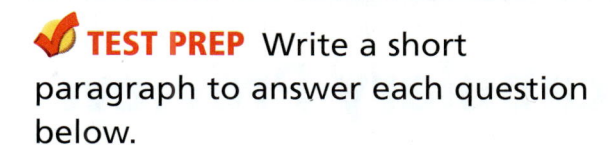

✓ **TEST PREP** Write a short paragraph to answer each question below.

15. **Evaluate** Do you think entrepreneurs should start businesses only to earn a profit? Explain your answer.

16. **Draw Conclusions** Do you think that Arkansas's heritage has changed over time? Why or why not?

Activities

Art Activity Carroll Cloar based many of his paintings on photographs of people and buildings in Earle. Find a photograph of a person or building in your community. Draw a picture of it. Include as many details as you can.

Writing Activity Find out more about a person you read about in this chapter. Write a paragraph about their life and achievements.

Technology
Writing Process Tips
Get help with your writing at:
www.eduplace.com/kids/hmss/

Chapter 7 Government in Arkansas

Technology
e • word games
www.eduplace.com/kids/hmss/

Vocabulary Preview

legislative branch
Members of Arkansas's **legislative branch** work in the capitol building in Little Rock. There, the General Assembly meets to write, discuss, and pass laws.
page 136

budget
To keep track of the state's money, officials make a **budget.** They use it to figure out how much money to spend and how much money to collect in taxes.
page 144

Reading Strategy

Summarize Use this strategy to focus on important information.

Quick Tip As you read, look for details that support the main ideas in each lesson. Write down these main ideas and details.

volunteer

A citizen may help his or her community by becoming a **volunteer.** Some volunteers work to keep Arkansas's parks and wilderness areas clean and beautiful.
page 151

republic

In a **republic,** citizens participate by voting in elections. Arkansas voters elect local, state, and national representatives to serve in government.
page 152

Core Lesson 1

The United States Government

VOCABULARY

legislative branch
executive branch
judicial branch
political party
primary

Vocabulary Strategy

legislative branch

The words **legislative**, **legal**, and **legislature** are related. They all have to do with laws.

READING SKILL
Problem and Solution Identify problems faced by the United States government. List ways in which the Constitution provides solutions.

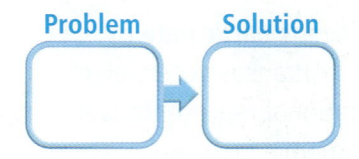

Problem → Solution

Build on What You Know On a team, players agree to follow the rules. The states and citizens of the United States have agreed to follow the rules laid out in the nation's plan of government.

The Federal Government

Main Idea The Constitution is the plan for the government of the United States.

After the American Revolution, the leaders of the United States wrote a plan for government. It was known as the Articles of Confederation. This plan gave most of the power to the states and very little to the national government. In fact, the states acted as separate countries rather than as one nation. As a result, conflicts took place among them. Many state leaders agreed that they had to find a better way to work together.

In 1787, state delegates met to change the Articles of Confederation. They knew that they had to unite the states under one government. However, they also wanted to protect each state's right to take care of its own matters. After several months, the delegates came up with a new plan. This plan, the Constitution of the United States, has lasted for more than 200 years.

Agreement The states had to ratify, or agree to, the plan described in the Constitution.

134 • Chapter 7

The U.S. Constitution

The Constitution provides for a federal system of government. The national, or federal, government shares power with state governments in a federal system. The Constitution explains the powers that the federal government has. It also explains the things that states have the power to decide.

The federal government deals with issues that affect the nation. Federal departments print money, control the military, make treaties, and oversee trade with other countries. The federal government collects taxes. It uses tax money to provide public services. A public service is something done for the good of people in the nation.

States have the power to set up state and local governments. These governments make decisions about state and local matters. They carry out federal laws, and write state and local laws.

Although the Constitution protects state powers, some states refused to approve the document. These states agreed to ratify the Constitution only if it protected individual rights. The first ten amendments to the Constitution, known as the Bill of Rights, were added to protect citizens' rights. Later amendments added more rights for more people. These protections help limit government power.

REVIEW In what way do federal and state governments share power?

Writing the Constitution George Washington (1) addressed delegates from twelve of the original thirteen states at the Constitutional Convention. Among the delegates were Benjamin Franklin (2), James Madison (3), and Alexander Hamilton (4).

135

Balancing Power

Main Idea The three branches of federal government balance one another's power.

Under the Constitution, the federal government has three branches, or parts. These branches work together to protect and provide for the entire nation. The U.S. Congress makes up the legislative branch. The **legislative branch** legislates, or makes laws. The President heads the executive branch. The **executive branch** executes, or carries out, laws. The U.S. Supreme Court is the highest court in the judicial branch. The **judicial branch** decides questions of law. A court is a group of people that hears cases of law.

Separate Roles Each branch of government has a different job. The U.S. Congress meets in the Capitol building in Washington, D.C., to make laws.

SKILL Reading Charts Which branch of government carries out laws?

Checks and Balances

Having three branches of government creates a system of "checks and balances." Each branch has an equal amount of power. Each branch can also check the power of the other two. To check means to limit. This system prevents any one branch from gaining too much power.

For example, the President appoints justices, or judges, to the Supreme Court. Congress reviews the President's choices and may reject them. Similarly, Congress passes laws. The President can veto the laws. To veto means to reject. The Supreme Court decides whether laws uphold the Constitution.

Three Branches of Government

Legislative	Executive	Judicial
Congress • passes laws	**President** • carries out laws	**Supreme Court** • decides questions of law

Washington, D.C.

Representation

Citizens of the United States choose lawmakers in elections. Candidates try to persuade citizens to elect them. A candidate is a person who wants to be elected.

The President is an elected official. Most presidential candidates are members of a political party. A **political party** is a group made up of people who have similar ideas about government. The two largest political parties in the United States are the Democratic and Republican parties.

These parties hold primaries. A **primary** is an election in which party members choose a candidate to run for President. Candidates then campaign, or compete to win support and votes. Every four years, citizens vote for presidential candidates in a general, or national, election. Most citizens vote for the candidate who shares their ideas about government.

Congress has two parts, the Senate and the House of Representatives. The citizens of each state elect two senators to the Senate. They also elect representatives to serve in the House. The number of representatives for each state depends on its population. In 2007, Arkansas had four representatives.

REVIEW What is the purpose of a political party?

Lesson Summary

The Constitution lays out the plan for the government of the United States.

- Three branches of government
- Checks and balances
- Elected representatives

Why It Matters...

The U.S. Constitution guides the government of the nation and protects citizens' rights.

Lesson Review

1. **VOCABULARY** Explain the roles of the **legislative, executive,** and **judicial branches** of federal government.

2. **READING SKILL** What **solution** does the Constitution provide for the **problem** of protecting citizens' rights?

3. **MAIN IDEA: History** Why did state delegates want to replace the Articles of Confederation with the Constitution?

4. **MAIN IDEA: Government** How do the three branches balance one another's power?

5. **CRITICAL THINKING: Analyze** Why did early political leaders decide both to strengthen and to limit the power of the federal government?

RESEARCH ACTIVITY Make a poster showing at least three public services provided by the federal government. Add a caption explaining each service.

Skillbuilder
Identify Primary and Secondary Sources

A **primary source** comes from a person who witnessed an event. For example, journals, photos, letters, original artwork, speeches, and direct quotes are all primary sources. A **secondary source** is written by someone who did not witness the event. Examples include biographies, encyclopedias, and textbooks. Primary and secondary sources can offer different points of view on the same topic. The sources below present different accounts of the passing of the Constitution of the United States.

Passage A

I agree to this Constitution with all its faults, if [it has any]; because I think a [national] Government [is needed] for us. . . . I doubt too whether any other [group] . . . [could] make a better Constitution . . . . [C]an a perfect [document] be expected? It [surprises] me, Sir, to find this [Constitution] . . . so near to perfection. . . . Thus I [agree], Sir, to this Constitution because I expect no better, and because I am not sure, that it is not the best. . . .

—Benjamin Franklin, Constitutional Convention, September 17, 1787

Passage B

In 1787, state delegates met to revise the Articles of Confederation. They wanted to make a stronger national government. The lawmakers came up with a new plan, the United States Constitution. Many states did not want to approve the new plan. Some people thought that the national government would have too much power under the Constitution. Others worried that the Constitution did not include a bill of rights. Supporters of the Constitution persuaded enough lawmakers to ratify it. They promised to add a bill of rights to protect individual freedoms.

—from a textbook summary, 2007

Apply Critical Thinking

Learn the Skill

Step 1: Read the sources carefully. What is their subject?

Step 2: Identify the primary source. Look for words such as **I, my, we,** and **our.** Also look for personal details. These hint that the writer was actually at the event being described.

Step 3: Find the secondary source. Secondary sources do not include personal information about the event. Often, secondary sources summarize and analyze an event.

Practice the Skill

Use the passages on page 138 to answer the questions.

1. Which is the primary source, and which is the secondary source? What information helps you identify each?
2. Which facts are the same in both sources?
3. What details do you learn from the secondary source that you do not find in the primary source?

Apply the Skill

Using a newspaper, find one example of a primary source and one example of a secondary source. Write a paragraph explaining how the two sources are similar and how they are different.

139

Core Lesson 2

State and Local Government

VOCABULARY

common good
jury
bill
county
budget

Vocabulary Strategy

common good

Common means "relating to the community." The **common good** means the good of the community.

READING SKILL
Compare and Contrast List ways in which the governments of Arkansas and the United States are alike and different.

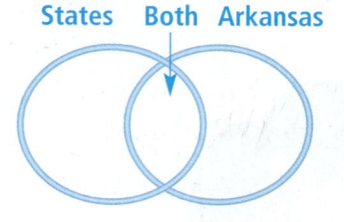

United States Both Arkansas

Build on What You Know Teachers and students follow rules to keep the classroom safe. What rules does your classroom have? Your community and state have rules, called laws, that protect and help citizens.

The Constitution of Arkansas

Main Idea Arkansas's constitution explains the plan for state government and protects the common good and citizens' rights.

Like the United States, Arkansas has a constitution. It lays out a plan for state government. It explains how laws are made and how state and local governments raise and spend money. Arkansas lawmakers wrote the first state constitution in 1836 when they applied for statehood. Since then, the constitution has been rewritten four times. Arkansans approved the fifth constitution, still in use today, in 1874. The state constitution includes a way to change laws. Since 1874, Arkansans have changed the constitution more than 80 times.

The Capitol Members of state government work in this building in Little Rock.

140 • Chapter 7

Arkansans' Basic Rights and Freedoms

Bill of Rights of the United States	Declaration of Rights of the State of Arkansas
First Amendment: Freedom of religion	Section 24: [N]o preference shall ever be given, by law, to any religious establishment, denomination [group] or mode of worship, above any other.
First Amendment: Freedom of the press	Section 6: The liberty of the press shall forever remain inviolate [untouched].
First Amendment: Freedom to gather peacefully	Section 4: The right of the people peaceably to assemble [gather]… shall never be abridged [reduced].
Sixth Amendment: Right to a speedy and public trial	Section 10: In all criminal prosecutions, the (person) accused (of a crime) shall enjoy the right to a speedy and public trial.

SKILL **Reading Charts** Which section of the Declaration of Rights protects the right of newspapers to print information and opinions?

The Common Good and Individual Rights

National, state, and local governments do two main jobs. They work for the common good and they protect individual rights. The **common good** means the good of the whole population. For example, Arkansas's state and local governments pass laws to keep people safe. They make traffic laws that require people to drive at safe speeds and wear seatbelts.

The U.S. Constitution lists citizens' rights in the Bill of Rights. Arkansas's constitution lists citizens' rights in the Declaration of Rights. The Declaration of Rights says that all people are equal. It protects basic freedoms, including the right of citizens to speak and gather freely.

According to the Declaration of Rights, citizens can also practice their religions and ask the government for change. Citizens have the right to a trial by jury. A **jury** is a group of citizens who decide a case in court. The Declaration of Rights also protects the rights to own property and to print information and opinions in writing.

Arkansas lawmakers thought that these rights were important so they made the Declaration of Rights the second part of the state constitution. Officials and citizens in Arkansas must work together to balance the common good and individual rights.

REVIEW What two main jobs do all levels of government do?

141

Sharing Power Members of the General Assembly write and pass laws that affect business, health care, education, and family life.

Arkansas's Government

Main Idea State and local governments share power in Arkansas.

How does the state constitution balance the common good with individual rights? It provides for a representative government. This means that citizens elect lawmakers.

The state constitution also provides for three branches of government. The legislative branch makes laws. The executive branch carries out laws. The judicial branch decides questions of law.

The General Assembly makes up the legislative branch. Like the U.S. Congress, it has a House of Representatives and a Senate. These two bodies work together to write and pass laws. The House has 100 elected members. The Senate has 35 elected members.

Members of the House of Representatives and the Senate represent different parts of the state, called districts. Each representative serves for two years. Each senator serves for four years.

The governor of Arkansas heads the executive branch. The governor approves or vetoes bills passed by the General Assembly. A **bill** is a written idea for a law. The governor oversees agencies that carry out the state's laws. Arkansans elect the governor to serve for four years.

Many courts of law make up the judicial branch. The Arkansas Supreme Court is the highest state court. It decides questions of law that have been raised in other state and local courts. Citizens elect six justices and one chief justice to serve for eight years.

Cities and Counties

Arkansas state government shares power with local governments. Cities, towns, and counties have local governments that protect citizens, provide public services, and keep communities running. A **county** is a smaller part of a state with its own government. Arkansas has 75 counties and many city and town governments.

Local governments carry out state and national laws. They also write their own local laws. Counties and cities pass many building and tax laws. Local governments manage city and county money. They decide how much money to spend on public services. These services include libraries, trash collection, road maintenance, and police and fire protection.

In Arkansas, an elected county judge leads the executive branch of county government. Other elected officials include a sheriff to maintain public peace and safety, and a treasurer to keep track of county spending. Elected justices of the peace meet together in a body called the quorum court. This court advises the county judge. It also has some legislative power.

Many cities and towns elect a mayor and city council. The mayor heads the city or town government. The city council advises the mayor and has some lawmaking power. Some cities elect only a city council. The council members appoint a city manager.

REVIEW What responsibilities do city councils have?

Public Services Local governments use tax money to pay for public schools and fire protection.

State Money at Work Arkansans enjoy state parks and other services provided by the state government.

Other Responsibilities

Main Idea State and local governments also raise money to pay for public services, and work with other cities, states, and nations.

State and local governments provide public services to help citizens. In addition to fire and police protection, they pay for roads, public schools and libraries, certain health care programs, parks and wildlife areas, and public transportation. These services cost large amounts of money.

The national government gives money for some public services. These include fixing highways and helping public schools. However, governments at all levels get most of their money by collecting taxes from people and businesses.

National and state governments collect income taxes. An income tax is a tax on money that businesses and workers earn. The state also collects sales taxes on certain goods and services that people buy. Local governments collect sales taxes and property taxes. A property tax is a tax on some kinds of property, such as houses and cars.

State and local governments use budgets to keep track of their money. A **budget** is a plan for collecting and spending money. Budgets help officials figure out how much money they can spend on public services each year. Budgets also help governments decide when to collect money or cut spending. At the state level, the governor and members of the General Assembly work together to write and pass a budget.

Arkansas and the World

Several Arkansas cities take part in the Sister Cities program. This program links two cities to help them learn about each other's economy, culture, and government. Arkansas's sister cities include Fort Smith, Arkansas, and Cisterna, Italy; Little Rock, Arkansas, and Hanam City, South Korea; and Hot Springs, Arkansas, and Hanamaki, Japan. People in these cities work together on projects in business, health care, and education.

Sometimes Arkansas lawmakers travel to other nations. They visit lawmakers, learn about other countries, and help find solutions to shared problems. In 2006, Governor **Mike Huckabee** visited Iraq, Afghanistan, and Pakistan. He met with Arkansas military troops and political leaders.

Lottie Shackelford was the first female African American mayor of Little Rock. She went on to observe elections in Romania. She also observed political activities in the former Soviet Union and West Germany.

REVIEW How does state government raise money to pay for public services?

Lesson Summary

State and local government
- State constitution provides plan.
- Officials share power.
- Taxes help pay for public services.

Why It Matters...

State and local governments make decisions and pass laws that affect the ways in which Arkansans live.

Lesson Review

1 VOCABULARY Choose the correct words to complete the sentences.

jury   bill   budget

Lawmakers in the General Assembly make a law by writing and passing a _____. They use a _____ to keep track of the state's money.

2 READING SKILL Use your diagram to **compare** ways in which the governments of Arkansas and the United States are alike.

3 MAIN IDEA: Government What part of Arkansas's constitution lists the rights of individuals?

4 MAIN IDEA: Government What powers do state and local governments share?

5 FACTS TO KNOW How are the governor and members of the General Assembly selected?

6 CRITICAL THINKING: Synthesize Describe jobs done by elected officials in each branch of state government.

ART ACTIVITY Draw a diagram that shows the different branches of state government. Identify important bodies or officials for each branch.

145

Extend Lesson 2
Citizenship

Symbols of Arkansas
★ ★ ★

Arkansas is a beautiful land with a rich history. The state flag and other symbols represent the beauty of the state, and the pride, and courage of Arkansans in the past and present.

Mount Magazine

Arkansans value their environment, so they adopted the nickname "the Natural State." At 2,753 feet, Mount Magazine is Arkansas's tallest mountain and a symbol of the Natural State's beautiful resources. Located in the Ouachita Mountains, Mount Magazine overlooks the Arkansas and Petit Jean rivers. American settlers first came to the mountain in the early 1800s. They farmed corn and other crops. Today, Mount Magazine State Park includes a visitor's center as well as many campsites, cabins, and trails that attract visitors throughout the year.

Arkansas State Flag

School teacher Willie Kavanaugh Hocker designed the state flag in 1913. The colors are the same as those of the United States. The diamond shows that Arkansas has the nation's only diamond mines. The twenty-five stars show that Arkansas was the 25th state to join the nation. The four stars in the center represent the four nations to which the Arkansas Territory has belonged over the years.

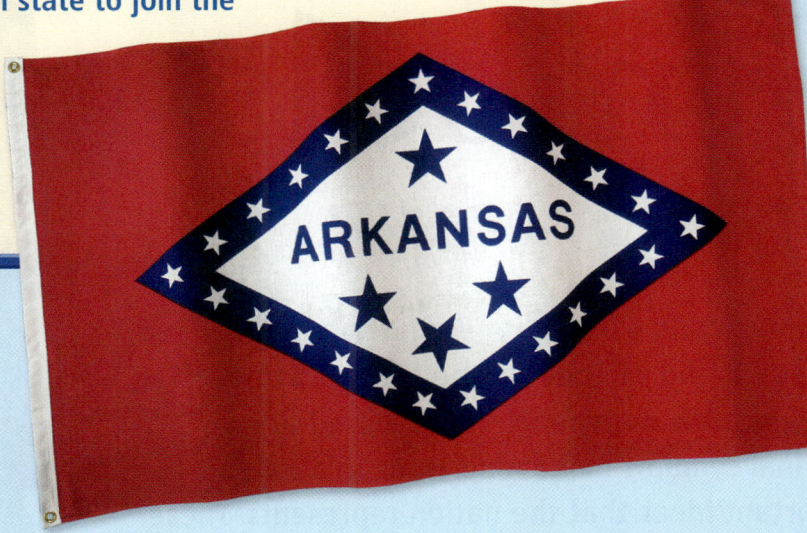

Little Rock Nine Monument

In 1957, nine African American teenagers challenged a governor, a state, and a nation to end school segregation. In 2005, the state placed this civil rights memorial, known as "Testament," on the state capitol grounds. It honors the courage of Melba Pattillo Beals, Elizabeth Eckford, Ernest Green, Gloria Ray Karlmark, Carlotta Walls Lanier, Dr. Terrence Roberts, Jefferson Thomas, Minnijean Brown Trickey, and Thelma Mothershed-Wair.

> " Their act of courage opened doors symbolically all over segregated America. "
> — "Testament," the Little Rock Nine monument

National Symbols

Americans often feel proud when they see the stars and stripes of the United States flag waving high overhead. The flag and other national symbols make Americans think about the important ideas that the nation represents. These ideas include freedom, democracy, and civil rights.

★ The Statue of Liberty

The people of the United States received the Statue of Liberty as a gift from the people of France in 1885. For millions of immigrants arriving in New York, "Lady Liberty" was the first thing they saw. It suggested that they could find freedom and opportunity in America. The words below are at the base of the statue.

"Give me your tired, your poor, Your huddled masses yearning to breathe free...."
— from "The New Colossus" by Emma Lazarus

148 • Chapter 7

The United States Flag

In 1777, Congressman Francis Hopkinson designed the first national flag with 13 stripes and 13 stars. These represented the 13 colonies that declared independence from Britain. Since then, the flag has changed almost 30 times. Today's flag still has 13 stripes, but it has 50 stars, one for each state. Citizens often say the Pledge of Allegiance to the flag to show their loyalty to the nation.

The Liberty Bell

The Liberty Bell arrived in Philadelphia in 1752. It rang when the Declaration of Independence was first read in public. Later, people fighting against slavery named it "The Liberty Bell." It has become a symbol of our nation's struggle for freedom.

Look Closely The Liberty Bell has cracked twice. The first time, it was melted down and made again.

Activities

1. **STEP INTO IT** Notice the torch in Lady Liberty's hand. Discuss what this shining light might mean.

2. **STUDY IT** Read the Pledge of Allegiance in the Citizenship Handbook on page R2. Break up the pledge into phrases or parts. Explain the meaning of each phrase. Then, write a paragraph explaining what the pledge makes you think about the nation and your responsibilities as an active citizen.

Technology Visit Education Place for more primary sources: www.eduplace.com/kids/hmss/

CITIZENSHIP

Core Lesson 3

Good Citizenship

VOCABULARY

democracy
volunteer
totalitarian
dictatorship
republic

Vocabulary Strategy

democracy

Democracy comes from a Greek word meaning "rule by the people."

READING SKILL

Categorize As you read, list information about citizens' rights and citizens' responsibilities.

Rights	Responsibilities

Build on What You Know Think about group projects on which you have worked. Such groups work much as a government does. To complete a project, group members must work together.

Rights and Responsibilities

Main Idea Citizens of the United States have many rights and responsibilities.

Americans often say that they live in a free country. They mean that the United States is a representative democracy. A **democracy** is a system in which people hold the power of government. In a representative democracy, people elect leaders to represent them. Arkansas's state motto is "The people rule." It shows the democratic spirit of government in the United States and Arkansas.

People in the United States enjoy many rights and freedoms. These include the right to gather peacefully and the freedom to tell their opinions. The nation's founders protected people's rights and freedoms by adding the Bill of Rights and other amendments to the U.S. Constitution.

Protecting Rights The Bill of Rights guarantees freedom of speech and other rights.

150 • Chapter 7

Participation Serving on a jury is a serious responsibility, but volunteering to help the community can be fun.

Government and Citizens

Along with rights come responsibilities. For a representative democracy to work, citizens must participate in government. Citizens can participate by voting. Learning about candidates and choosing representatives are important responsibilities.

Citizens have a responsibility to pay taxes. Governments use tax money to provide public services. Citizens may be asked to serve on a jury. People who serve on juries protect the right to a trial by jury.

All citizens have a responsibility to respect the rights of other people. To protect citizens' rights, people must obey laws. People should work to change laws that they think are unfair.

People can work for change by calling or writing their representatives. They can also write their ideas in a document called a petition. People who agree with the ideas sign the petition. The signed petition goes to government officials.

Citizens who are too young to vote can participate by obeying laws, sharing their opinions, and going to school. All people can be responsible citizens by working as volunteers. A **volunteer** is a person who provides a service without being paid for his or her time and effort. Volunteers pick up litter, give out food, and do other important jobs.

REVIEW Why do citizens in a representative democracy have responsibilities? What are they?

151

Elections Citizens can voice their opinions by voting in local and national elections.

Why We Vote

Main Idea Voting is a right and a responsibility for citizens of a republic.

Many nations around the world protect citizens' rights. However, some do not. In some countries, people do not have the freedoms that Americans have. People ruled by totalitarian [toh tah lih TAYR ee uhn] governments can go to jail for disagreeing with political leaders. **Totalitarian** means that the government uses force to control people's lives. Totalitarian governments decide what information people can share and what activities they can do.

The founders of the United States did not want the government to control the people. The founders did not want a dictatorship. A **dictatorship** is a form of totalitarian government in which one ruler makes all the decisions for a nation.

To provide for a representative democracy, the nation's founders set up a republic. A **republic** is a form of democratic government in which people choose leaders to represent them. These leaders work together to make decisions for the nation. In a republic, no one person can gain too much power.

Voting is an important right. It is also a citizen's most important responsibility. For the people to have power, they must vote and participate in government. Candidates for government office share their opinions about issues that affect people's lives. Citizens learn about candidates' ideas. Then they vote for the candidates with whom they agree. They also vote directly on some laws. By voting for candidates and laws, citizens decide how their government will work.

152 • Chapter 7

Votes Count

Citizens vote in national, state, and local elections. Every vote helps decide who will become the President in a national election, or who will become a state or local lawmaker.

In the presidential election of 2000, just a few hundred votes in the state of Florida made the difference in who became the next President. The election in Florida was so close that the votes had to be counted again. However, the U.S. Supreme Court stopped the counting. As a result, **George W. Bush** became President.

In Arkansas politics, Governor Huckabee won the 2002 election by fewer than 50,000 votes. That amounts to less than two percent of the population of Arkansas. In a democracy every vote is important.

REVIEW In what way do totalitarian governments control people's lives?

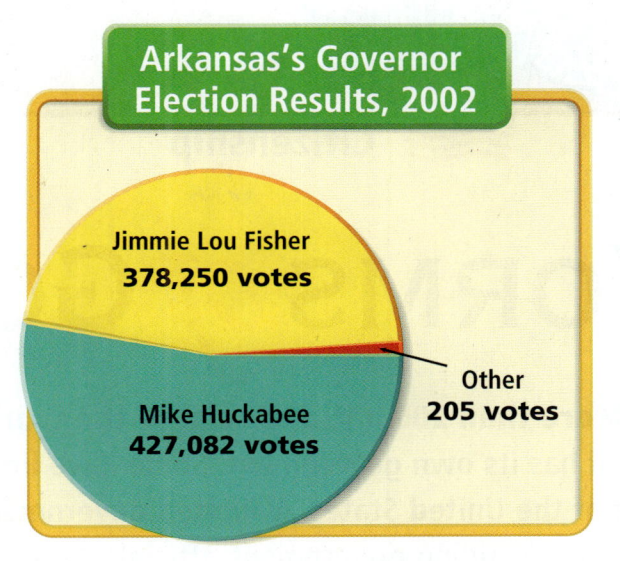

Arkansas's Governor Election Results, 2002

- Jimmie Lou Fisher 378,250 votes
- Mike Huckabee 427,082 votes
- Other 205 votes

Close Race Jimmie Lou Fisher came very close to becoming the first female governor of Arkansas.

Lesson Summary

In the United States, citizens have many rights and responsibilities. Voting is an important right. It is also a key responsibility that helps make the nation a representative democracy.

Why It Matters...

The United States government depends on citizens' participation.

Lesson Review

1. **VOCABULARY** Write a few sentences explaining ways in which a **republic** and a **dictatorship** differ.

2. **READING SKILL** Look at the list of responsibilities you **categorized.** Name the two responsibilities that you think are most important and explain why.

3. **MAIN IDEA: Citizenship** In what ways can young people participate in a representative democracy?

4. **MAIN IDEA: Citizenship** Why is voting such an important responsibility?

5. **CRITICAL THINKING: Draw Conclusions** What characteristics do people need to be active and responsible citizens?

WRITING ACTIVITY Write letters to two elected officials. Ask about each officials' responsibilities. Share your findings with the class.

Extend Lesson 3
Citizenship

FORMS *of* GOVERNMENT

More than 200 nations exist in the world. Each nation in the world has its own government. Some have limited governments like that of the United States. A **limited government** is one in which all citizens, including government officials, must obey laws. Other countries have unlimited governments. An **unlimited government** is one in which government leaders do not have to obey the laws.

Unlimited Government	Limited Government
One person or a small group of people control government.	Many people participate in government.
Rulers make and change laws when they want to.	A process exists for officials to make and change laws.
Rulers do not have to obey laws.	All citizens and officials must obey laws.
A constitution may or may not exist but rulers do not have to follow it.	A constitution explains what the government can and cannot do.
Citizens have few if any rights.	Citizens have protected rights.
Citizens cannot disagree with or change government safely.	Citizens can disagree with and work to change government peacefully.
Rulers may or may not be elected.	Most officials are elected.

Unlimited Government Joseph Stalin was a dictator. He and his supporters ruled the former Soviet Union from 1924 through 1953. Under Stalin's dictatorship, the government controlled most farms, industries, businesses, schools, and news media.

Dictatorship

Democracy

Limited Government The United States is a republic. A republic is a representative democracy. Citizens elect leaders to represent them in Congress and other branches of government. Many people work together to make decisions for the nation.

Activities

1. **TALK ABOUT IT** Discuss features of governments that might make them limited or unlimited. Why are democratic forms of government limited?

2. **RESEARCH IT** Research the governments of two nations other than the United States. Prepare a presentation in which you describe the forms of government for each nation. What roles do citizens play?

Chapter 7 Review and Test Prep

Visual Summary

1.–3. Write a description of each item identified below.

Government

- United States Constitution
- Arkansas Constitution
- Cities and Counties

Facts and Main Ideas

TEST PREP Answer each question below.

4. **History** Why did the United States replace the Articles of Confederation with the United States Constitution?

5. **Government** In what ways can the three branches of federal government check one another's power?

6. **Government** What jobs do state and local governments share?

7. **Citizenship** How can citizens participate in government?

Vocabulary

TEST PREP Choose the correct word from the list below to complete each sentence.

primary, p. 137
jury, p. 141
democracy, p. 150

8. Responsible citizens who serve on a _____ help decide a court case.

9. Political party members vote in a _____ to choose a presidential candidate.

10. In a _____, people hold the power of government.

156 • Chapter 7

Apply Skills

✓ **TEST PREP** **Study Skill** Read the passages below. Use what you have learned about primary and secondary sources to answer each question.

> We the People of the United States, in Order to form a more perfect Union . . . do ordain [enact] and establish this Constitution for the United States of America.
> —Constitution of the United States, 1787

11. This passage is an example of which of the following?

    A. a primary source
    B. a newspaper article
    C. a secondary source
    D. an encyclopedia entry

12. Which of the following is a secondary source?

    A. a speech
    B. a treaty
    C. an encyclopedia entry
    D. a journal entry

Critical Thinking

✓ **TEST PREP** Write a short paragraph to answer each question below.

13. **Summarize** Describe the jobs of the legislative, executive, and judicial branches of Arkansas's state government. Identify what official or body runs each branch.

14. **Compare and Contrast** Name two ways in which state government is similar to and two ways in which it is different from federal government.

Activities

Art Activity Research the history of the American flag and the Flag Code. Make a poster showing one of the proper ways to handle or display an American flag.

Writing Activity Write an essay explaining what you think the state motto, "The people rule," means. Think about how a representative democracy is supposed to work.

Technology
Writing Process Tips
Get help with your essay at:
www.eduplace.com/kids/hmss/

157

Chapter 8: Understanding Economics

Vocabulary Preview

Technology
e • word games
www.eduplace.com/kids/hmss/

capital resources
Industries in Arkansas rely on **capital resources** to make goods. Machines and trucks are two examples of capital resources.
page 161

export
A good sent from Arkansas to another nation is an **export.** Important exports from Arkansas include rice and poultry.
page 162

158 • Unit 3

Reading Strategy

Question Use this strategy as you read the lessons in this chapter.

Quick Tip List questions you have. When you finish reading, go back to find the answers.

opportunity cost

People have to make choices when they buy goods or services. The **opportunity cost** is the thing that people must give up when they choose something else.
page 168

productivity

Improved knowledge and training can help increase workers' **productivity.** Workers can produce more goods or provide more services in a shorter time.
page 169

Core Lesson 1

Arkansas's Economy

VOCABULARY

specialization
capital resources
human resources
export
import

Vocabulary Strategy

export

The **ex-** in export means "outside." An **export** is a product that exits, or is sent outside, a country.

READING SKILL
Main Idea and Details
List details about industries in Arkansas.

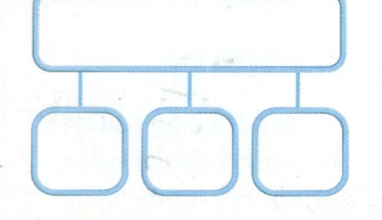

Build on What You Know Look at the label on your shoes, clothing, or backpack. Where was this item made? The goods that people buy come from Arkansas and all over the world.

Industries in Arkansas

Main Idea Arkansas's industries use resources to produce goods and services.

Arkansas's many industries help make the state's economy strong. More than one million people have jobs in Arkansas. They make goods and provide services that are used all over the world.

Specialization can help Arkansas's industries sell their goods or services. **Specialization** means that a business makes only a few goods or provides just one service. For example, a company might make auto parts, but not whole cars. By focusing on just a few parts, the business can become more expert at making them. It can make and improve its products at a lower cost.

Natural resource

160 • Chapter 8

Industry and Resources

Industries in Arkansas use productive resources to make goods and provide services. Industries use three kinds of resources: natural, capital, and human. **Capital resources** are things made by people that help workers make goods or provide services. Machines, tools, money, and buildings are capital resources. **Human resources** are the skills, knowledge, and hard work that people bring to their jobs.

The lumber industry in Arkansas uses all three productive resources. For example, lumber comes from trees. Trees are natural resources. Arkansans use capital resources such as saws to turn trees into lumber. The people who use the saws are human resources.

The mining industry also uses all three productive resources. Minerals and gemstones, such as bromine and diamonds, are natural resources. To dig them up, miners use capital resources such as machines and tools to remove soil and rock.

Minerals are nonrenewable resources. They cannot be replaced. Scarcity of natural resources affects companies' decisions about what to produce. When the natural resources that a company needs are no longer available, the company may decide to close. Or they may move to where those natural resources are still plentiful and therefore less expensive.

REVIEW In what ways are capital resources used to make lumber?

Productive Resources When an entrepreneur uses natural, human, and capital resources together, he or she can turn trees into goods such as furniture.

Human resource

Capital resource

161

World Trade

Rice Exports Exports such as rice are an important part of Arkansas's economy.

Oil Imports Arkansas depends upon oil from other countries, such as Canada.

Arkansas's Trade

Main Idea Arkansas trades goods and services with other countries.

People in different countries often trade goods and services. They do this to get the resources they need and want. They also trade with each other to buy goods at lower costs.

Every year, businesses in the United States export goods and services that are worth hundreds of billions of dollars. An **export** is a product that is sent out of a country to be sold or traded. People in the United States also spend hundreds of billions of dollars on imports each year. An **import** is a product brought in from another country. For example, many Americans wear clothes that are imports from China.

Imports and exports are important to the economy of the United States. They are also important to Arkansas's economy. Thousands of people in Arkansas work to produce exports. These include rice, poultry, and auto parts.

In 2005, Arkansas's top exports were transportation equipment, food, and chemicals. Companies sold these to people in Canada, Mexico, France, and other places. Canada bought over one billion dollars of these and other goods.

Arkansas also imports goods from other countries. For example, Arkansas imports petroleum from Canada because the state does not produce enough of its own. Petroleum is oil found underground. Other imports include metal products and medical supplies.

Using Money People can easily buy goods with money because it is portable and divisible.

Buying Goods and Services

Countries use money to pay for goods or services. Money has four main features. It is portable, divisible, durable, and uniform.

Portable means that money is easy to carry. People can carry large amounts of paper money. Divisible means that money can be divided into smaller units. A thousand dollar bill can be divided into smaller bills. Durable means that material from which money is made lasts a long time. For example, coins do not crumble over time. Finally, uniform means that everyone agrees on what money is worth.

REVIEW Why do countries trade with one another?

Lesson Summary

To produce goods and services, industries use natural, human, and capital resources. All of these resources are used to produce exports. Countries buy exports with money.

Why It Matters...

By exporting and importing goods, Arkansas participates in a global economy.

Lesson Review

1 VOCABULARY Use **export** in a sentence about goods that Arkansas businesses produce.

2 READING SKILL List two **details** about capital resources used by Arkansas's industries.

3 MAIN IDEA: Economics Why is specialization important to many industries?

4 MAIN IDEA: Economics What goods are imported to Arkansas from other countries?

5 FACTS TO KNOW What are nonrenewable resources?

6 CRITICAL THINKING: Draw Conclusions In what way does trade with other countries affect your daily life?

RESEARCH ACTIVITY Use an encyclopedia or the Internet to find the productive resources that go into the production of a product from Arkansas, such as poultry. Write a one-page report about what you learn.

163

Extend Lesson 1
Readers' Theater

Money AND Banks

How much do you know about banks and money?
Mrs. Fuller's class is studying money. She and her students visit a bank to learn more.

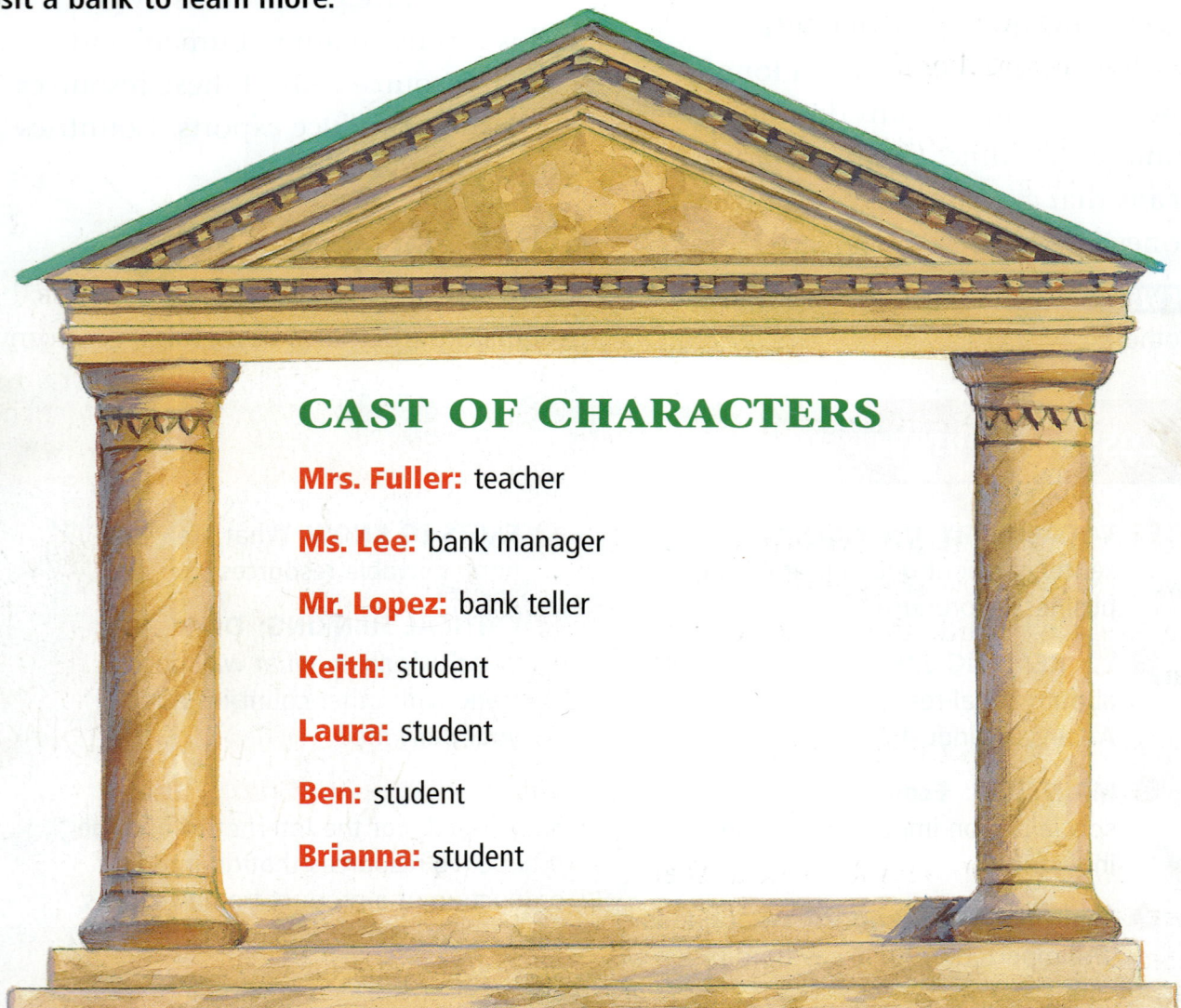

CAST OF CHARACTERS

Mrs. Fuller: teacher

Ms. Lee: bank manager

Mr. Lopez: bank teller

Keith: student

Laura: student

Ben: student

Brianna: student

Ms. Lee: Welcome to our bank! Everything at a bank is related to money.

Mrs. Fuller: What exactly *is* money? Keith, can you tell us?

Keith: Money is coins and bills that have a certain value. We use money to buy the things we want.

Mrs. Fuller: Good! Coins and bills are one kind of money. The money people keep in their checking accounts is another kind.

Laura: Where do coins and bills come from? Do you make them at the bank?

Ms. Lee: No, the government does that. They print paper money, and they mint coins.

Keith: But aren't banks part of the government?

Mrs. Fuller: No, banks are privately owned businesses. The government has rules that guide the decisions banks make.

Laura: What exactly do banks do, then?

Ms. Lee: We help people to keep their money safe. Our big vault is a lot safer than a sock or a mattress! Also, when you put your money in the bank, it earns interest.

Brianna: What's interest?

Mrs. Fuller: Interest is an amount of money the bank pays to customers who keep their money here. But banks also receive interest when they make loans.

Ben: Banks make loans? I don't get it. I thought they kept money safe for people. Why do they loan it out?

READERS' THEATER

165

Ms. Lee: Well, suppose a person wants to buy something expensive, like a house or a car. The person might not have enough money to pay for it all at once. So, the bank gives the person a loan for the whole amount. Then the person pays the money back slowly over time, with interest.

Mrs. Fuller: The person must pay back more than he or she borrowed. That's the interest. That's how the bank earns money.

Ms. Lee: All kinds of people in the community want loans, including farmers, business people, and factory owners.

Mrs. Fuller: That's one reason banks are so important in the community. They provide the funds for big projects that people and businesses couldn't afford on their own.

Brianna: Ms. Lee, when I put my money in the bank, how do I get it out again when I want it?

Ms. Lee: That's a great question. Let's go talk to Mr. Lopez. He'll tell you about deposits and withdrawals.

Mr. Lopez: Hello! I'm a bank teller. I work at the counter here and help people when they want to put money into their accounts or take it out.

Keith: Putting money in is called making a deposit, right? Taking money out is called making a withdrawal.

Mr. Lopez: That's right. When you make a deposit or a withdrawal, I update your account by entering all the information into the computer. Then I give you a receipt.

Ben: Is a checking account the same as a savings account?

Laura: No! When you have a checking account you can write checks. Right?

Mr. Lopez: Right. Checks are notes promising that your bank will pay money from your account in the amount written on the check. It's a good way to pay when you don't want to use cash.

Mrs. Fuller: Well, thank you so much for talking to us about banks. We all learned a lot.

Keith, Laura, Ben, and Brianna: Yes, thank you!

Activities

1. **TALK ABOUT IT** Describe the reasons why people save money in banks.

2. **THINK ABOUT IT** Make a list of businesses in your area. Then list the kinds of resources each business might buy with a bank loan.

Core Lesson 2

Arkansans at Work

VOCABULARY

opportunity cost
supply
demand
productivity

Vocabulary Strategy

demand

When you **demand** something, you say that you want it. In economics, **demand** means that people will buy a certain good or service.

READING SKILL
Categorize As you read, list jobs in Arkansas for each category.

Manufacturing	Tourism

Needs People use the money they earn to buy the food they need.

Build on What You Know What kind of work would you like to do someday? Arkansans find jobs in the state's many different industries.

Wants and Needs

Main Idea Workers in Arkansas earn money to pay for wants and needs.

Workers are paid money for their labor. With this money, workers buy things to meet their needs. A need is a good or service that people cannot live without, such as food, clothing, and shelter. Workers also may buy a good or service that they want but do not need, such as a television.

People cannot buy everything that they want. They have to make choices. Every choice has an opportunity cost. An **opportunity cost** is the thing that people give up in order to do what they want most. Suppose you buy a new jacket. You would then have less money to spend on other things, such as a new pair of shoes.

168 • Chapter 8

Supply and Demand at the Movies

Popcorn: $7 per box

Supply Greater Than Demand When the price of popcorn is too high, fewer people will want to buy it. The popcorn seller cannot sell his supply.

Popcorn: $1 per box

Demand Greater Than Supply When the price of popcorn is low, more people will want to buy it. The popcorn seller's supply is less than the demand.

Popcorn: $4 per box

Supply Equals Demand To earn the best profit, the popcorn seller should set a price where the demand for the popcorn equals the supply of popcorn.

Supply and Demand

Differences in price can help people make choices about which things to buy. Prices are the money value of goods and services. These prices are determined by supply and demand.

Supply is the amount of a product that businesses will make for a certain price. When they can sell a product at a high price, businesses make more. At lower prices, they make less, so the supply is smaller.

Demand is the amount of a product that people want to buy for a certain price. Demand affects the price a company will charge. If the demand is high, the company may charge a high price. However, at high prices, people may buy less. At lower prices, they usually buy more.

Earning and Saving

To buy what they need and want, many workers save some of the money they earn. By saving money over time, workers can set aside enough to make larger purchases that they could not afford otherwise.

Workers can also increase their earnings by gaining new knowledge or training. Improved knowledge and training lead to improved human resources. As workers increase their skills, they help increase productivity. **Productivity** is the amount of goods and services produced by workers in a certain amount of time. When productivity goes up, businesses can earn more money.

REVIEW In what ways can workers increase the amount of money they earn?

Manufacturing and Tourism Some Arkansans manufacture paper. Others play music for tourists who come to festivals, such as the Arkansas Blues and Heritage Festival.

Jobs in Arkansas

Main Idea Many Arkansans work in manufacturing or service industries.

Arkansas offers many jobs in manufacturing industries. These include the lumber, paper, furniture, automobile parts, and computer industries. **Steven M. Anthony** is the President of Anthony Timberlands, Inc., an Arkansas company that manufactures lumber. Today, almost one out of every five people who work in Arkansas work in manufacturing.

Each manufacturing industry has different kinds of jobs. For example, some people design products. Others, such as mechanics, make sure machines work correctly. Some people put parts together.

Tourism

Since the 1990s, more Arkansans have started working in service industries, such as tourism. Tourism is the business of getting travelers to visit an area and serving them when they come there. Some jobs in the tourism industry include travel agents who plan trips to Arkansas, hotel workers who provide a clean place for tourists to stay, and restaurant workers who feed them.

Arkansas's nickname—The Natural State—helps explain why so many tourists visit here. People come to enjoy the state's mountains, woodlands, and lakes. Tourists also come to Arkansas to visit places such as the Ozark Folk Center and to attend many of the state's cultural festivals.

The Future of Arkansas's Economy

Today, many Arkansans continue to work in agricultural jobs. Businesses in the manufacturing and service industries rely on crops and livestock raised by farmers and agricultural workers. In 2005, hundreds of thousands of people worked in agricultural jobs.

At the same time, science and technology are creating new types of jobs in industries such as medicine, space exploration, and computers. All three of these are high-tech industries. High-tech industries develop and use the most recent knowledge and equipment to make goods or provide services.

As the nation and world change, Arkansas and its economy will continue to change as well.

REVIEW What are three important manufacturing industries in Arkansas?

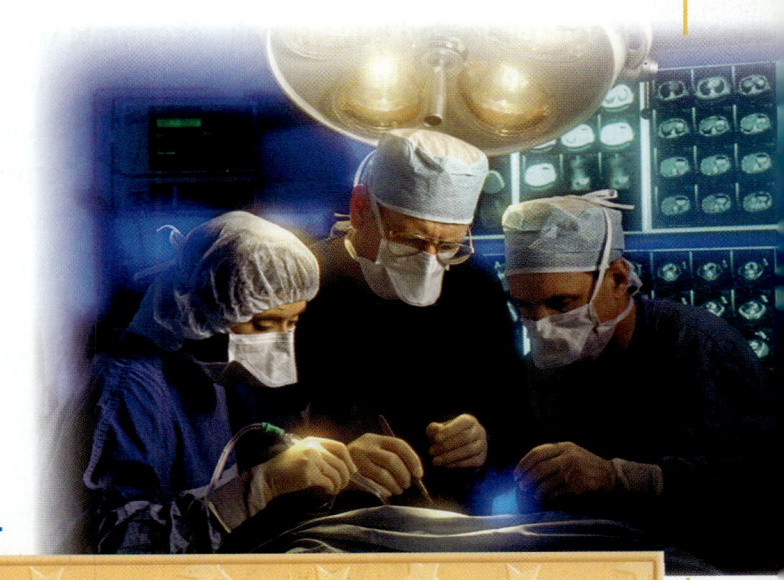

High-Tech Many jobs of the future lie in the high-tech industry. This industry includes medicine.

Lesson Summary

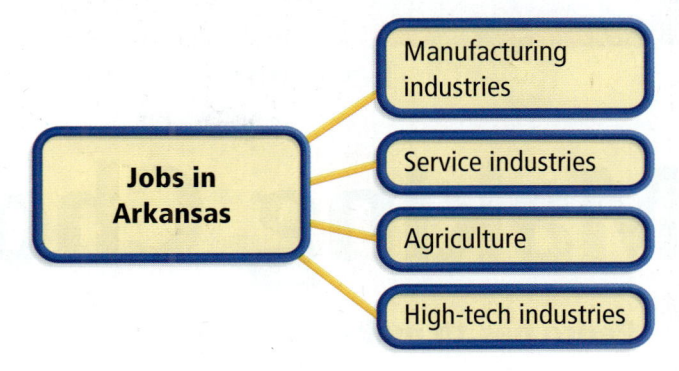

Jobs in Arkansas:
- Manufacturing industries
- Service industries
- Agriculture
- High-tech industries

Why It Matters...

Arkansas's economy provides Arkansans with jobs.

Lesson Review

1. **VOCABULARY** Use **supply** and **demand** in a sentence about Arkansas's industries.

2. **READING SKILL** Name three jobs you have listed in the **category** for manufacturing.

3. **MAIN IDEA: Economics** How do workers get the goods and services that they need and want?

4. **MAIN IDEA: Economics** What is tourism?

5. **CRITICAL THINKING: Cause and Effect** In what ways can supply and demand affect a community?

WRITING ACTIVITY Make a two-column chart of your wants and needs. Then prioritize your list of wants. Choose one want and write a sentence to identify an opportunity cost of your choice.

Extend Lesson 2
Economics

Making Choices

Pedro has to make a choice about what to buy. He is learning that people never have enough time or money to do everything they want. They must make choices. When people choose one thing, they often give up the chance to do something else.

Both sellers and buyers make economic choices. Sellers try to plan the best way to earn income from selling goods and services. They make choices among alternatives. The opportunity cost of the alternative they choose is the income that they could have earned from the alternative that they did not choose.

Buyers have opportunity costs, too. Let's look at Pedro. He has been helping his mom take care of his younger brother and has earned $12. The first choice he makes is whether to save his money or spend it now.

Pedro likes these action figures. However, he is saving for a robot construction kit, which costs almost $50. If he buys the action figures now, it will take him longer to save for the kit. In other words, the opportunity cost of buying the action figures now would be the chance to get a robot kit in the future.

172 • Chapter 8

Pedro decides to earn and save more money. He walks pets for neighbors and earns $10. When he has saved enough to buy a kit, he goes to several stores to find the best price. The kit he likes best costs $5 more than all the others.

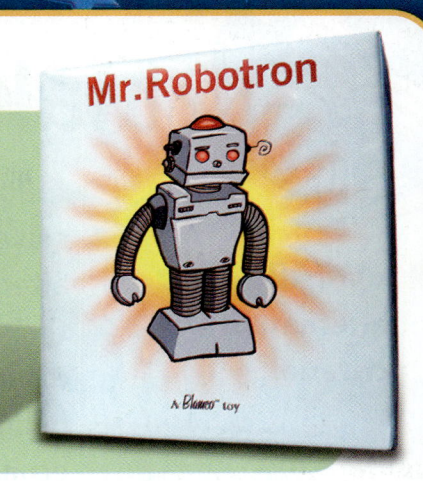

Pedro decides to get a less expensive kit that is almost as good. He saves the extra $5 to spend or save for something else. He can't have everything, but he's happy about the choices he made with his money!

Activities

1. **TALK ABOUT IT** Explain why Pedro didn't buy the action figures when he had $12.

2. **WRITE ABOUT IT** Write about a time when you chose between two things. Evaluate the consequence of the opportunity cost.

Citizenship Skills

Skillbuilder
Make a Decision

Business leaders in Arkansas make decisions about how to solve problems. To do this, they choose between different alternatives. An **alternative** is a choice. Business people base their decisions about alternatives on criteria. **Criteria** are sound reasons used to make decisions. Use the decision-making model below to help you think about alternatives and criteria in making economic decisions.

▶ **VOCABULARY**
alternative
criteria

Learn the Skill

Step 1: State the problem.

Step 2: Think about ways you could solve the problem. List the alternatives.

Step 3: State the criteria. Make a list of pros and cons for each of the alternatives. You might need to talk with other people or do research to find out more.

Step 4: Evaluate the criteria for each alternative.

Step 5: Make your decision about the best action to take.

The Decision-Making Model

Problem: A food company must decide what foods to sell.

Alternative 1: Specialize in selling fresh foods only

Alternative 2: Sell fresh, canned, and dried foods

Criteria: Specialization might help the company sell more goods at a lower cost to buyers. However, the company's research shows that in this neighborhood there are already two other stores specializing in fresh foods at low cost.

Criteria: There is a large local demand for fresh, canned, *and* dry foods. Out of 100 local people the company interviewed, 80 people said they preferred to do all their food shopping at once in one local store.

Evaluate the Criteria: Research shows that there may not be much demand for Alternative 1.

Final Decision: Sell fresh, canned, and dry foods

174 • Chapter 8

Apply Critical Thinking

Practice the Skill

Suppose you worked for a paper company that wants to earn more money. To do this, the company could raise the price of its paper, or it could lower its production costs. Make a decision about what the company could do. Think about the criteria of each of the alternatives. Use a chart like the one on page 174 to decide the best action.

Apply the Skill

An Arkansas company produces jewelry from Arkansas diamonds. Diamonds are a nonrenewable resource. The company worries that diamonds are growing more scarce. Use the steps that you have learned to think about possible alternatives and criteria to help solve the company's problem. Fill out a chart to help you make your decision. Then write a paragraph about your decision and how the scarcity of resources can impact production decisions.

Chapter 8 Review and Test Prep

Visual Summary

1. – 4. Write a description of each item named below.

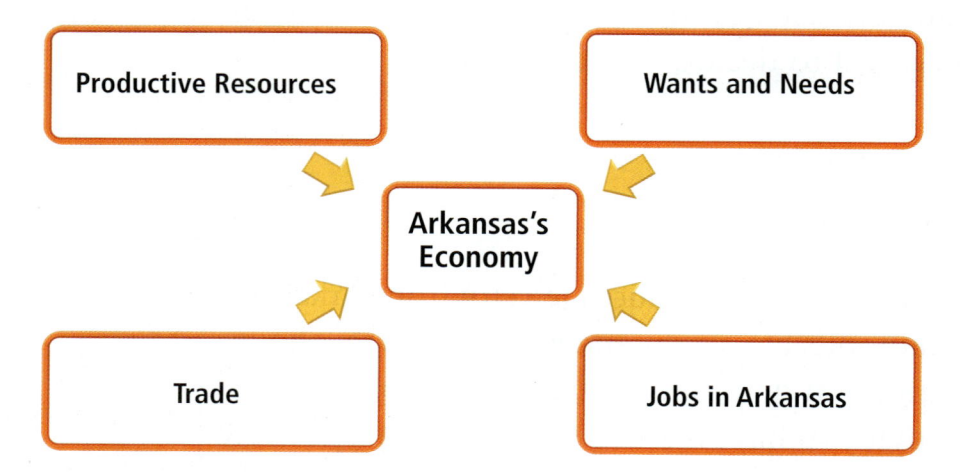

- Productive Resources
- Wants and Needs
- Trade
- Jobs in Arkansas

→ Arkansas's Economy

Facts and Main Ideas

TEST PREP Answer each question with information from the chapter.

5. **Economics** What are human resources?

6. **Economics** Describe the four main features of money.

7. **Economics** In what way is a need different from a want?

8. **Economics** What kind of industry is computer development?

Vocabulary

TEST PREP Choose the correct word from the list below to complete each sentence.

export, p. 162
import, p. 162
productivity, p. 169

9. Petroleum is an important _____ that Arkansas receives from other countries.

10. Improved human resources can help increase _____ .

11. Rice is an important _____ that Arkansas sells to other countries.

176 • Chapter 8

Apply Skills

✓ **TEST PREP** **Make Decisions** Use what you have learned about making decisions to answer the questions.

Problem: Should people in Arkansas continue to use trees for lumber?

Alternative 1: Yes

Alternative 2: No

Criteria: The lumber industry is very important to Arkansas's economy.

Criteria: The lumber industry may be harmful to the environment.

Evaluate the Criteria:

Final Decision:

12. Which of the following is the first step in making a decision?

    A. State the criteria.
    B. Identify the problem.
    C. Evaluate the criteria.
    D. List the alternatives.

13. What should people do next after evaluating the criteria?

    A. Create a chart.
    B. Evaluate more criteria.
    C. List more alternatives.
    D. Make a final decision.

Critical Thinking

✓ **TEST PREP** Write a short paragraph to answer each question below.

14. **Analyze** In what ways are capital resources used to produce goods and services?

15. **Compare and Contrast** Suppose that two companies make wood furniture. Company A trains its workers to use fast, new machines to build tables, desks, and chairs. Company B builds the same things using older machines. Compare the two companies' productivity.

Activities

Art Activity Look for images in newspapers, magazines and brochures and on the Internet that show Arkansas at work. Make a collage of jobs done in Arkansas.

Writing Activity Find out more about trade between the United States and other countries. Write a report detailing why the United States trades with other countries and how trade affects daily life in the United States and Arkansas.

Technology
Writing Process Tips
Get help with your report at:
www.eduplace.com/kids/hmss/

UNIT 3

Review and Test Prep

Vocabulary and Main Ideas

✓ **TEST PREP** Write a sentence to answer each question.

1. How do most **entrepreneurs** earn profits?
2. What arts make up the common **heritage** of the American people?
3. What is the highest court in the United States **judicial branch**?
4. What is a **democracy**?
5. In what way are **exports** important to Arkansas's economy?
6. What is **productivity**?

Critical Thinking

✓ **TEST PREP** Write a short paragraph to answer each question.

7. **Draw Conclusions** Why were the Little Rock Nine important in the struggle for civil rights?
8. **Evaluate** What are some of the benefits of living in a democracy?

Apply Skills

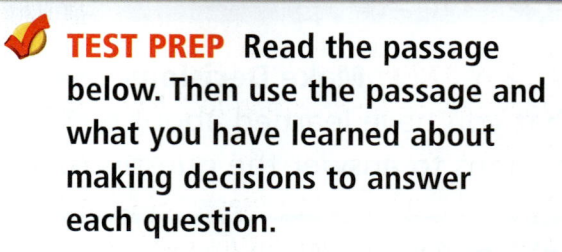

✓ **TEST PREP** Read the passage below. Then use the passage and what you have learned about making decisions to answer each question.

> A new company, the Natural State Mining Company, is looking for a place to build its headquarters. If it builds its headquarters in the West Gulf Coastal Plain region, it will be able to mine diamonds. If it builds its headquarters in the Arkansas River Valley region, it will be able to mine coal. The Natural State Mining Company decides to build its headquarters in the Arkansas River Valley.

9. What problem did the Natural State Mining Company face?

   A. where to look for diamonds
   B. where to build its headquarters
   C. whether or not it should leave the Arkansas River Valley
   D. whether or not it should leave the West Gulf Coastal Plain

10. What is the criteria for moving to the West Gulf Coastal Plain region?

    A. It will be able to mine diamonds.
    B. It will be able to mine coal.
    C. It will be able to add more jobs.
    D. It will be able to save money.

Unit Activity

Create a "Dream Job" Comic Strip

- Think about a job you would like to have in the future.
- Write the answers to these questions: Where will you work? What will you do in your job? What skills will you need? What will you like most about your job?
- Write a comic strip called "My Dream Job" in which you tell a friend all about your job. However, do not name the job!
- Have the class guess your dream job.

At the Library

Look for this book at your school or public library.

Little Rock Nine: Struggle for Integration by Stephanie Fitzgerald

Learn more about how the Little Rock Nine worked to end segregation in Arkansas and about the struggles they faced.

CURRENT EVENTS WEEKLY READER

Connect to Today

Create a display about equality in the United States.

- Find articles about the history of the civil rights movement in the United States.
- Write a paragraph summarizing what you learn.
- Find pictures that tell something about how more Americans gained their civil rights in the 20th century.
- Post your summary and pictures in a class display.

Technology
Weekly Reader online offers social studies articles. Go to:
www.eduplace.com/kids/hmss/

UNIT 4

The Land of the United States

The Big Idea

What do you like most about the place where you live?

"The thing that struck me most all over the United States was the physical beauty of the country, and the great beauty of the cities."

—Gertrude Stein, writer, 1937

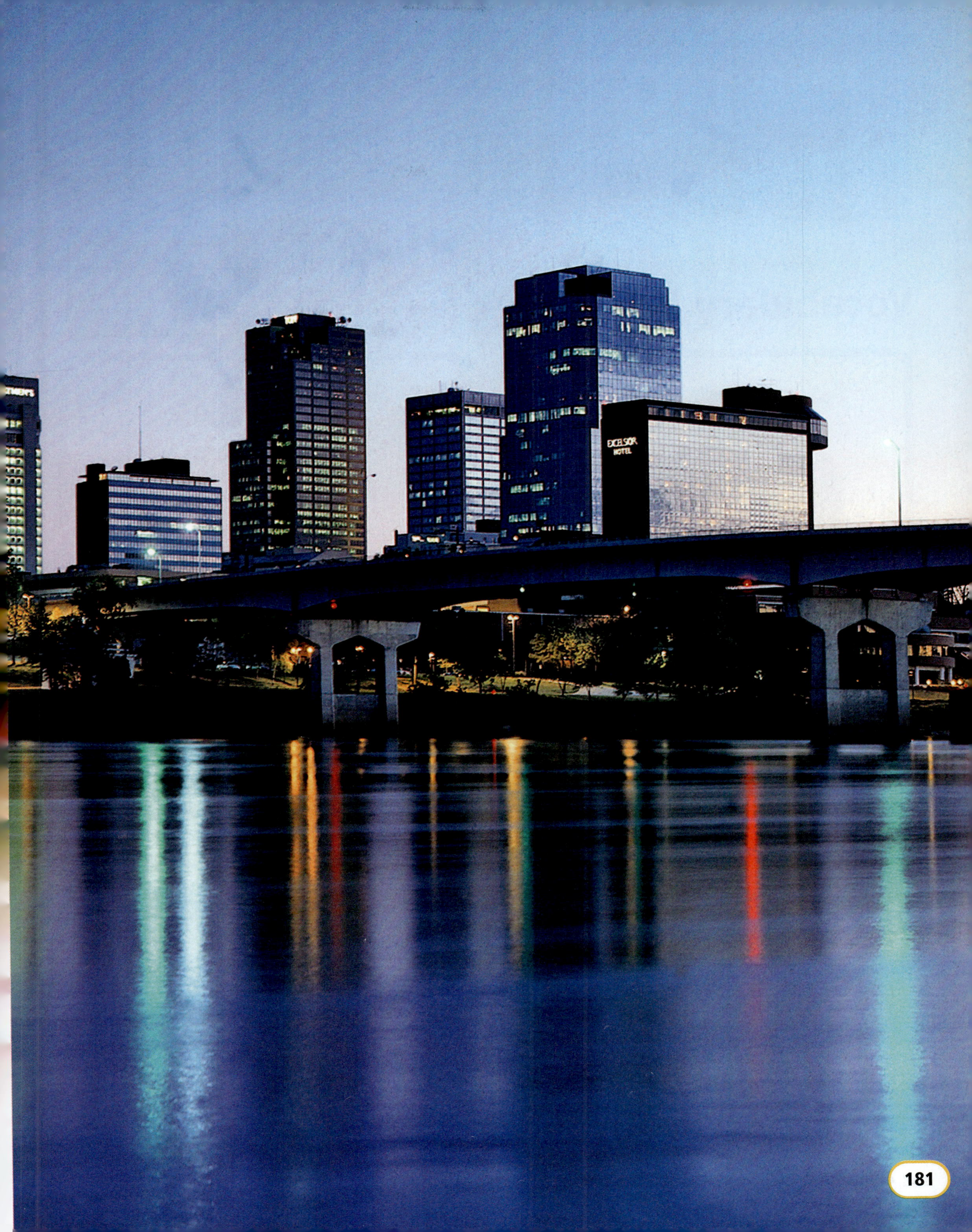

Chapter 9
An Overview of the United States

Vocabulary Preview

Technology
e • word games
www.eduplace.com/kids/hmss/

hemisphere
A **hemisphere** is one half of Earth's surface. Earth can be divided into four different hemispheres.
page 184

continent
The United States is part of the North American **continent.** Canada and Mexico are also part of this large body of land.
page 185

Reading Strategy

Predict and Infer Use this strategy as you read the lessons in this chapter.

Quick Tip Look at titles and pictures. What can you tell about the information you will read about?

interdependence
The United States Postal Service helps businesses serve customers from different regions. This leads to more regional **interdependence.**
page 193

prosperity
People from many countries trade and ship products around the world. The exchange of goods can help increase a nation's **prosperity.**
page 194

Core Lesson 1

Earth's Land

Build on What You Know How would you describe the place where you live? You can describe your location in different ways. You might tell the name of your town, state, and country.

VOCABULARY

hemisphere
continent

Vocabulary Strategy

hemisphere

The prefix **hemi-** means half. Hemisphere is half of a ball shape.

READING SKILL

Cause and Effect Chart the effects of human activity on climate.

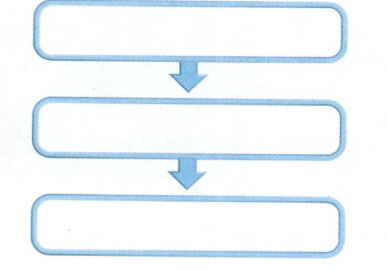

Dividing Land

Main Idea Earth can be divided into hemispheres, continents, countries, states, and regions.

If you could travel in space, you would see that Earth is shaped like a ball. This shape is called a sphere. Geographers divide Earth's surface into hemispheres. A **hemisphere** is one-half of Earth's surface.

Earth can be divided into two sets of hemispheres. One set consists of the Northern and Southern hemispheres. The other set consists of the Eastern and Western hemispheres. The equator divides Earth into the Northern and Southern hemispheres. The prime meridian divides Earth into the Eastern and Western hemispheres. You live in North America. North America lies in both the Northern and the Western hemispheres.

Earth This photo shows what Earth looks like from space.

The Continents

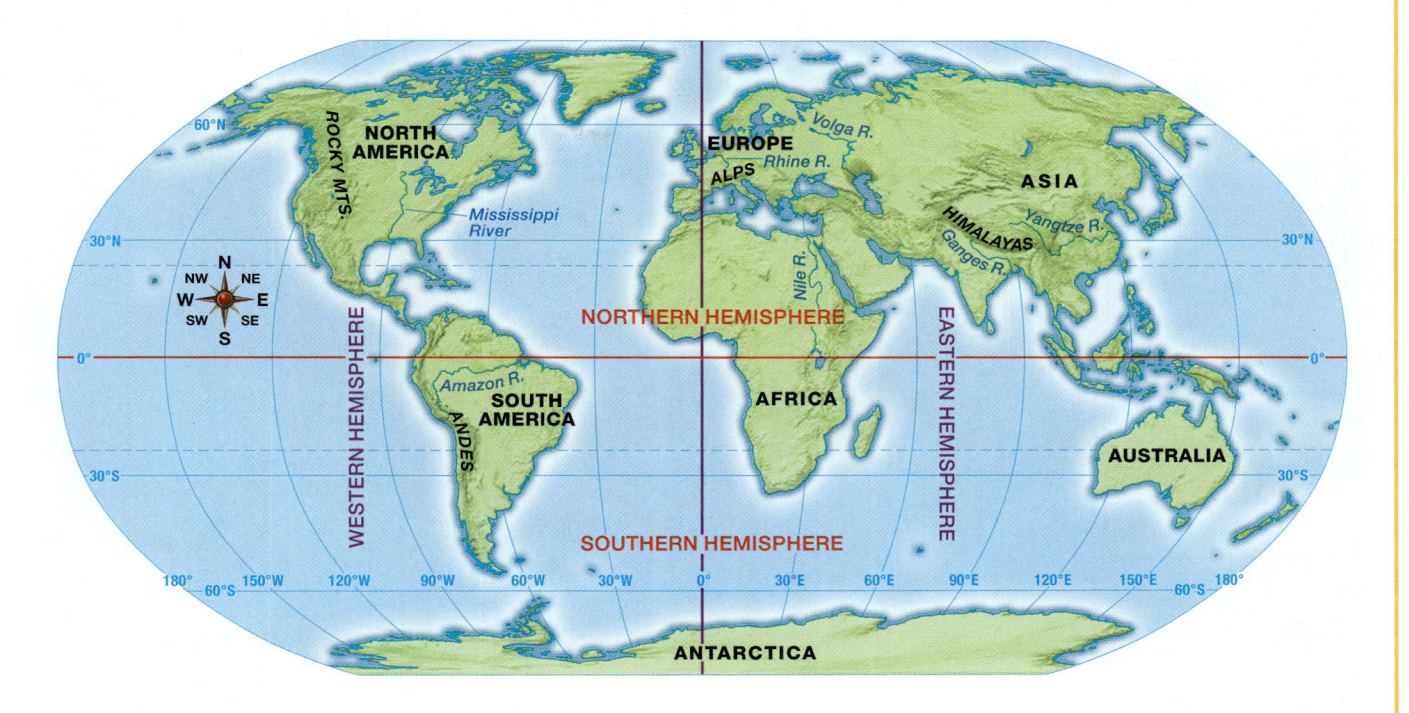

Our World The seven continents lie in different hemispheres.

SKILL Reading Maps In which two hemispheres is Australia located?

Continents and Countries

Earth has seven continents. A **continent** is a large body of land. The seven continents are Africa, Antarctica, Asia, Australia, Europe, North America, and South America. You can see on the map that some continents are surrounded by water and that some continents touch each other.

Most continents are made up of different countries. A country is a nation with its own government and laws. Africa has more countries than any other continent. North America is the third-largest continent. The United States is part of North America.

States and Regions

The United States is divided into 50 states. Groups of states make up different regions in the United States. Regions can be based on any shared feature. States within the same region are located close together. Those states are divided by state borders, but they often share natural features.

Five geographical regions make up the United States. These are the Northeast, Southeast, Midwest, Southwest, and West. Geographers use regions to show how places are alike and different.

REVIEW Explain the difference between a continent and a country.

U.S. Geographic Regions

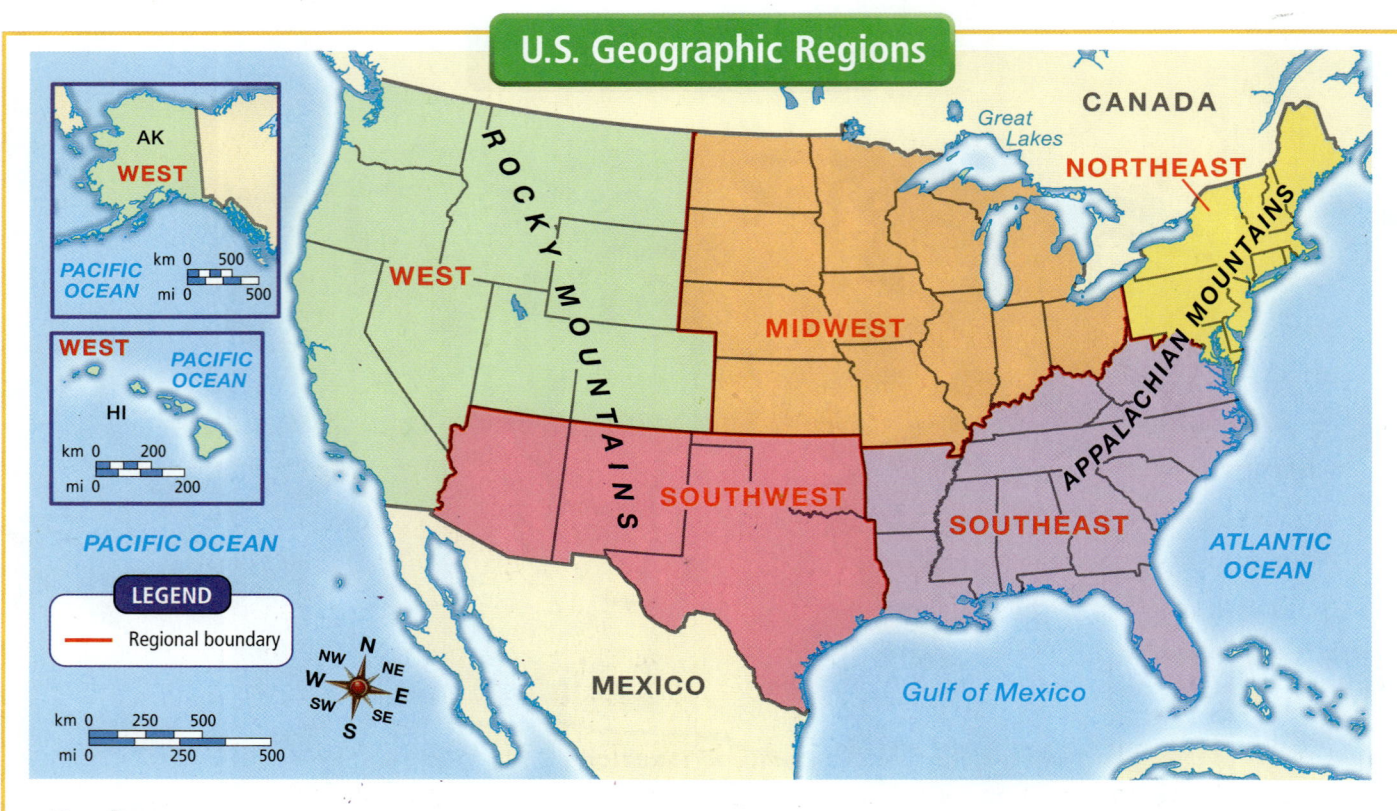

Regions The United States can be broken into five geographic regions.
SKILL Reading Maps Which two regions border the Gulf of Mexico?

Regions of the United States

Main Idea The United States has five regions with different physical features.

The five geographic regions of the United States have very different physical features. The Appalachian Mountains are a major mountain range in the Northeast. Most people in the Northeast live in the coastal states to the east of the Appalachians.

The Appalachians also extend into the Southeast. The Southeast has plateaus, hills, and valleys. The region also has low coastal plains and wetlands. The Mississippi River creates rich farmland in the Southeast.

The Mississippi River is also a major waterway for the Midwest. The Midwest lies between the Appalachian and Rocky mountains. Forests and farms cover these plains. Four of the Great Lakes are also in the region.

The Southwest has deserts, plateaus, and canyons. The Colorado River helped carve the Grand Canyon. The Rocky Mountains are found in both the Southwest and the West.

The West includes the Sierra Nevada and the Cascade mountains. The West is the largest U.S. region, and includes both Alaska and Hawaii. It has the most varied climates. These range from deserts to tropical forests and from glaciers to volcanoes.

186 • Chapter 9

Working for Change

Today, we know that we must use our natural resources more carefully and try not to waste them. People around the world are working to stop pollution, the thinning of the ozone layer, and global warming. Scientists are looking for safer ways to make and use energy. Scientists are also looking for ways to repair the ozone layer and protect Earth's climate.

How can you help? You can turn off lights when you leave a room. You can turn off the water while you brush your teeth. You can recycle the bottles, cans, and paper that you use. You can plant trees. You might also consider starting a recycling program or even a student environmental club. With your friends and family, you can work to help protect the environment.

REVIEW What activities have led to global warming?

Recycling Many products can be recycled, or made into new products, after people have used them.

Lesson Summary

Earth can be divided into hemispheres, continents, countries, states, and regions with different climates. People around the world are working to protect Earth's climate.

Why It Matters…

The way we care for Earth today affects the way we'll live tomorrow.

Lesson Review

1. **VOCABULARY** Use **hemisphere** and **continent** in a sentence about where you live.

2. **READING SKILL** What **effect** has human activity had on Earth's climate?

3. **MAIN IDEA: Geography** Would you expect the weather to be warmer in the Southwest or in the Northeast? Why?

4. **MAIN IDEA: Civics** In what ways can people protect the environment?

5. **CRITICAL THINKING: Synthesize** How does recycling protect natural resources?

HANDS ON **MAP ACTIVITY** Draw a map of the world. Locate one major river and one other physical feature on each continent.

Map and Globe Skills

Skillbuilder

Use Latitude and Longitude

VOCABULARY
latitude lines
parallels
longitude lines
meridians

Lines of latitude and longitude are imaginary lines drawn on a globe or map. Using these lines can help you give an exact location for any place in the world. Latitude lines, or parallels, run east and west and measure distances north and south of the equator. Longitude lines, or meridians, run north and south and measure distances east and west of the prime meridian.

Learn the Skill

Step 1: Study the latitude lines circling this globe. The parallel in the middle of the globe is called the equator. The equator is located at 0° (zero degrees) latitude.

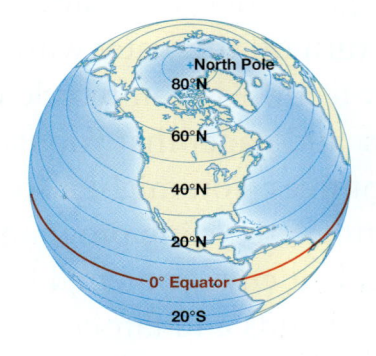

Step 2: Look at the longitude lines circling this globe. The prime meridian is located at 0° (zero degrees) longitude.

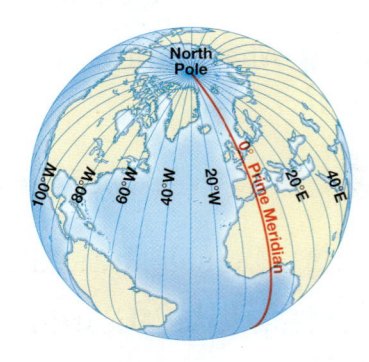

Step 3: Look at the map. You can record the location of a place by identifying the parallel and the meridian on which it lies. For example, New Orleans, Louisiana, is found at 30°N, 90°W.

190 • Chapter 9

Practice the Skill

Use the map to answer the questions.

1. What city is located at 35°N, 90°W?
2. What is the location of Denver, Colorado?
3. What is the estimated location of Chicago, Illinois?
4. Which two cities on this map lie between 95°W and 100°W?

Apply the Skill

Use the map on p. R22 to identify the approximate locations of three capital cities in the Western Hemisphere. Write the latitude and longitude for the places on an index card. Write the names of the capitals on the back. Switch cards with a classmate and check each other's work.

191

Core Lesson 2

Many Regions, One Nation

VOCABULARY

interdependence
prosperity

Vocabulary Strategy

interdependence

The prefix **inter-** means "between." **Interdependence** can mean dependence between people, or people needing each other.

READING SKILL

Draw Conclusions As you read, list facts that support this conclusion.

The government helps create links between Americans.

Build on What You Know Do you have friends or relatives who live in other parts of the country? Although you live far apart, do you feel connected? People all across our nation are connected, too.

Linking Regions

Main Idea Networks of communication, transportation, and trade link people of the United States.

Americans are linked in many ways. We live in the United States. We have a national government. We share the values of liberty, equality, and justice.

Our government has always searched for new ways to link states and regions. For example, early leaders created a postal system even before there was a United States. Our nation has built roads, canals, and railroads. We have phone systems, airports, and the Internet. These links change over time, but they have always had the same goal of connecting the states and regions of the country.

Making Connections The Internet and the United States Postal Service are two systems that link Americans.

192 • Chapter 9

United States Interstate Highways

Interstate Highways The Interstate Highway System has made transportation much easier.

Interdependence of Regions

Each link that connects states and regions leads to more interdependence. **Interdependence** is a relationship in which people or regions depend on each other. As more settlers moved west in the 1800s, communication became more important. From April 1860 to October 1861, the Pony Express delivered mail from Missouri to California. The route took about 10 days. By 1861, the telegraph system reached from coast to coast, and the Pony Express was no longer needed. The telegraph shortened delivery time and linked people across the United States.

The U.S. government has worked hard to create these links. Today, the Postal Service connects people and businesses across the country. It helps people communicate and transport goods. The mail handles billions of dollars in business every day.

The U.S. government has also helped build a network of roads called the Interstate Highway System. Many of these roads were built in the 1950s and 1960s. Interstate highways help people and goods move easily across the country.

REVIEW In what way does the Postal Service link the country?

193

Trade and Prosperity

Good transportation and communication systems help the nation's trade. Active trade helps bring prosperity to the country. **Prosperity** means wealth and success.

Both the government and private businesses promote trade in many ways. They help transportation and communication systems run smoothly. For example, the federal government manages our air-traffic control system. This helps airplanes travel safely. The government also sets basic rules for television and radio communications. Some private companies ship items. Others provide phone service, Internet access, and air transportation.

Another way our government helps trade is by providing a system of money and banking. This makes trade easier. Everyone agrees on how to pay for goods and services. People know what the money is worth.

Our Common Culture

Main Idea Regions in the United States have their own culture as well as a shared culture.

Americans are connected by their common heritage. Heritage includes the traditions that people have honored for many years. It includes language, food, music, holidays, and shared beliefs. Some parts of our heritage stretch back for centuries. The cultures of all who have lived here are part of the heritage we share.

Air Safety One responsibility of air traffic controllers is to keep planes a safe distance apart.

Sharing Traditions

Holidays show our shared heritage. People in every state celebrate Independence Day. Memorial Day parades happen all across the country.

Arkansans celebrate their heritage and traditions at festivals each year. The Hope Watermelon Festival and Bradley County Pink Tomato Festival each highlight Arkansas resources.

Holiday Celebration People throughout Arkansas celebrate Independence Day in much the same way as all Americans do.

Musical heritage is the highlight of the Arkansas Blues and Heritage Festival in Helena. Thousands of visitors come to Magnolia for the Magnolia Blossom Festival, which features the World Championship Steak Cookoff.

REVIEW In what ways do we show our shared culture?

Lesson Summary

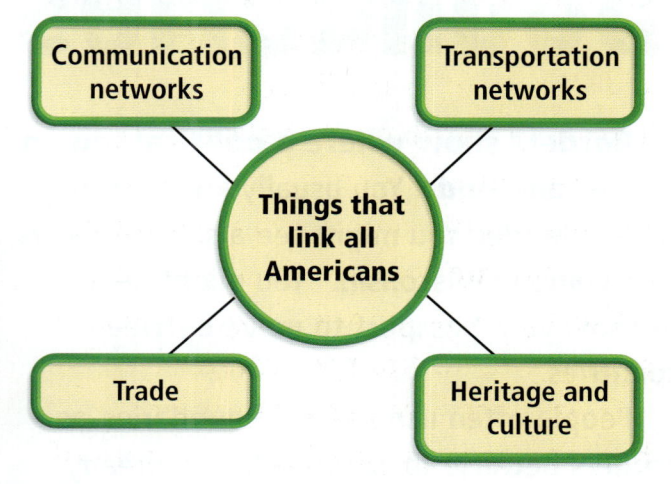

- Communication networks
- Transportation networks
- Trade
- Heritage and culture

Things that link all Americans

Why It Matters...

Though each region of the United States is different, we are linked together in many ways.

Lesson Review

❶ **VOCABULARY** Write a short paragraph that shows you know what **interdependence** and **prosperity** mean.

❷ **READING SKILL** What can you **conclude** about what the government does to help the economy?

❸ **MAIN IDEA: Geography** List three ways the government helps link different parts of the country.

❹ **MAIN IDEA: Culture** In what ways does heritage connect people?

❺ **CRITICAL THINKING: Draw Conclusions** Why do you think people celebrate so many festivals each year?

ART ACTIVITY What do you think it means to be an American? Make a poster with words and images that show our shared culture and heritage.

Extend Lesson 2

Geography

Borders and Boundaries

Borders show where a political region begins and ends. You usually know when you cross a border. You might see a sign that says "Welcome to Wisconsin." You might need to show your passport to move between countries.

People often use natural **boundaries** as borders because these boundaries already divide the land into regions. For example, a river called the Rio Grande (REE-oh GRAHN-day) forms part of the border between the United States and Mexico. Islands like Hawaii are surrounded by ocean on all sides.

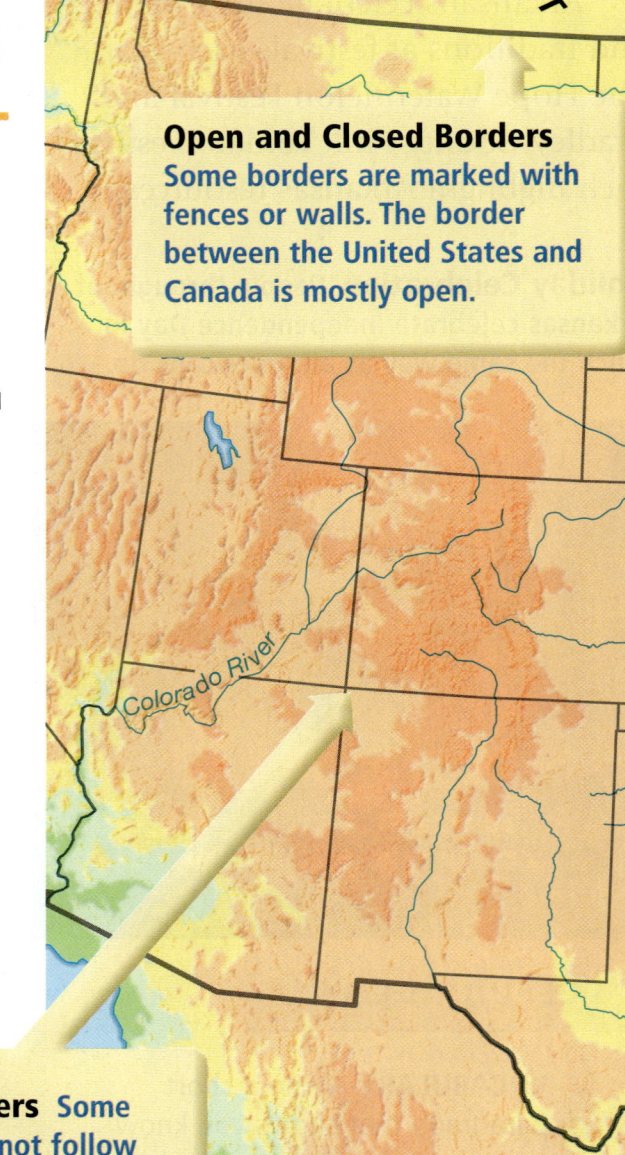

Open and Closed Borders Some borders are marked with fences or walls. The border between the United States and Canada is mostly open.

Four Corners Some borders do not follow any natural boundaries. They are simply lines drawn on a map. At Four Corners, the borders between four states meet in a +.

196 • Chapter 9

Borders Across Water The border between the United States and Canada crosses through several Great Lakes.

CANADA

Lake Superior
Lake Huron
Lake Michigan
Lake Ontario
Lake Erie

CENTRAL PLAINS

Platte River
Arkansas River
Red River
Mississippi River
Ohio River

APPALACHIAN MTS.

Wide Boundaries A boundary can be a gradual change between regions. For example, the boundary between mountains and plains may be a wide area of rolling hills.

Natural Boundaries as Borders Many states have rivers as borders. The Mississippi River serves as the eastern border of Arkansas.

GEOGRAPHY

Activities

1. **TALK ABOUT IT** What borders have you crossed? Discuss what it's like to cross a state border and to cross a national border.

2. **DRAW YOUR OWN** Draw a map of the land around your school. Note all the boundaries, including fences, roads, woods, and so on.

Chapter 9 Review and Test Prep

Visual Summary

1. – 3. Write a description of each item named below.

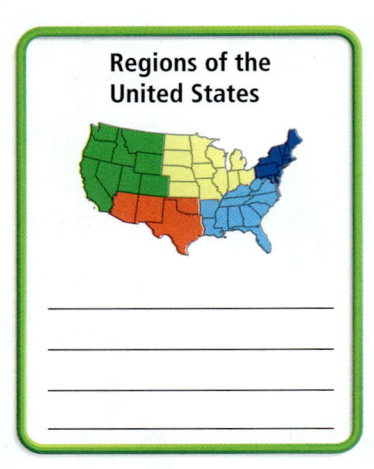

- Hemispheres
- Regions of the United States
- Interdependence

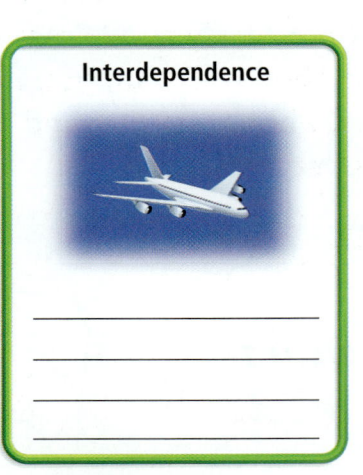

Facts and Main Ideas

TEST PREP Answer each question below.

4. **Geography** What are the seven continents?

5. **Geography** What physical features are found in the Southeast?

6. **Culture** What are some festivals held in Arkansas?

7. **Government** What is one way the U.S. government helps trade?

Vocabulary

TEST PREP Choose the correct word from the list below to complete each sentence.

hemisphere, p. 184
continent, p. 185
prosperity, p. 194

8. A _____ is one-half of Earth's surface.

9. _____ means wealth and success.

10. North America is the third-largest _____.

198 • Chapter 9

Apply Skills

✓ **TEST PREP Use Latitude and Longitude** Study the Missouri map below. Then use what you have learned about latitude and longitude to answer each question.

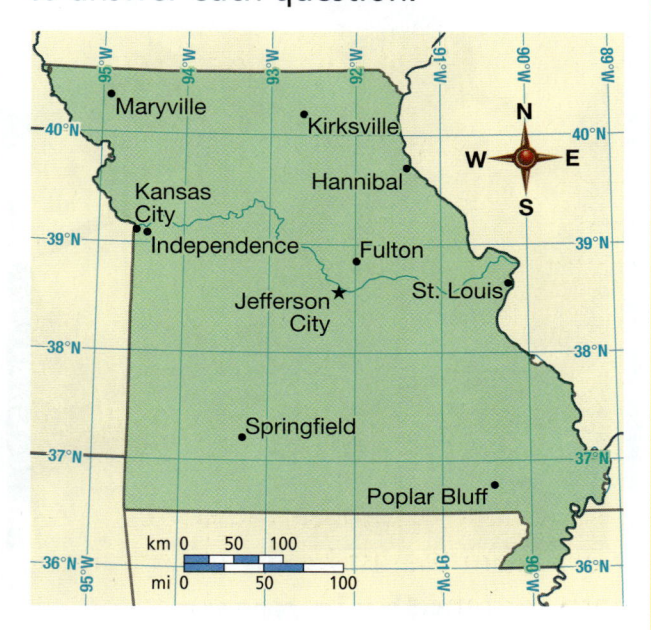

11. Which city on the map is closest to 37°N, 93°W?

    A. Jefferson City
    B. Maryville
    C. Hannibal
    D. Springfield

12. Which latitude and longitude lines are closest to the city of Fulton, Missouri?

    A. 37°N, 94°W
    B. 39°N, 92°W
    C. 40°N, 93°W
    D. 38°N, 92°W

Critical Thinking

✓ **TEST PREP** Write a short paragraph to answer each question below.

13. **Compare and Contrast** What are some ways in which the five major regions of the United States are different?

14. **Evaluate** What are the benefits of interdependence? Explain.

Activities

Research Activity Use library or Internet resources to find out more about the physical features of each region in the United States. Make a map that shows the location of each region and its major features.

Writing Activity Write a personal narrative telling how the climate in your area affects your daily life. Give an example from your own experience.

Technology
Writing Process Tips
Get help with your writing at:
www.eduplace.com/kids/hmss/

Chapter 10
The Southeast and Southwest

Technology
e • word games
www.eduplace.com/kids/hmss/

Vocabulary Preview

hub
Memphis, Tennessee, is a **hub.** From this busy center, people and businesses ship goods around the United States and beyond.
page 206

ethnic group
Today, people in the Lower Southeast represent many types of **ethnic groups.** For example, many Creoles live in Louisiana.
page 207

Reading Strategy

Monitor and Clarify Use this strategy as you read the lessons in this chapter.

Quick Tip Is the meaning of the text clear to you? Reread, if you need to.

mission

The Spanish built **missions** in the areas that they took over. Priests came to work and teach Christianity in the missions.
page 214

weathering

Much of the landscape in Arizona and Utah has been shaped by **weathering.** This process has shaped rock into tall forms.
page 216

Core Lesson 1

People of the Southeast

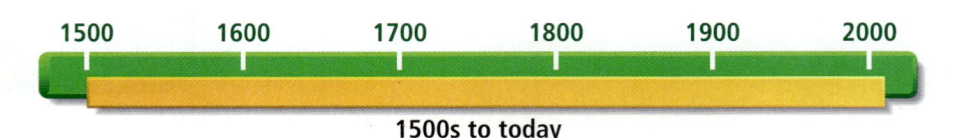

VOCABULARY

humid
hub
ethnic group

Vocabulary Strategy

hub

To remember the meaning of **hub,** think of the center of a wheel. A **hub** is the center of activity.

READING SKILL

Sequence Write the order in which groups settled in the South.

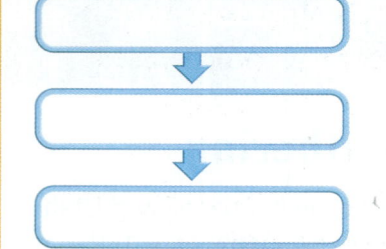

1500　1600　1700　1800　1900　2000

1500s to today

Build on What You Know When did your ancestors or relatives come to America? Where did they live? American Indians were the first people to settle in the Southeast.

First Peoples in the Southeast

Main Idea Both American Indians and European settlers depended on local resources to survive.

Before Europeans arrived, American Indians had lived in the Southeast for thousands of years. The early Eastern Woodlands people collected wild plants and seeds. They saved the best seeds for planting in the rich soil. Other American Indians learned how to farm from the Eastern Woodlands Indians.

Many American Indian nations in the Southeast became skilled farmers. The largest nations included the Choctaw, Cherokee, Creek, and Seminole. Most planted three important crops: corn, beans, and squash. After Europeans arrived, the Choctaw, Chickasaw, and Seminole traded fur and deerskins for cloth, weapons, and iron tools.

American Indians planted corn, beans, and squash. The beans climbed the corn stalks. The low squash plants kept the soil moist.

202 • Chapter 10

Jamestown, Virginia Today, visitors can tour a rebuilt Jamestown settlement and Powhatan village. People who lived in the Jamestown colony left behind this coin.

Early Colonies

In the 1500s, people from Europe began to settle in the Southeast. Spain built a permanent settlement in Florida in 1565. In 1607, the English established their first permanent colony at Jamestown, Virginia. The Southeast's warm weather and rich soil helped the people in Jamestown and other colonies survive. American Indians taught the Europeans how to raise corn.

The Europeans planted their first crop of tobacco in 1612. Soon, Southeastern farmers wanted more workers to help grow cotton, tobacco, rice, and other crops on the large plantations.

In 1619, a Dutch ship brought the first enslaved Africans to Jamestown. They had been captured in Africa, forced onto ships, and forced into slavery in the colony. Many lived and worked on southern plantations.

Tobacco soon became a major export and the southern colonies' most important crop. Within 20 years, thousands of pounds were being exported to England each year. The colonists also grew rice and other crops. Within 100 years, tobacco and rice made up almost two fifths of all exports from the colonies.

REVIEW Why did farmers in the Southeast grow tobacco and rice?

203

A Diverse Economy

Main Idea Manufacturing, services, tourism, mining, and agriculture make up the Southeastern economy.

The Southeast's economy once relied mainly on farming. Farming is still very important. North Carolina, Georgia, and Florida rank in the top ten states for farm income. Leading products include rice, cotton, tobacco, sugar cane, oranges, chickens, hogs, and cattle.

Many southeasterners work in manufacturing industries. Many people work in textile mills. In North Carolina alone, the cotton industry employs nearly 75,000 people. These workers make yarn, cloth, carpets, and rugs. Millions of acres of forests in Alabama, Arkansas, and Georgia provide jobs in the lumber and paper industries.

Many Industries

Top coal mining states include West Virginia and Kentucky. Coal and other resources help create power and energy. Thousands of southeasterners work in the oil industry. Florida ranks in the top four states for employment in the aerospace industry.

Tourism and service industries also play a vital role in the Southeastern economy. One of the leading service industries in the Southeast is ground and air transportation.

Hundreds of thousands of southeasterners work for the government. The U.S. government, including the military, is one of the largest employers in the Southeast. Most government employees in the Southeast live in Virginia and Florida.

SKILL Reading Graphs Which state has the most jobs from cotton?

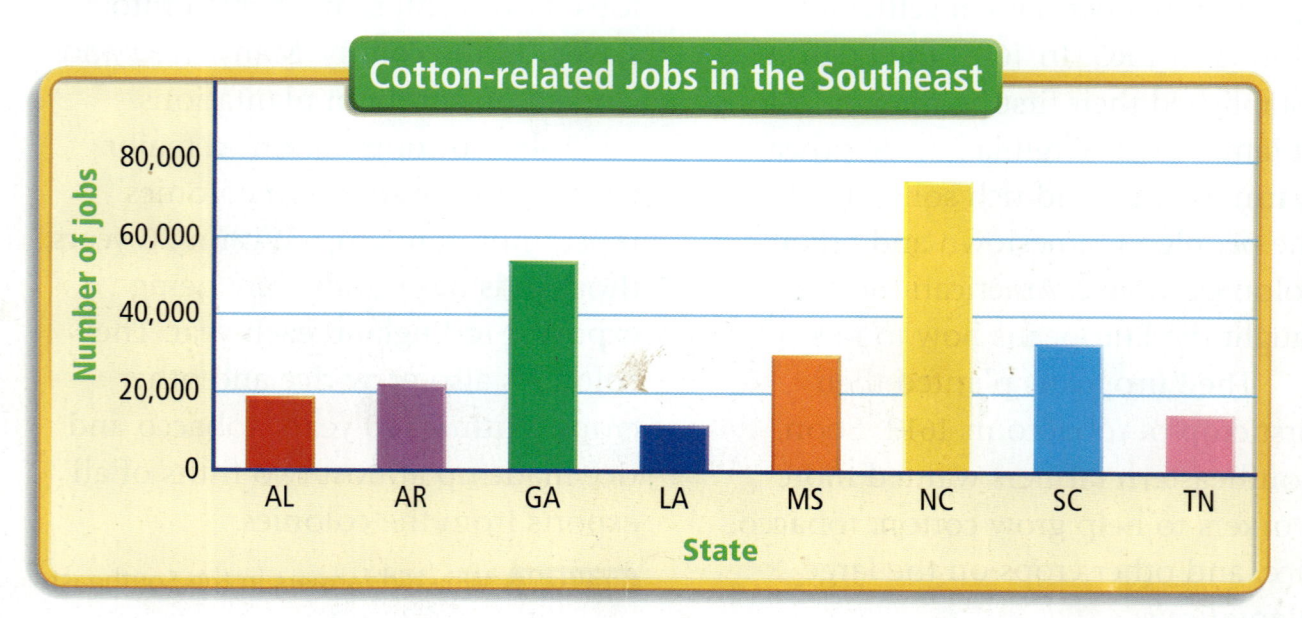

Cotton-related Jobs in the Southeast

State	Number of jobs
AL	~18,000
AR	~22,000
GA	~53,000
LA	~11,000
MS	~29,000
NC	~73,000
SC	~31,000
TN	~13,000

Climate and Wildlife

Main Idea The climate of the Southeast is warm, but it varies across the region.

The Southeast tends to be warmer and moister than northern regions. In winter, many people visit the Southeast to avoid cold northern temperatures.

The Southeast has more than one climate. Factors that control climate are latitude, elevation, and closeness to water. Because the Southeast is quite close to the equator, its climate is warmer than regions farther away from the equator. The southern latitude also results in a longer growing season than regions farther north. Farmers in coastal regions of the Southeast can grow crops for most of the year.

Coastal areas of the Southeast are usually warm. The ocean helps keep the air temperature steady. Winter is mild in the lowlands of the Mississippi Delta. Summer, however, is hot and humid. **Humid** means moist, or having a lot of water vapor in the air.

At higher elevations, winter is not as warm as in the coastal plains. The Ozark highlands can have severe weather. Frequent tornadoes strike in Arkansas and Florida.

The Southeast has many tropical storms that can cause heavy flooding and other damage. Most start in the Atlantic Ocean. Some grow into hurricanes. Between 1900 and 1996, Florida had 57 hurricanes.

REVIEW How does the climate affect the Southeast?

Hurricane Damage Hurricanes bring strong winds, heavy rain, and large ocean waves. They can cause damage to buildings, trees, and anything else in their path.

The Upper Southeast

Main Idea The Upper Southeast is a region of sharp contrasts, from country and forested areas to many large cities and suburbs.

The Upper Southeast is made up of six states: Arkansas, Kentucky, North Carolina, Tennessee, Virginia, and West Virginia. Much of the land in these states is forested. Arkansas, for example, is known as "The Natural State" because mountains, valleys, forests, and farm fields cover much of its land. Many people live in the country, but most people live in cities and towns.

In both Arkansas and Tennessee, more than half of the people live in urban areas. Many of these cities are important business centers. Memphis, Tennessee is a distribution hub. A **hub** is a major center of activity. Many people in Memphis work to distribute, or ship, goods throughout the world.

Water Transportation The Mississippi River provides transportation of people and goods through Memphis, Tennessee.

Life in the Upper Southeast

Farmers in the Upper Southeast grow cotton, tobacco, and rice. They also raise chickens, cattle, and horses. In Kentucky, champion racehorses graze on the area's lush grass. Many horse farms also dot the countryside in Tennessee and Virginia.

The natural environment of the region offers various activities. People can fish and raft in the many rivers. They can hunt for diamonds, hike in the Smoky Mountains, or explore Mammoth Cave.

Folk culture in the Appalachians includes storytelling, quilting, and fiddle or banjo music. Music lovers may attend festivals or visit the Grand Ole Opry in Nashville to hear country music. Every year, thousands of people visit Memphis to see Graceland, the home of **Elvis Presley.**

REVIEW How is the environment important to people in the Upper Southeast?

The Lower Southeast

Main Idea People who live in the Lower Southeast come from a variety of cultures with their own traditions.

The Lower Southeast includes six states: Alabama, Florida, Georgia, Louisiana, Mississippi, and South Carolina. The climate of the Lower Southeast is mostly warm and damp.

Many ethnic groups live in the Lower Southeast. An **ethnic group** includes people who share the same culture. For example, hundreds of thousands of Cuban Americans live in Florida. African Americans, Puerto Ricans, and Seminole Indians live there, too. Creoles, descendants of early French and Spanish settlers, live in Louisiana. Cajuns, descendants of early French Canadians, also live in Louisiana.

The Mississippi Delta region is famous as the birthplace of the blues. African American musicians in New Orleans, Louisiana, developed jazz in the early 1900s. Cajun and zydeco music are also popular. Zydeco blends the music of French, Caribbean, and African American cultures.

REVIEW How do ethnic groups shape the culture of the Lower Southeast?

Lesson Summary

- The Southeastern economy relies on manufacturing, tourism, mining, agriculture, and the service industry.
- Many ethnic groups make their home in the Southeast.

Why It Matters...

The Southeast is one of the fastest growing regions in the United States.

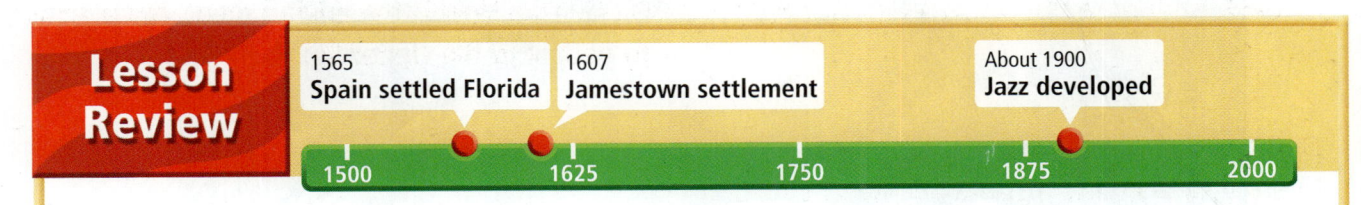

Lesson Review

1565 Spain settled Florida
1607 Jamestown settlement
About 1900 Jazz developed

1500 — 1625 — 1750 — 1875 — 2000

1 **VOCABULARY** Use the term **ethnic group** to describe the Southeast.

2 **READING SKILL** In what **sequence** did people settle in the Southeast?

3 **MAIN IDEA: Geography** Describe one way that early colonists used the resources of the Southeast?

4 **MAIN IDEA: Economy** What crops and livestock do farmers in the Upper Southeast raise?

5 **TIMELINE SKILL** How many years after the Spanish settled in Florida did Europeans settle in Jamestown?

6 **CRITICAL THINKING: Infer** How did Memphis's location help it become a transportation and distribution center?

SPEAKING ACTIVITY Find a recording of jazz, Cajun, or zydeco music at the library. Listen to the music and discuss why you like it or don't like it.

Extend Lesson 1
Geography

Gulf Coast Hurricanes

Conditions need to be just right for hurricanes to form. First, they need warm ocean water. The air above must be cooler than the water. The wind must be blowing in one direction and at a constant speed. These conditions occur in several places around the world. One place is in the Gulf of Mexico.

Two major hurricanes formed in this region in 2005. Hurricanes Katrina and Rita caused many billions of dollars of damage in Louisiana and nearby states. They changed the landscape and economy of the region, as well as the lives of people living there.

Hurricane Katrina This photograph was taken from space. It shows Hurricane Katrina heading towards the Gulf Coast. When it made landfall in Louisiana, wind speeds were as high as 145 miles an hour.

Sending Supplies Chris Duhon, a basketball player from Slidell, Louisiana, organized many boxes of supplies to be sent to Louisiana. After every big hurricane, citizens help out by donating money and supplies. Students can help by working on community service projects to distribute supplies or clean up neighborhoods.

Building Houses About 250,000 homes were damaged or destroyed by Hurricane Katrina. Many people, like these students from New Orleans, worked together to build new homes on the Gulf Coast.

Activities

1. **TALK ABOUT IT** In what ways can knowing how hurricanes form help people prepare for hurricanes in the future?

2. **CREATE IT** Find out more about how hurricanes form. Make a model or diagram showing what you learned.

GEOGRAPHY

209

Skillbuilder
Distinguish Fact from Opinion

VOCABULARY
opinion
fact

A writer may express opinions about a topic. An **opinion** is a belief or a feeling. An opinion is neither true nor false. A writer tries to support an opinion with facts. A **fact** is information that can be proven true. Thoughtful readers understand the difference between a fact and an opinion.

Learn the Skill

Step 1: Read what the writer wrote.

Step 2: Find words that signal an opinion. Examples include *I think, I believe,* and *We should.* Other examples are words that suggest feelings or beliefs, such as *terrible, wonderful, proud, worst,* and *best.*

Step 3: Decide what the writer's opinion about the topic seems to be.

Step 4: Find facts, such as names or dates, that the writer has used. Think about how you could check each fact.

To the Editor,

Most people believe that the age of aviation began when the Wright brothers made their first short flight. I believe that the commercial age of aviation began on January 1, 1914. On that date, pilot Tony Jannus took off in an airboat from downtown St. Petersburg, Florida. The airboat had a seat for one passenger. Jannus flew his thrilled passenger on a 23-minute flight to Tampa. That flight marked the start of the airline industry. Surely, Tony Jannus deserves as much fame as the Wright brothers. We should be proud of him.

—A Fan of Aviation History

Practice the Skill

Read the letter to the editor on this page. Then answer these questions.

1. What words does the writer use to tell you an opinion?
2. What does the writer want you to agree with?
3. What are two facts that support the opinion? How could you check them?

Apply the Skill

Write a statement of opinion about aviation in the Southeast. Use information in Lesson 1 to write supporting facts.

Core Lesson 2

People of the Southwest

VOCABULARY

irrigation
ceremony
mission
weathering

Vocabulary Strategy

weathering

Weather affects daily activities. **Weathering** is the effect that weather has on rock.

READING SKILL
Main Idea and Details
As you read, keep track of details that support the first main idea.

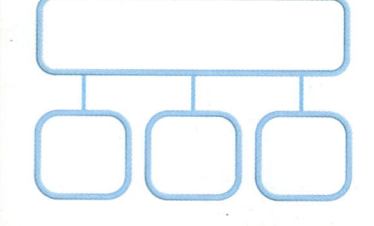

1300 1400 1500 1600 1700 1800 1900 2000

1300 to today

Build on What You Know Water is important to life. Suppose you had to change how you use water. Southwestern Indians used their water carefully.

Early Peoples of the Southwest

Main Idea American Indians of the Southwest, such as the Pueblo and the Hopi, used their resources wisely and have rich traditions.

Arizona, New Mexico, Texas, and Oklahoma make up the Southwest region. The landscape includes mountains, deserts, plateaus, and other dramatic landforms. The Southwest has large cities in the middle of deserts. It also has large rural areas.

Several American Indian groups lived in the Southwest region when Europeans first came to North America. Many still live there today. Hundreds of years ago, the Hohokam (huh HO kuhm) built canals to water their crops. Centuries later, settlers found the canals and rebuilt the settlement, which is now part of Phoenix, Arizona.

The Comanche (kuh MAN chee) moved to the Southwest from Wyoming. By the 1700s, they had spread across large parts of what are now Oklahoma and Texas.

212 • Chapter 10

A Closer Look at Pueblo Villages

About 700 years ago, people we now call the Pueblo (PWEHB loh) lived in the Rio Grande area of present-day New Mexico. This area is arid. Yet the Pueblo were skilled farmers. They built irrigation ditches and dams to control water. **Irrigation** means supplying land with water. They grew corn, beans, squash, and cotton. They also gathered wild plants and hunted animals.

Pueblo homes looked like huge apartment buildings. People built them using adobe (uh DOH bee), a type of clay brick. Some buildings had hundreds of rooms. The Pueblo were skilled at weaving baskets. They also made bowls, serving dishes, and jars from pottery. They painted them with colors made from plants and minerals. People traded these items for salt, food, and animal hides.

Pueblo Village Buildings in Pueblo villages often stood several stories tall.

A Closer Look at Hopi Life

The Hopi were living in the northeastern part of present-day Arizona by the 1300s. They are one of several groups known as Pueblo Indians because of their large buildings.

The Hopi were potters and farmers. They dug clay and shaped it into large and small pots to store their food and water. They used irrigation to grow beans, squash, and corn, which was their most important crop. The Hopi respected and took care of the land.

Modern-day Hopi still follow many of their cultural traditions. Most Hopi live in towns in the Southwest. They continue to take part in dances and ceremonies. A **ceremony** is a special event at which people gather to express important beliefs.

REVIEW Why was irrigation important to the Southwest Indians?

- Rear wall of cave
- Multi-story tower
- Kiva for religious activities

213

Spanish Settlements

Main Idea Spain influenced the architecture, customs, and food of the Southwest.

In 1521, Spanish soldiers conquered the American Indians in the area of present-day Mexico. They named the area New Spain. Then they traveled north. They reached present-day Kansas and also followed the Pacific coast to present-day Canada. Many hoped to find gold. Others wanted to claim more land for Spain. Spanish priests traveled north, too. They wanted to teach Christianity to the American Indians.

New Spain Today, the culture in many places still shows Spain's influence.

SKILL Reading Maps Which mission was farthest north?

The Spanish made a settlement at Santa Fe in 1610. They spread into Arizona and California. New Spain grew to include land that today makes up the Southwest states, Texas, and Florida.

As the Spanish moved into an area, they came into conflict with the American Indians who lived there. The Spanish wanted to control both the land and its people. They used force to achieve these goals. Many American Indians died.

The Spanish wanted American Indians to accept Christianity. To do this, they set up missions. A **mission** is a settlement for teaching religion to local people. Many missions grew into cities. Both Santa Fe and San Antonio started as missions.

Spanish Territory

LEGEND
- New Spain
- Present-day borders
- ▲ Mission

214 • Chapter 10

Cultural Influences

The priests who ran the missions often taught more than religion. Some insisted that American Indians give up their cultures and live like Europeans. They taught them to speak Spanish. They taught them trades and crafts. Pueblo Indians raised Spanish crops, such as grapes and wheat. They raised Spanish animals, such as sheep, horses, and cattle.

The Spanish also learned from the American Indians. For example, they learned to build with adobe and to make tortillas and other foods.

Spain lost control of its American colonies in the 1800s. In 1821, Mexico won independence from Spain. Mexico at that time included land in the Southwest.

Spanish Missions The Spanish built at least 26 missions in Texas.

Fifteen years later, Texas gained independence from Mexico. In 1845, Texas became part of the United States. The following year, the United States went to war with Mexico. The United States won. In 1848, it forced Mexico to give the Southwest region and California to the United States. In return, Mexico received $15 million.

The influence of the mission days is still strong in the Southwest. Many places have Spanish names. Many towns are built around an open square, just as they are in Spain. Many people speak Spanish. Some foods and festivals in the region came from Spain and Mexico. Many people from Mexico and other Latin American countries still move to the West.

REVIEW Why did the Spanish build missions in New Spain?

The Southwest Today

Main Idea Water in the Southwest has shaped both the land and people's lives.

The Southwest is known for wild rivers, high mountains, and beautiful canyons. Over millions of years, erosion, rivers, and weathering have shaped this desert land. **Weathering** is the breakdown of rock caused by wind, water, and weather. In Arizona, the Colorado River helped carve the mile-deep Grand Canyon. Erosion also shaped Big Bend National Park in Texas.

Each year, millions of tourists visit the region to view the scenery. Many of them hike or bike in the mountains and canyons. Others paddle the rivers and swim in the lakes.

Monument Valley Erosion created tall mesas and other landforms in Arizona and Utah.

Using Water

Water is scarce in the Southwest. Some areas, such as Las Vegas, Nevada, receive only about four inches of rain each year. Rivers are few in this region and are often overused. Many have been dammed to create reservoirs. Reservoirs are lakes used to store water.

The Colorado River and its reservoirs supply water to about 25 million people in the United States. It provides water for nearly four million acres of farmland. Because people use every drop the river holds, it actually dries up before reaching the sea.

Roosevelt Dam Water from the Roosevelt Dam irrigates thousands of acres of desert in Arizona.

Conserving Water

Southwesterners work hard at water conservation. Cities such as Phoenix, Arizona, often use local plants in their parks and public spaces. These plants have adapted to the dry region and do not need extra watering. Farmers conserve water by using drip irrigation. Instead of flooding the fields, water slowly soaks the soil.

Drip Irrigation System Southwestern farmers use drip irrigation, which drips water slowly at the roots of plants.

Things to Do and See

Southwesterners value their land, culture, and history. Many people speak Spanish or American Indian languages as well as English. People attend rodeos and American Indian festivals. They visit national parks and old abandoned towns. At the Arizona-Sonoran Desert Museum, people view the region's animals and plants.

REVIEW How do people conserve water?

Lesson Summary

- The Spanish, Mexicans, and American Indians have influenced the culture of the Southwest.
- Water in the Southwest has shaped both the land and its people.

Why It Matters...

The Spanish, Mexican, and American Indian cultures are an important part of life in the Southwest.

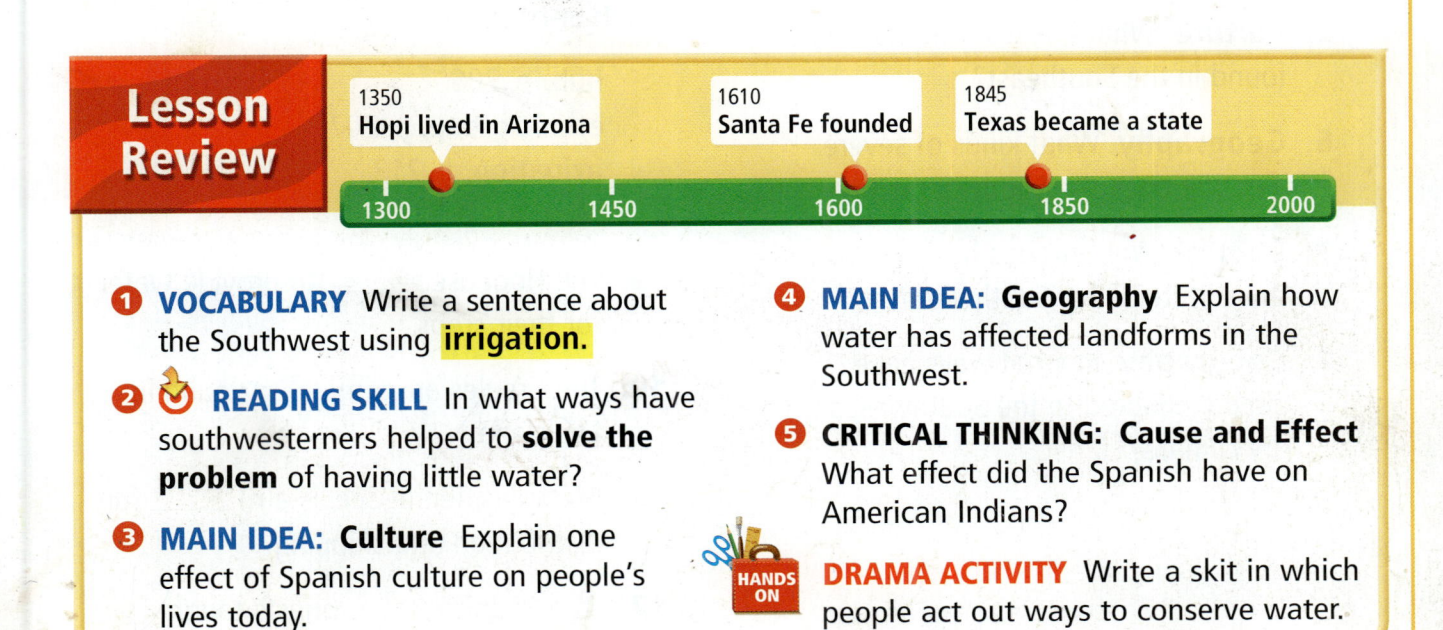

Lesson Review

1350 Hopi lived in Arizona
1610 Santa Fe founded
1845 Texas became a state

1300 — 1450 — 1600 — 1850 — 2000

❶ VOCABULARY Write a sentence about the Southwest using **irrigation**.

❷ READING SKILL In what ways have southwesterners helped to **solve the problem** of having little water?

❸ MAIN IDEA: Culture Explain one effect of Spanish culture on people's lives today.

❹ MAIN IDEA: Geography Explain how water has affected landforms in the Southwest.

❺ CRITICAL THINKING: Cause and Effect What effect did the Spanish have on American Indians?

HANDS ON DRAMA ACTIVITY Write a skit in which people act out ways to conserve water.

Chapter 10 Review and Test Prep

Visual Summary

1. – 4. Write a description of each item named below.

People of the Southeast
- History _____
- Geography _____

People of the Southwest
- History _____
- Geography _____

Facts and Main Ideas

TEST PREP Answer each question below.

5. **Culture** What musical traditions are found in the Southeast?

6. **Geography** What kinds of severe weather does the Southeast experience?

7. **Culture** What groups have influenced the culture of the Southwest?

8. **Geography** In what ways have people adapted to the Southwest's dry climate?

Vocabulary

TEST PREP Choose the correct word from the list below to complete each sentence.

hub, p. 206
ethnic group, p. 207
irrigation, p. 213
mission, p. 214

9. The Hopi used _____ to provide water for their crops.

10. The Creoles are a(n) _____ found in Louisiana.

11. Memphis, Tennessee, is a(n) _____ for distribution and shipping.

12. At a Spanish _____ priests taught American Indians their religion.

218 • Chapter 10

CHAPTER SUMMARY TIMELINE

- **1607** English settle Jamestown
- **1610** Spanish settle Santa Fe
- **1848** United States buys Southwest region from Mexico

1550 — 1600 — 1650 — 1700 — 1750 — 1800 — 1850

Apply Skills

✓ **TEST PREP** **Distinguish Fact from Opinion** Read the passage below. Then use what you have learned about distinguishing fact from opinion to answer the questions that follow.

> Water is scarce in the Southwest. The region has few sources of water and millions of people who need it. Many rivers have been dammed to make reservoirs. The Colorado River and its reservoirs provide water for 25 million people and four million acres of farmland. People use so much of the river's water that it dries up before it reaches the ocean. People use too much water. They should practice more conservation.

13. Which of the statements is an opinion?
    - A. The region has few sources of water.
    - B. Many rivers have been dammed to make reservoirs.
    - C. The Colorado River and its reservoirs provide water for 25 million people.
    - D. People use too much water.

14. Which fact supports the opinion?
    - A. Water is scarce in the Southwest.
    - B. Many rivers have been dammed to make reservoirs.
    - C. People use so much of the river's water that it dries up before it reaches the ocean.
    - D. They should practice more conservation.

Critical Thinking

✓ **TEST PREP** Write a short paragraph to answer each question below.

15. **Compare and Contrast** In what ways are the cultures of the Upper and Lower Southeast alike and different?

16. **Draw Conclusions** What challenges did early settlers face in the Southwest? What challenges do people face today?

Timeline

Use the Chapter Summary Timeline to answer the question.

17. How many years after the English settled in Jamestown did the Spanish settle Santa Fe?

Activities

Art Activity Make a model of an early settlement in the Southwest. Make a second model of a major city in the Southwest today. Consider important features, such as buildings and roads.

Writing Activity Write a persuasive essay to convince people to move to the Southeast or the Southwest.

Technology
Writing Process Tips
Get help with your writing at:
www.eduplace.com/kids/hmss/

219

Chapter 11 Northeast, Midwest, and West

Technology
e • word games
www.eduplace.com/kids/hmss/

Vocabulary Preview

university
Harvard is a well-known **university** in the Northeast. Each of the different colleges at Harvard teach one main area of study.
page 226

homestead
Settlers bought plots of land called **homesteads.** Many houses on homesteads were built from prairie earth.
page 231

Reading Strategy

Summarize Use this strategy as you read the lessons in this chapter.

Quick Tip Note the most important information and then put it into your own words.

assembly line

On an **assembly line,** each worker does only one small part of the manufacturing process.
page 232

wagon train

Pioneers on the Oregon Trail traveled by **wagon train.** These lines of wagons were pulled by oxen or horses.
page 238

Core Lesson 1

People of the Northeast

VOCABULARY

finance
university
immigration

Vocabulary Strategy

university

The prefix **uni-** means one. A **university** is one large school that is made up of many small colleges.

READING SKILL

Cause and Effect As you read, show the effects of the natural environment on American Indian cultures.

Cause	Effect

1500 1600 1700 1800 1900 2000

1500s to today

Build on What You Know Suppose you want to build a fort. Your first step is to look around and see what materials are available. The first people to live in a region must also learn to use the available resources.

First Peoples

Main Idea Natural resources affected American Indian cultures in the Northeast.

Many groups have helped shape the culture of the Northeast. American Indians have lived in the Northeast for thousands of years. In the past, nations such as the Haudenosaunee (hoh deh noh SHAW nee) used the resources of the land to survive. They governed themselves and traded with other nations.

Haudenosaunee Longhouse Longhouses were 200 to 300 feet long. Inside, each family had its own living area.

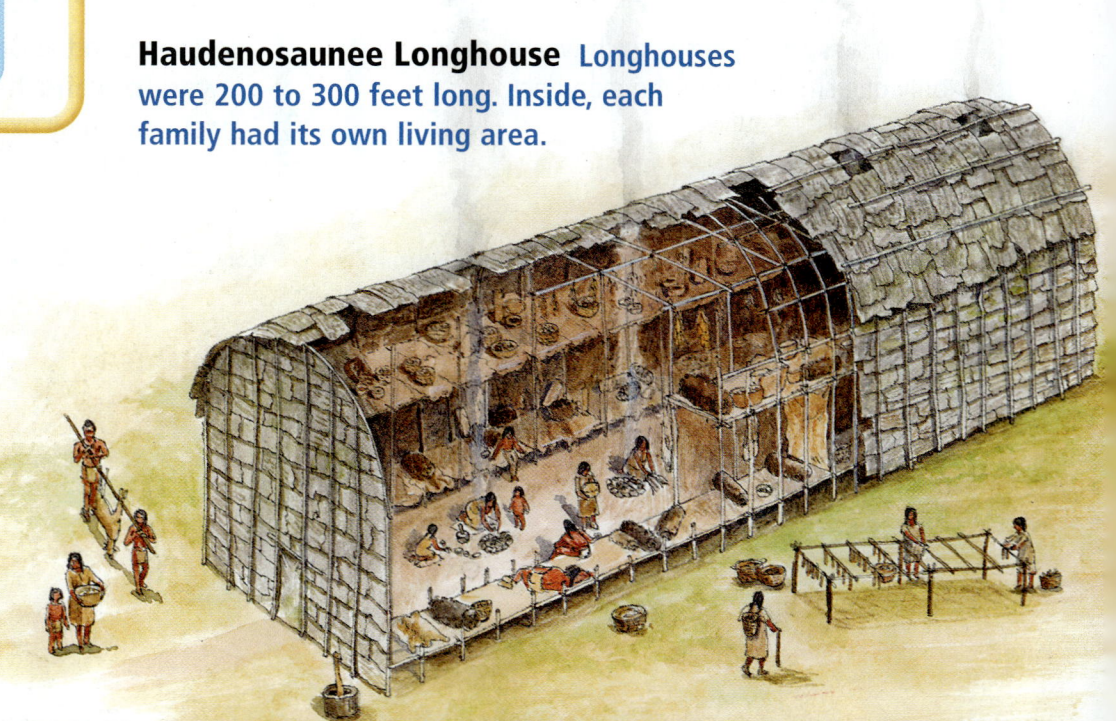

222 • Chapter 11

Natural Resources and Culture

American Indian nations used natural resources differently. In the north, the growing season was short. So, nations such as the Micmac mostly hunted to get food. They moved often to follow the animals. In the winter, the Micmac hunted sea mammals and land animals. They also fished and collected plants and shellfish.

In the south, where the growing season was longer, the Lenni Lenape (LEHN-ee LEHN-uh-pee) grew both corn and tobacco. Families came together to fish and farm during the long summer growing season. Families hunted separately in the winter. Large family groups lived together in longhouses. A chief and a council led each community. The rich natural resources of the region could support larger groups of people.

Today, American Indians in the Northeast have a modern lifestyle. At the same time, they work to preserve their cultures. Some groups, such as the Wampanoag (wahm puh NOH ag) of Massachusetts, have their own governments.

REVIEW How did climate and natural resources affect American Indian cultures in the past?

Two Language Groups
Coastal nations in the Northeast spoke Algonquian. Central Woodland nations spoke the Iroquoian language.

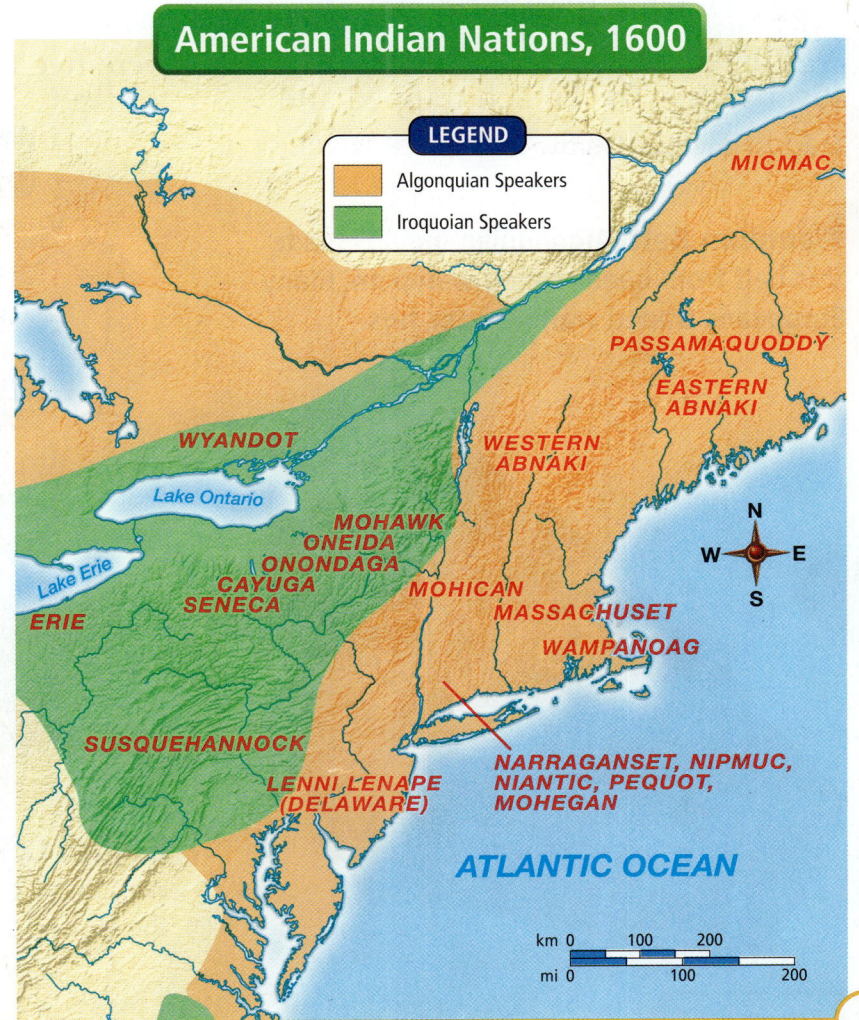

American Indian Nations, 1600

LEGEND
- Algonquian Speakers
- Iroquoian Speakers

MICMAC
PASSAMAQUODDY
EASTERN ABNAKI
WYANDOT
WESTERN ABNAKI
MOHAWK
ONEIDA
ONONDAGA
CAYUGA
SENECA
MOHICAN
MASSACHUSET
ERIE
WAMPANOAG
SUSQUEHANNOCK
LENNI LENAPE (DELAWARE)
NARRAGANSET, NIPMUC, NIANTIC, PEQUOT, MOHEGAN

ATLANTIC OCEAN

Colonies and Industry

Main Idea European colonists settled the Northeast and built a new nation.

By the 1500s, explorers from Europe reached North America. The first English colonists, or settlers, arrived in the East in the early 1600s. One group, the Pilgrims, came to Massachusetts in 1620. The Pilgrims were seeking a place to practice their religion freely. Another religious group, the Puritans, soon followed.

Around the same time, the Dutch and the French began to trade with American Indians. American Indians traded furs for pots, cloth, tools, and beads. Dutch settlers lived mainly on Manhattan Island and in the Hudson River valley. The French trapped and traded along the St. Lawrence River.

Wampum Belt Algonquian Indians made this belt from beads called wampum. Many Europeans traded wampum for furs.

Conflict in the Colonies

The English colonies grew as more Europeans arrived. They built towns and started farms and businesses. Sometimes they fought with American Indians over land and resources. Although there were times of peace, there were also some terrible wars. Finally, American Indians in the Northeast were forced to give up most of their land.

By the mid-1700s, many colonists disliked English rule. War between the Americans and the English broke out in Massachusetts. It spread to the other colonies. In 1776, American leaders met in Philadelphia. They declared that the colonies should rule themselves. When the Revolutionary War ended, Americans were free to govern themselves.

The Thirteen Colonies

English Colonies After the Revolutionary War, these colonies formed the new nation of the United States.

Factories and Workers

By the end of the 1700s, new inventions began to change life in the Northeast. Before then, most people worked on farms or made things by hand. To get goods such as textiles, or woven cloth, Americans traded with England. This cloth was made in factories with large machines.

Then, in 1790, **Samuel Slater** built the first water-powered spinning machine in the United States. This machine made yarn from cotton. Other entrepreneurs soon built textile mills alongside rivers in the Northeast. Rhode Island and Pennsylvania had dozens of these mills. Machines could make yarn much faster and more cheaply than people working by hand.

In 1813, **Francis Cabot Lowell** brought the power loom to the Northeast. A loom is a machine that weaves cloth. Lowell first saw the loom in an English textile mill. When he returned to Massachusetts, he built a loom with the same design. Now cotton could be spun into yarn and then woven into cloth in one big factory. Lowell hired young, unmarried women to work in his factories. Many of these women moved from farms to the growing mill towns to take these jobs.

REVIEW How did the Revolutionary War change colonial government?

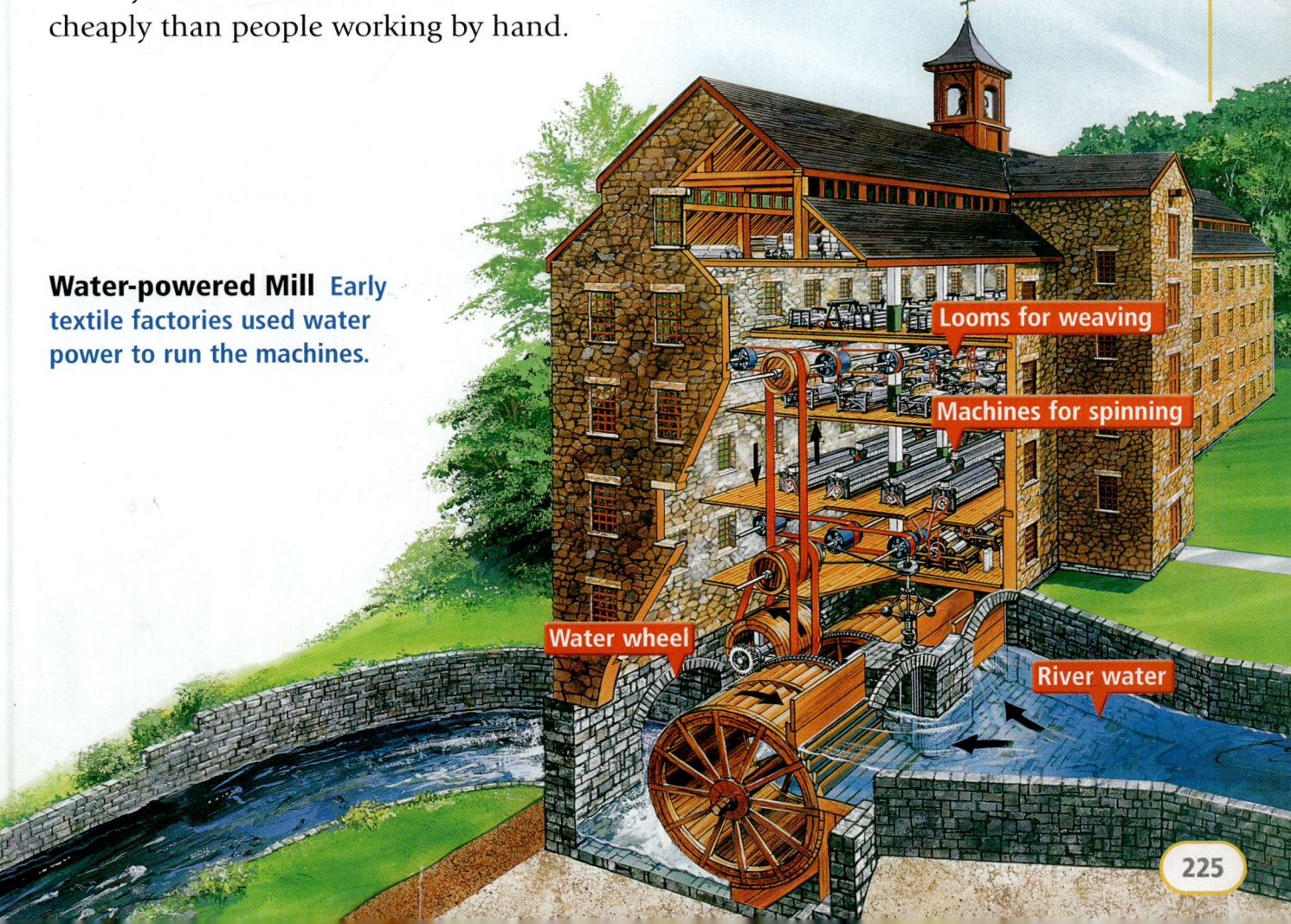

Water-powered Mill Early textile factories used water power to run the machines.

- Looms for weaving
- Machines for spinning
- Water wheel
- River water

225

Regional Growth

Main Idea The Northeast region quickly grew into an economic center of the nation.

The growth of the textile industry led to more industries. People built factories to make textile machines and other tools. These new industries needed even more workers. People moved from farms to cities.

By the late 1800s, millions of Europeans had come to the United States looking for factory jobs. Many of these immigrants settled in the Northeast. **Immigration** is when people move from one country to another. Immigrants from southern and eastern Europe wanted to escape war and poor living conditions. They hoped to find better lives in America. Soon, others wanted to join their families in America.

Beginning in the 1960s, many textile and manufacturing industries gradually moved out of the region. At the same time, the region's computer and healthcare industries grew greatly.

New England

Six states in the Northeast form the region called New England. These states are Connecticut, Maine, Massachusetts, New Hampshire, Rhode Island, and Vermont.

The capital of Massachusetts is Boston. It is New England's largest city. Boston's first settlers helped make the city an important shipping center. Today, the city is the trade and finance center of New England. **Finance** is the management of money.

The Puritans who settled Boston developed strong social institutions. In 1635, Puritans built the first free school in America. A year later, they built Harvard, the first American college. Harvard later became a university. A **university** is a school with several colleges.

Today, New England has hundreds of colleges and universities. It also has many churches, mosques, synagogues, and other places of worship.

Boston Many businesses today are located along Boston Harbor.

The Mid-Atlantic

The Mid-Atlantic region contains Delaware, Maryland, New Jersey, New York, Pennsylvania, and Washington, D.C. This region has the most people per square mile. New York City is the largest city in the nation. New York's location at the mouth of the Hudson River led to its growth. European settlers used the river and New York's harbor to move goods. Today, New York is a world center for banking, publishing, advertising, and technology.

Suburbs surround the major cities of the Mid-Atlantic. People began to move from cities to the less-crowded suburbs in the 1800s. Forest and farmland fill large areas, too. The soil here is easier to farm than it is in New England. Mid-Atlantic farms produce flowers, chickens, and dairy products.

REVIEW Why did people move to the suburbs in the 1800s?

Lesson Summary

- **1500s**—American Indians in the Northeast hunted, farmed, and fished.
- **1600s–1700s**—Europeans arrived. English colonies grew into a new nation.
- **1800s**—Growth in industries brought people to cities to work in factories. Suburbs grew.
- **1900s–Today**—Northeastern cities are centers for banking, publishing, and technology.

Why It Matters...

England's colonies in the Northeast grew into the United States of today.

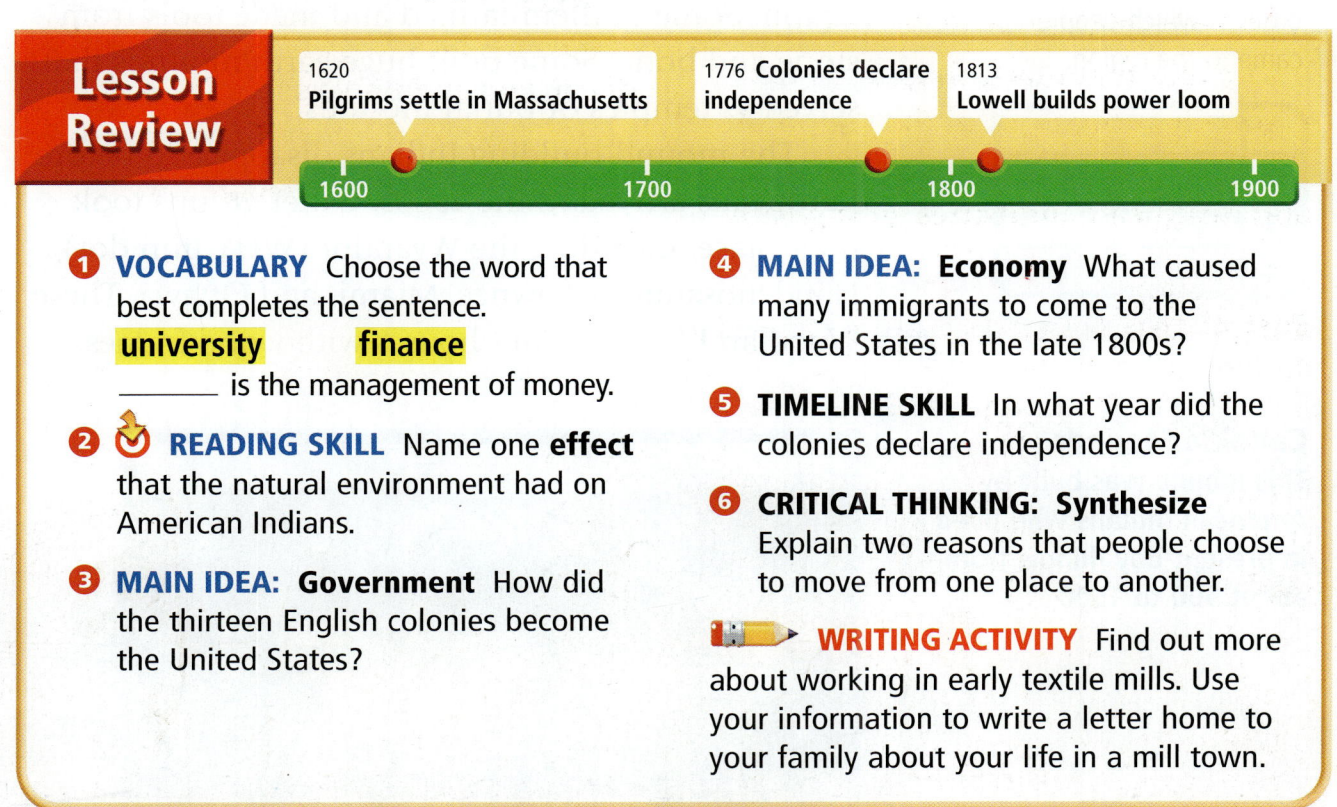

Lesson Review

1620 Pilgrims settle in Massachusetts
1776 Colonies declare independence
1813 Lowell builds power loom

1600 — 1700 — 1800 — 1900

❶ **VOCABULARY** Choose the word that best completes the sentence.
  university   **finance**
  _____ is the management of money.

❷ **READING SKILL** Name one **effect** that the natural environment had on American Indians.

❸ **MAIN IDEA: Government** How did the thirteen English colonies become the United States?

❹ **MAIN IDEA: Economy** What caused many immigrants to come to the United States in the late 1800s?

❺ **TIMELINE SKILL** In what year did the colonies declare independence?

❻ **CRITICAL THINKING: Synthesize** Explain two reasons that people choose to move from one place to another.

WRITING ACTIVITY Find out more about working in early textile mills. Use your information to write a letter home to your family about your life in a mill town.

Core Lesson 2

People of the Midwest

VOCABULARY

homestead
reservation
assembly line

Vocabulary Strategy

assembly line

To **assemble** something means to put it together. An **assembly line** is made up of workers who put a product together.

READING SKILL

Sequence Who first lived in the Midwest? Chart the order in which people came to the region.

1	
2	
3	
4	

800 1100 1400 1700 2000

900 to today

Build on What You Know What would happen if your family moved to a new town? You would need to make some changes in your life. The first people in the Midwest had to change their lives in many ways.

The Midwest's First People

Main Idea Many American Indian nations lived in the Midwest region.

People have lived in the Midwest for centuries. Early American Indians lived in the Great Lakes region. Some of them farmed and made tools from stone and bone. Some built huge earth mounds that served as temples or burial mounds.

The mound-building Indians disappeared before Europeans arrived in the 1600s. Other groups took their place, including the Wyandot (WHY uhn dot), Haudenosaunee, Shawnee, Miami, and Ottawa. These Woodland Indians built houses with wood frames.

Cahokia Mounds
This mound was built by American Indians who lived in present-day Illinois from about 900 to 1500.

228 • Chapter 11

The Plains Indians

Other American Indian nations lived on the Great Plains. Some built homes and farmed. Others were nomadic. This means they traveled from place to place.

Nomadic Plains Indians followed and hunted the buffalo. In the 1500s, Spanish explorers brought horses to North America. Plains hunters quickly learned to use these animals. Horses made it much easier to hunt buffalo.

When they traveled, Plains Indians carried their homes with them. These homes, called tepees, were easy to take apart and move. They were made of poles covered with animal skins.

Tepee Nomadic Plains Indians carried their homes with them when they moved.

Struggles for Control

American Indians traded with the arriving Europeans. The American Indians wanted knives and tools. The Europeans wanted furs and land. Some were willing to take the land by force.

In the mid-1700s, England and France went to war for control of the Ohio region. The British won in 1763, when the two countries signed the Treaty of Paris. **Pontiac,** an Ottawa chief, had fought with the French. After the war, he kept fighting the British until 1765.

REVIEW How did horses change the lives of the Plains Indians long ago?

Early Settlers

Main Idea The Midwest attracted a large population.

In 1783, the United States gained control of the Northwest Territory from the British. This area included most of the present-day Great Lakes region.

Then, in 1803, President **Thomas Jefferson** bought the Louisiana Territory from France. This doubled the size of the United States. Jefferson sent **Meriwether Lewis** and **William Clark** to explore the region. They returned from their 8,000-mile journey in 1806.

Lewis and Clark brought back information about the region, its plants and animals, and American Indian cultures. Settlers soon moved into these new areas. They came for many reasons. Eastern farmers came looking for new land. Soldiers came to claim land promised to them by the government.

Many Germans and Scandinavians also immigrated to the Midwest. They wanted religious freedom and better lives. By 1880, more than 70 percent of Minnesota's non–American Indian population was made up of immigrants and their children.

A Growing Nation The United States greatly increased in size between 1787 and 1803.

SKILL Reading Maps In which direction did the Louisiana Territory expand the United States?

Northwest and Louisiana Territories

LEGEND
- United States, 1787
- Northwest Territory, 1787
- Louisiana Purchase, 1803

230 • Chapter 11

Homesteaders on the Great Plains

Settlers did not rush to the Great Plains at first. However, in 1862, Congress passed the Homestead Act. A **homestead** is a piece of land given to someone to settle and farm there. The Homestead Act offered Great Plains land for a small fee to people who would live there for five years. People learned to farm this treeless land.

Life was hard for homesteaders. They often had to deal with harsh weather, prairie fires, and clouds of grasshoppers. Because there were too few trees to build wooden houses, people built houses of sod. Sod is large chunks of soil held together by plant roots.

In spite of the hardships, many homesteaders continued to arrive. They pushed American Indians off the land. Hunters had killed nearly all of the buffalo, the American Indians' main food supply. Some American Indians fought, but most were forced to move to reservations. A **reservation** is land that is set aside by the government for American Indians.

REVIEW What were two reasons that the United States grew?

Sod School House Sod houses could be small and dirty. Snakes and mice often lived in the walls.

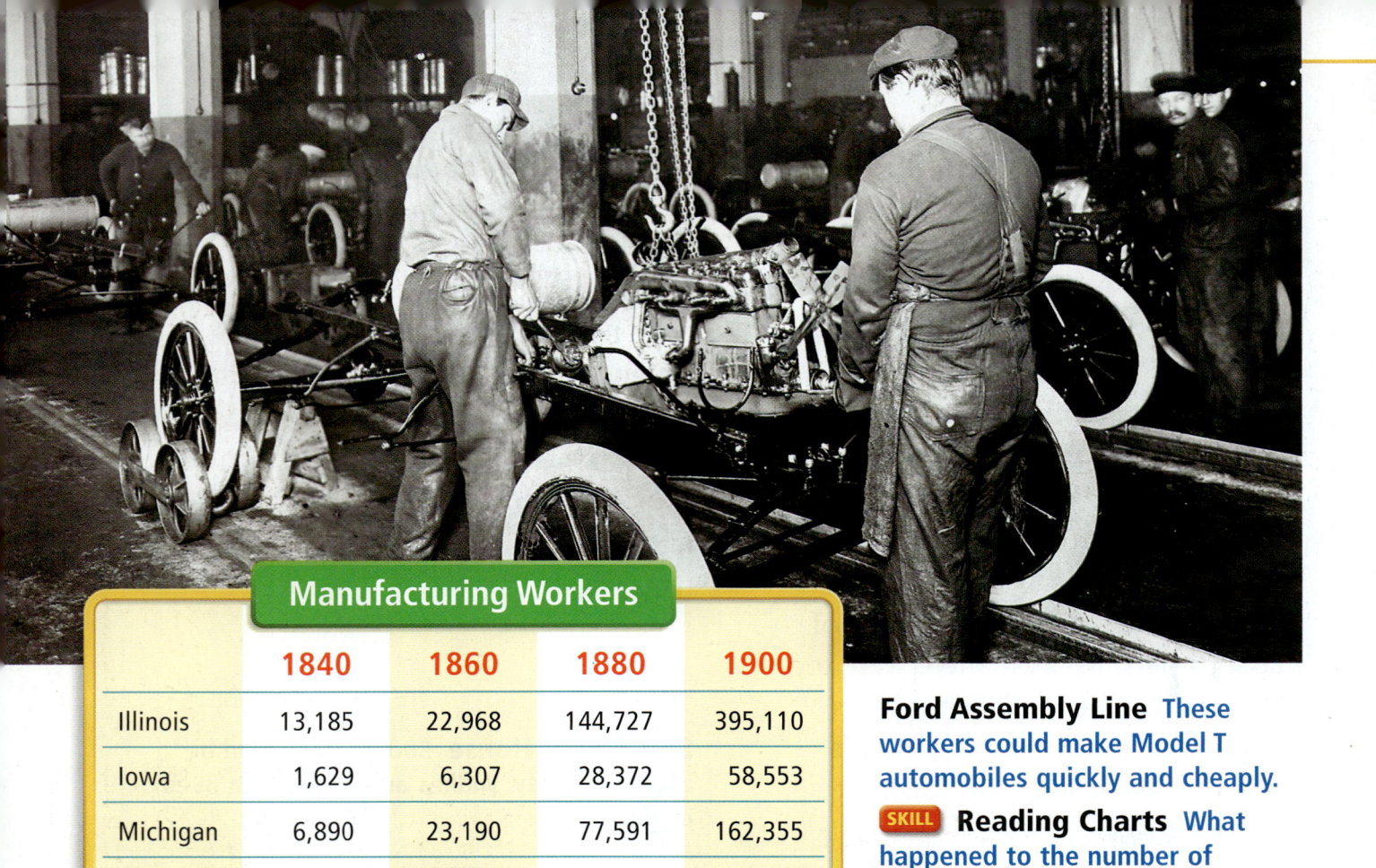

Manufacturing Workers

	1840	1860	1880	1900
Illinois	13,185	22,968	144,727	395,110
Iowa	1,629	6,307	28,372	58,553
Michigan	6,890	23,190	77,591	162,355
Missouri	11,100	19,681	63,995	134,975

Ford Assembly Line These workers could make Model T automobiles quickly and cheaply.

SKILL Reading Charts What happened to the number of manufacturing workers in the Midwest between 1840 and 1900?

Midwestern Cities

Main Idea Midwestern cities grew because of industry and good transportation routes.

In the late 1800s, many Americans moved from farms to cities. City factories needed workers. In Detroit, **Henry Ford** improved the assembly line for his automobile factory. On an **assembly line**, each worker does one small part of the job as a product moves along the line.

New settlers helped midwestern cities grow. After World War I, for example, many African Americans moved from the South to the Midwest. They hoped to get good factory jobs.

St. Louis, Missouri

St. Louis lies just south of where the Missouri River flows into the Mississippi. It began as a French fur-trading post in 1764. Later, many western settlers stopped there for supplies. Today, the Gateway Arch stands as a monument to the pioneers who passed through St. Louis.

Transportation helped St. Louis become an important city. Steamboats and trains brought goods and people from all over the country. By the 1890s, skyscrapers rose above busy downtown streets. St. Louis remains a transportation hub and an industrial center today.

Minneapolis, Minnesota

Minneapolis grew along the Mississippi River during the mid-1800s. Waterfalls provided power for mills that turned wheat into flour and timber into lumber. By the 1880s, the city was producing millions of barrels of flour each year. During the 20th century, manufacturing, food processing, computers, and health services became major industries.

Today, more than 380,000 people live in Minneapolis. In bad weather, people can walk in the city's enclosed skyway system. Visitors to the Mill City Museum learn how flour mills helped the city grow.

REVIEW Why did midwestern cities grow?

Minneapolis The Mississippi River flows through Minneapolis.

Lesson Summary

- American Indians lived in Midwest
- United States gained Northwest and Louisiana territories
- Homesteaders and immigrants came to Midwest
- Big cities and industry grew

Why It Matters...

Many people have moved to midwestern cities for better jobs.

Lesson Review

Timeline:
- 1783 Northwest Territory
- 1803 Louisiana Territory
- 1862 Homestead Act

(1780 — 1795 — 1810 — 1825 — 1840 — 1855 — 1870)

❶ **VOCABULARY** Write a paragraph contrasting a **homestead** and a **reservation**.

❷ **READING SKILL** Show the **sequence** of events that led to St. Louis's growth.

❸ **MAIN IDEA: Government** What government actions brought people to the Great Plains?

❹ **MAIN IDEA: Economics** What factors help explain why Minneapolis grew?

❺ **TIMELINE SKILL** Which territory did the nation gain first, the Northwest or Louisiana?

❻ **CRITICAL THINKING: Evaluate** Would you rather work on an assembly line or make something all by yourself? Why?

WRITING ACTIVITY Many homesteaders kept journals. Write a journal entry that one of the children might write. Describe a funny or scary event.

233

Map and Globe Skills

Skillbuilder

Use a Special Purpose Map

Some maps have a special purpose. They use different symbols to tell about the special features of a place. The map below tells you about resources in the Midwest, one of the five regions of the United States.

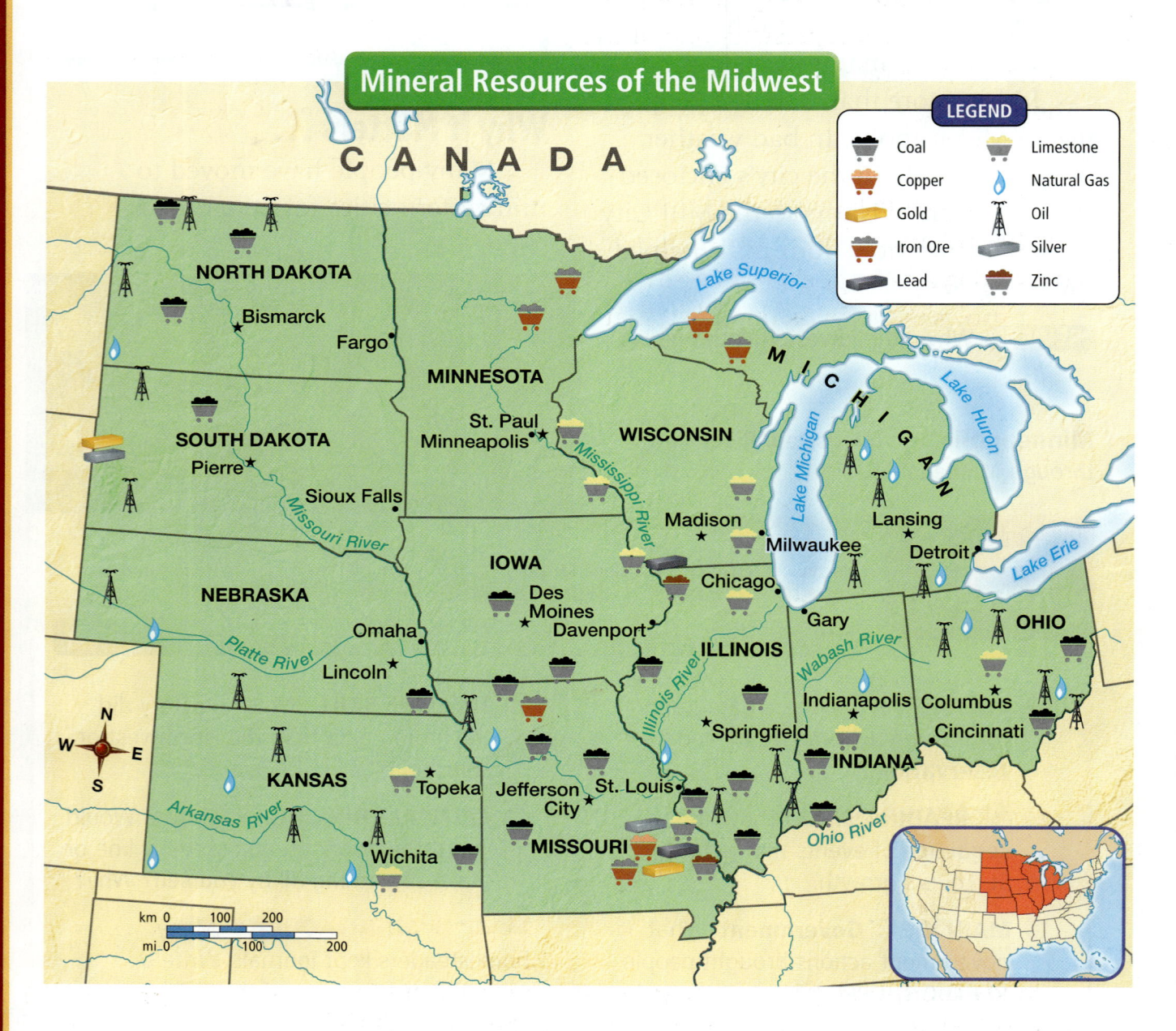

Mineral Resources of the Midwest

LEGEND
- Coal
- Copper
- Gold
- Iron Ore
- Lead
- Limestone
- Natural Gas
- Oil
- Silver
- Zinc

234 • Chapter 11

Learn the Skill

Step 1: Read the map title to find out what kind of information is shown on the map.

Mineral Resources of the Midwest

Step 2: Study the map's legend. Notice that each symbol represents one of the different mineral resources found in the Midwest.

LEGEND
- Coal
- Copper
- Gold
- Iron ore
- Lead
- Limestone
- Natural gas
- Oil
- Silver
- Zinc

Step 3: Note where the symbols from the legend appear on the map. For example, the coal symbol appears in North Dakota. This shows that coal is mined in that state.

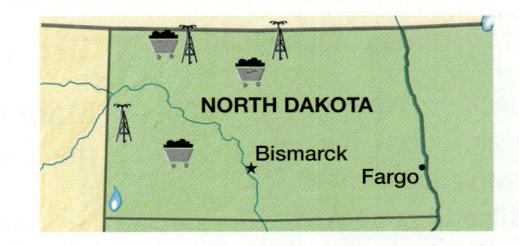

Practice the Skill

Use the map on page 234 to answer the questions.

1. Look at the legend. Name seven mineral resources that are found in the Midwest region.
2. According to the map, which mineral resources are found in the state of Wisconsin?
3. Based on this map, which mineral resource is found most widely in the Midwest?

Apply the Skill

Study the special purpose map on page 19. Then write a paragraph that summarizes the information shown on the map.

235

Core Lesson 3

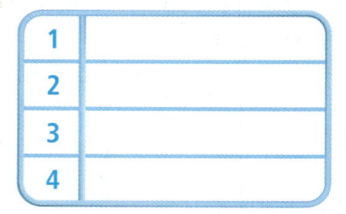

People of the West

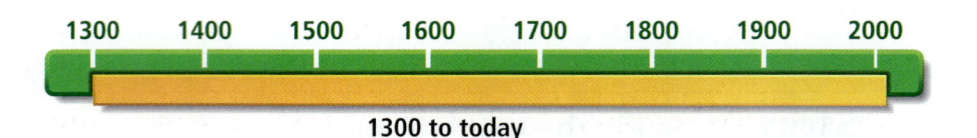

VOCABULARY

wagon train
transcontinental railroad
rural
migrant worker

Vocabulary Strategy

transcontinental railroad

The prefix **trans-** means across. The **transcontinental railroad** ran across North America.

READING SKILL

Sequence Chart the order in which the groups arrived in the West.

1	
2	
3	
4	

1300 1400 1500 1600 1700 1800 1900 2000

1300 to today

Build on What You Know Suppose you moved to a land you knew nothing about. What would you need to survive? How would you spend your free time?

Early Peoples of the West

Main Idea American Indians of the West, such as the Miwok, the Yokut, and the Tlingit used natural resources wisely.

Many scientists think that people first came to the West 15,000 years ago. Some scientists believe they crossed over a land bridge that once connected present-day Asia and Alaska. Over the centuries, people spread through the continent. In the West region, these people included the Aleut (al YOOT) and Inuit (IHN oo iht) in the north and the Yokut (YO kut) and Kitanemuk (ki ta na mook) in the south.

The first settlers of Hawaii were Polynesians. They came by a different route. They crossed thousands of miles of Pacific Ocean in canoes. Unlike the many groups on mainland North America, they shared a common culture. However, they too adapted to their new home.

Resources in the Valley This image shows an artist's idea of how the Central Valley plant and animal life might have looked 500 years ago.

A Closer Look at Central Valley Life

The Miwok (ME wahk) and the Yokut lived in a large, flat valley in the middle of California. This place is called the Central Valley. The climate there was mild with fresh water and many food resources. Miwoks and northern Yokuts gathered acorns. People also gathered wild grasses, nuts, and roots for food.

Miwoks and Yokuts hunted for elk, rabbits, and birds. Some Yokut towns were built near the marshy wetlands of the southern valley. People here used boats made of reeds to fish for trout. Yokuts in the northern valley trapped salmon with nets.

Some people wove reeds and grasses to make their houses. In the north, houses were dug into the earth. In the south, people built towns. Some houses held one family. Other houses were very long and held ten or more families. In such houses, each family had its own fireplace and door.

A Closer Look at Tlingit Life

On the northwest coast of the present-day United States, the Tlingit (TLING giht) lived in large wooden houses. The Tlingit did not raise crops. They got food by gathering wild plants, hunting, and fishing. The Tlingit used spears, bows, harpoons, and traps to catch animals. They also traded seal oil for furs from inland groups.

The Tlingit were fine artists. They wove baskets, hats, and blankets. Tlingit blankets showed a figure that had special meaning to the weaver's family or village group. Their blankets and their religious stories helped the Tlingit pass on their traditions to their children. Their traditions remain alive today.

Miwok, Yokut, Tlingit, and other American Indian groups still live in the West. Many still practice the skills of their ancestors. At the same time, they live and work in the modern world.

REVIEW What did different groups who settled the West have in common?

The Oregon Trail

Oregon Trail People met at the start of the trail in Missouri. They joined wagon trains, elected captains, and hired guides for the journey.

More People Go West

Main Idea People traveled west to find gold, get land, or work on the railroads.

Small groups of trappers and traders had roamed the West since the early 1800s. After the United States took control of the region, many more people moved there.

The West attracted new settlers for many reasons. In 1848, gold was discovered in California. Thousands of Americans, Chinese, and Europeans went to look for gold. Others came west to buy cheap land. They made a difficult six-month trip on the Oregon Trail in wagon trains. A **wagon train** was a line of wagons that carried settlers and everything they owned. Some came west for religious freedom. One group, the Mormons, set up their own government in Utah.

The westward expansion affected American Indians. Settlers overran their hunting grounds. The new settlers wanted to own the land. Most American Indians believed that people could use land but could not own it.

Fighting soon broke out between American Indians and settlers. The U.S. Army drove the American Indians off their land. The government forced them to live on reservations, where many still live today.

Gold Nuggets During the Gold Rush, over 80,000 people went to California hoping to find gold.

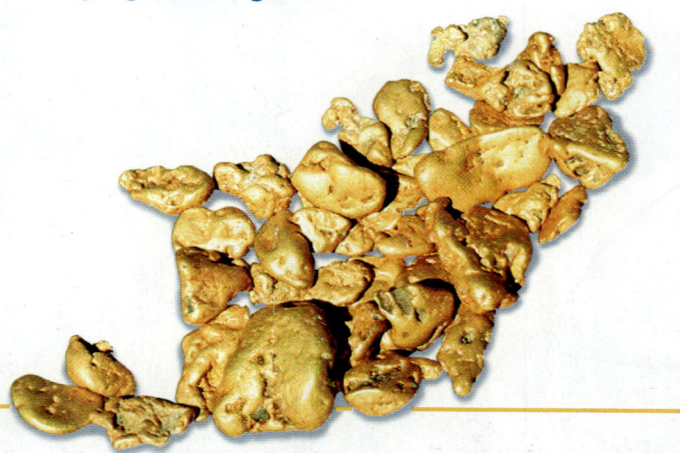

The Fifty States

As the West grew, the United States government helped two companies build a transcontinental railroad. The **transcontinental railroad** was the first train system to link the East and West. Many Chinese immigrants helped build the railroad. Their hard work helped finish the job in 1869.

Good transportation helped the West's population grow faster. The railroad moved people and goods from one coast to another in under a week. Before the railroad, people traveled over land by horse, wagon, or on foot. Their journeys took weeks and even months.

The West continued to grow. When a territory's population grew to a certain point, its people could ask Congress to make it a state. In 1959, the territories of Alaska and Hawaii became the last of the 50 states to join the nation.

People from many cultures shaped the history of the West. Today, it is a region of great diversity.

REVIEW How did the transcontinental railroad affect population growth in the West?

The Pacific States

Main Idea Major coastal cities in the Pacific States are ports and centers of industry.

The Pacific States are Alaska, California, Hawaii, Oregon, and Washington. The ocean affects the climate and economy of this region. Seattle and other cities are major seaports. Since the 1800s, many Asian immigrants have entered the United States through these cities. Today, many Asian Americans live in the region.

Port cities in the Pacific States trade with many countries. Together the ports of Los Angeles and Long Beach, California, move more cargo than the Port of New York. Shipping is not these cities' only industry. San Francisco is a major international banking center. Los Angeles is home to the movie and television industries. Seattle and Portland have software and high-technology businesses.

Seattle The Space Needle and Mount Ranier are two features of the Seattle skyline.

Visiting the Mountain States Tourism helps the economy of the Mountain States.

Agriculture and Tourism

The climates of the Pacific region let farmers in rural areas grow many types of crops. **Rural** means an area in the country with few people, houses, and businesses. Many farmers in this region depend on migrant workers to pick their fruits and vegetables. A **migrant worker** moves from place to place doing seasonal work. Cities also support the rural agriculture industry. Canning factories and other businesses process raw foods into products that are shipped around the world.

The Pacific States have many areas of natural beauty. Alaska's Arctic Wildlife Refuge preserves wilderness areas. Hawaii Volcanoes National Park has Mauna Loa, a huge active volcano. Washington's Olympic National Park is known for its many glaciers.

The Mountain States

Main Idea Most people in the Mountain States live in large cities and towns.

Why are Colorado, Idaho, Montana, and Wyoming called the Mountain States? The Rocky Mountains run through them. There are also hills, plateaus, plains, and valleys. Few people live in rural areas because of the rugged land and harsh winters. Most live in cities or towns.

In the Mountain States, many activities in rural areas take place outdoors. Millions of cattle and sheep graze on ranches. National parks, forests, wildlife refuges, and wide-open land cover much of the region. Many people visit these areas to enjoy the wildlife or participate in outdoor activities such as hiking or rock climbing.

Life Today

Cities in the Mountain States are centers for industry, entertainment, and services such as health care. Many have colleges. People enjoy art exhibits, sporting events, plays, operas, and museums. Jackson, Wyoming, has a ski area in the middle of the town.

Many people work in the farming, mining, and forestry industries. In recent years, tourism has become very important to the economy. Each year, millions of visitors come to the national parks, ski resorts, and vast wilderness areas. These tourists spend money at businesses such as hotels and restaurants. This creates jobs.

REVIEW Name two things the four Mountain States have in common.

Lesson Summary

- The resources of the West influenced the life and culture of the people who lived there.
- A growing population forced American Indians from their land and formed new states.
- Today, the West has a very diverse culture.

Why It Matters...

Settling the West helped make the United States a large, powerful nation. It also brought many cultures together to create a unique American culture.

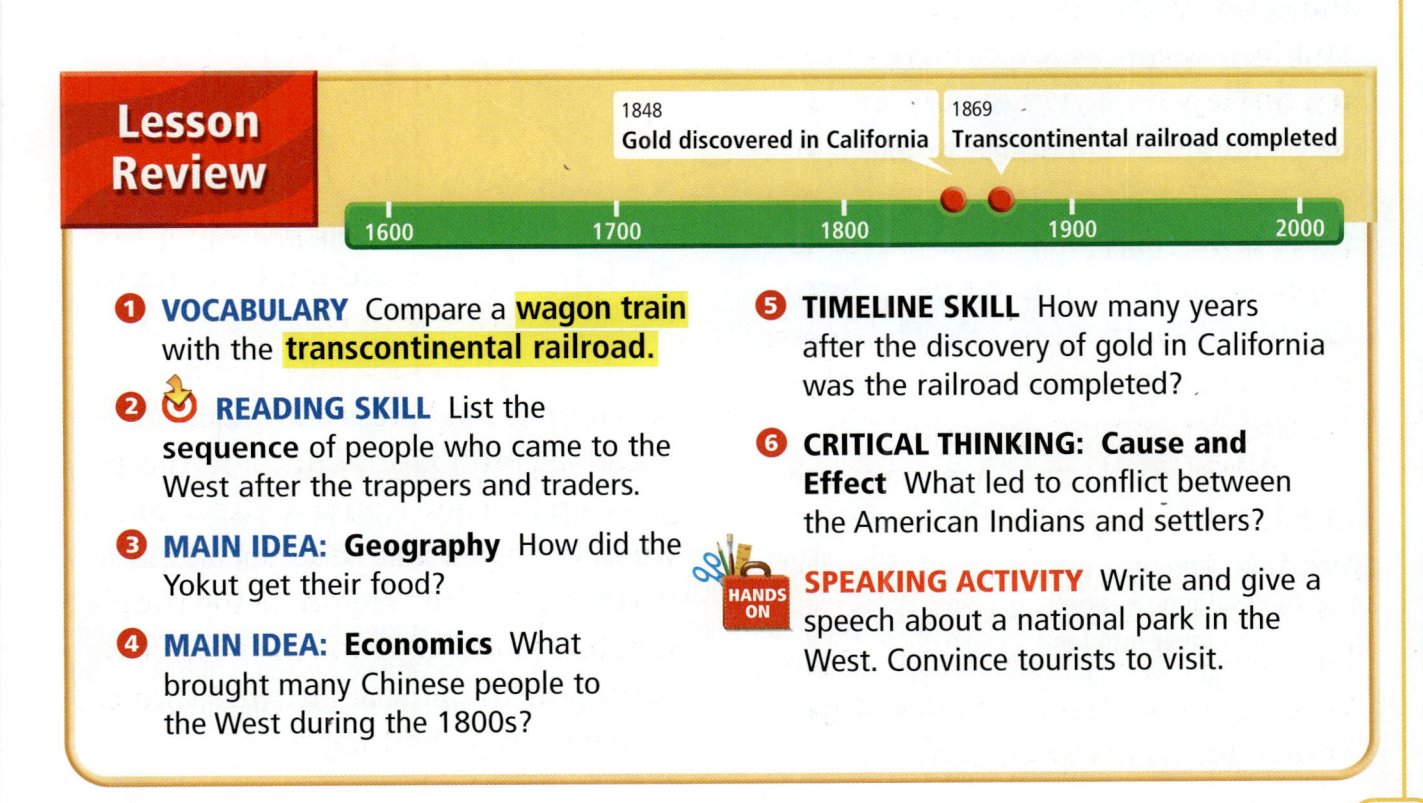

Lesson Review

1848 Gold discovered in California
1869 Transcontinental railroad completed

1600 — 1700 — 1800 — 1900 — 2000

1 VOCABULARY Compare a **wagon train** with the **transcontinental railroad.**

2 READING SKILL List the **sequence** of people who came to the West after the trappers and traders.

3 MAIN IDEA: Geography How did the Yokut get their food?

4 MAIN IDEA: Economics What brought many Chinese people to the West during the 1800s?

5 TIMELINE SKILL How many years after the discovery of gold in California was the railroad completed?

6 CRITICAL THINKING: Cause and Effect What led to conflict between the American Indians and settlers?

SPEAKING ACTIVITY Write and give a speech about a national park in the West. Convince tourists to visit.

Extend Lesson 3
History

Lewis AND Clark

President Thomas Jefferson bought the Louisiana Territory in 1803. At the time, he knew little about the huge piece of land he had bought. He sent Meriwether Lewis and William Clark to explore and map the land west of the Mississippi River.

The journey of Lewis and Clark was a major event in U.S. history. Their explorations led others to journey to the West. Trace their journey on the map, starting in St. Louis.

Meriwether Lewis **William Clark**

"Ocean in view! O! the joy!"

— William Clark, November 7, 1805

Map locations:
- 5 Fort Clatsop
- Columbia River
- Traveler's Rest
- 4 Missouri River
- Great Falls
- Three Forks
- Lemhi Pass

❶ May 1804:
The Journey Begins!
Lewis, Clark, and their team of more than 40 men headed up the Missouri River into land unexplored by Europeans. It would be a two year trip.

❷ September 1804:
Across the Plains
In the grasslands of what is now South Dakota, the group saw "new" animals such as prairie dogs, pronghorn antelope, coyotes, and jackrabbits. They also saw herds of thousands of buffalo.

❸ October 1804–April 1805:
The First Winter
The group built a winter fort near the villages of the Mandan and Hidatsa people. Here, a Shoshone Indian woman named Sacagawea (sak uh guh WEE uh) helped the men find food.

242 • Chapter 11

HISTORY

Legend:
- Lewis and Clark's journey west
- Louisiana Territory

Map locations:
1. St. Louis / Camp Dubois
2. (along Missouri River)
3. Fort Mandan
- Floyd's Grave

The United States Mint honored the 200th anniversary of Lewis and Clark's expedition with a new nickel.

④ June 1805:
The Great Falls

Five huge waterfalls blocked the group's travel. It took a month to carry boats and supplies 18 miles to a safe spot up the river.

⑤ December 1805–March 1806:
The Pacific!

The group spent the winter at Fort Clatsop, waiting for the right time to head home. By the time they completed their journey in September 1806, they had traveled about 8,000 miles.

Activities

1. **CONNECT TO TODAY** Lewis and Clark showed **courage** by going on their journey. Talk about someone you know who has done something courageous.

2. **RESEARCH IT** Read more about Lewis and Clark's journey. Write a series of journal entries about why Sacagawea helped the expedition.

243

Chapter 11 Review and Test Prep

Visual Summary

1. – 3. Write a description of each item named below.

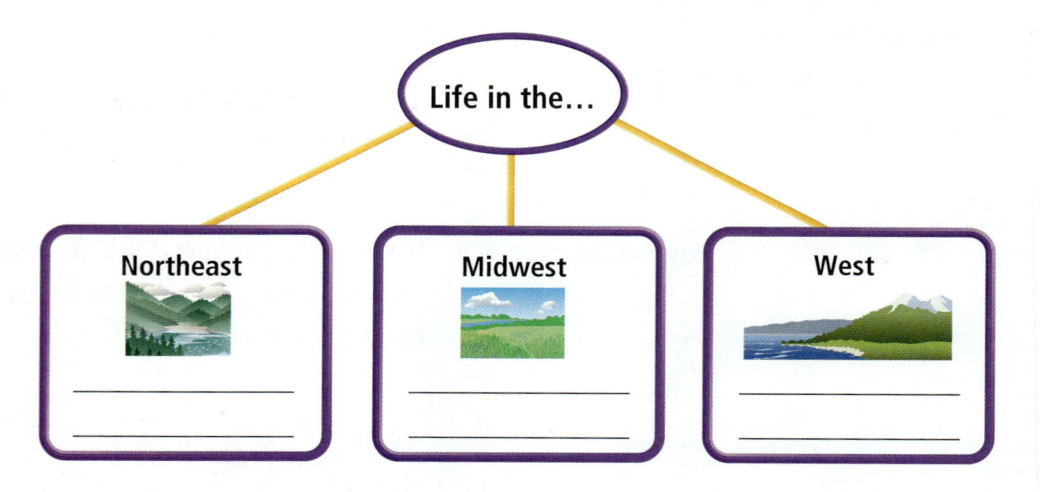

Life in the...

- Northeast
- Midwest
- West

Facts and Main Ideas

TEST PREP Answer each question below.

4. **History** Why did the Pilgrims come to North America?

5. **Technology** In the 1800s, why did many people move to cities in the Northeast?

6. **History** What effect did gaining the Northwest Territory and the Louisiana Purchase have on the United States?

7. **Technology** What types of transportation helped settlements in the Midwest grow?

8. **History** Why did many Americans, Chinese, and Europeans move to the West in the mid-1800s?

Vocabulary

TEST PREP Choose the correct word from the list below to complete each sentence.

finance, p. 226
assembly line, p. 232
transcontinental railroad, p. 239

9. In a(n) _____, each worker does one small part of the whole job.

10. Boston became a center of _____ and trade in New England.

11. The completion of the _____ helped the West's population grow.

244 • Chapter 11

CHAPTER SUMMARY TIMELINE

- **1620** Pilgrims arrive in Massachusetts
- **1776** Colonies declare independence
- **1869** Transcontinental railroad completed

1600 — 1700 — 1800 — 1900

Apply Skills

✓ **TEST PREP** **Read a Special Purpose Map** Study the Crystal Lake Beach map below. Then use your map skills to anwer the question.

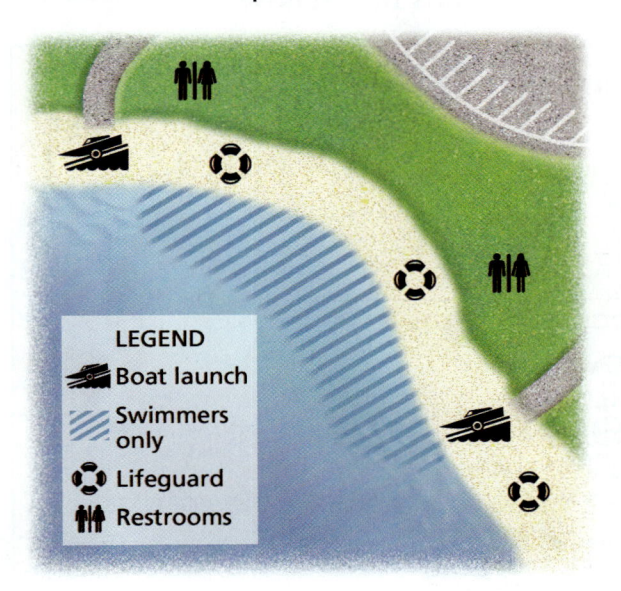

LEGEND
- Boat launch
- Swimmers only
- Lifeguard
- Restrooms

12. What is the purpose of the map?
    A. to sell boats
    B. to provide a guide for visitors
    C. to keep people out of the lake
    D. to identify wildlife

13. How many places for people to put their boats into the water does the map show?
    A. two
    B. three
    C. four
    D. none

Critical Thinking

✓ **TEST PREP** Write a short paragraph to answer each question below.

14. **Compare and Contrast** Why did many people in the Northeast settle along the coast or near rivers?

15. **Infer** Why do you think Seattle, Los Angeles, and Long Beach are such important seaports?

Timeline

Use the Chapter Summary Timeline to answer the question.

16. In what year did the colonies declare independence?

Activities

Art Activity Make a poster divided into three sections. In each section, illustrate one way that people in the Northeast, the Midwest, and the West use natural resources.

Writing Activity Write a dialogue between a person who lives in the city and a person who has moved to the suburbs. Discuss the advantages and disadvantages of life in a suburban area.

Technology
Writing Process Tips
Get help with your writing at:
www.eduplace.com/kids/hmss/

245

UNIT 4 Review and Test Prep

Vocabulary and Main Ideas

✓ **TEST PREP** Write a sentence to answer each question.

1. The United States is located on what **continent** in what **hemispheres?**

2. How did the Pony Express and the telegraph system support **interdependence** in the United States?

3. What cultural features are shared by people in an **ethnic group?**

4. Why do farmers in the Southwest use drip **irrigation?**

5. What is the difference between a **homestead** and a **reservation?**

6. What role did **wagon trains** and the **transcontinental railroad** play in western settlement?

Critical Thinking

✓ **TEST PREP** Write a short paragraph to answer each question.

7. **Draw Conclusions** Why is it important for the United States to find new sources of energy?

8. **Compare and Contrast** Compare and contrast the ways in which people adapted to the geography and climate of two regions.

Apply Skills

✓ **TEST PREP** Use the Great Lakes Industries map below and what you have learned about special purpose maps to answer the questions that follow.

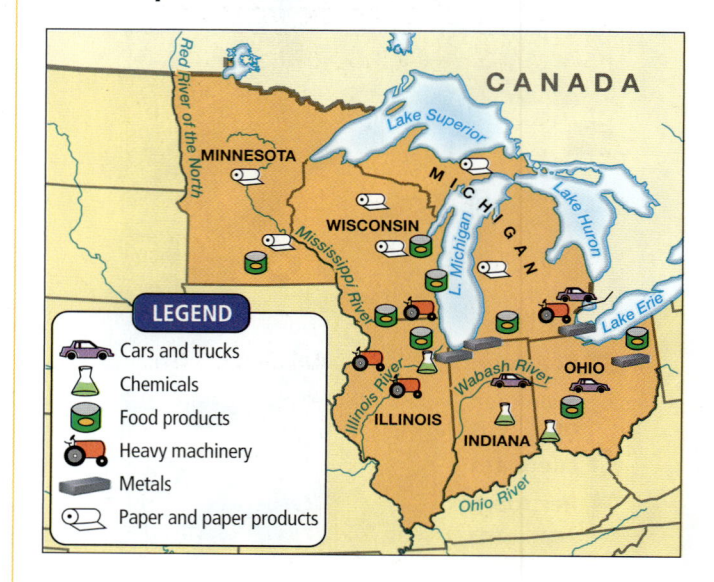

9. Which states are major producers of paper and paper products?

   A. Illinois, Indiana, Ohio
   B. Illinois, Minnesota, Wisconsin
   C. Michigan, Indiana, Ohio
   D. Michigan, Minnesota, Wisconsin

10. Which state produces heavy machinery, cars, trucks, and paper products?

    A. Indiana
    B. Ohio
    C. Michigan
    D. Wisconsin

Unit Activity

The Big Idea

Make a Travel Brochure

- Choose a place in the country that you think has interesting features.
- Fold a sheet of paper in half. Write the name of the place on the front cover. Draw a picture or map of the place.
- For the inside of the brochure, research and list interesting facts about the place and the region in which it is located.
- Find or draw pictures of the place and its region. Add captions.
- Post the brochure in your classroom.

At the Library

Look for this book at your public library.

Hottest Coldest Highest Deepest by Steve Jenkins

Explore some of the most unique places on Earth through illustrations, maps, and brief text.

CURRENT EVENTS WEEKLY READER

Current Events Project

Learn about countries from each of the four hemispheres.

- Using a world map or globe, choose one country from each of the four hemispheres.
- Research each country to find out basic information about its geography, culture, and economy.
- Make a display in which you use images, drawings, and text to describe each of the four countries.
- Include a world map on which you identify the location and hemisphere of each country. (Hint: Draw grid lines across the map to mark the four hemispheres.)

Technology
Weekly Reader offers social studies articles. Go to:
www.eduplace.com/kids/hmss/

247

References

Citizenship Handbook

Pledge of Allegiance R2
   English, Spanish, Tagalog, Russian, Arabic, Chinese

Character Traits R4

Arkansas Governors R6

Arkansas Counties R9

History Makers—Biographical Dictionary R12

Citizenship Handbook

Resources

Geographic Terms R16

Atlas R18

Glossary R32

Index R36

Acknowledgments R45

Pledge of Allegiance

I pledge allegiance to the flag of the United States of America and to the Republic for which it stands, one Nation under God, indivisible, with liberty and justice for all.

Spanish

Prometo lealtad a la bandera de los Estados Unidos de América, y a la república que representa, una nación bajo Dios, entera, con libertad y justicia para todos.

Russian

Я даю клятву верности флагу Соединённых Штатов Америки и стране, символом которой он является, народу, единому перед Богом, свободному и равноправному.

Tagalog

Ako ay nanunumpa ng katapatan sa bandila ng Estados Unidos ng Amerika, at sa Republikang kanyang kinakatawan, isang Bansang pumapailalim sa isang Maykapal hindi nahahati, may kalayaan at katarungan para sa lahat.

Arabic

ادين بالولاء لعلم الولايات المتحده الامريكيه والى الجمهوريه التي تمثلها دولة واحدة تؤمن باللة متحدة تمنح الحرية والعدالة للجميع

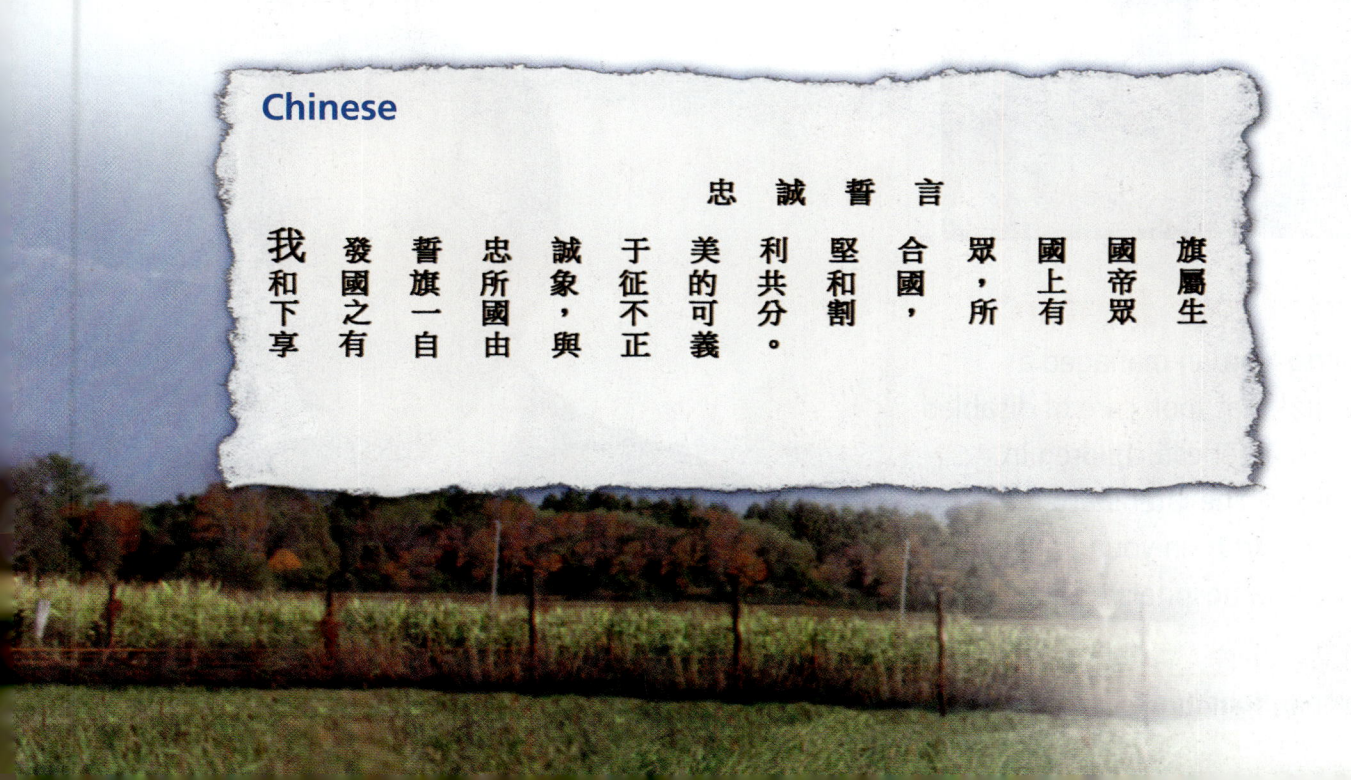

Chinese

忠 誠 誓 言

美的可義利共分國，所國上有
于征不正堅和割合國， 國帝眾
誠象，與 眾， 旗屬生
所國由
忠旗一自
誓發國之有
我和下享

Character Traits

Character includes feelings, thoughts, and behaviors. A character trait is something people show by the way that they act. To act bravely shows courage, and courage is one of several character traits.

Positive character traits, such as honesty, caring, and courage, lead to positive actions. Character traits are also called "life skills." Life skills can help you do your best, and doing your best leads to reaching your goals.

Dale Bumpers
Civic virtue Bumpers served the people of Arkansas as a governor and a senator. In both of these roles, Bumpers worked with other politicians to help improve life in Arkansas.

Lena Lowe Jordan
Caring Jordan managed a hospital that took care of disabled African American children in Arkansas. She later started a program to train young nurses to work in hospitals.

Character Traits

Courage means acting bravely. Doing what you believe to be good and right, and telling the truth, requires courage.

Patriotism means working for the goals of your country. When you show national pride, you are being patriotic.

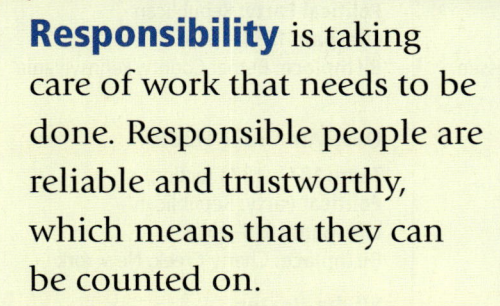

Responsibility is taking care of work that needs to be done. Responsible people are reliable and trustworthy, which means that they can be counted on.

Respect means paying attention to what other people want and believe. The "golden rule," or treating others as you would like to be treated, shows thoughtfulness and respect.

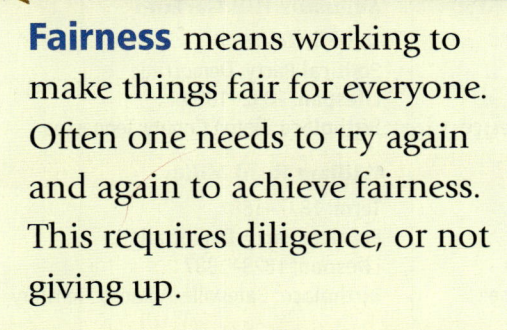

Fairness means working to make things fair for everyone. Often one needs to try again and again to achieve fairness. This requires diligence, or not giving up.

Civic virtue is good citizenship. It means doing things, such as cooperating and solving problems, to help communities live and work well together.

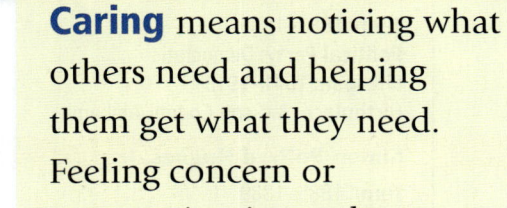

Caring means noticing what others need and helping them get what they need. Feeling concern or compassion is another way to define caring.

Arkansas Governors

Territorial Governors

James Miller
Term: 1819–1825
Political Party: None
Lifespan: 1776–1851
Birthplace: Peterborough, New Hampshire

George Izard
Term: 1825–1828
Political Party: None
Lifespan: 1776–1828
Birthplace: London, England

Robert Crittenden
Term: 1828–1829 (acting)
Political Party: None
Lifespan: 1797–1834
Birthplace: Woodford County, Kentucky

John Pope
Term: 1829–1835
Political Party: Democratic
Lifespan: 1770–1845
Birthplace: Prince William County, Virginia

William Savin Fulton
Term: 1835–1836 (acting)
Political Party: Democratic
Lifespan: 1795–1844
Birthplace: Cecil County, Maryland

State Governors

James Sevier Conway
Term: 1836–1840
Political Party: Democratic
Lifespan: 1796–1855
Birthplace: Greene County, Tennessee

Archibald Yell
Term: 1840–1844
Political Party: Democratic
Lifespan: 1799?–1847
Birthplace: Jefferson County, Tennessee (disputed)

Samuel Adams
Term: 1844 (acting)
Political Party: Democratic
Lifespan: 1805–1850
Birthplace: Halifax County, Virginia

Thomas Stevenson Drew
Term: 1844–1849
Political Party: Democratic
Lifespan: 1802–1879
Birthplace: Wilson County, Tennessee

Richard C. Byrd
Term: 1849 (acting)
Political Party: Democratic
Lifespan: 1805–1854
Birthplace: Hawkins County, Tennessee

John Seldon Roane
Term: 1849–1852
Political Party: Democratic
Lifespan: 1817–1867
Birthplace: Wilson County, Tennessee

Elias Nelson Conway
Term: 1852–1860
Political Party: Democratic
Lifespan: 1812–1892
Birthplace: Greeneville, Tennessee

Henry Massie Rector
Term: 1860–1862
Political Party: Democratic
Lifespan: 1816–1899
Birthplace: Fountain Ferry, Kentucky

Harris Flanagin
Term: 1862–1864
Political Party: Democratic
Lifespan: 1817–1874
Birthplace: Roadstown, New Jersey

Isaac Murphy
Term: 1864–1868
Political Party: Unionist
Lifespan: 1799–1882
Birthplace: Pittsburgh, Pennsylvania

Powell Clayton
Term: 1868–1871
Political Party: Republican
Lifespan: 1833–1914
Birthplace: Bethel County, Pennsylvania

Ozra Amander Hadley
Term: 1871–1873 (acting)
Political Party: Republican
Lifespan: 1826–1915
Birthplace: Cherry Creek, New York

Elisha Baxter
Term: 1873–1874
Political Party: Republican
Lifespan: 1827–1899
Birthplace: Rutherford County, North Carolina

Augustus Hill Garland
Term: 1874–1877
Political Party: Democratic
Lifespan: 1832–1899
Birthplace: Tipton County, Tennessee

William Read Miller
Term: 1877–1881
Political Party: Democratic
Lifespan: 1823–1887
Birthplace: Batesville, Arkansas Territory

Thomas James Churchill
Term: 1881–1883
Political Party: Democratic
Lifespan: 1824–1905
Birthplace: near Louisville, Kentucky

James Henderson Berry
Term: 1883–1885
Political Party: Democratic
Lifespan: 1841–1913
Birthplace: Jackson County, Alabama

Simon Pollard Hughes, Jr.
Term: 1885–1889
Political Party: Democratic
Lifespan: 1830–1906
Birthplace: near Carthage, Tennessee

State Governors (cont.)

James Philip Eagle
Term: 1889–1893
Political Party: Democratic
Lifespan: 1837–1904
Birthplace: Maurin County, Tennessee

William Meade Fishback
Term: 1893–1895
Political Party: Democratic
Lifespan: 1831–1903
Birthplace: Jeffersonton, Virginia

James Paul Clarke
Term: 1895–1897
Political Party: Democratic
Lifespan: 1854–1916
Birthplace: Yazoo County, Mississippi

Daniel Webster Jones
Term: 1897–1901
Political Party: Democratic
Lifespan: 1839–1918
Birthplace: Bowie County, Texas

Jefferson Davis
Term: 1901–1907
Political Party: Democratic
Lifespan: 1862–1913
Birthplace: near Rocky Comfort, Arkansas

John Sebastian Little
Term: 1907
Political Party: Democratic
Lifespan: 1851–1916
Birthplace: Sebastian County, Arkansas

John Isaac Moore
Term: 1907 (acting)
Political Party: Democratic
Lifespan: 1856–1937
Birthplace: Lafayette County, Mississippi

Xenophon Overton Pindall
Term: 1907–1909 (acting)
Political Party: Democratic
Lifespan: 1873–1935
Birthplace: Monroe County, Missouri

Jesse M. Martin
Term: 1909 (acting)
Political Party: Democratic
Lifespan: 1877–1915
Birthplace: London, Arkansas

George Washington Donaghey
Term: 1909–1913
Political Party: Democratic
Lifespan: 1856–1937
Birthplace: Oakland, Louisiana

Joseph Taylor Robinson
Term: 1913
Political Party: Democratic
Lifespan: 1872–1937
Birthplace: near Lonoke, Arkansas

William Kavanaugh Oldham
Term: 1913 (acting)
Political Party: Democratic
Lifespan: 1865–1938
Birthplace: Richmond, Kentucky

Junius Marion Futrell
Term: 1913 (acting)
Political Party: Democratic
Lifespan: 1870–1955
Birthplace: Jones Ridge, Arkansas

George Washington Hays
Term: 1913–1917
Political Party: Democratic
Lifespan: 1863–1927
Birthplace: Camden, Arkansas

Charles Hillman Brough
Term: 1917–1921
Political Party: Democratic
Lifespan: 1876–1935
Birthplace: Clinton, Mississippi

Thomas Chipman McRae
Term: 1921–1925
Political Party: Democratic
Lifespan: 1851–1929
Birthplace: Mount Holly, Arkansas

Thomas Jefferson Terral
Term: 1925–1927
Political Party: Democratic
Lifespan: 1882–1946
Birthplace: Union Parish, Louisiana

John Ellis Martineau
Term: 1927–1928
Political Party: Democratic
Lifespan: 1873–1939
Birthplace: Clay County, Missouri

Harvey Parnell
Term: 1928–1933
Political Party: Democratic
Lifespan: 1880–1936
Birthplace: Orlando, Arkansas

Junius Marion Futrell
Term: 1933–1937
Political Party: Democratic
Lifespan: 1870–1955
Birthplace: Jones Ridge, Arkansas

Carl Edward Bailey
Term: 1937–1941
Political Party: Democratic
Lifespan: 1894–1948
Birthplace: Bernie, Missouri

Homer Martin Adkins
Term: 1941–1945
Political Party: Democratic
Lifespan: 1890–1964
Birthplace: Jacksonville, Arkansas

Benjamin Travis Laney, Jr.
Term: 1945–1949
Political Party: Democratic
Lifespan: 1896–1977
Birthplace: Jones Chapel, Arkansas

Sidney Sanders McMath
Term: 1949–1953
Political Party: Democratic
Lifespan: 1912–2003
Birthplace: Columbia County, Arkansas

Francis Adams Cherry
Term: 1953–1955
Political Party: Democratic
Lifespan: 1908–1965
Birthplace: Fort Worth, Texas

Orval Eugene Faubus
Term: 1955–1967
Political Party: Democratic
Lifespan: 1910–1994
Birthplace: near Combs, Arkansas

Winthrop Rockefeller
Term: 1967–1971
Political Party: Republican
Lifespan: 1912–1973
Birthplace: New York City, New York

State Governors (cont.)

Dale Leon Bumpers **Term:** 1971–1975 **Political Party:** Democratic **Lifespan:** 1925– **Birthplace:** Charleston, Arkansas	**William Jefferson Clinton** **Term:** 1979–1981 **Political Party:** Democratic **Lifespan:** 1946– **Birthplace:** Hope, Arkansas	**Mike Huckabee** **Term:** 1996–2007 **Political Party:** Republican **Lifespan:** 1955– **Birthplace:** Hope, Arkansas
Bob Cowley Riley **Term:** 1975 (acting) **Political Party:** Democratic **Lifespan:** 1924–1994 **Birthplace:** Little Rock, Arkansas	**Frank Durward White** **Term:** 1981–1983 **Political Party:** Republican **Lifespan:** 1933–2003 **Birthplace:** Texarkana, Texas	**Mickey Dale "Mike" Beebe** **Term:** 2007– **Political Party:** Democratic **Lifespan:** 1946– **Birthplace:** Amagon, Arkansas
David Hampton Pryor **Term:** 1975–1979 **Political Party:** Democratic **Lifespan:** 1934– **Birthplace:** Camden, Arkansas	**William Jefferson Clinton** **Term:** 1983–1991 **Political Party:** Democratic **Lifespan:** 1946– **Birthplace:** Hope, Arkansas	
Joe Purcell **Term:** 1979 (acting) **Political Party:** Democratic **Lifespan:** 1923–1987 **Birthplace:** Warren, Arkansas	**James Guy Tucker, Jr.** **Term:** 1991–1992 (acting), 1992–1996 **Political Party:** Democratic **Lifespan:** 1943– **Birthplace:** Oklahoma City, Oklahoma	

Arkansas Governors

Arkansas Counties

County	County Seat	Year Organized	Population, 2005	Origin of Name
Arkansas	DeWitt, Stuttgart	1813	20,073	for the Quapaw Indian nation
Ashley	Hamburg	1848	23,178	for Senator Chester Ashley
Baxter	Mountain Home	1873	40,330	for Governor Elisha Baxter
Benton	Bentonville	1836	186,938	for Senator Thomas Hart Benton of Missouri, who played a key role in Arkansas's admission to the United States
Boone	Harrison	1869	35,793	for the idea that the county would be a "boon" or benefit to its residents
Bradley	Warren	1840	12,192	for Hugh Bradley, a soldier in the War of 1812
Calhoun	Hampton	1850	5,589	for Vice President John C. Calhoun
Carroll	Berryville, Eureka Springs	1833	26,999	for Senator Charles Carroll of Maryland, one of the first signers of the Declaration of Independence
Chicot	Lake Village	1823	13,027	for Point Chicot on the Mississippi River
Clark	Arkadelphia	1818	22,916	for William Clark, explorer and governor of the Missouri Territory
Clay	Corning, Piggott	1873	16,578	for state Senator John Clayton
Cleburne	Heber Springs	1883	25,391	for Confederate General Patrick Ronayne Cleburne
Cleveland	Rison	1873	8,903	for President Grover Cleveland
Columbia	Magnolia	1852	24,695	for Columbia, the female personification of the United States
Conway	Morrilton	1825	20,739	for Henry Wharton Conway, a delegate from the Arkansas Territory to Congress
Craighead	Jonesboro Lake City	1859	86,735	for Senator Thomas Craighead
Crawford	Van Buren	1820	57,630	for William Harris Crawford, a U.S. statesman and judge

Arkansas Counties

County	County Seat	Year Organized	Population, 2005	Origin of Name
Crittenden	Marion	1825	51,882	for Robert Crittenden, first secretary and acting governor of the Arkansas Territory
Cross	Wynne	1862	19,237	for Edward Cross, territorial judge, or David C. Cross, Confederate soldier
Dallas	Fordyce	1845	8,524	for Vice President George Mifflin Dallas
Desha	Arkansas City	1838	14,358	for Benjamin Desha, a soldier in the War of 1812
Drew	Monticello	1846	18,693	for Governor Thomas Stevenson Drew
Faulkner	Conway	1873	97,147	for Sanford C. "Sandy" Faulkner, Confederate soldier and composer of "The Arkansas Traveller"
Franklin	Charleston, Ozark	1837	18,218	for Benjamin Franklin
Fulton	Salem	1842	11,934	for William Savin Fulton, governor of the Arkansas Territory
Garland	Hot Springs	1873	93,551	for Governor Augustus H. Garland
Grant	Sheridan	1869	17,348	for President Ulysses S. Grant
Greene	Paragould	1833	39,401	supposedly for Nathaniel Greene, a general in the Revolutionary War
Hempstead	Hope	1818	23,383	for Edward Hempstead, a delegate from the Missouri Territory to Congress
Hot Spring	Malvern	1829	31,264	for hot springs within the county at the time of its formation
Howard	Nashville	1873	14,552	for state Senator James H. Howard
Independence	Batesville	1820	34,737	for the Declaration of Independence
Izard	Melbourne	1825	13,430	for Governor George Izard
Jackson	Newport	1829	17,601	for President Andrew Jackson
Jefferson	Pine Bluff	1829	81,700	for President Thomas Jefferson
Johnson	Clarksville	1833	24,042	for Benjamin Johnson, a judge in the Arkansas Territory
Lafayette	Lewisville	1827	8,027	for the Marquis de Lafayette, a French ally of the United States

County	County Seat	Year Organized	Population, 2005	Origin of Name
Lawrence	Walnut Ridge	1815	17,153	for Captain James Lawrence, a naval officer in the War of 1812
Lee	Marianna	1873	11,545	for Confederate General Robert E. Lee
Lincoln	Star City	1871	14,262	for President Abraham Lincoln
Little River	Ashdown	1867	13,227	for the Little River
Logan	Booneville, Paris	1871	22,944	for James Logan, an early settler
Lonoke	Lonoke	1873	60,658	for a "lone oak" tree used as a landmark
Madison	Huntsville	1836	14,962	for President James Madison
Marion	Yellville	1835	16,735	for General Francis Marion of the Revolutionary War
Miller	Texarkana	1874	43,162	for James Miller, governor of the Arkansas Territory
Mississippi	Blytheville, Osceola	1833	47,911	for the Mississippi River
Monroe	Clarendon	1829	9,302	for President James Monroe
Montgomery	Mount Ida	1842	9,274	for General Richard Montgomery of the Revolutionary War
Nevada	Prescott	1871	9,550	for the state of Nevada
Newton	Jasper	1842	8,452	for U.S. Marshall Thomas Willoughby Newton
Ouachita	Camden	1842	27,102	for the Ouachita River
Perry	Perryville	1840	10,468	for Commodore William Hazard Perry of the War of 1812
Phillips	Helena	1820	24,107	for Sylvanus Phillips, a representative to the Arkansas Territorial Legislature
Pike	Murfreesboro	1833	11,038	for explorer Zebulon Pike
Poinsett	Harrisburg	1838	25,349	for Joel Roberts Poinsett, a statesman, scientist, and botanist
Polk	Mena	1844	20,176	for President James K. Polk
Pope	Russellville	1829	56,580	for John Pope, governor of the Arkansas Territory
Prairie	Des Arc, DeValls Bluff	1846	9,113	for prairies found in the area

Arkansas Counties

County	County Seat	Year Organized	Population, 2005	Origin of Name
Pulaski	Little Rock	1818	366,463	for Count Casimir Pulaski, a Polish general in the Revolutionary War
Randolph	Pocahontas	1835	18,465	for John Randolph of Virginia
St. Francis	Forrest City	1827	27,902	for the St. Francis River
Saline	Benton	1835	91,188	for the salt works started in the area
Scott	Waldron	1833	11,150	for territorial Supreme Court Justice Andrew Scott
Searcy	Marshall	1838	7,969	for Richard Searcy, a civil servant, major landowner, and circuit court judge
Sebastian	Fort Smith, Greenwood	1851	118,750	for William K. Sebastian, a U.S. Circuit Court judge
Sevier	De Queen	1828	16,456	for Senator Ambrose Sevier
Sharp	Ash Flat	1868	17,397	for Ephraim Sharp, an early settler
Stone	Mountain View	1873	11,716	for the many rocks and stones in the area
Union	El Dorado	1829	44,186	for the concept of "union"
Van Buren	Clinton	1833	16,529	for President Martin Van Buren
Washington	Fayetteville	1828	180,357	for President George Washington
White	Searcy	1835	71,332	for Senator Hugh L. White of Tennessee, a presidential candidate
Woodruff	Augusta	1862	8,098	for William Woodruff, editor of the *Arkansas Gazette*
Yell	Danville, Dardanelle	1840	21,391	for Governor Archibald Yell

Arkansas Counties

Biographical Dictionary

The page number after each entry refers to the place where the person is first mentioned. For more complete references to people, see the Index.

A

Angelou, Maya 1928–, Arkansas writer. (p. 125)
Anthony, Steven M. 1961–, president of Anthony Timberlands, Inc. (p. 170)
Armstrong, Neil 1930–, Astronaut; first person to set foot on the moon. (p. 106)

B

Bates, Daisy 1913?–1999, civil rights leader and writer. (p. 117)
Bates, Lucious 1904–1980, publisher of the *Arkansas State Press*. (p. 117)
Bonaparte, Napoleon 1769–1821, French ruler who agreed to the Louisiana Purchase. (p. 73)
Bush, George W. 1946–, 43rd President of the United States, 2000–. (p. 155)

Daisy Bates

C

Caraway, Hattie Wyatt 1878–1950, Arkansas Senator; first woman elected to the U.S. Senate. (p. 118)
Cash, Johnny 1932–2003, singer and songwriter from Arkansas. (p. 126)
Clark, William 1770–1838, explored Louisiana Purchase with Meriwether Lewis. (p. 73)
Clinton, Bill 1946–, 42nd President of the United States, 1993–2001; 40th and 42nd governor of Arkansas, 1979–1981, 1983–1992. (p. 119)

Johnny Cash

Clinton, Hillary 1947–, New York senator and former First Lady of Arkansas and the United States. (p. 119)
Cloar, Carroll 1913–1993, Arkansan artist. (p. 125)
Columbus, Christopher 1451–1506, Italian explorer; reached the Americas. (p. 48)
Cotnam, Florence Lee Brown 1865–1932, women's rights leader from Arkansas. (p. 103)

D

De Soto, Hernando 1500–1542, Spanish explorer. (p. 49)
De Tonti, Henri 1650–1704, French explorer; started Arkansas's first European settlement. (p. 54)
Douglass, Frederick 1817–1985, abolitionist and writer. (p. 90)

E

Eisenhower, Dwight 1890–1969, 34th President of the United States, 1953–1961. (p. 117)

F

Flanagin, Harris 1817–1874, 7th governor of Arkansas, 1862–1865. (p. 93)
Franklin, Benjamin 1706–1790, American writer and statesman. (p. 68)
Fulbright, William 1905–1995, Arkansas senator. (p. 118)
Fulton, William 1795–1844, 5th and last territorial governor of Arkansas, 1835–1836. (p. 82)

Benjamin Franklin

R13

Kerry George

G

George, Kerry Arkansas teacher; works to improve the lives of disabled children. (p. 117)

Gibbs, Mifflin Wistar 1823–1915, the first African American city judge elected in the United States. (p. 118)

Grey, William H. 1829–1888, Arkansas state representative and senator. (p. 99)

Grisham, John 1955–, Arkansas writer. (p. 125)

H

Hancock, John 1737–1793, first signer of the Declaration of Independence. (p. 66)

Huckabee, Mike 1955–, 44th governor of Arkansas, 1996–2007. (p. 145)

J

Jefferson, Thomas 1743–1826, 3rd President of the United States, 1801–1809; wrote the Declaration of Independence. (p. 66)

Johnson, Andrew 1808–1875, 17th President of the United States, 1865–1869. (p. 96)

Johnson, John H. 1918–2005, Arkansas entrepreneur; started *Ebony* magazine. (p. 120)

Jolliet, Louis 1645–1700, French explorer; sailed down the Mississippi River with Jacques Marquette. (p. 50)

Jones, Jerry 1942–, owner of the Dallas Cowboys. (p. 127)

John H. Johnson

K

Keohane, Nannerl 1940–, Arkansas educator; first woman president of Duke University. (p. 121)

King, Martin Luther, Jr. 1929–1968, civil rights leader. (p. 117)

Kountz, Samuel Lee 1930–1981, Arkansas doctor. (p. 121)

L

La Salle, René-Robert Cavelier, Sieur de 1643–1687, French explorer; claimed land around Mississippi River for France. (p. 51)

Law, John 1671–1729, Scottish merchant; his Company of the West controlled trade in French Louisiana. (p. 55)

Lewis, Meriwether 1774–1809, explored Louisiana Purchase with William Clark. (p. 73)

Lincoln, Abraham 1809–1865, 16th President of the United States, 1861–1865; issued Emancipation Proclamation. (p. 91)

Lozano-Yancy, Maura 1962–, Arkansas entrepreneur; started ¡Hola! Arkansas, Arkansas's first statewide Spanish-English newspaper. (p. 120)

Abraham Lincoln

M

Madison, James 1751–1836, 4th President of the United States, 1809–1817; helped write the Constitution. (p. 68)

Marquette, Jacques 1637–1675, French explorer; sailed down the Mississippi River. (p. 50)

Massie, Samuel 1919–, Arkansas educator; first African American professor at the United States Naval Academy. (p. 121)

McClellan, John 1896–1977, Arkansas senator. (p. 118)

Miller, James 1776–1851, first governor of the Arkansas Territory, 1819–1825. (p. 78)

Murphy, Isaac 1799–1882, eighth governor of Arkansas, 1864–1868; voted against secession from the Union in 1861. (p. 91)

John McClellan

P

Pippin, Scottie 1965–, professional basketball player and six-time NBA national champion; played basketball for University of Central Arkansas. (p. 127)

Pope, John 1770–1845, third governor of the Arkansas Territory, 1829–1835. (p. 82)

Pryor, David 1934–, 39th governor of Arkansas, 1975–1979. (p. 119)

John Pope

R

Rockefeller, Winthrop 1912–1973, 37th governor of Arkansas, 1967–1971. (p. 119)

Roosevelt, Franklin Delano 1882–1945, 32nd President of the United States, 1933–1945. (p. 104)

S

Sacagawea 1784–1884?, interpreter for Lewis and Clark. (p. 73)

Sevier, Ambrose 1801–1848, Arkansas's territorial representative to the U. S. Congress; supported statehood. (p. 82)

Shackelford, Lottie 1941– , first female African American mayor of Little Rock. (p. 145)

Steenburgen, Mary 1953–, film and television actress; won an Academy Award for her work in *Melvin and Howard*, 1981. (p. 126)

Stephens, Charlotte Andrews 1854–1951, formerly enslaved woman who became the first free African American teacher in Little Rock. (p. 98)

Stowe, Harriet Beecher 1811–1896, author of *Uncle Tom's Cabin*. (p. 90)

Charlotte Andrews Stephens

T

Tubman, Harriet 1820–1913, formerly enslaved woman who helped enslaved African Americans escape to freedom. (p. 90)

Tyson, John 1953–, Arkansas businessperson; chairman of Tyson Foods. (p. 120)

W

Walker, Hazel 1914–1990, professional basketball player; founded a women's professional basketball team in 1948; selected for the Women's Basketball Hall of Fame, 2001. (p. 127)

Walton, Sam 1918–1992, Arkansas entrepreneur; started Wal-Mart. (p. 120)

Washington, George 1732–1799, general of the Continental Army during American Revolution; 1st President of the United States, 1789–1797. (p. 66)

Sam Walton

Williamson, "Sonny Boy" 1899?–1965, musician; rose to fame in the 1940s playing blues harmonica. (p. 126)

Geographic Terms

basin
a round area of land surrounded by higher land

bay
part of a lake or ocean that is partially enclosed by land

canyon
a valley with steep cliffs shaped by erosion

cape
a piece of land that points out into a body of water

coast
the land next to a sea or ocean

coastal plain
a flat area of land near an ocean

delta
land that is formed by soil deposited near the mouth of a river

desert
a dry region with little vegetation

fault
a break or crack in Earth's surface

▲ **glacier**
a large ice mass that pushes soil and rocks as it moves

gulf
a large area of sea or ocean partially enclosed by land

hill
a raised area of land

highland
an area of land in a high elevation

island
an area of land surrounded by water

isthmus
a narrow piece of land connecting two larger land areas

lake
a large body of water surrounded by land

lowland
an area of low land surrounded by higher land

mountain
a raised mass of land with steep slopes

ocean
a large body of salt water that covers much of Earth's surface

peninsula
a strip of land surrounded by water on three sides

plain
a large area of flat land

plateau
a high, flat area of land

prairie
a flat area of grassland with few trees

rain forest
a thick forest that receives heavy rainfall throughout the year

river
a body of water that flows from a high area to a lower area

river basin
an area that is drained by a river

swamp
a low area of wet land with trees and shrubs

tectonic plate
a huge slab of rock in Earth's crust that can cause earthquakes and volcanoes when it moves

tributary
a river or stream that flows into another river

valley
a low area of land between hills or mountains

▲ **volcano**
an opening in Earth's surface through which melted rock and gases escape

wetland
an area that is soaked with water, such as a swamp

plateau
plain
cape
bay
peninsula
coastal plain

Geographic Terms

R17

Atlas

The World: Political

ALB.	—Albania
AZER.	—Azerbaijan
BOS. & HERZ.	—Bosnia & Herzegovina
CEN. AFR. REP.	—Central African Republic
DEM. REP. OF CONGO	—Democratic Republic of Congo
FR.	—France
IT.	—Italy
LIECH.	—Liechtenstein
LUX.	—Luxembourg
NETH.	—Netherlands
N.Z.	—New Zealand
REP. OF CONGO	—Republic of Congo
SERB. & MONT.	—Serbia & Montenegro
SLOV.	—Slovenia
SWITZ.	—Switzerland
U.A.E.	—United Arab Emirates
U.K.	—United Kingdom
U.S.	—United States

R18 • Resources

ARCTIC OCEAN
ICELAND
RUSSIA
ASIA
Area of index
EUROPE
KAZAKHSTAN
MONGOLIA
GEORGIA
UZBEKISTAN
KYRGYZSTAN
ARMENIA
TURKEY
AZER.
TURKMENISTAN
TAJIKISTAN
CHINA
N. KOREA
S. KOREA
JAPAN
PACIFIC OCEAN
TUNISIA
CYPRUS
LEBANON
SYRIA
IRAQ
IRAN
AFGHANISTAN
MOROCCO
ISRAEL
JORDAN
KUWAIT
PAKISTAN
BHUTAN
NEPAL
ALGERIA
LIBYA
EGYPT
QATAR
SAUDI ARABIA
U. A. E.
BANGLADESH
TAIWAN
WESTERN SAHARA (Morocco)
AFRICA
MAURITANIA
OMAN
INDIA
MYANMAR
LAOS
Northern Mariana Islands (U.S.)
MARSHALL ISLANDS
SENEGAL
GAMBIA
GUINEA BISSAU
GUINEA
SIERRA LEONE
LIBERIA
MALI
BURKINA FASO
NIGER
CHAD
SUDAN
ERITREA
YEMEN
THAILAND
VIETNAM
CAMBODIA
PHILIPPINES
Guam (U.S.)
FEDERATED STATES OF MICRONESIA
IVORY COAST
GHANA
TOGO
BENIN
NIGERIA
CEN.AFR. REP.
DJIBOUTI
ETHIOPIA
SOMALIA
SRI LANKA
BRUNEI
PALAU
KIRIBATI
CAMEROON
EQU. GUINEA
SAO TOME AND PRINCIPE
GABON
REP. OF CONGO
DEM. REP. OF CONGO
UGANDA
KENYA
RWANDA
BURUNDI
TANZANIA
MALDIVES
MALAYSIA
SINGAPORE
INDONESIA
PAPUA NEW GUINEA
NAURU
SOLOMON ISLANDS
EAST TIMOR
TUVALU
COMOROS
ANGOLA
MALAWI
ZAMBIA
MOZAMBIQUE
ZIMBABWE
INDIAN OCEAN
VANUATU
FIJI
New Caledonia (Fr.)
NAMIBIA
BOTSWANA
MADAGASCAR
MAURITIUS
Reunion (Fr.)
AUSTRALIA
SWAZILAND
LESOTHO
SOUTH AFRICA
km 0 1000 2000
mi 0 1000 2000
NEW ZEALAND
ATLANTIC OCEAN
ANTARCTICA

FINLAND
SWEDEN
NORWAY
RUSSIA
ESTONIA
km 0 150 300
mi 0 150 300
NORTH SEA
DENMARK
LATVIA
LITHUANIA
RUSSIA
UNITED KINGDOM
IRELAND
NETH.
BELARUS
POLAND
GERMANY
BELGIUM
LUX.
CZECH REPUBLIC
UKRAINE
SLOVAKIA
LIECH.
AUSTRIA
FRANCE
HUNGARY
MOLDOVA
ATLANTIC OCEAN
SWITZ.
SLOV.
CROATIA
ROMANIA
SAN MARINO
BOS. & HERZ.
MONACO
SERB. & MONT.
BULGARIA
Corsica (Fr.)
ITALY
ANDORRA
MACEDONIA
ALB.
PORTUGAL
Balearic Islands (Sp.)
Sardinia (It.)
GREECE
SPAIN
TURKEY
Sicily (It.)
GIBRALTAR (U.K.)
MEDITERRANEAN SEA
MOROCCO
ALGERIA
TUNISIA

The World: Physical

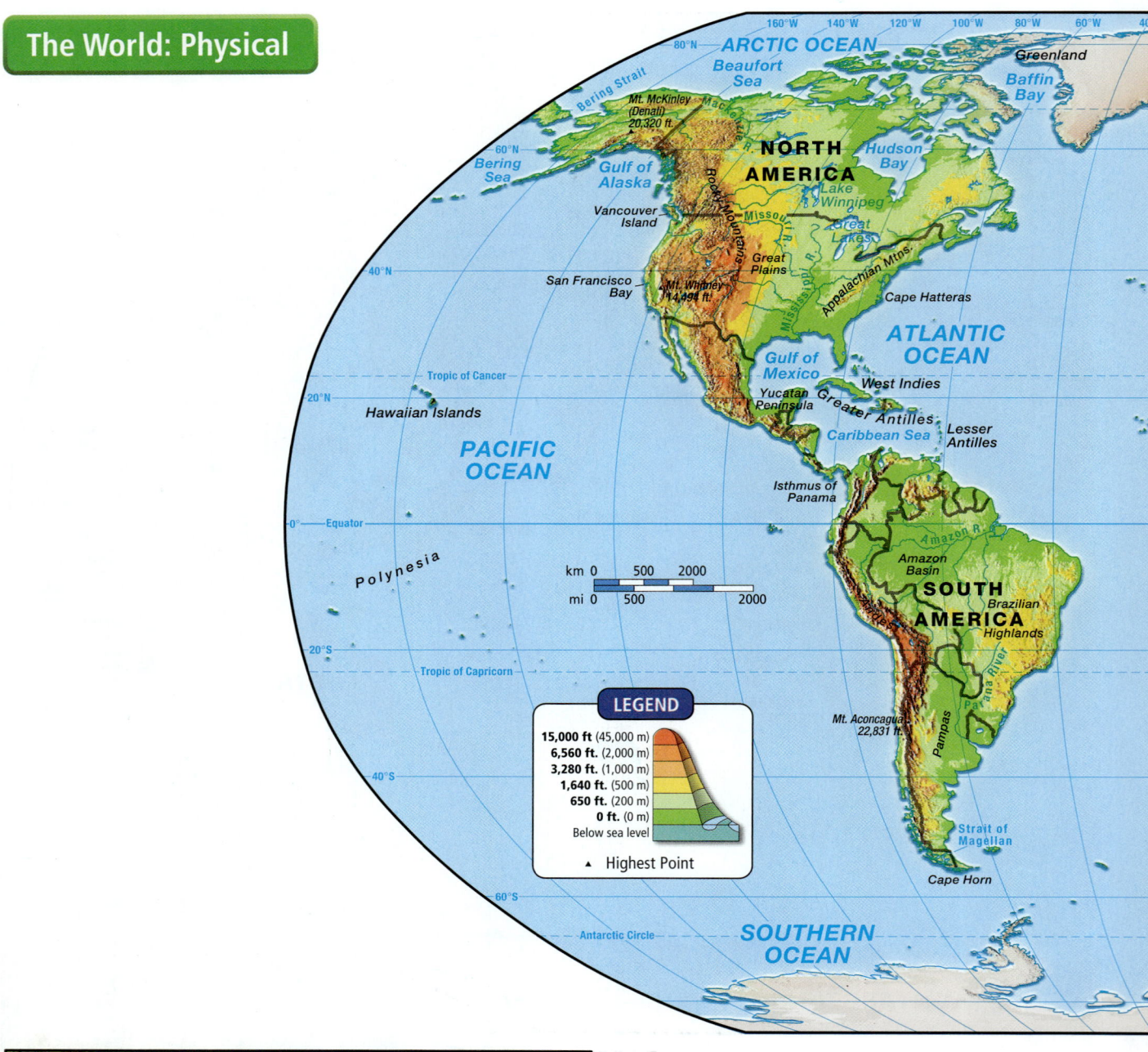

Atlas

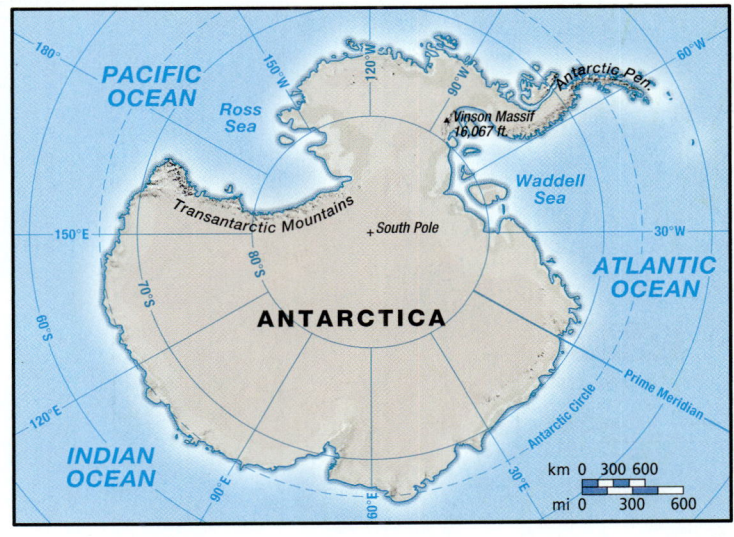

World Physical Map (Eastern Hemisphere)

ARCTIC OCEAN

- Iceland
- Arctic Circle
- Barents Sea
- North Sea
- **EUROPE**
  - Northern European Plain
  - Ural Mountains
  - Volga River
  - Danube River
  - Alps
  - Pyrenees
  - Strait of Gibraltar
  - Atlas Mtns.
  - Mediterranean Sea
  - Black Sea
  - Caucasus Mountains
  - Mt. Elbrus 18,510 ft.
  - Caspian Sea
- **ASIA**
  - Ob River
  - Yenisey River
  - Central Siberian Plateau
  - Lake Baikal
  - Amur River
  - Sea of Okhotsk
  - Kamchatka Peninsula
  - Aral Sea
  - Gobi Desert
  - Plateau of Tibet
  - Himalaya Mountains
  - Mt. Everest 29,035 ft.
  - Huang He
  - Chang Jiang
  - Ganges River
  - Sea of Japan
  - East China Sea
  - South China Sea
  - Bay of Bengal
  - Arabian Sea
  - Red Sea
- **AFRICA**
  - SAHARA
  - SAHEL
  - Niger River
  - Nile River
  - Congo River
  - Lake Victoria
  - Great Rift Valley
  - Mt. Kilimanjaro 19,340 ft.
  - Madagascar
  - Kalahari Desert
  - Cape of Good Hope
  - Prime Meridian
- **PACIFIC OCEAN**
  - Tropic of Cancer
  - Micronesia
  - Philippine Islands
  - Melanesia
  - Equator
- Sumatra
- Borneo
- Java
- Strait of Sunda
- New Guinea
- **INDIAN OCEAN**
- Coral Sea
- **AUSTRALIA**
  - Great Sandy Desert
  - Nullarbor Plain
  - Darling River
  - Mt. Kosciusko 7,310 ft.
- Tasman Sea
- North Island
- South Island
- Tropic of Capricorn
- **ATLANTIC OCEAN**
- Antarctic Circle
- **ANTARCTICA**

Antarctica Inset Map

- **PACIFIC OCEAN**
- Ross Sea
- Transantarctic Mountains
- South Pole
- Vinson Massif 16,067 ft.
- Antarctic Pen.
- Weddell Sea
- **ATLANTIC OCEAN**
- **ANTARCTICA**
- **INDIAN OCEAN**
- Antarctic Circle
- Prime Meridian

km 0 300 600
mi 0 300 600

R21

Western Hemisphere: Political

LEGEND
- ⊛ National capital
- — National border

km 0 500 1000
mi 0 500 1000

R22 • Resources

Western Hemisphere: Physical

United States: Political

Atlas

ARCTIC OCEAN
- RUSSIA
- ALASKA
  - Yukon River
  - Fairbanks
  - Anchorage
  - Juneau
- CANADA
- Aleutian Islands
- PACIFIC OCEAN

km 0 250 500
mi 0 250 500

Compass: N, NE, E, SE, S, SW, W, NW

WASHINGTON
- Seattle
- ★ Olympia
- Columbia R.

OREGON
- Portland
- ★ Salem

IDAHO
- ★ Boise
- Pocatello
- Snake River

MONTANA
- Helena ★
- Billings

WYOMING
- Casper
- Cheyenne ★

CALIFORNIA
- Sacramento ★
- San Francisco
- Reno
- Los Angeles
- San Diego

NEVADA
- Carson City ★
- Las Vegas

UTAH
- Salt Lake City ★
- Provo

COLORADO
- Denver ★
- Colorado Springs
- Pueblo
- Colorado River

ARIZONA
- ★ Phoenix
- Tucson

NEW MEXICO
- Santa Fe ★
- Albuquerque
- El Paso
- Rio Grande

PACIFIC OCEAN

LEGEND
- ⊛ National capital
- ★ State capital
- • Major city
- ━ National boundary
- ─ State boundary

HAWAII
- Kauai
- Niihau
- Oahu — Kailua
- Honolulu ★
- Molokai
- Lanai
- Maui
- Kahoolawe
- Hawaii — Hilo

PACIFIC OCEAN

km 0 50 100
mi 0 50 100

Gulf of California

MEXICO

R24 • Resources

CANADA
St. Lawrence River
Lake Superior
Lake Michigan
Lake Huron
L. Ontario
Lake Erie
NORTH DAKOTA
Bismarck
Fargo
MINNESOTA
SOUTH DAKOTA
Pierre
Sioux Falls
Minneapolis
St. Paul
WISCONSIN
Madison
Milwaukee
MICHIGAN
Grand Rapids
Lansing
Detroit
NEW HAMPSHIRE
VERMONT
MAINE
Augusta
Burlington
Montpelier
Portland
Concord
Manchester
Boston
NEW YORK
Albany
Rochester
Buffalo
MASSACHUSETTS
Hartford
Providence
New Haven
RHODE ISLAND
CONNECTICUT
IOWA
Cedar Rapids
Des Moines
Missouri R.
NEBRASKA
Omaha
Lincoln
Chicago
ILLINOIS
Springfield
PENNSYLVANIA
Newark
New York
Harrisburg
Trenton
Pittsburgh
Philadelphia
NEW JERSEY
Cleveland
OHIO
Columbus
Indianapolis
INDIANA
Cincinnati
Baltimore
Dover
DELAWARE
Annapolis
Washington, D.C.
MARYLAND
WEST VIRGINIA
Charleston
Richmond
Norfolk
VIRGINIA
Kansas City
Topeka
Kansas City
Jefferson City
St. Louis
Louisville
Ohio R.
Frankfort
KANSAS
MISSOURI
KENTUCKY
Greensboro
Raleigh
NORTH CAROLINA
Nashville
TENNESSEE
Memphis
Tulsa
Oklahoma City
OKLAHOMA
Fort Smith
ARKANSAS
Little Rock
Mississippi River
MISSISSIPPI
Columbia
SOUTH CAROLINA
Charleston
Atlanta
GEORGIA
Birmingham
Dallas
TEXAS
Jackson
Montgomery
ALABAMA
Savannah
LOUISIANA
ATLANTIC OCEAN
Jacksonville
Mobile
Tallahassee
Baton Rouge
New Orleans
Austin
Houston
San Antonio
FLORIDA
Tampa
Miami
Gulf of Mexico
BAHAMAS
km 0 100 200 300 400 500
mi 0 100 200 300 400 500
CUBA

United States: Physical

CANADA
St. Lawrence River
Mesabi Range
Lake Superior
Lake Michigan
Lake Huron
L. Ontario
Lake Erie
Mississippi River
Des Moines River
Missouri River
Platte River
Sand Hills
Mt. Washington 6,288 ft.
White Mtns.
Adirondack Mountains
Connecticut R.
Hudson R.
Catskill Mtns.
Nantucket
Martha's Vineyard
Long Island
Delaware River
Susquehanna River
Delaware Bay
Chesapeake Bay
ALLEGHENY PLATEAU
APPALACHIAN MOUNTAINS
BLUE RIDGE MOUNTAINS
CENTRAL PLAINS
Ohio R.
Wabash River
OZARK PLATEAU
Arkansas River
OUACHITA MOUNTAINS
Red River
Mt. Mitchell 6,684 ft.
Cumberland Plateau
Tennessee R.
FALL LINE
ATLANTIC COASTAL PLAIN
Savannah R.
Oconee R.
Altamaha R.
Chattahoochee River
Alabama R.
Tombigbee R.
Pearl River
Sabine River
Brazos River
Colorado River
GULF COASTAL PLAIN
Galveston Bay
Mobile Bay
Pensacola Bay
Tampa Bay
ATLANTIC OCEAN
Gulf of Mexico
Everglades
Florida Keys
BAHAMAS
CUBA
km 0 100 200 300 400 500
mi 0 100 200 300 400 500

Arkansas: Political

MISSOURI

- BENTON
- CARROLL
- BOONE
- BAXTER
- FULTON
- RANDOLPH
- CLAY
- MARION
- IZARD
- SHARP
- GREENE
- Fayetteville
- MADISON
- SEARCY
- LAWRENCE
- WASHINGTON
- NEWTON
- STONE
- INDEPENDENCE
- Jonesboro
- MISSISSIPPI
- CRAWFORD
- JOHNSON
- VAN BUREN
- CLEBURNE
- CRAIGHEAD
- FRANKLIN
- POINSETT
- Fort Smith
- POPE
- JACKSON
- LOGAN
- CONWAY
- CROSS
- SEBASTIAN
- FAULKNER
- WHITE
- WOODRUFF
- CRITTENDEN
- SCOTT
- YELL
- PERRY
- PRAIRIE
- ST. FRANCIS
- Pulaski
- Little Rock
- LEE
- GARLAND
- SALINE
- LONOKE
- MONROE
- POLK
- Hot Springs
- PHILLIPS
- MONTGOMERY
- HOT SPRING
- GRANT
- JEFFERSON
- ARKANSAS
- HOWARD
- Pine Bluff
- Arkansas River
- PIKE
- CLARK
- DALLAS
- CLEVELAND
- LINCOLN
- DESHA
- SEVIER
- HEMPSTEAD
- NEVADA
- CALHOUN
- DREW
- LITTLE RIVER
- Red River
- Ouachita River
- MILLER
- OUACHITA
- BRADLEY
- COLUMBIA
- UNION
- ASHLEY
- CHICOT
- LAFAYETTE
- Mississippi River

OKLAHOMA
TEXAS
LOUISIANA
MISSISSIPPI
TENNESSEE

Compass: N, NE, E, SE, S, SW, W, NW

LEGEND
- ★ State capital
- • City
- County boundary

Scale: km 0 30 60 / mi 0 30 60

Atlas

R28 • Resources

Arkansas: Physical

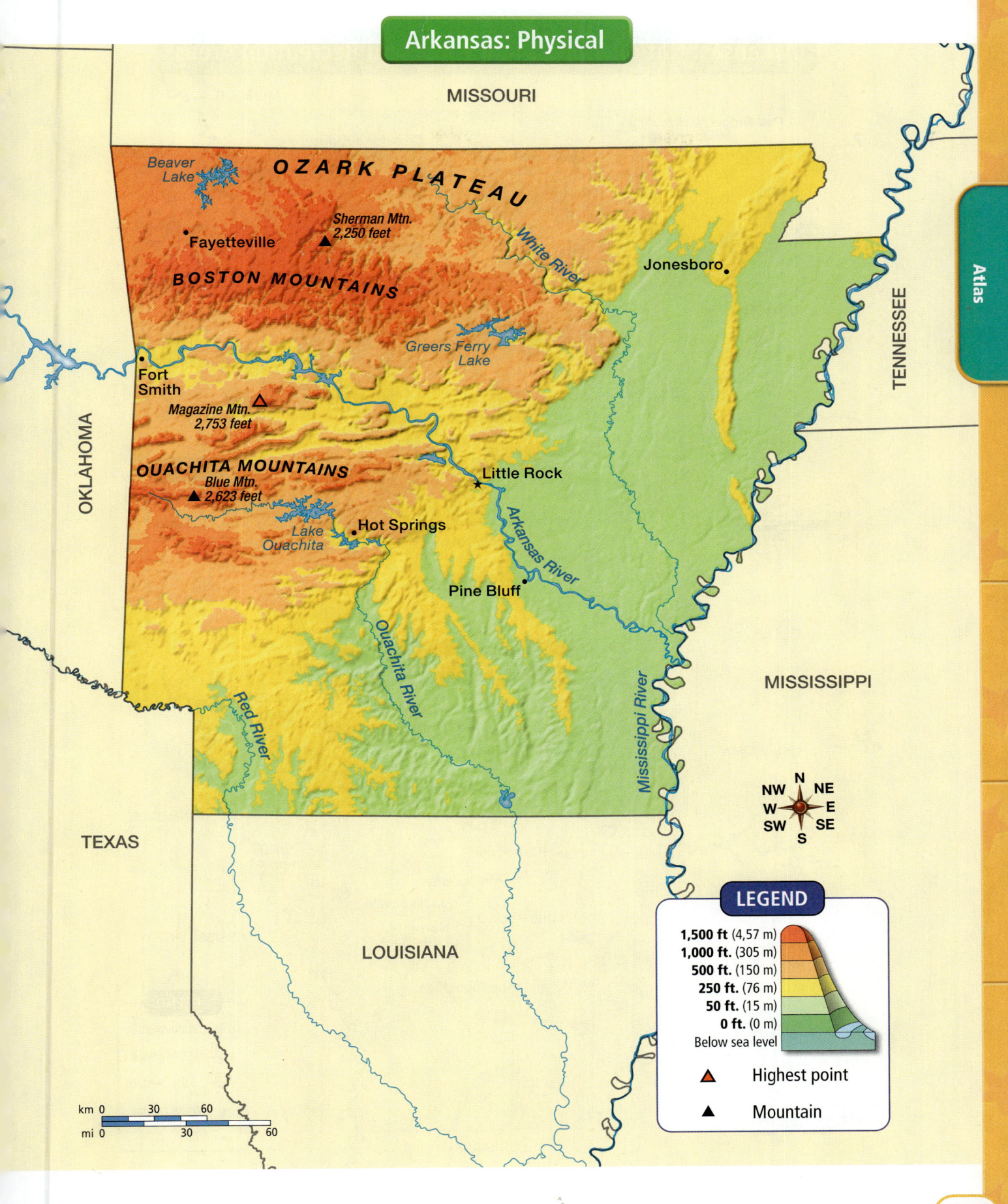

MISSOURI

Beaver Lake

OZARK PLATEAU

Sherman Mtn. 2,250 feet

Fayetteville

White River

Jonesboro

BOSTON MOUNTAINS

Greers Ferry Lake

Fort Smith

Magazine Mtn. 2,753 feet

OUACHITA MOUNTAINS

Blue Mtn. 2,623 feet

Little Rock

Lake Ouachita

Hot Springs

Arkansas River

Pine Bluff

OKLAHOMA

Ouachita River

Red River

Mississippi River

TENNESSEE

MISSISSIPPI

TEXAS

LOUISIANA

LEGEND

- 1,500 ft (457 m)
- 1,000 ft (305 m)
- 500 ft (150 m)
- 250 ft (76 m)
- 50 ft (15 m)
- 0 ft (0 m)
- Below sea level

△ Highest point
▲ Mountain

km 0 30 60
mi 0 30 60

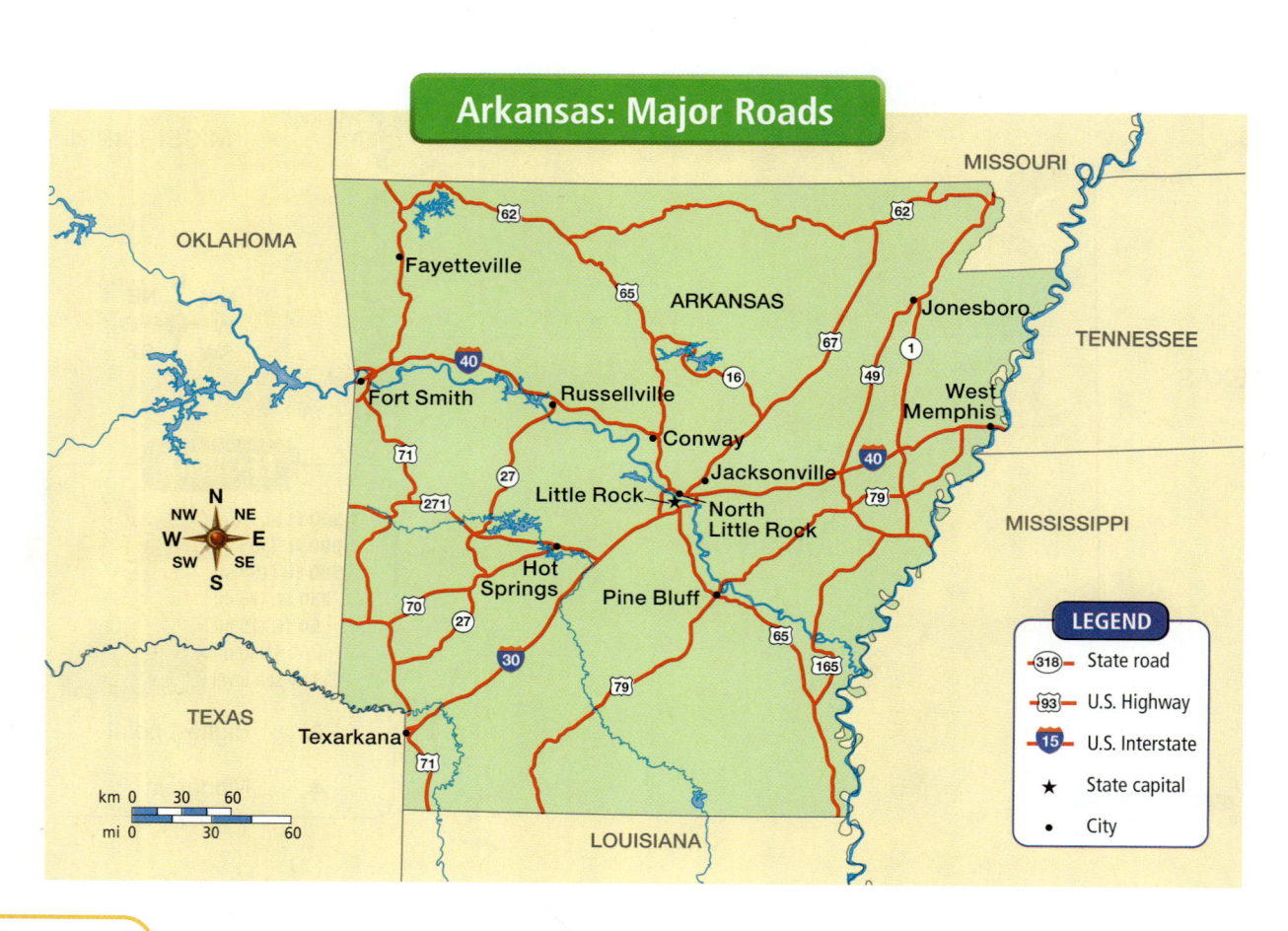

Arkansas: National and State Parks and Recreation Areas

- Pea Ridge National Military Site
- Ozark Folk Center State Park
- Crowley's Ridge State Park
- Devil's Den State Park
- Fort Smith National Historic Site
- Village Creek State Park
- Louisiana Purchase Historic Monument
- Hot Springs National Park
- Crater of Diamonds State Park
- Jenkins' Ferry Battlefield Historic Monument
- Arkansas Post National Monument
- Old Washington Historic State Park

LEGEND
- National park
- State park

Arkansas: Major Roads

Cities: Fayetteville, Jonesboro, Fort Smith, Russellville, Conway, West Memphis, Jacksonville, Little Rock, North Little Rock, Hot Springs, Pine Bluff, Texarkana

LEGEND
- State road
- U.S. Highway
- U.S. Interstate
- State capital
- City

R30 • Resources

Arkansas: Land Use

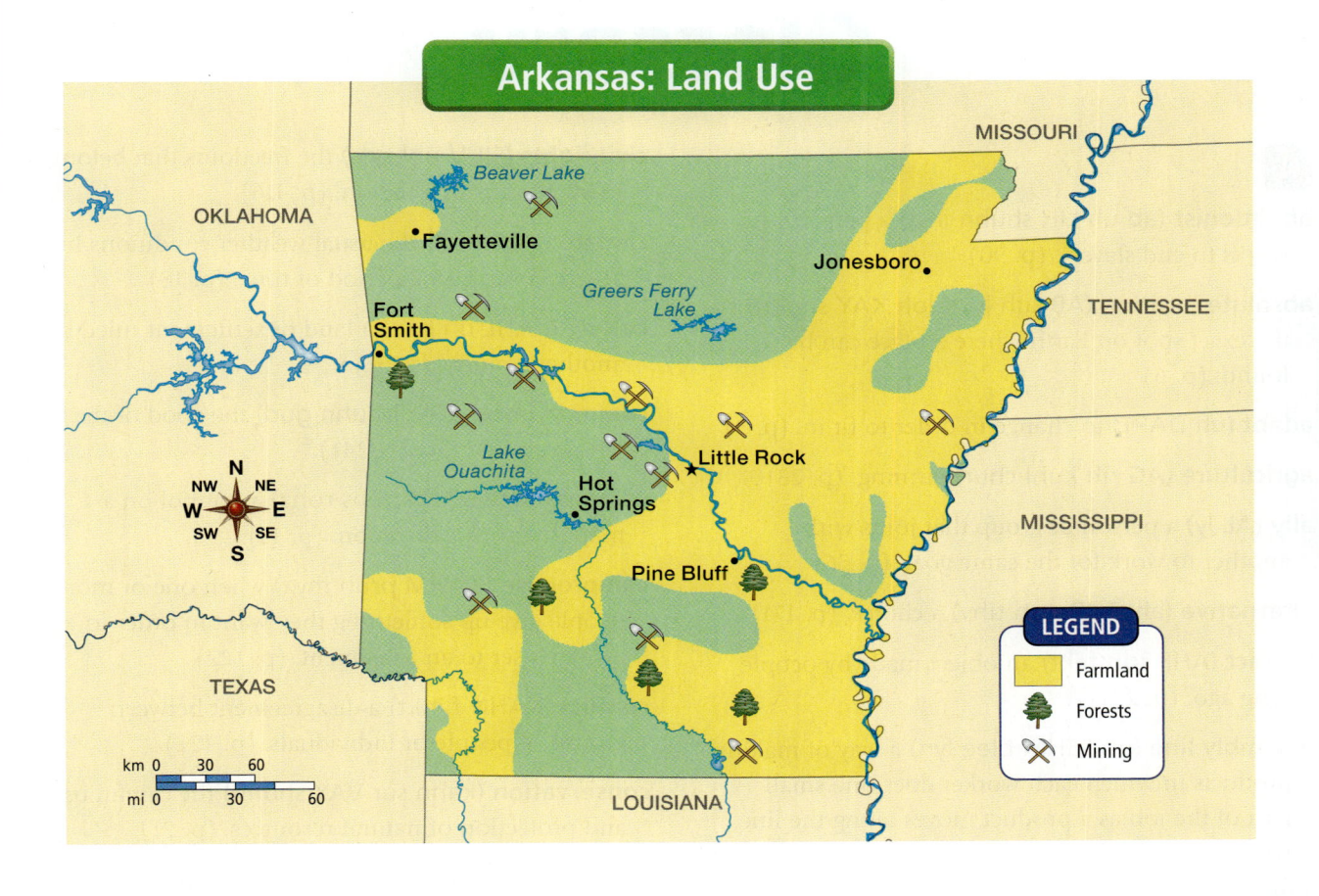

LEGEND
- Farmland
- Forests
- Mining

Arkansas: Population Density

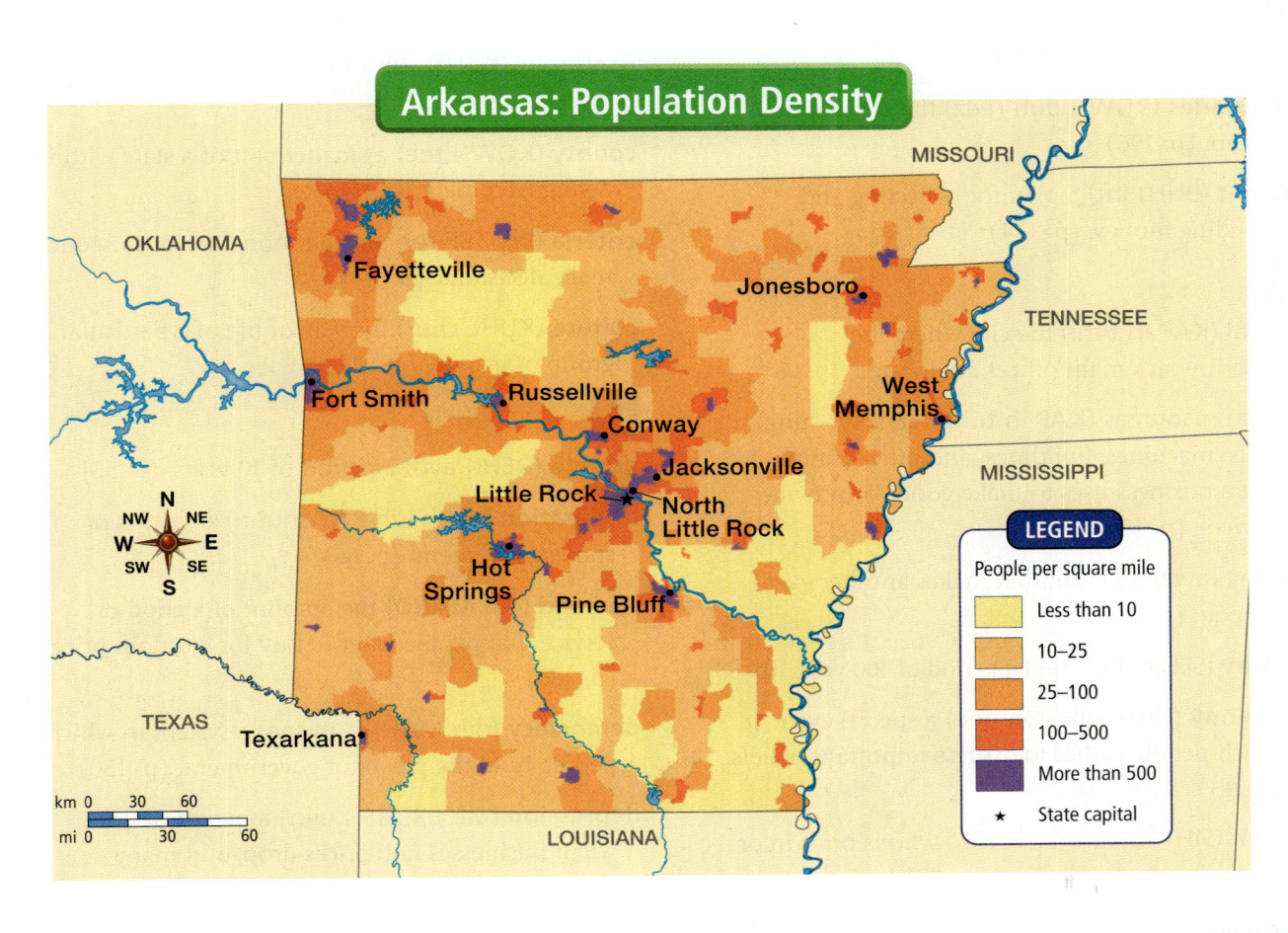

LEGEND

People per square mile
- Less than 10
- 10–25
- 25–100
- 100–500
- More than 500
- ★ State capital

R31

Glossary

A

abolitionist (ab uh LIH shuhn ihst) a person who works to end slavery. (p. 90)

absolute location (AB suh loot loh KAY shuhn) the exact spot on Earth where a place can be found. (p. 6)

adapt (uh DAPT) to change in order to fit in. (p. 9)

agriculture (AG rih kuhl chur) farming. (p. 28)

ally (AL ly) a person or group that joins with another to work for the same goal. (p. 56)

alternative (ahl TUR nuh tihv) a choice. (p. 174)

artifact (AHR tuh fakt) an object made by people long ago. (p. 27)

assembly line (uh SEHM blee lyn) a way of making products in which each worker does one small part of the job as a product moves along the line. (p. 232)

B

bill (bihl) a written idea for a law. (p. 142)

boundaries (BOWN duh reez) the edges of a region. (p. 196)

budget (BUHJ iht) a plan for collecting and spending money. (p. 144)

C

capital (KAP ih tuhl) the city where the government's main offices are located. (p. 78)

capital resources (KAP ih tuhl REE sawr suhz) the tools, machines, buildings, and other equipment that a business uses to make goods or provide services. (p. 161)

cause (kawz) an event that makes another event happen. (p. 76)

century (SEHN chuh ree) a period of 100 years. (p. 58)

ceremony (SEHR uh moh nee) a special event at which people gather to express important beliefs. (p. 213)

citizen (SIHT ih zuhn) a person who is born in or swears loyalty to a nation. (p. 97)

civil rights (SIHV uhl ryts) the freedoms that belong to all citizens of a nation. (p. 116)

climate (KLY miht) the usual weather conditions in an area over a long period of time. (p. 18)

colony (KAHL uh nee) a land or settlement ruled by another country. (p. 51)

common good (KAHM uhn gud) the good of the whole population. (p. 141)

compass rose (KUM puhs rohz) a symbol on a map that shows direction. (p. 11)

compromise (KAHM pruh myz) when one or more people give up something they want in order to move closer to an agreement. (p. 122)

conflict (KAHN flihkt) a disagreement between groups of people or individuals. (p. 122)

conservation (kahn sur VAY shuhn) the careful use and protection of natural resources. (p. 21)

constitution (kahn stih TOO shuhn) a plan for creating and running a government. (p. 225)

continent (KAHN tuh nuhnt) a large body of land. (p. 185)

county (KOWN tee) a smaller part of a state with its own government. (p. 143)

criteria (kry TEE ree ah) the sound reasons used to make decisions. (p. 174)

culture (KUHL chur) the way of life of a particular group of people. (p. 34)

D

decade (DEHK ayd) a period of 10 years. (p. 58)

declaration (dehk luh RAY shuhn) a written or spoken statement. (p. 66)

demand (dih MAND) the amount of a good or service that people want to buy for a certain price. (p. 169)

democracy (dih MAHK ruh see) a system in which people hold the power of government. (p. 150)

depression (dih PREHSH uhn) a period of time when businesses fail, prices drop, and many people lose jobs. (p. 104)

R32 • Resources

dictatorship (dihk TAY tur ship) a form of totalitarian government in which one ruler makes all the decisions for a nation. (p. 152)

discrimination (dih skrihm uh NAY shuhn) the unfair treatment of a group of people. (p. 103)

E

economy (ih KAHN uh mee) the way that people use an area's resources to produce goods and services. (p. 98)

effect (ih FEHKT) an event or action that is the result of a cause. (p. 76)

election (ih LEK shuhn) a process by which voters choose government leaders. (p. 67)

entrepreneur (ahn truh pruh NUR) a person who takes a risk to start a business. (p. 120)

environment (ehn VY ruhn muhnt) the water, land, air, and living things that surround us. (p. 4)

erosion (ih ROH zhuhn) the process of wearing away rock and soil. (p. 13)

ethnic group (EHTH nihk groop) people who share the same culture. (p. 207)

executive branch (ig ZEHK yuh tihv branch) the part of government that executes, or carries out, laws. (p. 136)

expedition (ehk spih DIHSH uhn) a journey for a specific reason. (p. 49)

explorer (ehk SPLOR ur) a person who travels to an unknown area for the purpose of discovery. (p. 49)

export (EHK sport) a product that is sent out of a country to be sold or traded. (p. 162)

F

fact (fakt) a statement that can be proven true. (p. 209)

finance (FI nans) the management of money. (p. 226)

G

geography (jee AHG ruh fee) the study of people, places, and environment. (p. 4)

glacier (GLAY shur) a huge mass of slowly moving ice. (p. 186)

goods (gudz) products that people exchange in trade or buy and sell for money. (p. 36)

governor (GUHV ur nur) the leader of a state or territory. (p. 78)

H

harvest (HAHR vihst) to gather crops that are ripe or ready to eat. (p. 35)

hemisphere (HEHM ih sfeer) one-half of Earth's surface. (p. 184)

heritage (HEHR ih tihj) traditions that people have passed down to each other for many years. (p. 124)

homestead (HOHM stehd) a piece of land given to someone to settle and farm. (p. 231)

human resources (HYOO muhn REE sawr suhz) the skills, knowledge, and hard work that people bring to their jobs. (p. 161)

hub (huhb) a major center of activity. (p. 206)

humid (HYOO mihd) having a lot of water vapor in the air. (p. 205)

I

immigrant (IHM ih gruhnt) a person who leaves one country to live in another country. (p. 102)

immigration (ihm ih GRAY shuhn) the movement of people from one nation to another. (p. 226)

import (IHM pawrt) a product brought in from another country. (p. 162)

indentured servant (ihn DEHN churd SUR vuhnt) a person who agreed to work for a number of years in exchange for a trip to the Americas. (p. 55)

independence (ihn dih PEHN duhns) freedom from rule by someone else. (p. 66)

industry (IHN duh stree) a group of businesses that provide certain goods and services. (p. 88)

inflation (ihn FLAY shuhn) a condition that occurs when a nation has more money than it has goods to buy. (p. 92)

interdependence (ihn tur dih PEHN duhns) a relationship in which people, states, or nations depend on each other. (p. 193)

irrigation (eer ih GAY shuhn) supplying land with water. (p. 213)

J

judicial branch (joo DIHSH uhl branch) the part of government that settles disagreements about laws and what they mean. (p. 136)

jury (JUR ee) a group of citizens who decide a case in court. (p. 141)

L

legend (LEHJ uhnd) a table or list that tells what the symbols on a map mean. (p. 11)

legislative branch (LEHJ ih slay tihv branch) the part of government that makes laws. (p. 136)

limited government (LIHM uh tuhd GUHV urn muhnt) one in which all citizens, including government officials, must obey the law. (p. 154)

line graph (lyn graf) a graph that shows change over time. (p. 38)

M

manufacturing (man yuh FAK chur ihng) making goods from other materials. (p. 98)

meridians (muh RIHD ee uhnz) lines of longitude that run north and south and measure distances east and west of the prime meridian. (p. 190)

migrant worker (MY gruhnt WUR kuhr) a person who moves from place to place doing seasonal work. (p. 240)

migration (my GRAY shuhn) a movement from one place to another. (p. 74)

mission (MIHSH uhn) a settlement for teaching religious beliefs to local people. (p. 214)

mound (mownd) a pile of soil, stones, and other material. (p. 28)

multicultural (muhl tee KUHL chuhr uhl) of many cultures. (p. 124)

N

natural resources (NACH ur uhl REE sawr suhz) things found in nature that people use. (p. 19)

nomad (NOH mad) a person who has no permanent home but moves from place to place in search of food and water. (p. 27)

O

opinion (uh PIHN yuhn) an idea or belief. (p. 209)

opportunity cost (awp ur TOO nih tee cawst) the thing that people give up in order to do what they want most. (p. 168)

P

parallels (PAIR uh lehlz) lines of latitude that run east and west and measure distances north and south of the equator. (p. 190)

plain (playn) a large area of flat land. (p. 14)

plateau (pla TOH) a high, mostly flat area of land. (p. 13)

point of view (point uhv vyoo) the way someone looks at a topic or situation. (p. 100)

pollution (puh LOO shuhn) anything that dirties the land, air, or water. (p. 20)

population (pahp yuh LAY shuhn) the number of people who live in an area. (p. 20)

political party (puh LIHT ih kuhl PAHR tee) a group made up of people who have similar ideas about government. (p. 137)

politician (pahl ih TIHSH uhn) a person who takes part in government or has an elected position. (p. 118)

port (pawrt) a place along a body of water where ships can dock. (p. 72)

primary (PRY mehr ee) an election in which party members choose a candidate to run for President. (p. 137)

primary source (PRY mehr ee sawrs) an account written by someone who witnessed an event. (p. 138)

productivity (proh duhk TIHV ih tee) the amount of goods and services produced by workers in a certain amount of time. (p. 169)

prosperity (prah SPEHR ih tee) wealth and success. (p. 194)

R

Reconstruction (ree kuhn STRUHK shuhn) the period following the Civil War when the Confederate states rejoined the Union. (p. 96)

region (REE jehn) an area that shares one or more features. (p. 5)

relative location (REHL uh tihv loh KAY shuhn) the location of one place in relation to other places. (p. 6)

report (rih PORT) writing that presents information that has been researched. (p. 32)

republic (rih PUHB lihk) a form of democratic government in which people choose leaders to represent them. (p. 152)

reservation (rehz ur VAY shuhn) land that is set aside by the government for American Indians. (p. 231)

revolution (reh vuh LOO shuhn) a fight to remove a government from power. (p. 66)

route (root) a way to go from one place to another. (p. 48)

rural (ROOR uhl) an area in the countryside with few people, houses, and businesses. (p. 240)

S

scale (skayl) a ruler that shows distances on a map. (p. 11)

scarcity (SKAYR sih tee) a situation that occurs when there are not enough resources to provide a product or service that people want. (p. 48)

secede (sih SEED) to separate from a country and form a new nation. (p. 91)

secondary source (SEHK uhn dair ee sawrs) an account written by someone who did not witness an event. (p. 138)

segregation (sehg rih GAY shun) the separation of people based on race. (p. 116)

sharecropping (SHAIR krahp ihng) a system in which a landowner provides a farmer with land, tools, seeds, and other equipment to grow crops. In exchange, the farmer gives the landowner a share of the harvest. (p. 98)

slavery (SLAY vuh ree) a cruel system in which people are bought and sold and forced to work without pay. (p. 55)

specialization (spehsh uh lih ZAY shuhn) a situation in which a business makes only a few goods or provides just one service. (p. 160)

squatter (SKWAH tur) a person who settles on land without permission. (p. 80)

suburb (SUHB urb) a community that develops near a city. (p. 106)

supply (suh PLY) the amount of a product that businesses will make for a certain price. (p. 169)

T

tariff (TAR ihf) a tax on trade goods. (p. 91)

tax (taks) money that people or businesses pay to support the government. (p. 65)

territory (TEHR ih tawr ee) a part of the United States that is not a state. (p. 74)

trade (trayd) to exchange things. (p. 27)

trading post (TRAYD ihng pohst) a place where people exchange goods. (p. 54)

transcontinental railroad (trans kahn tuh NEHN tuhl RAYL rohd) the first train system to link the East and the West of the United States. (p. 239)

transportation (trans pur TAY shuhn) the act of moving people and goods from place to place. (p. 37)

totalitarian (toh tah lih TAYR ee uhn) describes a government that uses force to control people's lives. (p. 152)

U

university (yoo nuh VUR sih tee) a school with several colleges. (p. 226)

unlimited government (uhn LIHM uh tuhd GUHV urn muhnt) a government in which rulers do not have to obey the laws. (p. 154)

V

volunteer (vahl uhn TEER) a person who provides a service without being paid for his or her time and effort. (p. 151)

W

wagon train (WAG uhn trayn) a line of wagons that carried settlers and everything they owned. (p. 238)

weathering (WEHTH ur ihng) the breakdown of rock caused by wind, water, and weather. (p. 216)

Index

Note: Page numbers followed by an "m" refer to a map. Page numbers in *italic* type refer to photographs, illustrations, or charts.

A

Abolitionists, 86, 90
Absolute location, 6
Acid rain, 188
Actors, 126
Adaptation, 9, 18–21, 27
Aerospace, 204
Africa, 185, 185m
African Americans
 civil rights movement, 116–117
 in Civil War, 92
 jobs of, 98, 112, 120, 121
 in Lower Southeast, 207
 migration to cities, 103, 226, 232
 in politics, 99, 118, 119, 145
 rights of, 86, 97, 99
 segregation and, 98, 114, 116–117, 125
 as sharecroppers, 98
 World War II and, 105
Africans
 culture, 89
 enslaved, 55, 89–90, 92, 203
 See also Slavery
Agriculture, 28, 120, 186
 of American Indians, 28, 34, 35, 36, 37, 202, 212, 213, 223
 of Archaic Indians, 27
 of Arkansas, ix, R31
 Arkansas Post and, 55, 56
 in Arkansas Territory, 80
 Columbian Exchange and, 52–53
 crops of, 19, 19m, 88–90
 Great Depression and, 104
 in the Mid-Atlantic states, 227
 Mississippi River and, 14, 16
 in the Mountain States, 241
 of the Pacific States, 240
 plantations, 88–90
 sharecropping, 98
 in the Southeast, 203–204, 205
 of the Upper Southeast, 206
 in West Gulf Coastal Plain, 15
 World War II and, 105
Air conditioning, 9
Air-traffic control system, 194
Air travel, 7, 192, 194, 204
Alabama, 204, 207
Alaska, 186, 236, 239, 240
Aleut, 236
Alluvial, 14
Ally, 47, 56
Alps Mountains, 185m, 189, R21m
Alternative energy sources, *188*, 189
Amazon River, 185m, 189, R20m
Amendments to the U.S. Constitution
 Bill of Rights, 69, 135, 150
 Thirteenth, 96
 Fourteenth, 96
 Fifteenth, 96
 Nineteenth, 103
American Indians, 47
 Archaic Indians, 27
 of Arkansas, 35m
 Caddo, 34, 35, 35m
 Cherokee, 202
 Chickasaw, 56
 Choctaw, 202
 civil rights of, 117
 Columbian Exchange and, 52–53
 Comanche, 212
 conflict between in Arkansas Territory, 79
 conflict over land, 224, 229, 238
 Creek, 202
 Eastern Woodland Indians, 202
 European diseases and, 56
 European settlers and, 203, 229
 explorers and, 49, 50
 French and Indian War and, 56, 229
 Haudenosaunee, 222
 Hidatsa, 242
 Hohokam, 212
 Hopi, 212, 213
 horses and, 229
 Indian Removal Act, 81
 Mandan, 242
 migration into Arkansas, 74
 Mississippian Indians, 29
 mound builders, 24, 28–29, 35, 228
 move to reservations, 81, 231, 238
 of the Northeast, 223m
 Osage, 35m, 36
 Paleoindians, 27
 Plains Indians, 229
 Proclamation of 1763 and, 70
 Pueblo, 212, 213, 215
 Quapaw, 35m, 36, 54
 of the Southeast, 202
 of the Southwest, 212–213
 Spanish settlers and, 214–215
 trade at Arkansas Post, 54, *55*
 trade with Europeans, 224
 Trail of Tears and, 81
 Tunica, 35m, 37
 use of natural resources, 223
 of the West, 236
 Woodland Indians, 28
American Red Cross, 104
American Revolution, 66–67, 224
Andes Mountains, 185m, 189, R20m
Angelou, Maya, *124*, 125, R13
Annual Dermott Crawfish Festival, 195
Antarctica, 185, 185m
Anthony, Steven M., 113, R13
Appalachian Mountains, 70, 71m, 186, 186m
Apple blossom, x
Archaeologists, 27, 30–31
Archaic Indians, 27, 28
Arctic Wildlife Refuge, 240
Arizona, 212, 214, 216
Arizona-Sonora Desert Museum, 217
Arkansas, 10m, 28, 206, 221, R14, R28m–R31m
 after World War II, 106
 agriculture of, ix, 19m, R31m
 arts and, 124–126, 128
 athletes of, 127
 Bull Shoals Dam, *8*
 capital, ix, 63, 1 R28m
 capitol, xix
 Civil War and, 91–93
 climate of, 18, 205
 constitution of, 140–142
 counties of, R9–R12, R28m
 culture of, 25, 124–127, 195
 early people in, 27–29
 economy of, ix, 98, 160–170
 educators and doctors of, 121
 entrepreneurs, 120, 161
 European settlement of, 54–55
 explorers in, 49, 50
 first constitution of, 82–83
 first people in, 26–29
 flag of, 146, *147*
 forest of, 204
 governors of, R6–R8
 in Great Depression, 104
 immigrants in, 102
 Indians of, 34–37, 35m
 industry in, 160–161, 170, 171
 jobs of citizens of, 168, 170, 171
 land area, ix
 landforms of, 206, R29m
 Little Rock, 6, 82, 117, 145
 mining in, 98, 105, 161, 206, R31m
 motto of, ix, 150
 Mount Magazine, 146
 movement into, 7
 naming of, 54
 national and state parks of, 15, 21, 30–31, 146, R30m
 natural resources of, 19, 19m, R31
 nickname of, ix, 170
 political leaders of, 118–119
 population, ix, *83*, 102, R31m
 postal abbreviation, ix
 Reconstruction in, 97
 regions of, 12–15, 13m, 186
 seal of, ix
 second constitution of, 97
 segregation and, *116*
 slavery in, 83, 89
 songs of, ix
 state government of, 140–142
 statehood, 63, 81
 symbols of, x, 146–147
 tourism in, 170
 trade of, 158, 162–163
 transportation in, R30m
 and the world, 145
 World War I and, 103
 World War II and, 105
 See also Arkansas Post; Arkansas Territory
Arkansas Blues and Heritage Festival, 195
Arkansas Indians, 25

R36 • Resources

Arkansas Post, 46, 54
American Revolution and, 67
as capital of Arkansas Territory, 78
flooding of, 57, 82
founding of, 54–55
French soldiers at, 56
move to Écores Rouges, 56, 57
settlement of, 59
Spanish control of, 57
Arkansas River, 13, 14, 36, 57, 74, 119
Arkansas River Valley, 12, 13, 13m
Arkansas Road, 80
Arkansas Territory, 74m
conflicts over lands in, 81
Fort Smith, 79
government of, 78
population of, 74, 78, 82, *83*
settlement of, 74–75, 79–80
Washington (town), 80
Armstrong, Neil, 106, R13
Art, *29, 33,* 36, 115, 129, 213
Art Activities, 131, 157, 219, 245
Articles of Confederation, 68, 134
Artifacts, 24, 27, *30,* 30–31, *31,* 80, 237
Ashmore, Henry Scott, 129
Asia, 185, 185m
Asian Americans, 239
Assembly line, 170, 221, 232
Athletes, 127
Atlas, R18–R31
Australia, 185, 185m
Automobile factory, 232

B

Banking, 164–167, 194, 239
Barracks, 56
Basin, R18
Bates, Daisy, 117, R13
Bates, Lucious, 117, R13
Battles
of Civil War in Arkansas, 92
of Lexington and Concord, 66
of Yorktown, 67
Bauxite, 105
Bay, R16–R17
Beals, Melba Pattiillo, 147
Beliefs, 5, 34
Big Bend National Park, 216
Big Ideas, 1, 44, 112, 180
Bill, 142
Bill of Rights, xxiii, 69, 135, 141, 150, *150*
Biography, 128–129, R13–R15
Blanchard Springs Caverns, 13
Blizzards, 187
Bolton, S. Charles, 1
Bonaparte, Napoleon, 73, R13
Boone, Daniel, *70*
Boone's Trace, *70*
Borders, 196–197
Boston, Massachusetts, 226
Boston Mountains, 13, R29m
Boston Tea Party, 65
Boundaries, 196–197
Bradley County Pink Tomato Festival, 195
Bralei Homes, 106
Brine, 35
Britain
colonies of, 56, 64–65, 65m, 203, 224, 224m

French and Indian War, 47, 56, 65, 229
Proclamation of 1763 and, 70
War of Independence and, 66–67
Budget, 132, 144
Buffalo, 229, 231
Bumpers, Dale, R4, R8
Bush, George W., 153, R13

C

Caddo, 34, 35, 35m
Cahokia Mounds, *228*
Cajuns, 207
California, 214, 237, 238, 239
Canada, 182, 214
Candidates, 137, 151, 152
Canoes, 25, 27, 28, 35, 36, 37
Canyon, R16, *R16*
Cape, R16, *R17*
Capital (city)
of Arkansas, ix, 63
of Arkansas Territory, 78
of the United States, *136,* 227
Capital resources, 158, 161
Capitol, xix, *132, 136, 140*
Caraway, Hattie Wyatt, 118, R13
Cardinal Directions, 10m, 11, 23m
Caring, R4, R5
Cars, 7, 19, 20
Cascade Mountains, 186
Cash, Johnny, 126, R13
Cause, 76–77
Caves, 13
Central Valley, California, 237
Ceremony, 213
Character traits, R4–R5
Chart Activities, 95
Checking accounts, 167
Checks and balances, 136
Chemicals, 188
Cherokee, 202
Chickasaw, 56, 67
China, 102
Chinese immigrant, 238, 239
Choctaw, 202
Choices, 168–169, 172–173
Christianity, 214–215
Churches, 226
Cisterna, Italy, 145
Cities. *See* Towns and cities
Citizens
of democracies, 155
rights and responsibilities of, 97, 133, 137, 150–153
Citizenship Activities, 109
Citizenship Skills
make a decision, 174–175
resolve conflicts, 122–123
symbols of Arkansas, 148–149
understand point of view, 100–101
City council, 143
City government, 143
City manager, 143
Civic virtue, R4, R5
Civilian Conservation Corps, 104
Civil rights, 116–117, 125, 148
Civil Rights Act, 117
Civil War, 91–93, 94–95
Clark, William, 73, 230, 242–243, R13
Climate
of Arkansas, 18

in the Central Valley, 237
changes in, 186, 188
geography and, 187
of Lower Southeast, 207
of Pacific States, 239
people's adaptation to, 27
of the Southeast, 205
Climatic regions, 186m
Clinton, Hillary, 119, R13
Clinton, William Jefferson (Bill), 112, 119, 125, R8, R13
Cloar, Carroll, 115, 125, R13
Closed borders, 196
Clothing, 18
Coal, 19, 105, 204
Coast, R18
Coastal plains, 186, 205, R16, *R17*
Colonial Williamsburg, 206
Colonies, 46, 71m, 224m
of the British, 56, 64–67, 65m, 203, 224, 224m
of the French, 51
French and Indian War in, 56
Louisiana, 54–57
Proclamation of 1763 and, 70
Colorado, 240
Colorado River, 186, 216
Columbian Exchange, 52–53
Columbus, Christopher, 44, 48, 52–53, R13
Comanche, 212
Common good, 140, 141
Communication systems, 107, 192, 193, 194
Communities, 5, 8, 35, 36
Company of the West, 55
Compass rose, 10, 11
Computers, 107
Concord, Battle of, 66
Confederate States of America (Confederacy), 91m, 91–95
Conflict, 122–123
Congress, 96–97, 117, 136, 137
Connecticut, 226
Conservation, 3, 21, 217
Constitution, 68
Constitutional Convention, 68, *135*
Constitution Day, xxii–xxiii
Constitution of Arkansas
changes to, 97, 140
Declaration of Rights and, 141
first, 82–83, 140
government and, 142
Constitution of the United States, xxii–xxiii, *xxiii,* 68, *134*
Bill of Rights and, 69, 135, 141, 150
government established by, 134–137
See also Amendments to the U.S. Constitution
Consumers, 172–173
Continental Army, 67
Continents, 182, 185, 185m
Cotnam, Florence Lee Brown, 45, 103, R13
Cotton, 88–90, *204,* 204, 206
Countries, R18m–R19m, 185
County, 143, R9–R12, R28m
County government, 143
County judge, 143
Courage, R4, R5
Courts, 136, 142, 143

Crater of Diamonds State Park

Crater of Diamonds State Park, 15, R30m
Creek, 202
Creoles, 207
Crops, 19, 19m
Crowley's Ridge, 12, 13m, 14, R30m
Cuban Americans, 207
Culture, 25, 34
   of Africans, 89
   of American Indians, 213
   American Indians, 223
   of the Appalachians, 206
   of Arkansas, 124–127
   of Arkansas's Indians, 34–37
   of early peoples of Arkansas, 26–29
   of Lower Southeast, 207
   of Polynesians, 236
   Spanish influence on, 215
   of the Tlingit, 237
   tourism and, 170
   of United States, 194–195
Current Events Projects
   Celebrate Arkansas's diversity, 111
   Countries of four hemispheres, 247
   Create an equality display, 179
   Design a brochure, 43
Customs. *See* Traditions

D

Dams, 8, 119, 213, 216
Debt, 98
Decade, 58
Decision-making model, 174–175
Declaration, 62, 66
Declaration of Independence, 62, 66
Declaration of Rights, 141
Degrees, 6
Delaware, 227
Delegates, 66, *68*, 135
Delta, R16
Demand, 169
Democracy, 148, 150–153, 155
Democratic Party, 137
Deposit, 166–167
Depression, 87
Deserts, 186, R16
De Soto, Hernando, 49, 50m, R13
De Tonti, Henri, 46, 54, 59, R13
Detroit, Michigan, 232
Diamonds, *x*, 15, 161, 206
Dictatorship, 152
Disabled people, 117
Discrimination, 103
Diseases, 56
Districts, 142
Diversity, 107
Divisibility, 163
Doctors, 121
Douglass, Frederick, 86, 90, R13
Drama Activities, 85
Drawing Activities, 53
Drip irrigation, 217
Drought, 104
Duhon, Chris, 209
Durability, 163
Durango, Colorado, 241
Dutch, 224

E

Early people
   in Arkansas, 27–29, 30–31
   in the Midwest, 228
   in the Northeast, 222–223
   in the Southeast, 202
   in the Southwest, 210–211
Earning, 169
Earth
   continents of, 182, 185, 185m, R20m–R21m
   countries of, R18m–R19m
   divisions of land of, 182, 184, R18m–R19m, R20m–R21m
   land of, 184–189
Earthquakes, 75
Eastern Hemisphere, 184
Eastern Woodland Indians, 202
Ebony, 120
Eckford, Elizabeth, 147
Economic decision-making, 174–175
Economics
   making choices, 172–173
   of North and South, 94–95
Economy
   of Arkansas, ix, 98
   future of, 171
   Great Depression and, 87, 104
   human resources and jobs, 167–170
   industry and, 160–161
   money and banks, 164–167
   of the Southeast, 204
   supply and demand, 168–170
   trade and, 162–163
   wants and needs, 168–169
Écores Rouge, 56, 57
Ecosystems, 188
Education, 98, 116–117, 119
Educators, 121
Effect, 76–77
Eisenhower, Dwight, 117, R13
Elections, 137
   in 2000 and 2002, 153
   in Arkansas, 142
   candidates, 137, 151, 152
   citizens' responsibilities in, 133, 151, 152–153
   constitution of Arkansas and, 82–83
   general, 137
   of Abraham Lincoln, 91
   of Washington, 67
   primary, 137
Elevation, 187, 205
E-mail, 107
Emancipation, 92
Emancipation Proclamation, 92
Employment, 161, 169, 170–171, *204*, 225–227, 232–233, 239–241
Energy sources, 19, *188*, 189, 204
England. *See* Britain
Enslaved people, 55, 89–90, 92, 203
Entertainers, 126
Entrepreneurs, 115, 120, 161, 225
Environment, 4
   adaptation to, 9, 18, 27
   changes in, 188
   movement and, 7
   peoples' relationships with, 8–9, 18–21
   protection of, 3, 21, 189

Equality, 116–117, 119, 125, 192
Equator, 6, 184, 187, 190, 205
Erosion, 13, 14, 216
Ethnic groups, 200, 207
Europe, 52–53, 87, 102, 185, 185m
   explorers from, 48–51
   immigrants from, 226
   See also Britain; France; Spain
Executive branch, 136, 142
Expedition, 46, 49, 73, 230, 242m–243m
Explorers, 49
   from France, 50–51
   Lewis and Clark, 73, 230, 242m–243m, 242–243
   routes of, 50m
   from Spain, 48–49
Exports, 158, 162, 163

F

Factories, 90
Facts, 210–211
Fairness, R5
Farming. *See* Agriculture
Fault, R16
Federal government
   branches of, 136
   communication and transportation systems and, 192–194
   Constitution and, 134–137
   taxes and, 144
Fertile soil, 19
Festivals, 170, 195, 215, 217
Finance, 226, 239
Fire protection, 143, 144
Fires, 231
First Continental Congress, 66
Flag
   of Arkansas, 146, 147
   of the United States, 148, 149
Flanagin, Harris, 93, R13
Flatboats, *78*
Floods
   Arkansas Post and, 57, 82
   hurricanes and, 205
   of Mississippi River, 17, 104
Florida, 203, 204, 205, 207, 214
Flour mills, 233
Folk culture, 206
Food, 9, 27–29, 35–37, 49, 52–53, *52–53*, 80, 88–89, 92, 103–105, 162, 168, 170, 171, 174, 194, *202*, 202–204, 206, 212–213, 215, 223, 227, 233, 237, 240
Ford, Henry, 232
Forests, *12*, 186, 188
   in Arkansas, 13, 15, R31
   of the Southeast, 204
   of the Upper Southeast, 206
Fort Clatsop, 243
Fort Smith, 79, 81, R28m–R31m
Fort Sumter, 91
Fossil fuels, 188
Founding documents, xxii–xxiii, 66, *66*, 68–69, *134*, 134–137, 138, 141, 150, *150*, 157
Founding fathers, 66–69, *66–69*, 71, 135, 138, 150, 152
Four Corners, *196*
France
   control of Louisiana, 54–57, 73
   explorers from, 50m, 50–51

R38 • Resources

French and Indian War, 47, 56, 65, 229
  sale of Louisiana Territory, 73, 230
  trade of, 47, 224
Franklin, Benjamin, 68, *135*, R13
Freedoms
  of African Americans, 97, 99, 116–117
  Bill of Rights and, 69, 135, 141, 150
  common good and, 141
  Declaration of Rights and, 141
  of democratic governments, 148
  French and Indian War, 47, 56, 65, 229
Fulbright, William, 118, R13
Fulbright Exchange Program, 118
Fulton, William, 63, 82, R6, R13
Fur trade, 36, 37, 50, 54, *55*, 224

G

Ganges River, 185m, 189, R21m
Gateway Arch, 232
General Assembly, 132, 142
General elections, 137
Geographers, 4, 5, 9, 184, 185
Geographic regions, 186m
Geographic terms, R16–R17
Geography, 2, 4
  borders and boundaries, 196–197
  divisions of Earth's land, 184–186
  Gulf Coast hurricanes, 208–209
  location, 6
  movement, 7
  place, 5
  regions, 5, 185
  relationships within places, 8–9
  themes of, 4–9
  weather and climate and, 187
George, Kerry, 117, R14
Georgia, 204, 207
Gibbs, Mifflin Wistar, 118, R14
G. I. Bill, 106
Glacier, R16
Global warming, 188, 189
Globes, *4*, 6, 10–11
Glossary, R32–R35
Gold and silver, 49, 238
Gold rush, 238
Goods
  economic choices about, 172–173
  exploration for trade routes and, 48–49
  importing and exporting of, 162–163
  industry and, 88
  inflation and, 92
  movement of, 7
  production of, 160
  supply and demand and, 168–170
  trade of, 36, 54
Gourds, 27
Government, 99
  in Arkansas, 83, 142–144
  branches of, 132, 136, 142
  of colonies, 64
  election of officials, 133
  employees of, 204
  federal, 134–137, 144, 192–194
  forms of, 154–155
  of the Haudenosaunee, 222
  jobs of citizens of, 141
  leaders of, 118–119
  of Lenni Lenape, 223
  limited, 154, 155
  local, 135, 143
  money and, 164–167
  paying for, 144
  rights and responsibilities to, 150–153
  state, 135, 140–142, 144
  of territories, 78
  totalitarian, 152
  unlimited, 154
Governors, 63, 78, 142, R6–R8
Graceland, Tennessee, 206
Grand Canyon, 186, 216
Grand Ole Opry, 206
Graph and Chart Skills
  line graph, 38–39
  make a timeline, 58–59
Graphic organizers, 4, 12, 18, 26, 34, 48, 54, 64, 72, 78, 88, 96, 102, 116, 124, 134, 140, 150, 160, 168, 184, 202, 212, 222, 226, 228, 236
Graphs, line, 38–39
Great Britain. *See* Britain
Great Depression, 87, 104
Great Lakes region, 186, 228, 230
Great Migration, 103, 103m, 226
Great Plains, 229, 231, 242
Green, Al, 128
Green, Ernest, 147
Grey, William H., R14
Grisham, John, 125, R14
Gulf, R16

H

Habitats, 188
Hamilton, Alexander, *135*
Hanamaki, Japan, 145
Hancock, John, 66, R14
Hands On Activities, 23, 41, 61, 85, 109, 131, 157, 177, 199, 219, 245
Harvard University, 220, 226
Harvest, 35
Haudenosaunee, 222
Hawaii, 186, 236, 239, 240
Healthcare industry, 226, 233, 241
Healthy Arkansas program, 113
Hemispheres, 182, 184, R22m–R23m
Henry, Natalie Smith, 129
Heritage, 115, 124, 194–195. *See also* Culture
Hidatsa, 242
Highlands, 12, R16
  Arkansas River Valley, 13, 13m
  Ouachita Mountains, 13m, 14
  Ozark Mountains, 13, 13m
High-tech industry, 171, 226, 233, 239
Highways, *7*, 106, 193, 193m
Hills, 12, 14, 186, R16
Himalayan Mountains, 185m, 189, R21m
Historical Maps, 10, 35m, 50m, 52m–53m, 65m, 71m, 74m, 91m, 103m, 214m, 223m, 224m, 230m, 238m, 242m–243m
Hocker, Willie Kavanaugh, 147
Hohokam, 212
¡Hola! Arkansas, 120
Homestead, 220, 231
Homestead Act, 231
Honesty, R4
Honeybee, *x*
Hopi, 212, 213
Hopkins, Francis, 149
Horses, 206, 229
Hot Springs National Park, 14, R30m
House of Representatives, 137, 142
Housing
  of Caddo, *34*, 35
  of enslaved people, 89
  of Haudenosaunee, *222*
  on homesteads, 220, 231
  of Miwoks and Yokuts, 237
  of Osage, 36
  of the Plains Indians, 229
  of Quapaw, 36
  of the Tlingit, 237
  of Tunica, 37
  of Woodland Indians, 228
  suburbs, 106
Hub, 200, 206, 232
Huckabee, Mike, 113, 145, 153, R8, R14
Hudson River, 227
Hudson River valley, 224
Human capital. *See* Human resources
Human characteristics, 5, 188–189, 192–195, 206–207, 216–217, 226–227, 232–233, 239–241
Human regions, 5
Human resources, 159, 161, 168, 169
Human settlement patterns. *See* Settlements
Humidity, 205
Hunter-gatherers, 27, 28, 35, 37, 223, 237
Hunting
  of Arkansas's Indians, 34, 35, 36
  on horseback, 52
  of Micmac, 223
  of Miwoks and Yokuts, 237
  of Osage, 36
  of Tunica, 37
Hurricanes, 187, 205, 208–209

I

Ice Age, 26
Idaho, 240
Immigrants and immigration, 87, 102, 107, 226
  from Asia, 239
  in the Midwest, 230
Imports, 162, 163
Inauguration, 125
Incentives for entreprenuership, 120
Income taxes, 144
Indentured servants, 55, 56
Independence, 66
Indian Removal Act, 81
Indian Territory, 79, 81
Individual rights, 141
Industry, 88
  in Arkansas after Civil War, 98
  in Arkansas now, 160–161
  cotton growing, 88
  Great Migration and, 103
  immigration and, 102
  jobs in, 170
  in the Midwest, 232, 233
  in the Mountain States, 240
  in the Northeast, 225–226
  in the Pacific States, 227, 239, 240

Inflation

Inflation
    in the Southeast, 204
    resources and, 161
    World War II and, 105
Inflation, 92
Information sharing, 107, 192–194
Interdependence, 183, 193
Interest, 166
Intermediate Directions, 10m, 11, 23m
Internet, 107, 192, 194
Interstate Highway System, 193, 193m
Inuit, 236
Inventions, 224
Iroquois, 228
Irrigation, 212, 213, 217
Island, R16
Isthmus, R17

J

Jackson, Andrew, 81
Jackson, Arkansas, 80
Jackson, Wyoming, 241
Jamestown, 203
Jefferson, Thomas, 66, 73, 147, 206, 230, 242, R14
Jobs. *See* Employment
Job training, 169
Johnson, Andrew, 96, R14
Johnson, John H., 112, 120, R14
Jolliet, Louis, 50, 50m, R14
Jones, Jerry, 127, R14
Jordan, Lena Lowe, R4
Judges, 118, 136, 142, 143
Judicial branch, 136, 142
Jump, Jive and Jamfest, 195
Jury, 141, 151
Justice (character trait), 192
Justices, 136, 142, 143

K

Kansas, 214
Karlmark, Gloria Ray, 147
Katrina (hurricane), 208–209
Kentucky, 206
Keohane, Nannerl, 121, R14
King, Martin Luther, Jr., 117, R14
Kitanemuk, 236
Knowledge, 169
Kountz, Samuel Lee, 121, R14

L

Labor, 168
Lakes, 5, 7, *R16*
Land
    area of Arkansas, ix
    conservation of, 21
    drought and, 104, 216–217
    erosion, 13, 14
    people's affect on, 20, 188, 189
Land bridge, 26, 236
Landforms, 5
    of Arkansas, 206
    movement and, 7
    regions and, 12
    of the Southwest, 212, 216
    weathering of, 201

Language, 5, 34, 207, 215, 223m
Lanier, Carlotta Walls, 147
La Salle, René-Robert Cavelier, Sieur de, 44, 50m, 51, 54, 59, R14
Latitude lines, 6, 190, 205
Law, John, 54–55, R14
Laws
    citizenship and, 151
    federal, 136
    in limited and unlimited governments, 154–155
    local, 143
    state, 132, 142
    voting on, 152
Lazarus, Emma, 148
Legend of maps, 10, 11
Legislative branch, 132, 136, 142
Lenni Lenape, 223
Levees, 17
Lewis, Meriwether, 73, 230, 242–243, R14
Lewis and Clark Expedition, 73, 230, 242m–243m, 242–243
Lexington, Battle of, 66
Liberty, 192
Liberty Bell, 147, 149
Library activities, 43, 111, 179, 247
Life skills, R4–R5
Lincoln, Abraham, 91, 92, 96, R14
Line graph, 38
Little Rock, Arkansas, 125, R28m, R29m, R30m
    as capital of Arkansas, ix, 63, 82, 132
    first female mayor of, 145
    location of, 6
    migration to, 80
    segregation in, 114, *116*, 117
    suburbs of, 106
Little Rock Nine, 114, *116*, 117, 147
Little Rock Nine Monument, 147
Loans, 166
Loblolly pine, x
Local government, 135, 143
Location, 6, 187
Loess, 14
Long Beach, California, 227
Longhouses, 36, *222*, 223
Longitude lines, 6, 190
Los Angeles, California, 227
Louisiana, 51, 207
    French control of, 54–57, 73
    growth and change in, 56
    hurricanes in, 208–209
    migration of Quapaw to, 81
    Spanish control of, 57, 73
    statehood, 74
    trade in, 54–55
Louisiana Purchase, 73–74, 74m, 77, 230, 242
Louisiana Territory, 73–74, 230, 230m, 242, 242m–243m
Lowell, Francis Cabot, 225
Lower Southeast, 207
Lowlands, 12, 13m, R17
    Crowley's Ridge, 13m, 14
    Mississippi Alluvial Plain, 13m, 14
    West Gulf Coastal Plain, 13m, 15
Lozano-Yancy, Maura, 115, 120, R14
Lumber industry, 98, 160, 161, 233

M

Madison, James, 68, *135*, R14
Magazine Mountain, 13, R29m
Magnolia Blossom Festival, 195
Maine, 226
Mammoth Cave, 206
Mammoth Springs, 13
Mandan, 242
Manhattan, 224
Manufacturing, 98, 170, 221
    in the Midwest, 232, 233
    in the Southeast, 204
Map activities, 23
Map and Globe Skills
    review map skills, 10–11
    use a special purpose map, 234–235
    use latitude and longitude, 190–191
Map legends, 10–11
Map scales, 10–11
Maps
    atlas, R18–R31
    list of, xxi
Marquette, Father Jacques, 50, 50m, R14
Maryland, 227
Massachusetts, 225
Massie, Samuel, 121, R14
Mauna Loa, 240
Mayor, 143
McClellan, John, *118*, 119, R14
Medical advances, 171
Memphis, Tennessee, 206
Mena, Ukraine, 145
Meridians, 6, 190
Mexican War, 215
Mexico, 182, 214, 215
Miami, 228
Micmac, 223
Mid-Atlantic States, 227
Midwest, 185, 186, 186m, 187, 234m
    early peoples of, 228
    settlement of, 230
Migrant workers, 240
Migration, 7
    of African Americans, 103, 226, 232
    of American Indians, 81, 231
    into Arkansas, 74, 83
Military, 135
Mill City Museum, 233
Miller, James, 78, 79, R6, R14
Minerals, 161
Mining, R31
    in Arkansas, 206
    of diamonds, 161
    environment and, 20
    in the Mountain States, 241
    in Reconstruction, 98
    in the Southeast, 204
    World War II and, 105
Minneapolis, Minnesota, 233
Minnesota, 230, 233
Missionaries, 50, 201
Missions, 201, 214–215
Mississippi, 207
Mississippi Alluvial Plain, 12, 13m, 14
Mississippian Indians, 24, 29, 30–31, *33*
Mississippi Delta, 205, 207

R40 • Resources

Mississippi River, 14, 16–17, 62, 81, 186
　cities on, 233
　exploration of, 49, 50–51
　flooding of, 104
　New Madrid Earthquakes and, *75*
　settlements along, 36, 54–57, 72, 88
　trade and travel on, 73
Mississippi River Valley, 54–56, 64, 72
Missouri River, 191m, 214m, 230m, 232, 234m, 238m, 242, 242m–243m, R23m–R27m
Missouri Territory, 74, 74m
Miwok, 236, 237
Mockingbird, *x*
Money, 135, 164–167, 194
　characteristics of, 163
Montana, 240
Monticello, 206
Mormons, 238
Mothershed-Wair, Thelma, 147
Motto, ix, 150
Mound builders, 24, 28–29, 35, 228
Mounds, 24, 28, 29, 31, 35, 228
Mountains, 5, 7, 12, 186, *R16*
Mountain States, 240
Mount Magazine, 146
Mount Magazine International Butterfly Festival, 195
Mount Magazine State Park, 146
Mount Rainier, *239*
Mount Vernon, 206
Movement, 7, 44
Multicultural state, 124
Murphy, Isaac, 91, 97, R6, R14
Music, 126, 128, 195, 206, 207
Musical instruments, 36

N

Nashville, Tennessee, 206
National government. *See* Federal government
National parks, 14, 21, 240, 241, R30m
National Road, 80
National symbols, 148–149
Natural boundaries, 196–197
Natural gas, 19
Natural resources, 123, 188
　American Indians and, 223, 236
　of Arkansas, 19, 19m, R31
　conservation of, 3, 20–21, 189
　industry and, 161
　of the Midwest, 234m
　renewable and nonrenewable, 19, 161
　scarcity of, 161
New England, 226
New Hampshire, 226
New Jersey, 227
New Madrid Earthquakes, 75
New Mexico, 212–217
New Orleans, Louisiana, 55, 62, 72, 73
New Spain, 214
New York, 227
New York City, New York, 227
Nickname, ix, 170
Nile River, 185m, 189, R21m
Nomads, 229
Nonrenewable resources, 19, 161
North America, 44, 182, 185, 185m
North Carolina, 204, 206

Northeast, 185, 186, 186m, 187, 220
　colonies of, 224, 224m
　first peoples in, 222–223
　Mid-Atlantic States, 227
　New England, 226
Northern Hemisphere, 184
Northwest Territory, 230, 230m

O

Oceans, 187, R17
Ohio region, 229
Ohio River, 71m, 72, 191m, 197m, 230m, 234m, R25m, R27m
Ohio River Valley, 72
Oil, 19, 20, 162, 204
Oklahoma, 212–217
Old Washington. *See* Washington, Arkansas
Olympic National Park, 240
Open borders, 196
Opinion, 210–211
Opportunity costs, 159, 168–169, 172
Oregon, 239
Oregon Trail, 221, 238m
Osage, 34, 35m, 36, 79
Ottawa, 228, 229
Ouachita Mountains, 12, 13m, 14, R29m
Ouachita River, 14
Overfishing, 188
Ozark Folk Center, 170
Ozark highlands, 205
Ozark Mountains, 12, 13, 13m
Ozone depletion, 188–189

P

Pacific states, 239
Painters, 125
Paleoindians, 27
Parallels, 6, 190
Paris, Treaty of, 67
Park Hill, 106
Parkin Archaeological State Park, 30–31
Participation, 151–153
Patriotism, R5
Pea Ridge battle, 92
Pearl Harbor, 105
Penninsula, R17
Pennsylvania, 225, 227
People, 186
　adaptation to environment, 9, 18, 27, 188
　movement of, 7, 8, 20, 26, 27, 44, 74, 81, 103, 103m
　relationship with environment, 8–9, 18–21, 188, 189
Petition, 151
Petroleum, 162
Phone systems, 192, 194
Physical characteristics
　of highlands, 12
　of lowlands, 12
　movement and, 7
　of regions in the United States, 5, 185, 186
Physical features. *See* Physical characteristics

Physical maps
　of Arkansas, R29m
　of the United States, R26m–R27m
　of Western hemisphere, R23m
　of the world, R20m–R21m
Physical regions, 5
Pilgrims, 64, 224
Pioneers, 221
Pippin, Scottie, 127, R15
Place, 5
Plains, 2, 14, 186, R17
Plains Indians, 229
Plantations, 89, 90, 203
Plateaus, 13, 186, R17
Pledge of Allegiance, 149, R2–R3
Points of view, 82, 100
Polar ice caps, 188
Political maps, 10
　of Arkansas, R28m
　of the United States, R24m–R25m
　of Western hemisphere, R22m
　of the world, R18m–R19m
Political party, 137
Politicians, 114, 118–119
Pollution, 20–21, 188, 189
Polynesians, 236
Pontiac, 229
Pony Express, 193
Pope, John, 45, 82, 83, R6, R15
Population, 20, R31m
　of American Indians and settlers, 56
　of Arkansas counties, R9– R12
　of Arkansas state, ix, 102
　of Arkansas Territory, 74, 78, 82, *83*
　of enslaved people in Arkansas, 89
　of Minnesota, 230
　representatives and, 137
　of the West, 239
　of Woodland Indians, 28
Port, 62, 72, R17
Portability, 163
Portland, Oregon, 239
Ports, 226, 227, 239
Postal system, 192, 193
Pottery, 25, 28, 29, 30, 31, *33*, 36, 213
Power loom, 225
Prairie, 13, R17
Prairie Grove battle, 92
Precipitation, 187, 188
President, 136, 137. *See also specific presidents by name*
Presley, Elvis, 206
Prices, 92, 169
Primary elections, 137
Primary sources
　Arkansas's symbols, 146–147
　national symbols, 148–149
　Parkin Archaeological Site, 30–31
　secondary sources and, 138–139
Prime meridian, 6, 184, 190
Proclamation, 92
Proclamation of 1763, 70–71, 71m
Producers, 172
Production decisions, 161
Production resources, *161*
Productivity, 159, 169–170
Profit, 120
Property rights, 141
Property taxes, 144
Prosperity, 183, 194
Pryor, David, 114, 119, R8, R15

Public services

Public services, 135, 143, 144, 151
Pueblo, 212, 213, 215
Puerto Ricans, 207
Puritans, 226

Q

Quapaw, 1, 25, 34, 35m, 36, 44, 47, 50, 54, 81
Quorum court, 143

R

Radio, 194
Railroads, 7, 98, 102, 192, 232
Rain forests, 123, R17
Ratify, 69, *134*, 135
Readers' Theater
    Money and Banks, 164–167
Reading and Thinking Skills
    distinguish fact from opinion, 210–211
    identify cause and effect, 76–77
Reading Skills, 226
    categorize, 124, 150, 168
    cause and effect, 12, 64, 184, 222
    compare and contrast, 4, 34, 78, 96, 140
    draw conclusions, 72
    main idea and details, 18, 54, 102, 160, 212
    problem and solution, 116, 134
    sequence, 26, 48, 88, 202, 228, 236
Reading Strategies
    monitor and clarify, 25, 87, 201
    predict and infer, 3, 183
    question, 63, 115, 159
    summarize, 47, 133, 221
Reconstruction, 96–99
Recreation, 17, 241, R30m
Recycling, *20*, 189
Red River Road, 80
Regions, 5
    of Arkansas, 12–15, 13m
    borders and boundaries of, 196–197
    of the United States, 185–186, 186m, 200–245
Relationships within places, 8–9
Relative location, 6
Religions, 5
Religious freedom, 64, 141, 224, 230, 238
Renewable resources, 19
Report, 32
Representation, 137, 142, 150, 152–153
Representative, 65, 66, 82, 142
Representative democracy, 155
Republic, 133, 152, 155
Republican Party, 137
Research Activities, 71, 242
Reservations, 231, 238
Reservoirs, 216
Resources, 1, R31m
    capital resources, 158, 161
    conservation of, 20–21
    human resources, 159, 161
    natural, 19, 19m, 20–21, 123, 161, 188, 189, 223
    renewable and nonrenewable, 19, 161
Respect, 151, R5
Responsibility, 150–153, R5
Revolutionary War, 66–67, 224
Rhine River, 185m, 189
Rhode Island, 225, 226

Rice, 203, 204, 206
Rights
    of African Americans, 86, 97, 99
    Bill of Rights and, xxiii, 141, 150, *150*
    Declaration of Rights and, 141
    of democratic governments, 148
    equality and, 119
    responsibilities and, 151–153
    See also Amendments to the U.S. Constitution; Bill of Rights; Civil rights; Voting rights
Rio Grande, 196
Rita (hurricane), 208
River basin, R17
Rivers, 5, *R16*, R17
    dams on, 8, 119, 213, 216
    erosion by, 13
    Mississippi River, 16–17
    movement and, 7
    pollution of, 188
    settlements near, 8, 17, 36, 74
    transportation on, 8, 16, 25, 27, 28, 29, 35, 36, 37, *88*
Roads, 20, 106, 192, 193, 193m
Roberts, Terrence, 147
Robert Thompson (steamboat), 79
Rockefeller, Winthrop, 119, R7, R15
Rocky Mountains, 186, 240
Roosevelt, Franklin Delano, 104, R15
Routes, 48, 50m, 80
Rural areas, 240

S

Sacagawea, 73, 242, R15
Sales taxes, 144
Salt, 35, 37, 213
San Antonio, Texas, 214
San Diego, California, 214
San Francisco, California, 239
Santa Fe, New Mexico, 214
Satellites, 106
Saving, 169
Savings accounts, 167
Scale on maps, 10, 11
Scarcity, 48, 50, 161
Schools, 226. *See* Education
Seal, *ix*
Seaports, 239
Seasons, 205
Seattle, Washington, 239
Secede, 91
Secondary sources, 138–139
Second Continental Congress, 66
Segregation, 114, 116–117, 125, 129, 147
Seminole, 202
Seminole Indians, 207
Senate, 137, 142
Service industry, 170, 204
Services
    economic choices about, 172–173
    importing and exporting of, 162–163
    industry and, 88
    production of, 160–161
    supply and demand and, 168–170
Settlements
    in Arkansas, 54–55, 64–65, 77
    in Arkansas Territory, 79–80, 146
    in British colonies, 64–65, 65m
    in the Midwest, 229
    near rivers, 8, 17, 36, 74

    in the Southeast, 203
    in the West, 72–75
Settlers, 220, 238
Severe weather, 187, 205
Sevier, Ambrose, 82, R15
Shackelford, Lottie, 145, R15
Sharecropping, 98
Shawnee, 228
Shipping, 226, 227
Sierra Nevada Mountains, 186
Sister Cities program, 145
Skills, 207
    citizenship skills, 100–101, 122–123, 174–175
    examine artifacts, 80
    graph and chart skills, 58–59
    map and globe skills, 10–11, 190–191, 234–235
    reading and thinking skills, 76–77, 210–211
    reading charts, 141, 232
    reading maps, 13, 19, 50, 74, 103
    reading visuals, 18
    study skills, 32–33, 138–139
    See also Reading Skills
Skyscrapers, 232
Skyway system, 233
Slater, Samuel, 225
Slavery
    abolitionists and, 86, 90
    in Arkansas, 83
    Civil War and, 91–92
    cotton production and, 88–90
    in French Louisiana, 55
Smoky Mountains, 206
Sod houses, 231
Soil, 14, 19
Solar energy, *188*
Songs, ix, 206
South America, 107, 185, 185m
South Carolina, 207
Southeast, 185, 186, 186m, 187
    climate of, 205
    colonies in, 203
    economy of, 204
    lower section, 207
    people of, 202
    rural life in upper section, 206
    upper section, 206
    wildlife of, 205
Southern Hemisphere, 184
Southwest, 185, 186, 186m
    landforms of, 216–217
    people of, 210
    Spanish settlements of, 214–215
    things to do and see, 217
    water in, 216–217
Southwest Trail, 80
Soviet Union, 106, 145
Space Needle, *239*
Space race, 106
Spain
    colonies of, 65m
    explorers from, 48–49, 50m, *51*
    introduction of the horse, 229
    settlements of, 203, 214m, 214–215
    territory controlled by, 57, 71m, 73
Speaking Activities, 177
Specialization, 160
Sphere, 184
Spinning machines, 225

R42 • Resources

Sports, 127, 206, 216, 240–241
Springs, 13, 14
Sputnik I, 106
Squatters, 80
State, 185
State government, 135, 140–142, 144
Statehood, 45, 63, 81, 239
State parks, 15, 21, R30m
States' rights, 90
Statue of Liberty, 148
Steamboats, 79, *88*, 232
Steenburgen, Mary, 126, R15
Stein, Gertrude, 180
Stephens, Charlotte Andrews, 98, R15
St. Lawrence River, 224
St. Louis, Missouri, 232
Stowe, Harriet Beecher, 90, R15
Study skills
    identify primary and secondary sources, 138–139
    write a report, 32–33
Suburbs, 106, 227
Supply and demand, 169
Supreme Court, 117, 136, 142, 153
Swamp, R17
Symbols
    of Arkansas, *x*, 146–147, *146–147*
    of the United States, 148–149, *148–149*

T

Tariffs, 91
Taxes, 144
    in British colonies, 65
    citizens' responsibilities and, 151
    city and county governments and, 143
    federal government and, 135
    tariffs, 91
Technology, 9, 171
Technology Activity, 61
Tectonic plate, R17
Telegraph system, 193
Television and movie industry, 194, 239
Temperature, 187
Tennessee, 206
Tepees, 36, 229
Territory, 74
Territory of Orleans, 74
Testament, 147
Test prep, 22–23, 40–41, 42, 60–61, 84–85, 108–109, 110, 130–131, 156–157, 176–177, 178, 198, 218–219, 244–245, 246
Texas, 212, 214, 215, 216
Textile industry, 225–226
Timelines, 46–47, 58–59, 62–63, 86–87, 200–201, 220–220
Tlingit, 236, 237
Tobacco, 203, 204, 206
Toltec Mound, *28*
Tools, *27*, 28, 34, 202, 228
Tornadoes, 205
Totalitarian government, 152, 154
Tourism, 170, 195
    of the Mountain States, 240, 241
    in the Southeast, 204
    in Upper Southeast, 206
Towns and cities
    development of in Northeast, 224
    growth of, 226
    in the Mid-Atlantic states, 227
    in the Midwest, 232–233
    of Mississippian Indians, 29
    of Miwoks and Yokuts, 237
    in the Mountain States, 240–241
    near rivers, 8, 17
    New Orleans, 54, 72, 73
    in the Pacific States, 227
    of Tunica, 37
    in the Upper Southeast, 206
    of Woodland Indians, 28
Trade, 183, 226
    of American Indians, 28, 35, 36, 37, 213, 222
    of Archaic Indians, 27
    of Arkansas, 162–163
    at Arkansas Post, 54, *55*, 56
    communication and transportation systems and, 194
    of Europeans, 224
    exploration and, 48–51
    federal government and, 135
    in French Louisiana, 55
    of Mississippian Indians, 29
    shipping and, 227
    at trading posts, 54
    of United States, 225
Trading posts, 47, 54
Traditions
    culture and, 34, 124, 194–195
    of enslaved people, 89
    of the Tlingit, 237
    See also Culture
Trail of Tears, 81
Training, 169
Transcontinental railroad, 239
Transportation, 25, 204, R30m
    adaptation to environment and, 9
    of Arkansas Indians, 35, 36, 37
    development of St. Louis and, 232
    of early peoples of Arkansas, 27, 29
    links between regions, 192
    movement of people and, 7, 8
    population increases and, 102
    of settlers, 79
    trade and, 8, 194
    transcontinental railroad, 239
    on water, 16, *88*, 206
    of Woodland Indians, 28
Treaties, 67
    between Cherokee and Osage, 79
    federal government and, 135
    with Quapaw, 81
    Treaty of Paris, 67, 229
Trial, 141, 151
Tributary, R17
Trickey, Minnijean Brown, 147
Tubman, Harriet, 90, R15
Tunica, 34, 35m, 37
Tyson, John, 120, R15

U

Uncle Tom's Cabin (Stowe), 90
Uniformity, 163
Union, 82, 91m, 92–93, 94–95
Union Army, 91, 97
Unit Activities
    Create a "Dream Job" comic strip, 179
    Make an "Early Arkansans and Their Environment" poster, 43
    Make a travel brochure, 247
    Make a "Why I Came to Arkansas" postcard, 111
United States, 180, *180–181*, 182, 193m, 230m, R24m–R25m, R26m–R27m
    Articles of Confederation, 68, 134
    Civil War in, 91–95
    Constitution of, xxii–xxiii, *xxiii*, 68, *134*, 134–137
    control of the West, 238
    establishment of, 67
    exports and imports of, 162
    flag, 148–149, *149*, R2–R3
    government of, 134–137, 144, 192, 192–194
    Great Depression, 104
    interstate highways, 193, 193m
    links between regions, 183, 192–195
    Louisiana Purchase, 73–74, 74m, 230
    national parks of, 14, 21
    Northwest Territory, 230
    Proclamation of 1763 and, 70–71
    Reconstruction, 96–99
    regions of, 185–186, 186m, 200–245
    space race, 106
    symbols of, 148–149
    trade, 135, 225
    Trail of Tears and, 81
    transcontinental railroad, 239
    treaties of, 67, 79, 81, 135
    War of Independence, 66–67, 224
    war with Mexico, 215
    westward expansion of, 72–75
    World War I, 103
    World War II, 105
    See also Lower Southeast; Mid-Atlantic states; Midwest; New England; Northeast; Southeast; Southwest; Upper Southeast; West
United States Postal Service, 183, 193
University, 220, 226
Upper Southeast, 206
Utah, 238

V

Valleys, 5, 12, 13, 186, *R16*, R17
Vermont, 226
Veto, 136
Virginia, 204, 206
Vocabulary strategies, 4, 12, 18, 26, 34, 48, 54, 64, 72, 78, 88, 96, 102, 116, 124, 134, 140, 150, 160, 168, 184, 212, 222, 226, 228, 236
Volcano, 186, 240, R17
Volcanoes National Park, 240
Volga River, 185m, 189, R22m
Volunteers, 133, 151, 209
Voting rights
    of African American men, 86, 92, 97, 99
    as a democratic responsibility, 133, 152–153
    under first constitution of Arkansas, 83
    for women, 45, 103

W

Wagon train, 221, 238
Walker, Hazel, 127, R15
Wal-Mart, 120

Walton, Sam

Walton, Sam, 120, R15
Wampum belt, 224
Wants and needs, 168–169
War of Independence, 66–67, 224
Washington (state), 239, 240
Washington, Arkansas, 80, 81
Washington, D.C., *136*, 227
Washington, George, *71*, 80, *135*, 206, R15
   at Constitutional Convention, 68
   at First Continental Congress, 66
   as President, 67
Waste, 20
Water
   affect on climate, 187
   borders and, 196, 197
   conservation of, 21, 217
   effect on climate, 205
   of Mississippi, 16
   people's use of, 20
   sources of, 16
   in the Southwest, 216
   transportation on, 8, 16, 25, 27, 28, 29, 35, 36, 37, *88*
Waterfalls, 233, 243
Watermelon Festival, 195
Water-powered mills, 225, 233
Weather, 187, 205
Weathering, 201, 216
Weaving, 237
Weekly Reader Projects. *See* Current Events Projects
West, 185, 186, 186m, 236–239
   Mountain States, 240
   Pacific States, 239–240

Western Cherokee, 74, 79, 81
Western Hemisphere, 184, R22m–R23m
West Gulf Coastal Plain, 12, 13m, 15
Wesward expansion, 55–56, 67, 70–71, 72–75, 79–82, 90, 102, 230–233, 238–239, 242–243
West Virginia, 206
Wetlands, 186, *R16*, R17
White River, 14, 74
White-tailed deer, *x*
Wide boundaries, 197
Wilderness areas, 21
Wilderness Road, *70*
Wildlife, 21, 205
Williamson, "Sonny Boy," 126, R15
Wind turbines, *188*
Withdrawal, 166–167
Women
   civil rights of, 117
   Civil War and, 92
   discrimination against, 103
   as educators, 98, 121
   in politics, 118, 119
   voting rights, 45, 103
   World War I and, 103
   World War II and, 105
Woodland Indians, 24, 28, 228
Woodlot, 35
Wooly mammoths, 26
Workers, 159, 168–170
Work slow-downs, 89
Works Progress Administration, 104
World, R18m–R19m, R20m–R21m
World War I, 103

World War II, 105
Writers, 125, 129
Writing Activities, 199
   description, 53
   dialogue, 245
   essay, 31, 61, 109, 157
   evaluation, 173
   letter, 129
   magazine article, 23
   paragraph, 131
   persuasive essay, 219
   report, 32–33, 177
   short story, 41
   summary, 85
Wyandot, 228
Wyoming, 240

Y

Yangtze River, 185m, 189
Yokut, 236, 237
Yorktown, Battle of, 67

Z

Zydeco music, 207

Acknowledgments

For each of the selections listed below, grateful acknowledgment is made for permission to excerpt and/or reprint original or copyrighted material, as follows:

Photography Credits

Cover (Arkansas State Capital) © Wesley Hitt/Alamy. (Statue of Liberty) © Herbert Spichtinger/zefa/Corbis. (compass) © HMCo./Michael Indresano. **Back cover** © Stockbyte/Getty Images. **Title page** (Arkansas State Capital) © Wesley Hitt/Alamy. **ix** One Mile Up. **x** (tl) Creativ Studio Heinemann/Getty Images. (tr) Tom Brakefield/CORBIS. (bl) Joe McDonald/ CORBIS. (cl) Don Farrall/Getty Images. (cr) Lawrence Lawry/Photo Researchers, Inc. (b) Paul A. Souders/CORBIS. **xi** (b) Photodisc/Getty Images. **xxii** (t) R. Krubner/ Robertstock. (b) Micheal Ventura/PhotoEdit. **xii-iii** AirPhoto. **xiii** (cr) Ohio Historical Society. (tl) Courtesy of the Old State House Museum/University Museum Collections, University of Arkansas. **xiv** (b) Science Museum/SSPL/Image Works. (tl) Houghton Mifflin Company. **xv** (t) NASA. (b) Babara Higgins Bond. **xvi** (b) AP Photo/Mike Winthroath. (t) Eddie Adams/CORBIS. **xvii** (b) Philip Gould/CORBIS. (tl) David Young-Wolff/PhotoEdit. **xviii** (cl) Tony Freeman/PhotoEdit. (bl) Frank Siteman/PhotoEdit. (t) Terry Smith/Mira. **xix** David Young-Wolff/PhotoEdit. **1** Arkansas Dept of Parks & Tourism. **2** (b) Kevin Anthony Horgan/Getty Images. (r) AirPhoto. **3** (l) Bill Barksdale/AGStockUSA. (r) David Young-Wolff/PhotoEdit **4** Michael Newman/PhotoEdit. **5** JP Laffont/Sygma/CORBIS. **7** Purcell Team/Alamy. **8** David Frazier/PhotoEdit. **11** Ray Boudreau. **12** William A. Bake/CORBIS. **14** AirPhoto. **15** R. Krubner/Robertstock. **18** AP Photo/Beth Hall. **19** Bill Barksdale/AGStockUSA. **20** David Young-Wolf/Photoedit. **24** (l) Marilyn Angel Wynn/Nativestock.com. (r) North Wind Picture Archives/Alamy. **25** (cl) Anthony Stein, Mississippian Moundbuilders and their Artifacts, http://mississippian-artifacts.com. (cr) Nez Perce National Historical Park, Spalding Idaho. **26** (b) Archives Charmet/Musee de l'Histoire Naturelle/Bridgeman Art Gallery. **27** (tl) Ohio Historical Society. (tr) Marilyn Angel Wynn/Nativestock.com. **28** (t) North Wind Picture Archives/Alamy. (l) Courtesy of the Old State House Museum/University Museum Collections, University of Arkansas. **29** Werner Forman/Art Resource, NY. **30** Arkansas Archeological Survey. **31** Arkansas Archeological Survey. **33** (t) Richard A. Cooke/CORBIS. (b) Ray Boudreau. **34** Texas Parks & Wildlife, Interpretation & Exhibits Branch. **36** (tl) Anthony Stein, Mississippian Moundbuilders and their Artifacts, http://mississippian-artifacts.com. (br) Bryan Haynes. **37** (r) Nez Perce National Historical Park, Spalding Idaho. (tr) Bridgeman-Giraudon/Art Resource. **44** Victoria & Albert Museum, London/Art Resource, NY. **45** (tl) Mathew Brady/Picture History. (bl) Visions of America, LLC/Alamy. (tr) Bettman. (br) The Granger Collection, New York. **46** (l) J.N. Marchand "Detial"/Library and Archives of Canada/ C-008486. (r) Arkansas History Commission. **47** (l) ©Lowell Georgia/CORBIS. (r) North Wind Picture Archives/Alamy. **48** Francis Back. **49** (t) Arkansas History Commission. (tr) Erich Lessing/Art Resource. **54** Arkansas History Commission. **55** (bl) Hussenot/PhotoCuisine/Corbis. (tl) ©Lowell Georgia/CORBIS. (cl) Courtesy of Lysa Oeters/Mazer Photography. (br) Marilyn Angel Wynn/Nativestock.com. (tr) ©Marilyn "Angel" Wynn/NativeStock. (cr) The Historical Shop. **56** North Wind Picture Archives/Alamy. **58** Ray Boudreau. **62** Bridgeman Art Library/Getty Images. **62** Bridgeman Art Library. **63** Old State House Museum. **63** Arkansas History Commission. **64** Getty Images. **65** The Granger Collection, New York. **66** (tl) The Granger Collection, New York. (tr) Bridgeman Art Library/Getty Images. **67** (t) The Granger Collection, New York. (tr) Christie's Images/CORBIS. **68** (tl) The Corcoran Gallery of Art/CORBIS. (tr) Bettmann/CORBIS. **70** George Caleb Bingham, "Daniel Boone Escorting Settlers through the Cumberland Gap, 1851-52. Oil on canvas, 36 1/2 x 50 1/4." Washington University of Art, St. Louis. Gift of Nathaniel Phillips, 1890. **71** Super Stock Inc. **72** Bridgeman Art Library. **73** Bridgeman Art Library. **75** Courtesy National Information Service for Earthquake Engineering, University of California Berkeley. **77** Ray Boudreau. **78** Bettmann/CORBIS. **79** Science Museum/SSPL/Image Works. **80** (t) Skip Stewart-Abernathy, Arkansas Archeological Survey. (b) Arkansas Dept of Parks & Tourism. **81** The Granger Collection, New York. **82** (tl) Arkansas History Commission. (tr) Arkansas History Commission. **86** (l) Smithsonian Institution/CORBIS. (r) Babara Higgins Bond. **87** (l) Carroll County Historical Society of Berryville. (r) CORBIS. **88** Courtesy of the Southwest Arkansas Regional Archives. **89** (t) Skip Stewart-Abernathy, Arkansas Archeological Survey. (cr) Collection of the Blue Ridge Institute & Museums, Ferrum College. **90** (tl) CORBIS, (tc) Schlesinger Library, Radcliff Institute, Havard University. (tr) Smithsonian Institution/CORBIS. **92** (t) Library of Congress. (cr) The Granger Collection, New York. **95** (t) The Granger Collection, New York. (b) Private Collection/The Bridgeman Art Library. **96** (bl) CORBIS. (br) The Granger Collection, New York. **97** (br) Babara Higgins Bond. **98** UCA Archive, Torreyson Library. **100** (all) Ray Boudreau. **102** Carroll County Historical Society of Berryville. **104** (tl) CORBIS. (tr) Civilian Conservation Corps (CCC) work crew at Devil's Den State Park, Washington County, Arkansas, 1934. Courtesy Shiloh Museum of Ozark History, Springdale Arkans/Billye Jean Scroggins Bell Collection (S-95-6-52). **105** (tr) K.J. Historical/CORBIS. (tl) Arkansas History Commission. **106** (all) NASA. **112** (tr) Wikipedia. (br) Courtesy EBONY Magazine. **113** (tl) AP Photo/Mike Winthroath. (bl) One Mile Up. (tr) Courtesy of Steven Anthony/Anthony Timberlands, Inc. (br) WidStock/Alamy. **114** (cl) ullstien bild/The Granger Collection, New York. (cr) AP Phot/Danny Johnson, File. **115** (cl) Courtesy HOLA! ARKANSAS Hlispanic Media and Publishing Company. (cr) Where the Southern Cross the Yellow Dog by Carroll Cloar/David Lusk Gallery. **116** ullstien bild/The Granger Collection, New York. **117** (tl) University of Arkansas Museum. (tr) Bettman/CORBIS. **118** (bc) Arkansas History Commission. (br) Hulton Archive/Getty Images. (bl) Butler Center for Arkansas Studies, Central Arkansas Library Systems. **119** (b) Arkansas History Commission. (br) Eddie Adams/CORBIS. **120** (tl) Courtesy HOLA! ARKANSAS Hlispanic Media and Publishing Company. (br) Louie Psihoyos/CORBIS. **121** Special Collections & Archives, Nimitz Library, USNA. **123** Ray Boudreau. **124** AFP/Getty Images. **125** Where the Southern Cross the Yellow Dog by Carroll Cloar/David Lusk Gallery. **126** (tr) Getty Images. (br) Hulton Archive/Getty Images. (bl) Photo by Chris Strachwitz all used by permission, all rights reserved. Courtesy Arhoolie Records, El Cerrito, CA, www.arhoolie.com <http://www.arhoolie.com>. **127** Johnathan Daniel/Stringer/Getty Images. **128** Frank Micelotta/Getty Images. **129** (r) AP Photo/News-Press, Lenn Wood, FILE. (tl) Courtesy Shiloh Museum of Ozark History/Martha Hall Collection (S-96-112-22). (tr) Courtesy Shiloh Museum of Ozark History (S-95-117). **132** (all) David Young-Wolff/PhotoEdit. **133** (l) Jeff Greenburg/Omni-Photo Communications. (r) AP Photo/Danny Johnston. **134** Aaron Haupt/Photo Researchers, Inc. **135** Virginia Museum of Fine Arts, Richmond. Gift of Edgar William and Bernice Chrysler Garbisch. Photo: Ron Jennings. **136** Joseph Sohm, Chromosohm Media Inc./PhotoResearchers, Inc. **141** Ray Boudreau. **142** David Young-Wolff/PhotoEdit. **144** AP Photo/Mike Winthroath. **145** (r) James H. Pickerell/The Images Works. (b) Peter Blakely/CORBIS SABA. **146** Courtesy Arkansas Dept of Parks & Tourism. **146-7** David Muench/CORBIS. **147** (tr) Royalty-Free/Getty Images. (bl) Wikipedia. **148** Artbase Inc. **149** (tr) David Young-Wolff/Alamy. (cl) Lee Snider/CORBIS. **152** Photodisc/Craig Brewer/Artbase Inc. **153** (cr) Jeff Greenberg/Omni-Photo Communications. (t) Ron Chapple/Getty Images. **154** (t) AP Photo/Danny Johnston. (b) Bettmann/CORBIS. **155** Brooks Kraft/CORBIS. **158** (l) Bill Barksdale/AGStockUSA. (r) Wesley Hitt/Mira. **159** (l) Arkansas Dept of Parks & Tourism. (r) Philip Gould/CORBIS. **160-1** (b) G.I. French/Robertstock. **161** (bc) Bill Barksdale/AGStockUSA. (br) Photodisc Green. **162** Wesley Hitt/Mira. (tr) Comstock. **163** David Young-Wolff/PhotoEdit. **165** Ray Boudreau. **166-7** Ray Boudreau. **168** Arkansas Dept of Parks & Tourism. **170** (tl) Philip Gould/CORBIS. (tr) Courtesy of Arkansas Dept of Parks & Tourism. **171** Bill Parsons/Mira. **172** (all) Ray Boudreau. **180-1** Bill Parsons/Mira.com. **182** (l) Kevin Anthony Horgan/Getty Images. (r) Images.com/CORBIS. **183** (l) Digital Vision, LLC/SuperStock. (r) Artbase. **184** Kevin Anthony Horgan/Getty Images. **187** Visions of America, LLC/Alamy. **188** (b) Glenn Allison/Getty Images. (r) Owaki-Kulla/CORBIS. **189** David Young-Wolf/PhotoEdit. **192** Digital Vision, LLC/SuperStock. **194** (b) Artbase. (r) Jack Hollingsworth/Getty Images. **195** Terry Smith/Mira. **196** Mark E. Gibson. **197** Brian Sytnyk/Masterfile. **200** (l) CORBIS. (r) Philip Gould/CORBIS. **201** (r) Artbase, Inc. (l) Tony Freeman/PhotoEdit. **203** (tl) Jeff Greenberg/PhotoEdit. (tr) Jeff Greenberg/PhotoEdit. (cr) Ira Block/National Geographic Image Collection. **205** Joe Skipper/Reuters Newmedia Inc./CORBIS. **206** Dennis MacDonald/PhotoEdit. **208** NOAA/Handout/Reuters/CORBIS. **209** ©2005 Randy Belice/NBAE/Getty Images. (b) AP Photo /Judy Bottoni. **210** Florida State Archives. **213** Grant Heilman Photography. **215** Tony Freeman/PhotoEdit. **216** (b) Artbase, Inc. (r) David Muench/CORBIS. **217** Bob Rowe. Progressive Image/CORBIS. **220** (l) Andre Jenny/Mira. (b) CORBIS. **221** (l) Bettman/CORBIS. (r) The Granger Collection, New York. **224** David Frazier/The Image Works. **225** Mathew Pippin. **228** Micheal S. Lewis/CORBIS. **231** CORBIS. **232** Bettman/CORBIS. **233** Bill Ross/CORBIS. **237** Luigi Galante. **238** Neal Mishler/Getty Images. **239** David Mendelsohn/Masterfile. **240** Frank Siteman/PhotoEdit. **242** (all) North Wind Picture Archives. **R0** (l) Panoramic Images/Getty Images **R0-R1** Arkansas Dept of Parks & Tourism. **R1** Photo Library International/CORBIS. **R2** LWA-Dann Tardif/CORBIS. **R4** (l) UAMS Library. (br) AFP/Getty Images. **R12** (c) University of Arkansas Museum. (bl) Hulton Archive/Getty Images. (br) The Corcoran Gallery of Art/CORBIS. **R13** (c) Wikipedia. (tr) CORBIS. (br) Hulton Archive/Getty Images. **R14** (tl) Mathew Brady/Picture History. (bl) UCA Archive, Torreyson Library. (cr) Louie Psihoyos/CORBIS. **R16** Michael Melford/The Image Bank/Getty Images. **R17** (t) R.T. Holcomb/CORBIS (b) Craig Aurness/CORBIS.